The
Nurse
Behind
the Gates

BOOKS BY SHARI J. RYAN

The Bookseller of Dachau

The Doctor's Daughter

The Lieutenant's Girl

The Maid's Secret

The Stolen Twins

The Homemaker

The Glovemaker's Daughter

The Perfect Nanny

LAST WORDS

The Girl with the Diary

The Prison Child

The Soldier's Letters

SHARI J. RYAN

The
Nurse
Behind
the Gates

bookouture

Published by Bookouture in 2024

An imprint of Storyfire Ltd.
Carmelite House
50 Victoria Embankment
London EC4Y 0DZ

www.bookouture.com

ISBN: 978-1-83525-491-2
eBook ISBN: 978-1-83525-490-5

This book is a work of fiction. Whilst some characters and circumstances portrayed by the author are based on real people and historical fact, references to real people, events, establishments, organizations or locales are intended only to provide a sense of authenticity and are used fictitiously. All other characters and all incidents and dialogue are drawn from the author's imagination and are not to be construed as real.

To my great-uncle, Hanuš...
Alone at seventeen, a month before the liberation of Dachau, the
world lost you—a brave warrior.
It would have been a privilege to know you.

To catch a glimpse of an infrequent daytime moon, one must be in a certain location at a specific time with clear conditions to discover evidence of what hides in the dark.

PROLOGUE

EMILIE, JULY 1942

Dachau, Germany

Over the past five months, Otto and I have driven past the foreboding black iron gates of Dachau countless times since moving here as newlyweds. I promised myself the location wouldn't be a bad omen for our new life together and I've done my best to avoid the sights since moving here, but this morning, sitting here now in front of this dismal spot, there's nowhere else to look.

The gates are within a stone's throw and though the air is hot and humid, a chill scurries up my arms like a spooked spider. Raindrops dribble down the iron rods, drawing my attention to a pattern melded into the bars, or...is it two patterns? An optical illusion, perhaps, depending on the perspective.

As a uniformed guard steps out from beneath the gated arch, my gaze clings to the words bent into the iron:

ARBEIT MACHT FREI.
Work will set you free.

Will the criminals ever be released from this concentration camp? The words on the sign don't depict the amount of work necessary to be set free.

A tall, hard-eyed Gestapo approaches Otto's car window and demands identification. Otto pulls out his papers and hands them over, and I can see the subtle nervous twitch of his right eyebrow. The guard's gaze flares, likely noticing my trembling hands.

"Heil Hitler," Otto says, saluting the man.

"Heil Hitler," the man replies. "What is the purpose of your arrival to Dachau?"

"You must be a new guard. We haven't met. I'm Dr. Berger, working in Block 5. Dr. Dietrich has requested that my wife, Emilie Berger, aid him with his work as I've been doing."

I hand my identification to Otto, feeling the blood drain from my face. No matter how many times I cross paths with a man in this particular uniform, I feel like a meek mouse from the terror they emanate. Can they see through me, and read my thoughts?

He pivots on his heels, taking a couple of steps toward the cement arched wall over us and pulls a hanging clipboard off a protruding nail. He draws his finger down the center, studying it intently. "Dr. and Frau Berger," he states, handing our identifications back to Otto. The guard steps back from the car and unlatches the gates for us to continue through. The way he referred to us made us sound much older than twenty-two.

I shouldn't be surprised to see SS officers and more Gestapo scattered around the open gravel area. The number of convicts lined in rows or walking in groups is astounding. How could there be so many criminals? As if this place isn't dreary enough, the inmates are soaked, with ragged garbs hanging from their shoulders. Of course, the SS and Gestapo have proper head covers and trench coats to keep them dry.

We arrive at a row of cars between two buildings, and my

stomach tightens, knowing this is where we get out and walk amongst the crowded compound.

I regret agreeing to this idea. I ought to have taken Otto's advice and stayed away from a conversation I shouldn't have been a part of, but it's too late to change my mind now.

Otto opens my car door, and props open an umbrella to shield me from the rain then takes my hand, his grip tight as if I might change my mind and run back home. He wouldn't be wrong. If I could, I would. I can't shake off the restless apprehension.

As the door closes behind me, my reflection in the neighboring car's window catches my eye. My curled hair, lipstick, and fitted dress makes me stand out among the drab surroundings. With Otto in black dress slacks, a white-collared shirt, and suspenders, we don't look as though we're visiting a concentration camp.

A long, dark-brown wooden building with narrow windows looms, swallowing us within its ominous presence. A formation of military planes flies overhead, low enough to leave a whizzing whistle behind in a tail of smoke. Not a day goes by when we aren't reminded of being trapped in the center of a hostile battle. There's no clearer definition of war than the sight of barbed wired fences surrounding dark fields muddied by the sky's tears. Uniformed, rigid men pace in every direction, and there's no way to distract myself from the truth—the fear I live in daily.

Groups of male inmates wearing blue and white striped uniforms watch us as we walk along the muddy, rubble pathway. I can't avoid the dread and grief in their eyes. They recoil upon eye contact, turning away as if it's a sin to look in our direction.

"Just focus on where you're walking, darling. Don't mind any of the prisoners walking about," Otto says, gripping my hand tightly. He leans in a bit closer to whisper into my ear.

"It's not every day these men catch a glimpse of gorgeous blonde beauty."

In any other place or time, my cheeks would blush from his compliment, but here, in this place, I would rather go unnoticed. "It looks like the winds have pushed rubble over the path, be careful not to trip."

The plaid red, black, and brown umbrella Otto is holding above my head does little to offer me comfort as we approach a new destination. A daunting wooden door with an iron handle stands between me and this solid confinement, a place I never imagined I would see.

"Is there a particular reason we're going into this specific building and not the others?" I inquire, turning to Otto with a timid smile. *Everything will be okay*, I remind myself.

He squeezes my hand gently and whispers, "Darling, it's the sick bay, as I mentioned earlier." His response carries a hint of tension.

I squint at the sign above the door, straining my eyes to make sense of the marking "B.5". My ankles ache in the heels I unwisely chose not realizing we'd be walking over wet rubble. "Are there different wings in this sick bay too?" My question comes across as mischievous, anticipating his response based on all the others he's given me.

Otto huffs a quiet laugh from his nose and responds in a hush. "Yes, indeed, there are several wings. There seems to be an abundance of ill criminals, requiring the need for expansion."

Though it's becoming more difficult to keep my cheerful grin in place, the questions keep coming of their own accord. "But I thought you said you didn't work with the patients?" I can't help but add, "You know you've been a bit mysterious about your days at work. I guess I can't help the questions."

"It's all right, darling. I did say I hadn't been working with the patients. That's correct," he says, reaching for the iron handle on the door. He pulls it open and waves me forward. "Go on."

Otto releases my hand to close the umbrella and steps inside after me. Sweltering sticky air clings to our skin as we walk over unfinished wooden floor panels, between matching walls, and beneath ceilings with dark beams crisscrossing in every direction. The stench of ammonia is the only familiarity in this setting. Nothing about this vacant space reminds me of a medical ward. An icy chill spreads up my arms.

A distressing moan echoes between the corridor walls and I can't tell how near or far from the source we are. "Oh my goodness. Whoever that is sounds to be suffering horribly. Is someone helping them?" I ask, peeking into dark windows as we pass closed doors.

Otto takes my hand back into his, caressing the pad of his thumb over my knuckles. "I'm sure someone is tending to them, and I know you're going to do so well here. You're the most brilliant nurse I know, and with the prettiest eyes, I might add. I can't think of anyone more qualified than you." Otto has a way of charming me, even if I'm overwhelmed with fear at the moment.

"I'm not a nurse." The reminder isn't necessary, but the words arise.

"Yes, but we both know how you spend your days. You and those medical books—well, they've gone right to your head, in fact." Otto's tease comes along with a belly laugh, but the humor is at my expense. I don't think he takes me as seriously as he once did, back when we were at university.

Another wailing moan carries down the hallway toward us. It isn't an unusual sound to hear in an infirmary, but no one wants to hear another person suffering.

Otto stops in front of a wooden door and my heart thumps in my chest as he pushes against the slab to reveal what's waiting on the other side. Before he steps forward, he pauses and peers down at me but doesn't make direct eye contact. "There are patients in here, but we'll be continuing on to the lab where I work. Don't look at any of them. It will give them a reason to talk to you. We shouldn't converse. I know that goes against your good nature, but these men are still criminals, even if they aren't the dangerous kind."

"I understand," I say. But I'm not sure I do.

Men line the walls: some are standing, others are sitting on the floor, heads hanging between bent knees. Most are wearing filthy yellowing-white prisoner uniforms with dark blue stripes. There's a damp, sweet smell in the air, forcing my throat to tighten as we continue forward. Our steps feel slow and unhurried, as if we're trekking through thick sand.

"Help," someone groans. "Please, miss. Help us."

"Ignore them. They do this to everyone who walks through that door," Otto mumbles beneath his breath.

I wish I could close my eyes or pinch my nose to avoid the stench of what must be a mixture of body odor and sickness, but I'm not that type of person. That would be rude and disrespectful, even to a criminal.

I do my best to block out the cries for help as we near the next door, but a distinct sound yanks me to a firm stop.

"A rare honeybee," I hear.

Groggily and softly spoken, those familiar words strike me like a punch to the gut. *A rare honeybee...the world couldn't survive without them.* I'd never forget that fact. I search for where the words came from. There are so many men, and they all look alike. My free hand flares to my chest and my breath catches in my throat as I search, knowing those precise words were meant for me to hear. I was sure there wasn't a single person here that I could possibly know. Not under these circumstances, but I must be wrong.

Otto stops alongside me, inspecting the area for whoever

spoke out, confirming he heard the words too. He wouldn't understand the meaning, though.

"Dr. Berger," another voice calls. Otto is addressed formally with a commanding inflection. "Might I have a word with you?"

"Yes, of course," Otto replies. "Go on and wait over by the office door ahead. I'll only be a moment." He's leaving me here, in the middle of an enclosed area filled with ill, desperate criminals... and the person who spoke *those* words. I clutch my hands to my stomach knowing I can't move any closer toward the office door yet.

From the corner of my eye, I see an inmate lift his limp arm, holding his palm toward me. I want to screw my eyes shut, to close off my ears.

But then I hear, "Is it really you?"

Unable to resist, I twist my neck slightly to the left, toward the man holding out his arm, and step in closer, his words pulling me over. My blood runs cold as I come to a stop in front of him, my brown leather day shoes scuffing against the dirty floor. He has no body hair, is malnourished, and pale. His eyes are heavy as if he hasn't slept in weeks, and...

Bile rises from my stomach, burning through my insides as I notice a small but prominent dent on the bridge of his nose. A dent along the bridge of his nose...that I know happened when he tripped on a knot-riddled log, landing face first in a pile of splintered wood, requiring eight sutures.

I shake my head furiously as my stomach drops. I'm mistaken. He wouldn't be here. He *couldn't* be here. With my eyes shut tightly, I pray that when I open them again, I'll see that my mind has been playing tricks on me.

But I know it's not.

Those eyes...I would recognize them anywhere—even here, in a place like this. My breaths become frantic, and my lungs struggle to inhale. A whimper rattles deep in my throat as tears burn at the back of my eyes. He looks close to death.

"No, no—" I whisper. The sensation of his name flickers across my tongue, a relic of nostalgia that sears in my brain.

"You're here," he utters, his voice dry and scratchy.

My brain catches up with what I'm seeing, and I hold a finger to my lips, signaling him to stay silent. A heavy wave of dizziness hits me, but I glance over my shoulder to find Otto still having a private conversation out of view.

I swallow against the thickness in my throat, keeping myself still so no one will notice our encounter.

"Why—why are you here?" I gasp. "Did you break the law? You wouldn't do that...you-you wouldn't," I whisper, my words fumbling as I try to ask everything all at once.

He tilts head to the side and the faint line of his eyebrows arch with despair. "Of course I haven't—"

"Tell me what's happened. Let me—" I swallow hard and peer back once more to see if Otto is returning, but he's not there. "Let me help. Why would anyone bring you here if you're not a criminal?"

His sharp, bony shoulders slouch forward, and he stares up at me for a long, painful second. A second I'll never forget.

"Emi, you must know why I'm here..."

ONE

EMILIE

Munich, Germany

Crystallized snowflakes cover the red, gray, and white cobblestones between my house and Otto's. Soon, we'll be calling these houses "our parents' houses, on the street we lived."

Avoiding my husband's concern, made obvious by the lines across his forehead, I stare down at my damp black oxfords, watching the flecks of snow melt away. Another sharp gust of wind slices through my stockings, making me shiver. *It's silly to be standing out in the cold like this.*

"Emilie, you're freezing," he tells me, rubbing his leather-gloved hands up and down the length of my cardinal-red wool-covered arms.

"Sweetheart, I'm so sorry. I'm not trying to be difficult. I'm struggling to understand all of this," I say. "I didn't think we'd be leaving so soon."

"But we're married now—husband and wife," Otto says. I can hear the smile in his voice. "It's time for us to start our married life properly."

"Of course, and I'm eager for every bit that's to come, but—"

"Moving out of Munich won't be so bad, I promise," Otto says, taking my hands into his, our fingers intertwining. "No matter where we go or what challenges come, we'll always have each other."

My heart warms at his words and I peer up at him, finding his hazel eyes full with determination and passion. It's becoming harder to resist his plea to join him in the car. He opens the passenger-side door, gesturing toward the leather interior.

We got married three weeks ago and, until last night, everything was going smoothly. But as I took my last bite of the pork roast I'd spent all day preparing, his words spilled out like water from an overflowing bucket.

"They've moved up the research job offer—my uncle's agency. They want me to start right away, and they're giving us a newly furnished house. A house, at no cost. I've been bursting at the seams, dying to tell you all day," he said, his cheeks flushing pink, eyes open wide, and hands balled into fists on the tabletop.

I sipped from my glass of water, taking a brief second to process everything he'd just revealed. "Right away?" I managed to ask through the tightening nerves in my stomach. I guess I didn't need to question his decision. Whatever happens, we rarely have time to think.

"Yes, I can take you to our new house tomorrow morning. They want me to start later this week if possible," he continued. A sheen of sweat was beginning to form along his forehead, as the expression on my face became sullen. He's always known I hate surprises.

"But how? This is so sudden..."

"Darling, we're sitting in your parents' kitchen, acting as if we live here alone. They're in the next room over. We're married! I wish you'd share my excitement for this opportunity."

"What about our classes at the university? Where will we be moving?" I began to spout off questions, percolating with each second longer we sat there between his announcement and my response. He has more classes than I do since the nursing program is slightly shorter than the doctor's. Still, neither of us is anywhere close to completion.

"We're just moving outside the city. We'll figure everything out."

I still believed I had a say in our future. But here we are, standing on our familiar street next to the packed car, and it's clear things are moving along quicker than anticipated.

"You haven't addressed how we will continue our classes in the city. Will we be driving into Munich every day? How will you do that if you're working? You can't keep telling me we'll make everything work without a plan. This wasn't our plan. Your father said that your uncle's agency was going to wait for you to obtain your medical degree. Why would that change?"

Just before we got engaged a year ago, we discussed a potential job opportunity to work alongside his father and uncle in a medical research role. I can still hear Otto's father, Herr Berger, proudly describing it as an "Evolving program...in a constant realm of development..." and his certainty that the governmental agency were offering Otto "a one in a million opportunity" since they were happy to wait for him to complete his degree. It all sounded so promising and exciting.

But this sudden rush to move everything along before we're ready doesn't.

Otto makes a show of looking around the quiet street off Munich's busy cityscape. "Look around, Emi...this city is falling apart." Our little nook among the city is still intact, but less than a five minute walk from here, the streets are swarming with Nazi rallies, propaganda, protests, and Gestapo overruling day to day life in general. "We're being sucked into a war we don't want to be a part of. The best thing we can do is put some space between us and Munich. By helping my vater and uncle in this position, we'll escape the city for a greater sense of safety."

I've gotten good at drowning out the background noise of sirens and commanding shouts in the streets, but it's still there. We can't escape it. The war will continue to close in around us, no matter where we are.

And it will be just Otto and me safe outside of the city. Not our families. I'm not sure I'll be able to sleep at night, knowing they're still here while I'm safe elsewhere.

"We will go back to our classes when we can. This isn't forever. It's for now. We can't control the war, nor do we want to be involved. Let's step aside and hope the end is near," he says, running out of breath as if we're running out of time to step into the car. "Emi, I want to share a beautiful life with you in a place we love. It's my promise to you and I won't break it."

We've been discussing this matter for countless hours, barely catching a wink of sleep last night, and yet, my curiosity persists... "Just help me understand, why now? What prompted your uncle to pull the plans forward like this?"

A plane flies overhead, zinging through the sky, stealing the silence around us as I wait for an answer.

Otto sighs. "My uncle Dietrich's agency has formed an additional alliance with the Luftwaffe. They have a need for a medical research team, so my uncle has to put one together quickly."

"The air force?" I consider my ever-present fear that Otto's medical courses won't be enough to keep him from being conscripted into the armed forces like many men his age have been. "I thought the agency was working toward finding a cure for cancer. What does the Luftwaffe have to do with that?"

Otto takes in a lungful of frigid air and holds it before exhaling with an answer in one quick breath. The truth, at last… "I'm not privy to much of the information around what's needed for the agency's medical research. I was told I'd find out shortly, but in the meantime, I must take this position, now," he says, his voice lowering an octave, embracing a serious tone I don't often hear from him. "If I finish my classes instead and the war is still in motion, I'll become an enlisted officer and won't have a say. This job with my father and uncle would have me working in way that benefits the country, thus keeping me off the front lines. Isn't that what we want, Emi?"

I've been shivering the entire time we've been outside, but now that a numbness has settled into my limbs, I'm stiff as a board. "So, you'll be forced to enlist if we don't go…" I repeat, staring at his rising and falling chest as he tries to catch the breaths he skipped.

"Citizens in this country have little control. You know this," he says, holding his arms out for me to curl into. I do, for the warmth I desperately need. "I understand your concerns and you have every right to be apprehensive, but my father has assured me—us—that we will be safe, and we will have the best house money can buy at the minute. Plus, we'll be living next to other doctors and medical professionals and their wives. They're all like us, wanting to make a difference by contributing to ground-breaking medical research. It'll be fun. A new group of friends, a new community."

It's hard not to question the validity of his words at a time like this. "Otto, no one is giving away houses, so there must be an explanation for why there's no cost to us."

Otto lowers his head. "Sweetheart, listen to me," he says pulling me into a full embrace, cloaked by his wool coat. "I'm trying my best to ensure our future pans out the way it should. I understand why you have so many questions, but the answers… they aren't something I can explain in a way that won't scare you."

"What do you mean?" I question, my voice faltering as sweat dampens my hands within my gloves.

"I didn't...I didn't want to scare you, but I'll be working in a field hospital, located inside Dachau."

"Doing what?" I say, feeling my tongue lodge in my throat. "In Dachau? The concentration camp the Nazis built to intern political protesters."

"Yes, but it's a location that happens to have additional lab space we can utilize. And I realize what you're thinking...those protesting criminals are fighting against this war and that's something we feel the same way about. So in my mind they aren't the type of convict you need to worry about me being near. They're like-minded people who spoke out of turn—something neither of us would do to avoid arrest. It's not a prison full of murderous criminals. The field hospital has extra lab space for us to conduct our work. I'll be helping the greater good without sacrificing our safety. This is for us, Emi."

If these people are in prison, there must be a reason beyond expressing their opinions.

"Well, if there's nothing to worry about, why does the house come as a benefit to this research job?" People only speak of Dachau in rumors. I don't know anyone who has seen the place from inside.

"My uncle negotiated funding, knowing it would provide us with safety." Otto kisses the top of my head. "I want to take care of you—it's all I've ever wanted. I've done nothing but try to prove that to you."

"You have, and with nothing but the best intentions. I just need a moment to get used to the change."

"I know you don't like surprises. You're a planner, and I'm sorry that I can't provide that comfort for you at the moment. But what is in my control is my devotion to you. I'll never let you down, Emi. I haven't yet, have I?"

He never has. We've always been side-by-side, in sync with

what we want and where we're going. "I'm sorry, I'll try to be more understanding," I say, squeezing my arms around him in his long tan wool coat.

"Don't apologize," he says, pushing me away a bit so he can stare into my eyes. A strand of his sandy hair falls over his forehead and he lifts my hand to kiss my knuckles. "We need to take a different path for a future that will benefit us after the war ends."

"I understand," I say, sweeping my cheek up in an angle against his coat to meet his firm, but endearing gaze.

"I think you'll be happy with the house. I know you would have rather picked it out yourself, but there weren't really options."

I'm not keen on surprises, even the well-intentioned ones. The thought of something unexpectedly shaking up my life used to make my stomach turn sour. But today isn't yesterday or the past. I know it's time to move forward. Even when I shared the sudden change with my parents this morning, they smiled and reminded me to be grateful to have a loving husband who wants to take care of me. Mama and Papa always want what's best for me. So, no more questioning this move. With a breath of chilly air, I smile and welcome the new life ahead as I slide into Otto's car.

TWO
EMILIE
FEBRUARY 1942

Dachau, Germany

We turn off the main road into a thickly wooded area with snow dusting the tree branches that reach up through the low-bearing clouds. With another sharp turn, the smooth terrain turns into a rubble covered road. Pebbles ping the undercarriage of the car and pop against the tires as we pass a shallow building peeking out from between the trees. The cream-colored concrete façade, crowned by a tall wooden watchtower, contrasts with its sharply sloped terracotta roof. The two-storied structure encases a stone arched opening secured by a Gothic iron gate. Dark windows line the top floor of the building above another row on both sides of the arch. The rest—whatever else there is to see—lurks behind tall shrubbery.

"What is this place?" I ask Otto.

"Well, that's the entrance to Dachau," he says, continuing past the building.

Tall oak trees line the road far into the distance, but there are sporadic gaps, exposing the continuation of the stone wall, barbed wire coiled along the top.

Otto releases my hand and presses on the brake to slow down before taking the next turn. "Almost there."

I wish we weren't, I think to myself as we continue down the road.

As if Otto senses my unease, he takes my hand from my lap and holds it tightly within his again. His hair feathers over his forehead, the pomade slick from this morning drying out. The imperfect sight distracts me, reminding me that I enjoy the unpolished moments only I get to see. "Everything is changing, but as long as we have each other—"

"We have everything," I complete his sentence, words we've comforted each other with since the start of our relationship. It's best we aren't living in the city, but my parents and friends are, which means I'll have to worry from afar—and worse, feel guilty that I'm somewhere safer than them.

"As I mentioned, the house is in a lovely neighborhood, surrounded by other couples and families. You'll make more friends."

It's hard to imagine anything past this moment, anything after driving past the mysterious building within the woods.

"I promise you'll be happy. I do."

"You don't have to remind me of that," I tell him, brushing the hair off his forehead.

"I know, but I can hear your thoughts, Emi...every single one." He gives me a quick smirk.

"Well, that's impossible because I haven't said a word," I squeak.

He taps his thumb repeatedly against the steering wheel. "Your silence is quite loud."

Otto pulls up in front of a charming two-story classic style house with a beige façade, dark trim and opulent style windows. A beautiful landscape of greenery with blooming flowers frames the house, except for a cobblestone walkway stretching out to the road. The terracotta roof is almost identical to the odd building we just passed and mirroring houses in alternating pastels surround us, giving off an overall quaint appeal.

With the car parked, Otto can't contain his excitement and practically leaps out of the car, rushing around the front to open my door. He's as eager as a child in front of a sweet shop.

"Oh my word, you're here!"

I spin around toward the sound of a woman's voice, my eyes growing wider as I spot her step out the front door of the house next to ours. She charges toward us, a blue polka-dotted apron looped around her neck and waist. Her hair is fiery red, and her personality already seems to radiate with a warm welcoming. She might be a bit older than us but maybe by only a few years or so.

She arrives breathless, having raced over to reach us. "I'm sorry, I'm sorry. I'm terrible. I'm sure you want to go gallivant through your gorgeous new home, but I had to come over and introduce myself. Everyone deserves a nice neighborly hello."

I extend my hand to shake hers but she cups her hand around my shoulder instead, offering me a sense of an immediate kinship. "It's a pleasure to meet you," I say, feeling the weight of nerves roll off my shoulders with her cheerful presence.

"I'm Ingrid, Ingrid Schmitt," she says. "You must be Emilie. My goodness, you're cute as a button. And that dress, it's stunning. I can already tell you're going to be my new shopping friend." Most people weren't doing much luxury shopping in Munich. I can't imagine it's much different here, but it's as if this street isn't living on the outskirts of a war.

"Thank you so much. That sounds lovely."

"And, Otto, it's delightful to meet you. My husband was telling me all about you two. He's excited to work alongside you. As he says: It's hard to find good men who don't want to spend their days focused on politics."

Otto must have already met her husband. I can't stop

myself from looking between the two of them, wondering if there's something I don't know. Although, aside from the concentration camp part, which he took his time to reveal, Otto has been up front with me about everything as it's unraveled.

"I'd rather focus on medical research than politics," Otto responds before turning to face me. "Darling, I'll be working with Herr Schmitt. We'll be in different labs, but in the same building, working beneath Dietrich," Otto tells me, filling in one blank.

"Oh," Ingrid says, flapping her hand at Otto. "You can call him Karl when he's home. Leave work at work. That's what I always say." She doesn't blink as she stares between the two of us, keeping her extra bright smile intact even though her chin trembles slightly.

"Okay then," Otto says. "It was lovely to meet you. We'll see each other again soon."

"Yes, soon," I echo Otto.

She smiles and presses her hands to her chest. "If you need anything, don't be afraid to ask. Congratulations, again." Without skipping a beat, she spins around and prances back toward her house.

"She seems so pleasant," I tell Otto, pressing my hand to my chest as a smile touches my lips. "We're off to a better start than I expected."

"See, I told you," Otto says with a wink. "You two will become great friends."

"I'm sure we will," I say with a sigh of relief.

"Are you ready for the grand tour?" He's beaming as he reaches into his pocket and retrieves a single gold key. Before I can blink, the door swings open into a beautiful foyer, adorned with ornate molding, oak trim, and sea-green wallpaper.

Each room flows into the next, all simply decorated and ready for a personal touch.

"Oh my. It's beautiful," I say, stopping at the base of the stairwell.

"You haven't seen all of it yet," Otto says, a smile lighting his words.

We continue through the maze of stunning rooms, free of dust, with shining walnut colored oak floors and new wallpaper. It's all quite perfect.

With the word "perfect" floating through my head, I recall what Mama used to tell me every time I became excited about something I knew too little about. She would say, "When a big picture appears perfect, take a closer look, because it's the little details that create the masterpiece of perfection."

* * *

I hang the last of Otto's dress shirts in the chestnut wardrobe that stills smells of sawdust inside. Then I move over to my travel trunk to remove the last of our bedroom items. It squeals open, releasing the scent of home—my old home. Lemon and vanilla. Mama always adds lemon zest and petals of lilacs to the bottle of house cleaner.

I wrapped my picture frames in newspaper print, just two or three to display on top of the bureau and nightstands. I place those down beside me and reach in for the folded linen to make up the beds and hang the drapes.

A cloud floats by the windowpane, revealing strong rays from the sun that bleed into the bedroom. A glistening orb catches my eye from within the trunk, drawing my attention to a gold-plated picture frame. I forgot I tossed this in. I haven't looked at it in so long, but I take in the nostalgia from the sepia-colored image of Danner and I smiling in front of the first bottle of honey I ever poured from his father's bee farm. I guess I packed this away in the trunk when Danner had to leave Germany. The reminder of his absence hurt too much. It's been four years since he was forced out of his home and ordered to live in Poland—where Polish-blooded Jews were sent. According to Hitler, they needed to return to where they came from. It's unfair. Everything in this war is unfair. Despite how long it's been since I last saw Danner, my memories are still sharp and clear. A smile touches my lips at the recollection of the day this photograph was taken.

"I hope wherever you are, you're okay, Danner." I kiss the tips of my fingers and press them to his face in the photograph.

THREE

EMILIE

Munich, Germany

There are six houses divided into two apartments each, sitting in the shape of a U on my street, with a total of twelve families occupying them. A thick line of trees frames our neighborhood and segregates us from the rest of the city. Our little street demonstrates the perfect working-class family life. The fathers have jobs in nearby factories, the moms stay home and take care of us, the kids, and we go to school, come home, then spend our time outdoors until dark.

Papa works for a chemical manufacturer, leading the factory line that produces materials used in communication devices. He always says that, between all the men on the street, they have all the necessary skills to run their own city. It's a fun dream to consider.

My four closest friends live within steps of my front door, which is more than any thirteen-year-old girl could ask for, especially since I'm an only child and have a bad habit of growing bored when sitting still for too long.

Our house is the only one in the half circle made from brick and without a distinctive façade, but it has the most room inside. Like the other houses, there are only two families occupying the divided space: mine and Gertrude Braun's family. We've made secret plans to knock down the wall between our two bedrooms so we can be roommates, but we're sure our parents wouldn't quite approve.

"It's cold out, Emilie... Gerty, I didn't even know you were here! Where are your coats, girls?" Mama catches us whooshing past the kitchen after doing our homework together in my bedroom, eager to get outside. I didn't realize what time it was and forgot she'd be in there starting dinner. We would have been quieter on the way to the front door. I stop short against my toes and Gerty stumbles over. We look at Mama, who's holding a dribbling whisk over the floor, waiting for a response.

"We're thirteen. We know when we're cold and if we should put on coats. Besides, it's March, and the temperature is above freezing. It's a known fact that cold air can increase blood circulation and increase an appetite for what smells like a delicious dinner."

"Emilie Marx...that is the most ridiculous thing—"

"I read about it. Do you want to see the textbook?" I ask.

"Of course you have proof. I have created a monster. That's what I've done."

"She's not a monster," Gerty argues. "She's a nurse in training and wants to prove scientific theories to be incorrect."

"That's not exactly right," I whisper to Gerty, hiding my mouth behind my hand.

"Mama, if we don't test out theories, how will we ever know if the textbook is correct?" I add, crossing my arms over my chest.

Mama tosses her head back with frustration. "Good God, you cannot argue your way out of everything in life," she laments.

"But you told me if I disagree with something, I can only argue if I have proof to back up my claim, which I do."

"You're as stubborn as me. God help me," she mutters. "Emilie, you can also get sick from being out in the cold too long."

"Where is your source?" I counter, tapping my finger against my chin with a smirk threatening to break into laughter.

"My source says you're thirteen and will do what I say. Coats, now," she says, pointing toward my bedroom.

"Okay, okay," I reply, making my way back to my bedroom where I dropped it on my lavender-quilted bed after school.

"I'll put mine on too, Frau Marx," Gerty says with a nervous chuckle.

Gerty hustles out the door in front of me before Mama enforces more rules she might also have to follow.

"Emi, don't stay outside too long. Dinner will be ready in an hour. You're staying in the area, yes?"

I secure the last button on my coat and stop at the opening of the kitchen where Mama is washing a pan over the sink. "You've never been worried about where I'm going before, and we don't usually eat dinner so early. Is everything okay?"

"Of course, but I don't want you going too far. The main streets are crowded. That's all."

"But why?"

She isn't telling me something. I can see it by the smudge of flour on her cheek. She only ends up with ingredients on her face when she's anxious.

She huffs, pressing her forearms against the sink. "Emilie, I'm not sure you understand the gravitas of the Reichstag's newest law, but any person who opposes Hitler's governing decisions will face consequences—brutal ones. You must understand the importance of keeping your thoughts to yourself."

"The talking mustache can't do anything to me. I'm on *my*

street in front of *my* house. I will think what I want, and I *think* he's a horrible man."

Mama drags her fingers through her frayed bangs. "I know I've always told you to speak your mind, but times have changed and you can't speak so freely now. Your father and I feel the same way, but we all need to keep quiet."

Before now, Mama has always said she wanted me to be a strong woman with a voice that could change the world. She's given me the ability to believe anything is possible, which is why I will become a lifesaving nurse someday. I will help people—help them to be good.

"It's not fair. We shouldn't—" I argue.

"That's enough. Go outside with your friends. Not another word about this."

My forehead strains, trying to understand why she's talking this way.

"You only have an hour. Don't waste it glaring at me."

I leave the entryway of the kitchen, trudging outside, perplexed.

Gerty is waiting for me on the front steps, avoiding the bickering between Mama and me. Until a couple of years ago it was always just the two of us, but when we turned eleven, the three boys who live here wanted to join us. Now there are five of us and more often than not, we're together, trying to formulate ideas to prevent death from boredom.

"It's time," Gerty says as I close my front door behind me. "Are you ready for today's performance?"

I laugh, knowing she's about to pull something magical out from behind her back. "I'm afraid to ask what it's time for," I say, shielding my eyes from the sun.

She retrieves a crystal ball from the step below and grins.

"Where did that come from?" I ask.

"It was buried at the bottom of the coat closet, and I found it yesterday. I grabbed it while you were talking to your mama. I figured since we've been reading fortunes regularly, using only playing cards, we should officially declare today...Fortune Friday," she shouts in proclamation, her hands shooting up into the air. We've been reading the boys' fortunes as a form of entertainment. They get a kick out of it, but not as much as Gerty and I do.

"Again?" Otto groans from his front door, slipping a sweater over his head. "Gerty, you ruined my week after your last fortune."

Gerty puckers her lips and scratches her ear. "How did I ruin your week?"

I elbow her in the side, recalling what she did. "You're so mean to him," I tease.

Otto grabs a milk crate and sets it down by our front stairs as a front row seat. "You said I would have a ton of homework and fail an exam."

Gerty holds her hands out to the side. "Did you?"

"Yes, but it's because you convinced me I would."

"That's not how this works," she says.

Danner and Felix both step out of their front doors at the same time. Danner takes slow steps toward us, and I can already tell he'll turn down hearing his fortune. He thinks it's bad luck to predict the future. Meanwhile, Felix thinks our fortunes are a golden door to tomorrow.

"It's time for Fortune Friday," Gerty announces.

Felix rubs his hands together and juts his tongue out.

I spot another milk crate and set it up at the base of the bottom step so Gerty can place the glass ball on it. She retrieves a deck of playing cards from her pocket and places those in front of the ball.

"Danner, you're up first," Gerty says. "I have a message coming in for you."

"No, no, no. Your prediction that I'm going to wet my pants next week is getting old and still hasn't happened, so I no longer need your services," Danner says as Gerty shuffles the playing cards.

"I bet you wouldn't turn down your fortune if Emilie offered it to you," Gerty teases in a singing tune.

"Gerty," I hiss at her, my cheeks burning.

Our girl-talk is supposed to be kept secret.

"He knows I'm not serious," she replies with a giggle.

Danner shrugs and takes a seat beside me, facing the pale green stone house he lives in with his parents and younger brother, David.

"Emi, did you ask your parents about Sunday?" Otto asks.

"What's on Sunday?" Gerty inserts herself.

"There's a festival. My parents told me I could bring a friend."

"Why didn't you ask me?" Gerty inquires.

"Because...I asked Emilie," he says with a raised brow.

"Oh," she says. "Well, I read your fortune, and it turns out, you're the one who will pee his pants this week."

"Liar," he argues.

"Maybe I am, maybe I'm not," she teases.

"Oh, right, the festival. I—I—uh, can't make it on Sunday. I'm sorry, Otto. My parents told me I need to stay nearby."

Gerty glances at me with curiosity. She left just before Mama said what she did.

"Oh, that's too bad," Otto says, scuffing the dirt with the tip of his boot. "Is it because of the new Aryan Paragraph regulation about cultural exclusion? Because my family and I would never go to a festival that supported something like that. I promise that's not something you have to dwell on."

"Jewish people aren't supposed to take part in any public event with this new regulation. I don't think any festival has a choice of whether they follow this law," Gerty says, placing the cards down to take in the news.

"That's what I heard too, but it's not like it's something we would ever participate in. We aren't supporting that law. It's not like that." Otto takes a cigarette and a lighter out of his pocket, turns away and lights up. When he turns back, he narrows his eyes, and silently whistles the smoke up toward the cloudy sky.

"Yeah," Felix says. "I wasn't aware of... Gerty, how come you didn't know about that if you can see the future?"

"I—I don't—we shouldn't be talking about this out loud," I say. Mama said not to disagree with anything where someone can hear us. I'm not sure who else could hear us, but I think it's best to find something else to talk about.

"I'm fooling around. I still want my fortune from you," Felix says, squatting down on the other side of the milk crate.

"Okay, you can be first," Gerty replies.

Otto takes another drag of his cigarette and stares at the side of Felix's face as if he's trying to read his fortune too.

"Okay, tell me what's going to happen next week," Felix says to Gerty.

Gerty holds her hands out, one on each side of the glass globe. He places his hands in hers and she holds on to them for a long moment. She has the role of fortune teller down pat as she meditates before offering an answer.

Danner nudges my shoulder with his. "What do you think it's going to be?" he whispers. "An ice age or a volcanic eruption that splits Europe into a dozen continents?"

I want to push my thoughts away from the racial exclusion news and Mama's warning about showing disagreement, but Hitler states his distaste for Jewish people, claiming they caused Germany to lose the war. We're supposed to take Hitler's side. I won't. Not ever, because Danner, the sweetest boy I know, is Jewish. I could never hate or dislike him. No one will force those feelings upon me.

"Oh my God. I'm going to die. I can see it in your eyes," Danner says.

I press my hand over my mouth, trying to stop myself from

laughing, bringing my thoughts back to the volcanic eruption or an ice age. Gerty comes up with the most ridiculous fortunes when she can't think of anything good to say. "Definitely a volcanic eruption."

"Okay then. I'll let you read my fortune," Danner says, keeping his voice low enough so Gerty doesn't hear. "I don't want to hear about natural disasters or peeing in my pants, though. Okay?"

I suppress laughter from bursting out of my nose and stare up toward the sky, thinking up a fortune for Danner. His initial reluctance for a fortune makes me think he's not up for anything that would scare him, so I have to come up with something in between scary and a natural disaster.

He takes my hands off my lap and clasps them with his. "Okay, go."

Chills coil up my arms as a light spring breeze washes over us. His hands are warm and consume mine. I've lost all trace of thought as I lower my gaze to find his eyes closed and his dimples punctuating the smile he's trying to hide.

"Well, I don't have a crystal ball or fortune cards, but I'm receiving a fuzzy message," I say. I'm not as good at this as Gerty. She is far more believable, despite the silly tales.

"Go on," Danner says, squeezing my hands a little firmer.

His eyelashes flutter over his cheeks.

"You're going to live a long, happy and healthy life, and beekeeping will make you and your dad world renowned for your famous honey."

Danner's eyes flutter open. "You were supposed to give me my fortune for next week, not the rest of my life. Now, nothing will ever come as a surprise. It's like reading the last page of a suspense book before making it past the first chapter." He's laughing as he speaks, but I sense a level of seriousness in his words—ones I don't particularly understand since I don't like surprises.

"I was only fooling you. Your real fortune is..."

Danner closes his eyes again, giving the appearance of allowing me one more chance.

"Next week—"

"I'm going to tell you that...I think you're the most beautiful girl in the world," he whispers, leaning in closer to my ear. His words steal my breath away.

"Me?" I respond quietly, realizing I'm now squeezing his hands much harder than he's squeezing mine.

Danner shrugs. "I hope it's okay that I said that." The gentle hush of his voice tickles my ear and his gaze drops to our hands. "I...I think about you a lot when we aren't together. We've always been honest with one another, so I think it's only fair I tell you that."

My cheeks heat and my heart pounds against the inside of my chest. He doesn't know how often I stare at his front door, wishing it would open and he'd appear. He's my favorite person to talk to. "I—I..."

"You don't have to—"

"I daydream about you during classes sometimes," I confess. "And I count the minutes until school is over and we can walk home together. So...I guess we feel the same way, right?"

Danner smiles, the kind of smile where his eyes follow the upward curve and his freckles smoosh together. I realize we're still holding hands and I glance over at Gerty, Otto, and Felix, curious if they noticed. I pull my hands away quickly, not wanting that form of attention from the three of them.

"Wait." Danner's eyes flash open. "What's my real fortune?"

I forgot we were even talking about his fortune. I shake the thoughts around in my head. "Oh, right. Um, well, you're going to receive news next week." The words burst from my mouth. I'm not sure what news he'll receive, but I'm sure something can be considered news.

"Well, I only want good news. Don't forget," he says.

"Oh, it'll be good."

"Emi, you can't stop there. What do you think it'll be?"

I catch myself staring into the depths of Danner's stormy eyes, feeling a heavy sensation in the pit of my stomach. The back of my neck grows warm, and I close my eyes. "I—well..." Another chill spreads through my body and I can't find my words.

"It's the worst news ever," Felix calls out, interrupting us. "It's my turn. Move over," he says, squeezing himself in between Danner and me.

"I just read your fortune!" Gerty shouts at Felix.

"I'm not taking in a stray cat next week. My father can't even be around them without breaking out into hives."

"Fine. Otto, I have your fortune ready."

He groans and tosses his head back. "I don't want to know."

Danner shoves Felix to the side and sits back down beside me. "I wasn't done yet," he tells him. "Emi, you have to tell me if it's good news or bad?" Danner asks again as Felix wraps his arm around Danner's neck, horse playing like usual.

It's bad news. I'm not sure why that thought is running through my head, but I'm trying to keep the words inside. There's no reason to say something like that. I force a smile and say, "It'll be good. I'm sure of it."

"Okay then, if that's the case...will you come to the bee farm with me on Sunday?"

His question takes me by surprise, but I answer without a second thought. "I'd love to!" My voice rattling with an awkward squeak as I startlingly remember my fear of bees. Danner winces at my response. He's aware of my silly fear.

"Are you sure?" he asks again, still wincing.

"It's time to get over my fear. I can do that," I tell him, forcing myself to sound more positive than I feel inside. Regardless, I couldn't imagine turning down an offer to spend time with him—bees or no bees.

* * *

"I'll keep you safe, I promise," he says as I step out the front door on this bright, sunny Sunday morning.

"I trust you," I say, unable to hide the blush blooming through my cheeks.

"Here, I brought you a pair of gloves and a hat with netting to protect your face and neck."

I'll look ridiculous wearing this, but I assume he'll be dressed the same way, so put my sense of style aside for today. We walk side by side toward the shallow woods that separate our homes from the rest of the city.

"Do you think you'll be a honey farmer like your papa someday?" I ask, curious since Danner doesn't talk much about his future dreams.

"I'm already a honey farmer. I'll prove it to you today. Papa said I'm as good as any other and I'll be well known for this honey someday."

The leaves crunch beneath our feet as we enter the woods. "I know you're scared of the bees, but are you aware that bees are one of the most important species on earth?"

I twist my lips to the side and raise my brow, questioning his statement, ready to argue the absurd fact. "I don't believe that," I say.

"It's true. Albert Einstein said that mankind would be extinct within four years if we lost all the bees."

"When did he say that?"

Danner shrugs. "It's a fact. I don't know. But I do know that bees are responsible for a third of the world's crops and agriculture. A honeybee's entire purpose in life is to keep our world from falling apart. Kind of like you. You talk about wanting to become a nurse so you can take care of people and keep them healthy. Some rare beings are born with a gift that keeps us all alive."

"Like honeybees?" I repeat.

"And maybe you too."

"I'm not a honeybee," I argue through a giggle.

"Sure you are, a rare one only a few are lucky to be acquainted with."

Danner takes my hand, intertwining his fingers with mine, making my heart leap into my throat as my pulse buzzes through every vein in my body.

The walk is shorter than I thought—and hoped for—and we quickly see his papa in the distance, already working with the hives. Our hands part, drifting down by our sides.

Danner slips into his protective gear and then helps me do the same. "This will prevent the bees from stinging us?" I ask.

Danner laughs through his netted mask. "Stop worrying so much."

"Emilie! You've finally agreed to let Danner teach you how to collect honey?" Herr Alesky shouts from across the open space.

"Yes," I say, hesitation clear in my voice. He laughs too, sounding like Danner.

Danner collects tools from his father's wooden crate and waves me over toward the buzzing hives. My heart pounds as I walk closer, wishing I could convince myself the bees won't hurt me. "Okay, the first thing we have to do is light up this smoker tool so we can puff out a cloud of smoke toward the hives."

"But why would you do that?" I ask, imagining bees swarming toward us out of anger.

"The bees will think there's a fire in the woods and they'll retreat to their hives for safety."

"Oh." I understand the logic, but still take a step backward as he prepares the smoker tool.

I watch as he performs the trick of getting the bees to hide inside their hives.

"Okay, now that they're all inside, we're going to pull out one of the wooden frames from inside the hive box. The bees will emerge with it, but you don't have to worry about them. I promise."

I take another step back, still terrified, but he gently slides the frame out, careful not to tap the sides. The bees come along, still attached, but he holds the piece out in front of him and gives it a little shake. Most of the bees return to the boxed hive. Danner pulls a brush-like tool out of his pocket and sweeps away the remaining bees. He's completely in his element. I'm so focused on watching Danner extract a perfect film of honeycomb that I forget about being terrified.

"You're doing great," he tells me, even though he's done all the work. "Come on over here." I follow him away from the hives and over to a tree stump with a metal bin and a crank. He hands me the bee-less frame and shows me where to slide it into the metal opening. "Okay, now you crank away for about twenty minutes or until your arms give out, I suppose. Then, like magic, you have fresh honey." He makes it all sound so easy when I know his father spends hours out here every day.

I'm eager to do this part, so I turn the wooden handle in circular motions, watching honey drip from the frame. Once I lose speed and traction Danner wraps his gloved hand around mine to help. I forget what I'm doing when I realize my back is against his chest and he's curled around me to help crank out the remaining honey. I could swear there's a hive worth of bees inside my chest, buzzing around, fluttering wings against my insides. The sweet, floral scent permeates the air around us and the warmth of his body embraces mine. It's a memory I'll never forget.

"Keep cranking, okay? I'm going to go grab the next few frames."

A void fills the space that he was standing in, and I wish he were back already. "You're right about the bees. They aren't coming after me. I guess I've been worried over nothing," I say, chuckling.

A dull thud, a clatter, and a forced sigh of wind expelling from lungs. I spin around, finding Danner face first on the ground, a knotted log wedged between his torso and the ground.

"Danner?" I shout, chasing after him, noticing he doesn't move after I call his name. Fearing he may be unconscious, I drop to my knees by his side and sweep his hair off the side of his face, finding him struggling to open his eyes.

"I'm okay," he mutters.

"What happened?" I cry.

I roll him to his side, finding a gash on the bridge of his nose and a couple smaller cuts on his lips. "Oh, Danner. Oh no."

"I'll be okay," he says against his swelling lip. "I just tripped."

I frantically try to find a handkerchief in my pocket but can't manage to do much with the thick gloves on my hands. I tear them off, despite the sporadic bees flying around us and grab the handkerchief from my skirt pocket. I press it to his nose to stop the bleeding and scoot behind him to help him onto his back so I can prop his head up. Danner, calm as could be, stares up at me, blinking slowly as if studying something he's never seen before. "You're so beautiful, Emi," he says.

Despite the heat flushing through my cheeks, taking the most flattering compliment while trying to keep my focus on his bleeding nose, I tell him to hush. Danner's father notices what's happening and rushes to my side, taking the handkerchief from my hand.

"He tripped," I tell him.

"That's going to leave a scar, son. We need to get you to the doctor." Danner's father is taller and bulkier than he is and can pull him up to his feet without much effort. "Young love should come with a warning label." Danner's father mutters the words quietly, but they were loud enough to embarrass us both.

"Will you stay with me?" Danner asks.

"Of course, for as long as you want me," I say as we walk toward the edge of the trees.

"Wait here while I get my truck," Herr Alesky says, leaving Danner leaning up against a tree and me by his side.

"I'm so sorry you're hurt." He takes the handkerchief away from his nose, finding the fabric soaked in blood. I take it from his hand and carefully dab up the blood on his lip too. "You'll be okay."

"I will. And you know what...at least I'll always have a scar now to remind me of today, you...making your first batch of honey on the same day I realized you will absolutely be the best nurse this world will ever have."

FOUR

DANNER

Munich, Germany

I've never had so much time to sit and think, and I've come to the conclusion that spending this much time with only my thoughts is unhealthy. Every day for the last fourteen months that I've been staying as a guest in Felix's house—ironically next door to where I grew up before being evicted by the Gestapo—I have spent hours sitting at his writing desk, staring at blank sheets of notepaper, imagining the words I could fill each one with. When I'm not staring at paper, I study hairline fractures along the honey-yellow walls of his bedroom until my vision blurs. That's when the guilt returns, like clockwork.

I remind myself I've left Mama and my brother, David, with a promise to find Papa and bring him back to reunite our family. I shouldn't have been so naïve to think I would find him so easily after his arrest four years ago, especially knowing so many Jewish citizens have been branded as criminals based on false accusations and sent to labor camps to serve their punishment. He could be anywhere, more unfortunately, a concentration camp for criminals.

I push the wooden chair away from the writing desk, grating the bottom of the legs against the wooden floor. Whenever I step out into the narrow hallway, I consider making my way to the front window to look outside, wishing to be back in a time when my friends would be waiting outside. It never takes long to bring myself back to the present and realize I'm not in my parents' house, which this one resembles so closely.

"Danner, is that you? Is everything all right?"

Felix's mom, Frau Weber, worries whenever I move from room to room during the day while Felix is at the textile factory working alongside his father. She must feel responsible for me, even though I wish she wouldn't worry so much. I promised to stay out of their hair and not cause them any extra work after they'd graciously offered to take me in.

"It's that time of the day again," I reply. "The porcelain throne awaits me and I mustn't keep it waiting."

"Danner, my goodness," she says, laughing at my remark. The thought of only moving about during the day to use the bathroom is depressing, but also humorous when I call out the facts.

Upon arriving at my new destination, two steps down the hall and through the door on the right, I close myself into the square space and lean over the protruding sink basin below a scratched-up mirror outlined by a silvering copper frame.

I push my fingers through my hair and take a closer look at the red web of veins branching across the whites of my eyes along with the sight of my long nose, high cheekbones, and what Mama would refer to as Ashkenazi eyes—heavy eyelids with thick lashes that cast a shadow over my cheeks. My muddy blonde hair color and reddish freckles might deceive anyone who tries to draw a conclusion on my heritage. One thing is certain though...I don't have the storybook features of a German Aryan and I no longer look like every other healthy twenty-two-year-old man.

People must think I'm closer to forty with the deepening worry lines branching out from the corners of my eyes and across my forehead. Every Jewish man, no matter what age they are, looks much older than they should. We live in a state of fear now, and it takes a toll.

It isn't easy to find too many reasons to stall when in the washroom, but I prefer to be alone in here rather than anywhere else. It's the one containment furthest away from the outside walls.

"If there's ever a threat of an incoming air raid or attack, the most central part of the building, the washroom will be the best place to be," Papa would often warn David and me. A man of the First World War generation was never less than prepared for the unexpected, until he was arrested.

I think of Papa's words whenever I hear gunshots or roundups of the disabled, non-white, homosexual, and Jewish citizens of this town. I yearn for his worldly advice, his words of wisdom, even his lectures on how to be a proper respectable man. It's all I have of him now.

I pull out the wrinkled, worn paper folded into a small square from my pocket and unfold the edges, one by one, careful not to tear it. Papa's messy handwriting spans from one side of the paper to the other.

Danner,

I've gone to the bakery for bread. I'll be back soon. Please switch out the water for the bees. I'll be home soon, son.

Love,

Papa

The first time I read this note was the last normal moment

of my life. The comfort I felt, the reminder to do something we did together every day, is something I never thought I would need to keep. Papa and I planned to grow the honey business and distribute within local territories, but that all came to a halting stop when the Gestapo decided to arrest him.

I pry my gaze away from the letter and back up to the mirror, and remind myself of what he would remind me if he were standing here:

I'm a proud Jew. This is who I am.

Except my passports and identification say otherwise. This letter in my hand burns against my skin, knowing the lies I hold on to as a safety harness. Without my altered identifications, I'm Danner Alesky, son of Sarah and Abraham Alesky, brother to David Alesky. With the updated papers, I'm Albert Amsler, living with a friend, Felix Weber, and his family in a city that is ridding its population of all Jewish inhabitants. I've been hiding under a fake name for so long that I question how many people could just look at me and see my truth.

A fist against the bathroom door causes a reflexive tremble in my knees. "Danner, is that you in there?"

"Yes, yes, I'm sorry," I say, drying my hands off on the hanging towel even though I'd dried them more than five minutes ago.

I open the door, coming face to face with Felix.

"What's wrong?" he asks, the lines in his forehead angled into the shape of a v.

"Nothing. I was washing up," I reply.

Compared to him, his grease riddled white shirt and sweat-drenched red face and wet hair, I don't have much reason for the use of soap. He's just arrived back home after a long shift at the automobile factory. I would be working alongside him if I weren't essentially hiding. The fewer people I face, the safer I'll be. Felix thinks my passport shows no sign of forgery.

He checks his watch as if there should be a certain time of day I choose to wash up. "You look nervous."

I pinch the bridge of my nose, a habit I've gotten into every time someone asks me if I'm okay. Ironically, I'm not checking to see if my nose looks like one that belongs to a Jewish man—though it is long and accentuated with the dented scar I earned years ago—instead, I worry that it might be growing like the wooden puppet, Pinocchio's, whose nose grew every time he lied. Mama used to read the story to me as a child in hopes that I would learn the importance of being honest. She wouldn't approve of my actions now.

Felix tilts his head in disagreement and chuckles. "Your nose isn't growing, mate. How many times do I need to tell you?"

I drop my hand, defeated that I've been called out by him once again. When a person has been friends with another for seventeen years, since the age of five, there aren't many ways to keep secrets. "I feel uneasy today. I can't quite put my finger on it, but my mind has been spinning in circles since I woke up this morning."

The sluggish sway of his shoulders tells me he wonders what I could be so worried about. Felix is aware of all that goes through my mind but feels confident I'm safe here, living under a false identity in their apartment. I don't think his parents feel the same as he does. I'm taking food from their mouths and unable to financially contribute. I try to take the bare minimum, but his mother isn't the type to allow a man in her house to be hungry, despite the rations we're subject to.

"Ed is having people over tonight," he says with a sigh.

Ed's become his closest friend in the time I was gone and Felix is trying to split his time between ensuring I'm not going stir-crazy here and hanging out with his friends like most twenty-two-year-old men want to do.

"Don't worry. I told him I couldn't make it. I don't want to leave you here after sitting in my room all day."

"You should go," I tell him.

Felix mentions this friend daily. They work at the factory together. He doesn't want to sit around here. I can't ask him to do that.

"No, no, we can play cards here or something, you and me," he says, patting me on the shoulder.

"I'm not up to playing cards. Go and have fun. Don't worry about me, okay?"

Felix tosses his head back, torn between his decision to be loyal to me or to live the life he deserves—and is free—to live. "You need to promise you aren't going to sit on the mattress popping open your father's pocket watch repeatedly as a form of entertainment. Or worse, stare at the radio like it's going to tell you what you want to hear?"

I'm certain the radio won't tell me where my father is being held prisoner, or if he's even still alive. I'm also sure I won't get much of an update about my mother or brother in Poland either. I'm not deluded enough to think it will tell me what I actually want to hear. My only hope is that the German radio station will be intercepted and the public informed that someone is making headway in stopping this war.

"Boys, dinner is almost ready," Frau Weber calls down the hallway to us.

I move away from the washroom so Felix can step inside to clean up before dinner. "You're going," I say, pushing him into the washroom and closing him inside.

The letter from my father is still hanging from my pinched fingers behind my back, so I fold it up and place it in my pocket and head down to the dinner table to help Frau Weber.

"Danner, you've been so quiet this afternoon. Is everything okay?"

Walking up behind Felix's mother reminds me of when I

would walk up behind my own, offering to help set the table or offer a hand with whatever she needed. She would wear her hair the same way, in a low knot, pinned to the base of her neck. Mama's hair is deep brown and Frau Weber's hair is a light honey shade of blonde. That's the only obvious difference, telling me I'm in someone else's home, approaching a woman who isn't my mother. Poland might as well be on the other side of the world considering how far I feel from Mama and David. This house is similar to how my home used to feel and I'm so grateful they took me in, but at the same time, the nostalgia constantly highlights what I've lost and am missing dearly.

"Of course, Frau Weber. I was just reading."

Well, I was trying to read, but my thoughts wouldn't allow me to absorb more than a sentence.

"Are you sure?"

"Yes, I was reading Felix's copy of *Cold Comfort Farm* again."

"I have other books you might enjoy. I'm happy to dig them out of my trunk if you'd like."

"Maybe some time," I say, taking the first two dinner plates out to the table.

"Did you hear about the questioning next door?" Herr Weber asks while turning the corner toward the dinner table. "Oh! Danner. I—I thought you were my wife."

"My ugly mug must have given you quite a scare then," I joke while acknowledging what he mistakenly asked me instead of his wife.

"You're just as lovely," Herr Weber quips back with laughter.

I can't get myself to laugh along with him. Not while I'm wondering what he was going to say. "What were the neighbors being questioned about?"

Herr Weber flaps his hand at me, then brushes his fist beneath his nose. "Oh, it was nothing. Nothing to worry about."

Which means it is something concerning. I appreciate them trying to protect me and keep me safe, but not being aware of what's happening around me isn't helpful. I should be aware if there are Nazis or Gestapo on the prowl in our enclosed neighborhood. Or at least have a sense of what they are looking for.

"What was that?" Frau Weber asks, joining us at the table with the other two dinner plates.

"It was nothing, dear." He lifts his brows in her direction, a gesture she must understand, and I don't, because she drops the subject. Normally, she would press for more information if he brushed a topic away.

"I'm going to visit Ed tonight. He's having people over," Felix says as he walks into the dining room with a clean face, combed hair, and a fresh pair of pants and shirt.

"Ed from the factory?" Herr Weber questions.

"Yes," Felix says, taking his seat. "You can lock up the house. I have a key."

Herr Weber clears his throat. "Why don't you stay in tonight? Keep Danner company."

"It's fine, Herr Weber, I told him he should go. I'll probably go to bed early anyway," I say, taking my spoon to the bowl of stew.

I catch a passing glimpse between Herr and Frau Weber, the look making more sense than their last exchange. Herr Weber closes his eyes for a moment and offers a subtle headshake as if fighting a chill.

"I think you should stay in as well, Felix. You'll see Ed at work tomorrow, won't you?" Frau Weber adds, giving Felix the same look Herr Weber just gave her.

Felix lifts his napkin and wipes it across his mouth. "Okay, I'll stay in," he agrees.

"What are you all being so discreet about? There's something you aren't saying." I frown.

"There's nothing for you to lose sleep over, son. You have

the proper papers and no reason to worry. The Gestapo makes rounds all the time." He wouldn't be concerned about us walking down the street tonight if I truly had nothing to worry about. Since the age of thirteen, all I've been able to do is watch my next step in hope of not falling into a trap.

The remaining moments of dinner fill with an orchestra of clanging dishes and silverware, slurps of stew, guzzles of water, and my heart hammering against my rib cage.

FIVE

DANNER

Munich, Germany

Mama has set out a bowl of chopped fruit, toast, and jam, ready for David and me to devour before running out of the house and racing to school. She would prefer we wake up earlier and take the time to sit down at the table and swallow the bites we take before continuing our mad dash, but she's given up the fight now that David is old enough to be following in my footsteps—sleeping too late and having to rush. He's three years younger but wants to do everything the same way I do. It can be annoying, but I try to take it as a compliment. He watches me like I'm his reflection in the mirror and copies my gestures, and even goes as far as smiling and scowling the same way. Mama said he'll find his own way soon enough and that ten years old is a hard age to navigate, being just a boy but wanting to be older like me.

Mama stands at the doorway with our bagged lunches in hand, but not with the typical tired smile she pins to her cheeks as we leave. She seems distressed. "What is it, Mama?"

"Yes, what's wrong, Mama?" David echoes.

"David, run along. Your brother will catch up in a moment. I need to have a word with him."

"Oh, you must be in trouble," David hoots as he skips out the door.

I don't think I'm in trouble. I would have had to do something wrong for that to be the case. This is something else, and I'm not sure it's going to be any better than me being in trouble. "What is it?" I ask, my voice stifled in my throat.

She places her hands on top of my shoulders as her eyes close for a long blink. She takes a deep breath and stares me straight in the face. "I'm not sure what events might unfold today, son. If you're told to go home, collect your brother, and do as you're told immediately without question. Do you understand?"

How could I understand? She's never said anything like this to me before. Why would someone tell me to go home?

Papa enters the kitchen just as Mama is trying to find the words to explain her statement. "Have you told him yet?" he says, straightening the knot on his tie.

"Told me what?" I ask, staring between the two of them. My stomach growls from hunger and nerves. I'm not even sure I'll be able to eat the toast I'm holding in my hand after they say what they need to say.

"I was trying to find the words," Mama says, folding her arms around her waist.

Dad rests his arm around Mama's back and leans down to stare me in the eyes like Mama was. "Son, the Führer made a statement yesterday that there were too many Jewish children in the public schools and that there's to be less than five percent of the student population going forward," Papa says. "We aren't sure how they plan to handle this new policy, but we want you to be prepared in case they ask you and your brother to leave. If they do, we will figure things out. It's not something you need to worry about."

"Too many Jewish children in school?" I repeat. "What difference does the number of Jewish children make?"

"It doesn't," Mama groans.

"Sarah," Papa utters. "We all feel the same way, but we don't have control over this."

"Can't I refuse to leave?" The question is rhetorical because I would never argue with a teacher.

"I'm afraid not, son. If you're told to leave, do so without a word."

I drop my chin already feeling the defeat. "Yes, Father."

He scruffs up my hair and kisses the top of my head. Mama then pulls me into a tight embrace. "I love you. It will be okay. Keep your chin up."

I don't think she believes those words. Her chin isn't up. She's staring down at the floor.

My shoulders feel heavier than when Papa's hands were resting on them, but I walk out the door, finding David running in circles around Emilie, Gerty, Otto, and Felix, who have waited for me. *I must be brave.*

Gerty wrangles her arms around David and captures him so he can't continue spinning around them. "Got you," she says with laughter.

I would prefer that no one knows what Mama and Papa just told me, but they might have already heard from their parents. "Gerty, Felix, Otto, and I were thinking of going to the theater tomorrow night. Can you go too?" Emilie asks.

"I should be able to," I say.

"Me too. I'm going with you too," David adds.

"We'll see about that," I mutter. Whenever David joins us, I end up having to watch him all night rather than having fun with my friends.

"You sound tired," Emilie says. "Did the math homework keep you up late?"

"No, no, I'm fine." She knows when I'm lying, but never

forces the truth out, which I appreciate. I offer her the same courtesy.

"I see," she says.

"I heard the radio last night," Felix injects. "It's not right. It's stupid is what it is."

Emilie stares over at Felix, giving him a look that I would take as a hint to stop talking.

"He's right. It is stupid, and if I could say the things I want say out loud—" Gerty adds with a grunt.

"Maybe it's best to assume you'll be part of the five percent, right?" Emilie asks.

I clear my throat, hoping she'll drop the subject. I don't want David asking questions. He'll walk right into his classroom and ask if they're going to send him home because he's Jewish. As young as he is, he would hope they would say yes just so he wouldn't have to go to school anymore. I don't think that's the way this will work.

My apprehension keeps me quiet throughout our walk, leaving Felix and Emilie to carry on a conversation about the film playing at the theater. I catch Emilie's lingering glance sweep over me once every few minutes. If she knows what I do, she understands the stress I'm feeling—the dread of walking in through the school doors, being told to stop and go home because I'm no longer wanted in the building.

David shouts his goodbyes as he runs ahead of us to make it inside the school hall first. If I walk slow enough, I might have more hope if he isn't sent back out the door, but I should be in there before he is in case anyone gives him grief.

I speed up to make it into the school, but Emilie catches my arm.

"I'll see you inside," Felix says, continuing on ahead.

Gerty is hesitant to leave but when she spots us having a quiet conversation, follows Felix into the school.

"Danner," Emilie says, "you don't deserve this...even just

the thought of it. It's not fair, and it's not right. I'll always stand behind you. I hope you know that."

I stare at her for a long moment, finding the truth welling up in her pretty blue eyes. "I do. This must be the news you were talking about in my fortune reading last week."

"No, no," she argues. She doesn't want to believe the gut feeling she must have had. Mama tells us to always trust what our gut is saying.

"Don't worry about me. I'll be okay," I tell her with words so forced it's obvious I'm lying.

"Look at me," she says, pressing her hand against my cheek. "Don't focus on what the government wants you to focus on. You'll be making their jobs easier. Whenever you feel like the world is against you, start counting your breaths. One breath every five seconds will show anyone who is watching that you haven't a worry in the world."

"One breath every five seconds?" I repeat.

"Yes, it keeps you calm, and no one will spot a hint of your worry."

"I can do that," I assure her before turning around and jogging toward the front door of the school.

I walk in through the door and hold my breath to try and slow the rush of air coming and going from my lungs even though I'm convinced even the walls are judging me for my religion. There are teachers in the corridor and every non-Jewish German child who walks in shouts, "Heil Hitler!" Along with their flat hand salute. No one told me I had to do so, which segregates me more, and I'm not just imagining that each one of the teachers I pass gives me a cold glare as I walk by. But no one stops me.

Frau Hunter, my teacher, could be the one with the power to send me away. My heart trembles as sweat trickles down the center of my spine while I walk into the brightly lit classroom.

The light of a projector is blaring against the blackboard even though the curtains are open too.

I walk past Frau Hunter's desk and smile at her, waiting for her mouth to open. "Guten Morgen, Herr Alesky. Have a seat."

Relief floods through me, my muscles relax, and I lose my grip, unsticking my fingernails from the palms of my hands.

I settle down into my seat and glance around the classroom, noticing empty desks scattered throughout the room. I shift my gaze to the clock just as the bell rumbles. The empty seats belong to the other Jewish kids who were in my class. I'm the only one left.

"Today we're going to be watching a presentation about the 'Aryan Paragraph.' I suggest you all take out your notebooks and pencils to jot down some notes as you will be quizzed on this information later."

The Aryan Paragraph. The new way of imposing regulations to exclude Jews from German society.

SIX

EMILIE

NINE YEARS AGO, APRIL 1933

Munich, Germany

From my view in the school yard, everything seems as it should be: children from the younger grade levels playing through laughter, bells dinging from the passing trolleys, and bicycle bells wavering against a bouncy ride. Even the faint perfume of the blooming flowers from a nearby garden mixed with the moisture left behind from this morning's rain shower paint a different picture to what's in front of me. The Germany I used to know is not the Germany I'm in.

The sun struggles to pierce through the heavy clouds, allowing only a few rays of light to leak through the trees and spill onto the grass. There are far fewer students standing around me than there were yesterday and there are distant echoes of police boots marching along cobbled roads.

It's no secret that many Jewish children were sent home today and I've been waiting for Danner along with Gerty, Otto, and Felix for nearly a half hour since school ended, but there's no sign of him anywhere.

"He might be home," Felix says. "No one else has exited the school doors in minutes. We should get going."

The six of us always walk home together. But not today.

As we start moving toward the sidewalk, I glance over my shoulder once more toward the school doors, seeing nothing more than a couple of papers floating around. Lost in thought, I fall behind the others, worried about what will happen to Danner if he was one of the Jewish students sent home from school. I'm not sure where he'll go. He loves school.

Otto slows his pace and waits for me to catch up to him. "I'm sure Danner is fine," he says.

"I hope so," I say.

Felix waits for us to catch up and yanks on the strap of my satchel, bouncing around as if he doesn't know what to do with his pent-up energy. "Do you think Danner was sent home?" he asks.

Felix and Danner are close, too. Their parents knew each other long before we were all born and that closeness carried over between the boys from a young age.

Gerty shuffles her feet to catch up with the three of us but meets me on my other side to avoid being knocked over by Felix. She locks arms with me and rests her cheek on my shoulder. "I don't think he was one of the kids sent home," she says. "But if he was, you and I will go marching right into the principal's office tomorrow and demand they take him back."

I'm afraid no one would listen to our demands. The decisions aren't being made by our principal. Mama and Papa said these are new German regulations. It's not fair to any of the kids this has happened to.

Otto shakes his head disapprovingly. "You can't barge into the school making demands right now. Besides, aren't you the fortune teller?" he replies. "Surely, you would have predicted that this would happen, yes?"

Gerty curls her lips and scrunches her nose. "I can't predict everything, you ding-dong."

Otto places his hands on his heart as if he's been offended by her words. "Well, I saw him close to the end of the day. We ran on the track together. He seemed okay to me."

"Did he mention anything about what happened today?" I ask.

"Not a word," Otto says.

Gerty and I give each other a look, one we exchange when we're both silently worrying about the same thing. "We're almost home. Hopefully he's already there so we can check to make sure everything is okay," Gerty says.

"Maybe we should have waited another few minutes," I say, feeling a twinge of guilt.

Just as we turn down our street, Otto's mother pops her head out their front door. "There you are," she hollers. "I was wondering what was taking you so long. You're late." She's standing squarely in her doorway now, her hands on her hips, watching as we approach.

"We were waiting for Danner, but—"

"He's home already," she says, whipping her dishrag off her shoulder.

I glance off to the left toward his bedroom window, curious to see if he's peeking out, but his drapes are closed.

"I made you kids apple fritters. Come on in before they get cold."

Still focused on Danner's house, I spot the front door crack open. I stop walking with the others and run across the stone road to see if he's okay. "Danner?"

When I'm close enough to catch a glimpse of the side of his face, he closes the door and secures the lock as if I'm some kind of monster chasing him.

I knock on the door, my heavy fist making a bong-bong

sound. "Let him be, Emilie," Otto's mother, Frau Berger, shouts across the street.

"Something is wrong. I need to see if he's okay," I say, knocking again. *Why won't he open the door?*

"Danner, it's me. Talk to me. Frau Berger made us apple fritters. Come on..."

"I can't, Emilie." His words are barely audible from the other side of the door.

"But why?" I question.

"Emilie, dear," Frau Berger hollers again. "I don't want to let the mice in, please come along."

"Go on, Emi. We'll talk later. I promise," Danner says, his voice weak and distraught from what little I can hear.

"I just need you to tell me if you're okay. Are you?"

"I'm fine," he says without hesitation. "Go to Frau Berger's for the apple fritters, then come over later."

I place my palm flat on his door, defeated he won't tell me what's happened. "I'll be back soon."

"Don't hurry on my account."

Those words are unlike anything Danner would say. He's always full of excitement and in a rush to get to wherever we're going or do whatever we might be doing. Today is the first day he's shied away from what's in front of him. Something must be wrong.

I fix my satchel over my shoulder so the bag rests on my back and hurry across the street to Frau Berger's open door, where she's still waiting. "I was just checking on Danner," I tell her.

"Of course," she says. "I understand."

Frau Berger closes the door after I step inside. Her house always smells of baked goods, mixed with a hint of tobacco from Herr Berger's pipe that he smokes before bed. The others are scattered around the kitchen, staring at the platter of fritters.

They look like they haven't eaten in a year. I'm not hungry, though.

Frau Berger places a stack of dessert dishes down on the counter and tells everyone to help themselves. I take a seat at their long wooden table and drop my satchel between my ankles.

Otto sits down beside me with his full plate. "Why didn't you take a plate?" he asks.

"I'm not hungry."

Felix and Gerty sit on the opposite side of the table with servings like Otto's. With everyone focusing on me and the fact that I didn't grab a plate, I see that it would have been better if I had just taken a small helping and picked at it rather than calling attention to myself for avoiding it all together.

"You're not eating," Gerty says, reaching across the table to rest her hand on top of mine.

"I'm just not hungry. I'm fine."

"You're a bad liar," Felix says, pointing at me. "And you're a worse fortune teller." He points at Gerty as he falls into a fit of laughter.

"It's Danner, isn't it?" Gerty asks, ignoring Felix's behavior.

"I'm worried about him. I can't imagine what he must be thinking right now, and I don't even know what happened today."

"Me too," she says. "No one should be treated any differently. No one citizen should be blamed for this war."

"What can we do to help him?" Otto asks, his mouth full. "We can't control the Jewish laws and regulations being imposed, but I feel terrible for what he's going through. It makes no sense. All we can do is stand by his side so he knows that no matter what happens, he will always have his friends to depend on."

"I agree," Felix says, his manners suddenly forgotten as well as he speaks with a full mouth.

"Yes, you're absolutely right," Gerty adds.

"Children," Frau Berger interrupts while placing the dry, cleaned baking dish away. "I don't mean to impose my opinions on the matter, but just as Otto was saying, we can't do much to control political changes. Defying rules and laws is a dangerous act. Danner might just be abiding to the enforcement, and you should all do the same, yes?"

"What enforcement?" I ask.

"The ones of our chancellor who is trying to fix the economy of our country."

Gerty chokes on the bite of food in her mouth, as shocked as I am to hear the words spill from Frau Berger's mouth.

"By removing the Jewish people from our schools to ensure jobs are distributed to the right population following a higher education?" Gerty rebuts.

Gerty is always a step ahead of the rest of us when it comes to understanding the German government and their priorities, concerns, and ways of preventing another war. Most of the time I would rather be in the dark about our reality, but we've gotten to a point where the reality of our country is slowly enveloping all of us.

"What exactly is the right population?" Felix asks. "We were all born here, including Danner, right?"

"That's not the point," Frau Berger says.

"What is the point?" I recoil.

She wasn't expecting my response but I'm not sure she understands what she's saying. Frau Berger has always been a kind woman with a big heart, which doesn't match the thoughts she's sharing with us now.

"My point is that we don't have much say against the chancellor's decisions. If we want to stand against him and the government, we might as well be standing alone."

Otto seems perplexed by his mother's opposing, unbalanced thoughts, and stares at her for a long moment. "If everyone is too afraid to do what's right, more Jewish people will be beaten and mortified on the streets like that poor lawyer, Dr. Siegel," he says.

"Otto, what are you talking about?" Frau Berger retorts as if he's making up a story. Except, we all heard and read about it in the newspaper.

"Dr. Siegel's friend, the owner of the Uhlfeder department store was taken away to a concentration camp because he's a successful businessman. Dr. Siegel was beaten then forced to walk down the street barefoot and nearly naked, holding a sign that said 'I'm a Jew, but will never again complain to the police'. How can we watch this happen?" Otto argues.

Mama always tells me that fear will eventually guide us all in one direction or another. I see that to be truer than ever now. The recollection of what happened to that poor doctor last month makes my stomach hurt, and thinking about Danner's family being treated the same way.

I stand up from the table and make my way over to the apple fritters. I take a piece and place it on a scrap of parchment paper, wrap it up and make my way out of the kitchen.

"Emi, where are you going?" Otto jumps up from his seat and follows me.

"To bring Danner a piece of the apple fritter he's missed out on because he's being held responsible for a failing economy, and the future of what could continue being a failing economy. It makes little sense, doesn't it?"

"I—I can bring it over there. He might be embarrassed if you—"

"Danner wouldn't be embarrassed in front of me," I tell him.

"What if he isn't here right now because he needed time alone after school? Shouldn't we respect that?"

"No," I say. Maybe I shouldn't be so quick to deny his statement because Danner was upset at the door, but friends are supposed to be the people who are there with you even when you want to avoid the world. We are supposed to hear the quiet thoughts that would go unheard if we didn't pay attention.

"I'll come with you," Otto suggests.

"You don't have to do that. You have friends over."

"Well, are you going to return? You're my friend, aren't you?" Otto takes my hand, something he's done a few times recently. His eyelids become heavy, and he appears hurt as he stares into my eyes.

"Of course we're friends, but Danner is—"

Gerty clears her throat and smirks at me, forcing me to glare with a plea to stop whatever she's about to say about Danner and me. I've told her what he said to me and what I said to him, but asked her to keep it just between us.

"Danner is going through a lot," Gerty says, changing direction.

I pull my hand out of Otto's and reach for the front door. "I'll see you later."

"Sure," he says, forcing a smile. "Tell Danner I said hello."

We live within a few steps of each other. There's no reason for such formality when we can walk out of our houses and shout each other's name to get a response. I guess there's something more bothering Otto too, but the changes in our country affect us all in one way or another.

I storm across the street, eager to talk to Danner. I'm sure he wasn't expecting me to return so soon. I rap my knuckles on his front door, a bit gentler this time in case he isn't the one sitting right by the door like I saw earlier.

Heels clomp across the wooden floors, and I'm not surprised to see Frau Alesky answer the door. "Emilie, sweetheart, you look like something has just scared you half to death. Come in, come in. Is everything all right?"

Frau Alesky is like my mother, a second mother to all the children who live in this little block. She wraps her arm around my shoulders and leads me into their living room. "Sit down. Do you want tea or cocoa?"

I shake my head. "No, thank you. I just wanted to come check on Danner."

"Of course. I'll find him," she says, pulling her shawl tighter around her shoulders. Their house is much colder than Otto's and I'm not sure why. "Have a seat, sweetheart." She waves her hand toward the sofa.

Just as I ease down onto their floral upholstered sofa, a ruckus storms into the living room. "Emilie," a young voice squeals as David soars in with a cape around his neck, blubbering like a jet plane. "What are you doing here?" David, the slightly smaller version of Danner, reminds me of the way he used to look and act just three years ago. It's strange to think we've all grown and matured so much over a short span of time. "Something smells good. What's in your hands? What's in the paper? Is it for me? Can I share?"

It's no wonder he arrives at school minutes before the rest of us do every morning. With the amount of energy he has, I can't imagine him sitting still for long.

"Your brother will share with you," I tell him. "How was school today?" I'm unsure if David had a similar day to Danner. I would think he might be less aware of changes if he weren't sent home, but it's hard to predict.

As if someone drained the energy straight out of David's body, his shoulders slump forward and he plops down on the sofa beside me. "Today wasn't a good day. My friends were sent home from school, and they won't be returning. And also, my teacher moved my desk, and I can hardly see the chalkboard from where I'm sitting now. Then Danner was in a bad mood on the way home too, so I think something sweet could cheer me up," he says, stretching his neck to peek over my arm at the paper wrapped goods.

"David," Danner hollers from down the hallway. "Leave her

alone," Danner continues as he walks out from around the corner. "You're already back?"

"I've been worried. I couldn't stay away."

Danner drops his head and scuffs his feet across the room to take a seat beside me. "David, go play. Emilie and I need to talk."

"But I want to stay, and she has something sweet in her hands."

"David," Frau Alesky calls his name. "Come see me in the kitchen, please."

David groans in defeat. "Fine, but save me some of what Emilie brought."

I almost giggle, but the grave stare in Danner's eyes steals every bit of happiness I was feeling just a second ago. "I've never seen you so look so upset," I tell him.

"I'm scared," he says, fear obvious within the croaks of his words. "The Führer hates Jewish people, and for that reason, I'm thankful I wasn't one of the many kicked out of school today, but the empty seats around me are a reminder that I'm no different to those kids and it might not be long before I'm one of them. I feel like there's a red flashing light on the top of my head. It's no secret I'm Jewish. It never has been, and I can't hide. I walked home before the rest of you today so you wouldn't have to feel uncomfortable walking with me. It's not fair to do that to you four. This is my problem, not yours."

I twist my position on the sofa to face Danner and grab his arm with both hands. "Don't ever say that again," I scold him. "You're an amazing person and no one should ever make you think otherwise. We're all different, and the person you are is what makes me want to spend all my free time with you. So, I need you to promise me you'll never change. Promise you'll always be the Danner we love."

Danner's bottom lip quivers and the despair riddled between his eyes breaks my heart. "But why? I don't even want to spend all my spare time with me," he says breaking through his visible pain with a small laugh. "Maybe I should be the one checking on you right now."

"Stop it," I say, shaking his arm. "You're bigger than this. You're better than the foolish regulations being imposed. The government is made up of mindless circus monkeys." I squeeze my hand firmer around his arm and lean forward to kiss him on the cheek, realizing it's the first time I've done that since exchanging our confessions a few days ago. My heart flutters and my stomach tightens as I think about my lips touching his cheek.

His face brightens with a scarlet hue and he pushes his sleeves up. "Emi," he chuckles. "You really have a way with your words."

I'm not sure it was my words that made him turn red, because mine feel like they might be on fire.

It takes me a moment to redirect my thoughts and pick up from where I left off with my comical lecture. "Well, in any case, no one, especially a mindless circus monkey will tell me who is important and who isn't. Especially a monkey with an awful mustache who screams at the top of his lungs just to speak."

Danner presses his hand over his eyes and laughs again. "A circus monkey?" he questions.

"I suppose that comparison is offensive to circus monkeys. But he does sound like one when he's shouting so loudly, doesn't he?" We both laugh so hard my stomach hurts by the time I need to stop so I can breathe.

"God, I'm not sure what I'd do without you," he says.

"You don't have to worry about that. And the others feel the same way. We're not going anywhere without you. Even Frau Berger wanted to share some of the apple fritter she made."

I never lie to my friends, but this time, it feels necessary to protect his heart.

SEVEN
EMILIE
FEBRUARY 1942

Dachau, Germany

I gaze at the kitchen clock's mahogany frame with its golden rings centered around the Roman numerals and scrollwork on the minute and hour hands. The pendulum's sway hypnotizes me, accentuating the depths of my thoughts. I've exhausted myself with house chores, and boredom creeps in. The house is clean, clothes ironed, and meals prepared.

As if the world knows I need an interruption, a startling thunk thunk rattles the front door, jolting me from my seat. I've met some of the neighbors but aside from Ingrid, I wouldn't imagine the others just popping by.

I adjust my apron on the way to the door, and through the rippled glass spot two figures. Alone in this house, would anyone hear me if I needed help?

I shake my head and take in a breath before opening the door a crack to peek outside.

"Mama! Gerty! What are you doing here?" I thrust open the door and jump into their arms, feeling as though I haven't seen or spoken to them in months. It's been just over a week.

"Well," Mama speaks first. "You sent us both letters on the first day you were living here, confessing your homesickness. So, we thought we should pay you a visit."

"I was going to visit sooner, but your mother told me newly-weds need a bit of space," Gerty says, tapping her thumb and fingers together in mockery of Mama.

"Your husband agreed with me as well," Mama defends herself to Gerty.

"Calvin did say I wouldn't want to walk into anything... There's nothing quite like being a newlywed." Gerty sighs and stares up at the ceiling.

I blush at the topic, and in front of my mother of all people. "Oh, goodness. Otto is at work all day. I've been doing a lot of cooking, cleaning, and studying my books. You certainly aren't interrupting much. Come in!"

I wave them both into the house, thrilled to have familiar company, especially Mama and my Gerty.

"I smell dumplings and stewed apples," Mama says, donning a proud smile and placing her hand over her heart. "I'm so proud."

I hold on to the smile from the excitement of seeing them, but I'd much rather Mama be proud of me for something more complicated than making dinner and keeping a house clean.

"Have you met any of the neighbors? Are they nice?" Gerty says, making herself at home as she removes her shoes and coat.

"Yes, they're all lovely, but not like my friends from home," I say, clearing my throat.

"Do they have children?" Mama asks.

"Next door does."

"Good, good. Maybe someday your kids will become friends."

"Mama," I interrupt, taking her coat that's sliding down to her elbows. "I'm in no rush."

"You're right to wait with the dreadful state of our country.

I couldn't imagine raising babies at a time like this. However, it doesn't make me any less eager to be a grandma so just put up with my comments and roll your eyes when I turn away, okay?"

Gerty chokes out a fake cough, pulling in our attention. She's grinning from ear to ear. "I won't take offense to anything you just said, Frau Marx, but it just so happens—"

"Oh my...no...yes? You are?" I shout, throwing my arms around Gerty.

"Yes! We're expecting. The doctor presumes I'm five months along." As she speaks, I feel the hard bulge of her stomach press up against me through our embrace.

"I'm ecstatic for you," I say, ignoring the twinge of unexpected jealousy. The thought of having children hasn't been on mind and what Mama said is true, but it doesn't mean I'm not sour about waiting out the war. My days of being lonely have only just begun and I can see how a baby would fix that.

Mama wraps her arms around the both of us. "Oh gosh, I can't wait to meet him or her," she says.

"It's a she. I can feel it."

"How?" I ask through a chuckle.

She smirks and holds her hands out to the sides. "I can see the future. Did you forget?"

"Oh, you girls and your fortune telling days..." Mama says.

"Come sit down. I'll put on some tea, and we can catch up."

I lead them into the family room and scoot the coffee table closer to the sofa so Gerty can put her feet up if she'd like.

"The house is beautiful, Emi. I adore the red floral décor wallpaper with the navy blue accents. It's modern and chic, but cozy in here too." The house came with some of the décor, including the wallpaper, but I added the drapes and artwork to offset the red hues.

I return with the tea set, waiting on the water to boil. "Thank you. I can't take all the credit, but it's beginning to feel more familiar, I suppose."

"Are you still homesick, dear?" Mama asks, taking a teacup and saucer for Gerty and then one for herself.

I lift my shoulders, knowing I'll always be a bit homesick. I've never lived anywhere but the city and it's quiet here. Very quiet, most of the time. "I miss you and Papa."

"He sends his love, sweetheart. His boss has him working extra hours at the factory. They have a worker shortage and he's picking up the slack."

"Poor Papa. He never seems to catch a break."

"He's better off being busy. I always say men are best on their feet, working so they stay out of trouble."

"I happen to agree," Gerty says, caressing her small baby belly.

The teapot whistles from the kitchen and I hop up from Otto's smoking chair to take the kettle off the stovetop.

"How's Munich?" The question aches in my throat, thinking about the familiar smells, sounds, and faces I miss. Although I must remember that many of those familiarities have been disappearing over the last few years too. Change is upon us regardless of whether we want it or not.

"It's only been a week," Gerty says with a giggle as I pour the tea water into the cups. "Not much has changed. There are still resistance leafless littering the streets and angry Gestapo eyeballing all the people passing by. You're not missing much."

"Is Otto enjoying his new job?"

"It seems so," I say, leaving my answer short and her question basically unanswered since I'm not sure I know myself with how tight-lipped he's been about his days.

"Good!" Gerty says, louder than necessary. "You must keep sending letters. I never get much mail these days and I was so excited to receive the last two you sent."

"Yes, same," Mama says with a raised brow, likely because she only received one letter.

"I promise to keep you updated on my riveting life here."

I'm not sure if the sarcasm is only extra loud in my mind or if they pick up on it too, but I don't think I've been shy about my slow progression to becoming a housewife.

I stare out the narrow side window, long after Gerty and Mama pull away from the house, wishing they could stay forever. Just as I take a step back from the window, a faint cry, or a whistle, grows in the distance. I press my ear to the window for a better sense of what I'm hearing. Another cry follows the last.

Without another thought, I whip open the front door, looking in every direction to see where the heart-wrenching sound is coming from. It isn't until I reach the curb that I spot a bike in the middle of the road and a child lying beside it. Another loud cry rolls down the hill as I charge toward him, reaching him just as Ingrid from next door runs outside too.

"Gunther," she shouts. "Mama is coming."

The little boy with ashy hair and pink cheeks has a gash across his forehead from where he must have hit the road after falling off his bicycle. He's conscious, but I don't want to move him until I check for any other injuries.

Ingrid falls to her knees by my side and lunges forward to scoop him up. "Thank you for coming down here," she tells me.

"Of course, but—you shouldn't move him just yet," I say.

"What do you mean? I need to get him out of the street," she says, breathlessly.

"Yes, but if he hit his head, it's critical to make sure we don't move him too fast."

"How are you so sure?" she asks, her question accusatory rather than curious.

"I was studying to become a nurse alongside Otto, but—"

"I wasn't aware," she says. "What should I do to help? I'm sorry for snapping. He's my baby."

Gunther stops crying. He's still whimpering, but he's making direct eye contact with Ingrid. "Gunther is your name?" I ask, gently.

He nods and his lip quivers.

"Where are you hurt? Can you show me?"

Ingrid stands up, holding her hand to her chest. "I'll go get the first aid kit."

"Yes, ice, and whatever else you have," I tell her.

I run my fingers through his hair. "You're okay. Just show me what hurts."

He reaches for his forehead, but I take his hand before he puts gravel in the wound. "Just your forehead?"

He nods again. I reach beneath his neck and feel around his spine to see if he flinches, but nothing seems to bother him, so I elevate his head enough to rest on my lap while we wait for Ingrid to return.

"I was riding my bicycle. Then a bird flew out of the tree and came right after me. I thought it was going to bite me right on the nose."

"I've heard that happens to a lot of kids, but it looks like the bird left you alone."

"The bird wanted to scare me," he says.

"After we put a bandage on your forehead, I can have a chat with that mean bird. How does that sound?"

"I think he flew away," Gunther says.

"The loud crash of your bicycle might have scared him off for good."

"Hopefully," he says, a tear rolling out of the corner of his eye.

Ingrid returns with a cloth-filled bag of ice and a small first aid kit. "Thank you for taking care of him. I guess I'm not helpful when it comes to injuries," she says.

"If he was my son, I would react the same way. You can't always think straight when you're worried."

"That explains why I can never think straight," Ingrid says with a chuckle. I wouldn't have pegged her as someone who worries often, not with the forward welcome she greeted us with.

"Do you worry about your husband a lot while he's at work?" Through my hours of first-hand training in the nursing program, I was taught to keep the patient and whoever is with them occupied with casual conversation. I'm not sure I'd consider this conversation casual chit-chat, but I can tell her thoughts have shifted direction.

"Oh, we all worry about our husbands while they're at work. It doesn't quite matter where they work these days. With so much uncertainty in our country, it's hard to avoid it, right?"

I suppose she has a point, but our husbands are putting themselves in more unnecessary danger than most.

"Can I sit up?" Gunther asks. "I don't want to lie here anymore."

"Just about done," I tell him, securing the bandage with one last piece of tape. "Can you tell me how many fingers I'm holding up?" I hold three fingers up over his face.

"Three," he says as if it's a race. I put one finger down without asking how many he can see. "Two." And then I put the third one back up. "Three! You can't trick me."

"I guess not. You're pretty fast. I want you to sit up nice and slow for me."

I slip my hands firmly behind his neck and back and let him do the rest. "You're wonderful with children," Ingrid says, crossing her hands over her chest. "It's a good thing we have such a lovely new neighbor living next door. Isn't that right, Gunther?"

He effortlessly pushes himself up to his feet and nods his head. "Thank you, Fräulein," he says.

"My pleasure, sweetheart."

I clean up the small mess of supplies and stand up beside

Ingrid. "Could I convince you to come over for tea? It's the least I can do to thank you for helping Gunther."

She scoops the rubbish out of my hands and reaches down for the first aid kit and ice wrap while waiting for me to respond.

"I'd like that," I say. "The house gets a bit too quiet for my liking sometimes."

"You're welcome to borrow my children whenever you'd like. You will never experience quiet again," she says with laughter.

"I'm happy to watch them for you if you ever need a break," I offer. "I would enjoy the company."

"I'll ask you again after you've been inside my house for an hour." Her smirk makes me wonder if her children misbehave often or if she's just venting as a tired mother.

I follow Ingrid and Gunther down the street and up her walkway that leads to the front door. They walk inside first, and I follow, finding her entryway lovely and much more lived in than mine. "How long have you and Karl been married?"

"About fifteen years, if you can believe it. We were young when we got married, like you and Otto."

We're only twenty-two—also young, but in a time of war, age is just a number. Or so everyone says.

Following Ingrid into her formal living room, I watch as she quickly turns a picture frame face down on the sideboard and then sweeps something off the tea table, but she moves so quickly I don't have a chance to see what either are.

"You don't need to tidy up on my behalf," I say, staring at the downward facing picture frame.

"Oh nonsense, take a seat. How do you take your tea?"

I'm trying to break my stare from the picture frame, but my eyes are like a magnet to that side table. "Honey, if you have it, would be wonderful. Thank you so much."

"Of course. Make yourself comfortable. I'm going to put the

water on. Gunther, why don't you show Frau Berger your favorite book?" Gunther has made a full recovery as he storms around in circles like a jet with accompanying rumbling noises. He reminds me of David when he was little, always trying to get in between Danner and me.

I watch him entertain himself while Ingrid is in the kitchen. If the side table wasn't so close to the arched entry of the kitchen, she might not have noticed if I meandered over for peek. I would never invade someone's privacy like that, but why would one feel the need to hide a framed photo of all things?

Ingrid returns with a tray of teacups and saucers. "So, have you met any of the other wives on the street?"

"No, I haven't. Is the street always so quiet?"

"Not always. None of the other ladies have young children, so they're out and about more than me. I have my hands full with three."

"My goodness. I can only imagine. Three children..." I say in wonder.

Ingrid chuckles following a sigh. "They certainly keep me busy. Gunther is seven, Ada is nine, and Marie is fourteen going on thirty."

The thought of taking care of just one child makes me dizzy. "It must be lovely to have a big family."

Ingrid grins, an expression I can't completely decipher.

A moment of awkward silence makes me brush my fingernails against the side of my neck as I try to control my focus from returning to the picture frame. "I'm sorry. I apologize if I'm being too forward, but I noticed you turned down a picture frame when we walked in. I can't stop myself from wondering about it. Is there a special story behind it?"

Ingrid's shoulders square and she tilts her chin upward, allowing me to see her struggle to swallow. She clears her throat and reaches up to fiddle with her pearl earring. "I wasn't expecting company," she says, her throat sounding dry. "The photo is something of a family secret, but the picture contains a memory of someone dear."

I shouldn't have been so nosy. I've been so consumed with everyone keeping secrets from me that it's the first thought I have when anyone does anything out of the ordinary. "How lovely. Memories are the greatest gift, aren't they?"

"Most of the time, yes," she says, curtly.

She's still staring at the ceiling, and the sunlight filtering in between the linen drapes twinkles across her eyes. Tears form. "I treasure my memories, especially from when I was a young girl, back when I could believe this world wasn't so scary."

Ingrid lowers her chin and presses the knuckle of her index finger beneath her eye. "Exactly. The photo is of my closest friend when I was a child. We were like sisters. Unfortunately, she passed away three years ago. I regret not keeping in touch with her like we promised to always do." She releases a heavy breath. "Anyhow, it's not a conversation starter, so I tend to put the photograph away when expecting company."

"I'm so sorry for your loss. Life only gives us the best of people for a short amount of time." *Like Danner.*

"That's what I think to myself all the time." Ingrid smiles and takes in a deep breath. "I suppose we must think alike."

"We must," I agree. "I'm happy to lend an ear whenever you'd like to talk."

As if I set off an alarm, a ferocious scream bellows from upstairs.

"Mama, my drawings are missing. Marie took them from me. Tell her to give them back!"

"Girls, we have a guest over. Please don't start a commotion. Marie, give your sister her drawings back if you took them," Ingrid says, keeping her voice chipper rather than replying with haste like I might do if I was embarrassed by my children.

A rumble grows from upstairs, and Ingrid lowers her head into her hand. "I apologize, Emilie." Gunther looks up toward the stairwell and smiles before running up the steps as quickly as he can. Before long, the three children are screaming at each other.

"They don't act like this when their father is here. It's only for my benefit," she says.

"How about I go pour the water into the teapot and you take a break for a moment?" I ask, standing from my seat.

"No, no, no. Please, sit back down. I'll take care of the water." She lunges from her chair, not so eloquently, and ambles into the kitchen.

Again, I stare at the upside-down picture frame and then peer down at the tea table, curious as to what she removed as we walked inside. I scan the room, finding landscape portraits hanging from the walls, a piano in the far corner, and a magazine rack by the piano bench.

I squint at the newspaper folded over the top, wondering if my eyes are deceiving me as I spot a copy of *Das Reich*, a paper that features Nazi propaganda and daily updates supporting the Führer's agenda.

EIGHT
EMILIE
FEBRUARY 1942

Dachau, Germany

As I fidget with the foil sealing the dinner plate, a deep rumble shakes the house and I grip the table for support. A startling pop follows the rumble and I collapse in front of the sink, trembling. I pull my knees into my chest and curl into a shaking ball. Even in Munich, we were far enough away from the resistance and Gestapo guarded streets. Though I've heard a fair share of fired shots over the last decade, none have been so close and consistent.

I pull myself up using the ledge of the sink and move across the hallway into Otto's study where I peer out between the drape and window frame, finding only darkness. Otto is late from work again, causing me to worry. Despite my racing pulse, I try to reassure myself everything is okay but I'm not sure it is. I kneel under the desk, counting heartbeats while longing for the comfort of my parents.

"Emilie?"

I unclench my fists and climb out from beneath the desk. I

straighten my dress, taking a deep breath, and make my way out to the foyer to greet Otto, thankful he's finally here.

"Thank goodness, you're home!" I say, running to greet him.

"I'm sorry I'm late, darling. We had a long day unfortunately."

"Of course," I say, swallowing against the tightness in my neck.

"You look upset. Is everything okay?"

"I've been listening to gunshots for the last hour. I don't know where it could be coming from but it was terrifying to hear."

Otto walks into the kitchen and takes a seat at the table. "Gunshots?" he questions, his eyebrows knit together into a v like shape pointing down his nose. "You know what...I think guards fire their pistols into the air if they're struggling to get the attention of the inmates."

"Why would they do such a thing? Is it necessary?" Wasting ammo doesn't sound like a logical way to gain attention.

"I'm not around that area of the camp. I'm not sure. I know it'll take a bit of time to feel familiar with the area and people. We'll get there."

"Yes, I suppose," I say, pulling the foil off our dinner plates before taking a seat across from him. "Mama and Gerty paid me a surprise visit. Then Ingrid invited me over for a cup of tea." Although something is amiss there too.

"How nice of your mother and Gerty to come by. That's one surprise I'm sure you enjoyed," he says with a wink. It *was* a nice surprise. "And tea with Ingrid sounds splendid. Her husband, Karl, is a great fellow. We get along quite well, in fact. His father got him into the field as well." Otto rushes through his brief description of Karl to inhale a heaping bite of the chicken and dumplings.

I've yet to meet the man or see him leave and come home from work.

"How nice," I say, convincing myself to smile. "Is he a real doctor?"

"No, in fact, he's self-taught, which is quite commendable."

I slip my fork out from between my lips and blink at him, questioning who Otto has become. Sure, we have known each other most of our lives, but something has drastically changed within him this past year.

"Well, I disagree. I don't think it's equally commendable. There's a lot to be learned in a classroom setting, as well with supervised direct training. Not everything can be taught out of a book." My heart races as the words pour out of my mouth. I'm speaking nothing but the truth and it has to be said.

NINE

EMILIE

SIX YEARS AGO, AUGUST 1936

Munich, Germany

The first day of a new school year is something I've always dreaded. People change over the summer break and are never the same again. Today is especially difficult because Gerty and I are in a different school now. Boys and girls are separated for educational purposes. At sixteen, none of us seems happy with the change.

Gerty gazes longingly out the classroom window, likely waiting for Jerald, her boyfriend of one year, to walk by. Though, he should be in his school too.

"At least we have each other," I remind her through a whisper and a smile.

"Thankfully, or I'd go mad being stuck here alone. Never ever leave me, okay?"

"Never leave me either," I say back, holding out my pinkie for her to grab and swear with.

A new teacher would make sense at a new school, and sure enough I don't recognize the woman walking into the classroom with her nose pointed to the ceiling. Every chair scrapes against the floor at once as we hop to attention, hailing her by extending our right arm toward the ceiling with a straight hand.

"Heil Hitler. Heil Hitler. Heil Hitler," we shout in unison before returning to our seats. Gerty and I share a look and roll our eyes, knowing the teacher hasn't turned to face the class yet.

"Heil Hitler," she replies, turning toward the chalkboard to scribble out her name. Frau Heine. "As you should already be aware, this class is a required general education class: Racial Awareness. You're all expected to learn your racial duties to serve the national community, understand biology, and politics. If you have any questions, the answer will be in the textbook, and if not, you may stay after class."

She hasn't made eye contact with anyone. She must not want to be here. Rather than focus on her, we're all forced to keep our focus straight ahead at the board where a large poster of Hitler hangs. The sight of him makes my stomach burn.

"I'll be passing out the textbooks now and we'll get started right away."

The thud of a book hits my desk and rattles my seat. I open the front cover, finding yet another display of Hitler's face. I blink for an extra-long second, and flip to the next page before returning my attention to the front board while the teacher continues handing out the books.

"Is that Danner?" Gerty whispers, covering her mouth with one hand and pointing out the window with her other.

I follow the tip of her finger, spotting Danner running past the school window toward the exit gates, dragging David by the arm. Despite whatever trouble I might get in, I scoop up my book and grab my satchel before escaping the classroom behind the teacher's back. She must see me leave but doesn't stop me.

I move through the hallway as fast as I can before pushing my way out the main door. "Danner, wait!" I shout after him.

"No, no, go back to class, Emi. Please."

"Stop running. Tell me what's wrong," I demand.

He slows down, but doesn't stop. He knows I'll keep running after him, which I do until I grab a hold of his arm.

"I told you to go back to class," he says, avoiding my stare.

I grab his chin and force him to look at me, finding tears in his eyes. "What happened?"

He closes his eyes and grits his teeth. David is oddly quiet beside him, shuffling his weight from one foot to the other. "His first class was on racial impurity with a focus on Jews and their inferior race," David says. "I have the same class, but it wasn't first on my schedule today. This is the government's way of getting us to leave on our own. It worked."

David suddenly sounds like an adult rather than the little boy flying around his living room like a jet. Not only is he catching up to Danner in height, but his voice has gotten deeper too. Regardless, for only thirteen, he knows much more than he should.

Danner's staring down at me but his gaze is vacant. "You can't let them win," I say.

"Them?" Danner finally speaks. "Them, Emi? Aren't we them? They are us? We're German, but I'm a German Jew, no longer the same as anyone else here."

"We both know your religion doesn't define you," I whisper the words that would get me into more trouble than I'd like to imagine.

"You can't stand on this side of the fence. I won't let you. You're going to get yourself hurt and in trouble. I've done what I can to fight off this blatant hatred, but they all stare at me in class. The teacher acted like my seat was empty and didn't give me papers or a textbook."

"I'll go get them for you," I tell him.

"No, you won't. Don't go in there. The school is for boys only and I can't have you going in there or anywhere to defend me. It's dangerous."

"Danner, please, you can't give up." Even I sound uncertain. Our altered curriculum without history, art, and library time, has been replaced by additional physical education. Danner may be better off learning on his own.

He takes a sharp breath and shakes his head before placing his hands on my shoulders. "Emi, look at me, now," he says. "Go back to your classroom. Tell your teacher you felt sick but you're okay now. David and I are going home. I'll be waiting for you at the end of the day, and we'll talk then. I need time to think about what's next for us. You're right to fight for everything you believe in, and I'll do the same, but only until it is too dangerous. I won't risk our lives for a fight we won't win. I know what side you're on and what side I'm on—we're on the same side and it's all that matters, okay?"

My eyes well up with tears as I listen to his wise words. But my heart shatters, knowing he's right when I wish him to be wrong. I can't fathom walking back into class to hear the hateful lectures about Jewish people. This is how Hitler plans to change Germany's youth. I won't go along with the hatred. I'm in this world to help and heal people. Therefore, I pray Hitler receives help for his instability and a cure for the evil blood running through his veins.

"We're supposed to go through life together," I tell Danner, my voice wobbling. "You told me we'd always be together."

We're only sixteen but I'm certain he's my future, and I'm his. We've said this for so long. I've known it since the day I knew he cared about me the same way I cared about him, back when we were thirteen.

"You still have Gertrude, Felix, and Otto. You aren't alone." He pulls me into his chest, wrapping his arms around me tightly. He's grown so tall, my ear must be parallel to his heart because I can hear the pounding loud and clear.

"I'm not worried about them. It's you I can't leave behind," I say.

"We might not have a choice, Emi, and it wouldn't be by my

say so or my desire because I can't imagine living life without you by my side. But look where we are—look at the laws being enforced. We cannot be in a relationship of any sort or we'll both be arrested. I won't let anything happen to you."

"No one needs to know about us," I say through gritted teeth. "We've kept our feelings for each other quiet for long enough. We can continue to hide the truth in public." Despite how badly I want to walk around the city hand in hand, it's not something we can chance. No matter where we are, we have to be discreet. Our parents and friends would worry for our safety and the public wouldn't approve. It's as if we're each trapped in a glass jar—two separate ones, reaching for each other, knowing there's nothing we can do to make our way any closer. We share our feelings. We hug, and sometimes there have been passing kisses on cheeks, but that's all there can be without a risk. I want to forget about the risks. I want to break down the glass walls and live out our dreams, which may only ever be dreams about him."

"It's too dangerous. Gerty teases you about us. She doesn't mean any harm, but she knows even if you haven't admitted it out loud. Felix and Otto have both said things to me too. They know, even though I didn't confirm. It's only a matter of time before more people notice the way I look at you, or the way your cheeks turn red every time you smile at me. This breaks my heart in more ways than I can possibly explain, but we have to follow the laws. We can't be together, not in the way we want to be. You need to be free from me despite what either of us want."

"I don't want to be free from you," I cry out.

Danner's chin trembles and he bites down on his lip. "God, Emi, this hurts too much. You know how much you mean to me. Don't ever question that...ever. Please, go back to school. Please. I feel like I can't breathe right now," he says, gasping for air.

"Stop talking like you're saying goodbye, Danner." I pull away and wipe the tears from my cheeks. "Don't ever say these things again, do you understand?" I clutch my hands against my chest, wishing I could tear my heart out to stop the pain.

A tear from his eye matches my own as he looks down between us. "Everything will be okay," he says, turning around and walking away. For what might be forever.

TEN

DANNER

Munich, Germany

The closer I am to the city hall, more red flags donning a centered white circle emblazoned with the Nazi's black swastika appear. The city is cloaked in blood-red flags rather than the familiar black, red, and yellow striped German flag. Nothing about this city resembles the Germany I used to be a citizen of. On each lamppost is a vibrantly colored poster with childlike illustrations propagating support of the regime and hatred against the Jews, naming us betrayers of the First World War.

But as usual, after checking the paper records that list deported or deceased male citizens of Munich for Papa's name, I feel the familiar sense of surprise and disappointment when I come up empty handed. I leave without an answer as to where he might be, as I always do. There's only so long I can remain in a state of denial that he wasn't deported and is still alive.

The winds are mild, and the thick clouds give way to warmth from the spring sun. If I close my eyes, I can remember the city as beautiful, flowers blooming everywhere, and cheerful citizens shuffling down the streets. But those memories are from when I was a child. Now, the streets are barren, colorless aside from the red, white, and black flags. There are fewer people and none of them stroll casually.

The scuffles from my borrowed shoes scrape along the pavement and I can't convince myself that I'm not making a racket and that I don't stand out amongst others. We're supposed to believe life has moved forward as usual, just without the Jewish population. Not all of us have. How many are like me, living with forged identification?

With heavy feet and heart, I amble around the back of the houses on the street I used to live on with Mama and Papa, the route I take to remain unseen by the neighbors. I'm just an intruder now—a temporary guest. The chains of a bicycle clatter and chirp as the rubber tires bounce along rubble behind me. If I didn't recognize the sound of Felix's bike, I'd be looking for a place to hide.

I peer over my shoulder, expecting him to whiz by me and pull up to his front door. Except this time he stops next to me, kicking up dirt from between the stones. He's out of breath, and since the spring season seems to be hiding behind winter's gloomy tail, steam pours out of his mouth like dry ice from a chemist's beaker. "You have to get inside and hide. I'm so sorry. I'm so—"

"Wh-what's going on. What happened?" I peer past him down the road, but I don't see anyone following him.

"Just go—go into the house, please," he says, his words frantic. He shoves his hand against my shoulder, urging me forward, and I obey his strong command, making my way into the house as fast as I can.

With one step inside the back door, I hear his bike crash against the side of the house and his boots clomping behind me.

I walk through the mudroom and out to the living room, considering my options for where to hide. Frau Weber rushes out of the kitchen, wiping her hands on her apron. "What in the world is going on?" Her cheeks flush with a dark red hue.

"I'm sorry, Mama," Felix says.

"For what?" she shouts in return.

"We need to hide Danner. Then I'll explain."

We all look at each other with fear and puzzlement because there's only one place to hide and apparently not much time. I lunge for the bookshelf along the stairwell. Felix helps me pull it away from the wall and search for the seam along the wall panels. It's taking too long to find the crevice and Frau Weber runs toward the kitchen, returning a moment later with a butter knife. She knows precisely where the seam is, stabs it and releases the loose wall panel. "Go on," she says, ushering me into the hole that's hardly big enough to store a dining table chair, never mind me. Just as the wall is pieced back into a seamless sight, the bookshelf scrapes against the floor until it hits the wall, vibrating the interior of this black hole I'm crouched into.

Sweat forms and trickles down my neck, then spine, and each of my limbs until I'm soaking wet.

"What happened, Felix?" I hear the muttering of their conversation through the wall.

"I—I'm not sure," he cries out. "When I was at Ed's house the other night—"

"You didn't go to Ed's house. You both stayed here," Frau Weber corrects him.

"No, Mama, I went alone after Danner went to sleep. I shouldn't have gone. I shouldn't have had anything to drink. We were all talking and—"

"You didn't," Frau Weber says, scolding him.

There's a pause before Felix answers his mother. "We were all friends and I mentioned Albert would be coming with me earlier in the day. Ed asked if my friend was still on his way, and I said he wasn't coming."

"Then what?" Frau Weber hurries him.

I can tell her what happened next. It's not Felix's fault. It's my own.

"There was a man there that Danner and I had gone to school with—a mutual friend of Ed's, I guess. He stepped into my conversation with Ed and asked me if I was still friends with Danner Alesky—the Jew I had grown up with. I said we were talking about someone named Albert. I might have stuttered or —I don't know, but Ed and the man Danner and I went to school with laughed at me as if I had no pants on. I wasn't sure what to make of it."

"So how did we get here, to hiding Danner?" Frau Weber shouts. I can picture her arms shooting out in every direction like she does when she's angry.

"I was at work and Ed asked me if Danner was living with us. I never told him his real name, but he suddenly knew it wasn't Albert like I had said, and he was sure about it. I'm not sure how he and the mutual person we know put these facts together. I didn't answer because he had a weird look in his eyes. But my silence must have been enough of an answer because he shook his head and said I should go home and figure out how to fix my living situation before it's too late. The man who was at that party—the one who went to school with us, is the son of an SS officer who's looking to fill a quota of removing Jews from Munich by the end of the week."

Though garbled and hysterical, I understand every one of Felix's words. I need to leave their house. I can't put them in danger for my sake. It doesn't sound like Felix knows when someone will come looking here for me. I can't get back to Mama and David in Poland, and Germany has been removing all the Jews for the last few months so there's nowhere good to go here.

"I haven't the faintest idea of what we're going to do," Frau

Weber says. "When will they be here?" Her voice trails off, making me assume she's moving around or pacing.

"You need to let me out. I'm leaving. I won't do this to your family," I shout from inside the hole.

"No, please no," Frau Weber cries out.

"I'll push over the bookcase if you don't let me out."

Never have I threatened a person, but I won't jeopardize their safety. No one responds, which means I must make a show of my word. I lurch my shoulder against the wall panel, using all my weight to move the hearty bookshelf. It begins to skate across the wooden floor, one small shift at a time until the bookshelf pulls away from the wall. I tumble out of the hole, catching myself with my palms against the floor. My nose hovers over the wood grains that I've never seen up so close before and when I push against my hands to pull my knees beneath me, I spot a pair of shiny boots close enough to catch the reflection of my startled wide eyes.

Felix and Frau Weber are nowhere in sight. It's me, an SS officer and a couple of guards I spot outside the open front door. "A stray Jew," he says, clicking his tongue against the roof of his mouth.

"Alesky is the name I've been given—son of Abraham Alesky. I assume you've been looking for your dear old vater, ja?"

I refuse to speak, give him an answer or anything he might want because he won't do me any favors.

The officer shoves the toe of his boot into my side, knocking me off my hands and knees. "He's dead."

The anger writhing through me sparks every nerve in my body and I pull myself up to my feet ready to knock this bloodsucker to the ground. He's lying. He doesn't know where Papa is. No one does. That's what they told me at city hall. It was stupid of me to keep checking for his whereabouts. No one unrelated would care so much and despite using a false name, the wallpaper lining these walls has more knowledge about this city than I do.

The other two guards join the fight. Except there isn't a fight. I'm defenseless against them and their armor-clad uniforms. I've never so much as hurt a fly, but I'm in the hands of the soulless now.

I fear the worst as I face the harsh light of day, the sun blinds me even after only being in the dark for a short amount of time. I don't see Felix or Frau Weber anywhere and I'm not sure what they've done with them. I pray they've spared them.

The hands gripping my arms shove me into the back of a metal truck, cloaking me in the dark just like the hiding hole in Felix's house.

He's not dead. Papa cannot be dead. They will say anything to infuriate us before locking us up—they were the sick children who taunted stray dogs then caged them before poking at them with a stick. That's who these boys have become—sick men with the idea of torture as a form of entertainment.

The truck moves along the bumpy road, and I slide around without anything to grip onto like a rubber ball, side to side until I hit a padded corner—a body that doesn't budge against the shock of my weight slamming into theirs. I shake the torso, unable to see anything within the opaque space, but my hand meets the cool fabric unaffected by the heat trapped within the truck's containment.

My body trembles beyond my control and I try to push myself away from the limp person I'm against, unsure if there are more at this end of the truck.

Please, God, don't let me die like this here. Please. I have more life to live. I'll do better. I'll do more.

I don't know where they're taking me, but at best it will be one of the labor camps, where they have taken so many others. No one knows much about what happens at those camps, but it's become clear no one returns to where they came from.

The rocks from beneath the truck ping against the under-carriage and echo harshly from every side of me. I'm cold and hot, sweating, and shivering, nauseous and scared to get sick. After a whiff of what I imagine to be a combination of death and body odor, I try to breathe only through my mouth, but maybe it's a smell I should get used to.

There were days I thought I would outsmart this war and outrun the Nazis. There's no hope for me now. I've been a fool to think otherwise.

ELEVEN
DANNER
MAY 1942

Dachau, Germany

The rear of the truck I've been bouncing around in opens, allowing in an abundance of sunlight, blinding me to my surroundings. After learning Papa had been arrested, I wanted to convince myself that he'd been taken to a common prison for criminals, but no one would truly believe that these days. Even Felix's house overflows with gossip and stories about the afore-mentioned concentration camps, places of internment for not only political opponents but Jewish people too. We don't know much about what happens at these locations because no one seems to return from them. That fact should have spoken for itself.

A Gestapo pulls me from the back of the truck and my feet hardly graze the ground before I'm being dragged toward a group of men. Most of them have a suitcase of belongings. I have nothing except for what's in my pockets.

SS guards stand before a tall metal iron gate, shouting at us to get into a single line. The others forming the line in front of and behind me appear bewildered, unknowing, and lost. No one can see much of what exists on the other side of the foreboding gates.

Minutes pass, standing here in the unnatural heat coming from a combination of crammed bodies, steam from the train, and smog settling beneath sun. I've gotten used to the missing scent of flowers, but the ash, smoke, and the sweet odor of something rotting is an unwelcome replacement. What would happen if I moved a foot forward— if I tried to run from the line, or collapsed in the act of falling faint? The guards don't try hard to conceal the weapons accessorizing their uniforms so I imagine I would be shot. The guards don't choose to fight. They choose to kill. We've been trained to know this and never question anything different.

When the gates whine and groan, opening enough for this line to pass through, we move in unison, like the legs of a caterpillar. Now on the other side, I spot lines of people wrapped around the long building to the right. To the left, in the distance are rows of wide buildings, most of which look identical to each other. Between the building to the right and the others to the left is a vast field of dry gravel, dust fogging up by our ankles each time we move forward.

"What do you think they're going to do with us?" the boy in front of me asks, keeping his voice to a quiet mutter. He must be around David's age, just a few years younger than me but seemingly even more in the dark than I am.

"I'm not sure," I reply just as quietly. The boy's eyes are wide, and he's shivering even though the air is anything but cold.

"I'm scared," he says.

My mind replaces his face with David's and the urge to hug him and tell him something that will keep him calm is strong but that won't help him, and it wouldn't help me if someone were willing to offer me the same.

A door from a wide, shallow building opens to the left of the line, and a different line of men exit, one in front of the other, in prison uniforms. They're holding objects I can't make out from here, but they catch the rays of the sunlight. Most of the men are shuffling their feet, dragging their weight as if tired and stripped of energy, leaving us to wonder what will happen to us once we step in through the doors we're slowly weaving into.

As we move closer to the façade of the building, I spot a sign calling the building Administration Office of Dachau.

Dachau. I've heard of the camp. The town isn't far from Munich, despite the amount of time it took to arrive here.

The initial room we step into isn't large, and I shouldn't be surprised to see the line I've been standing in snaking around the interior space. An SS guard in his green uniform stands at the front, questioning each person. I can't hear much from the other side of the room, but the struggle of the men trying to speak shows by the bobble of their Adams' apples.

If I had known I would end up here today, I would have eaten more of what Frau Weber offered me for breakfast. Hunger is already creeping in, like talons pinching my stomach, and I doubt I'll find food anytime soon here.

"I'm not some common criminal," a man shouts, standing before the SS guard. "My son is here somewhere, and he's innocent as well. I must find him at once." He tears a paper out of the guard's hand and tosses it in his face before spitting at him. "I won't comply with you pigs." The man, in dress shirt and loose slacks, steps away from the guard and turns around to face the opening we walked in through. "Jacob! It's Papa. Do you hear—"

A shot fires, the blast echoes against the four walls we're standing between and in the following silence, a body falls to the ground like a boulder plummeting from a high cliff.

"Next," the guard calls.

The man who said what we would all like to say is now nothing more than an obstacle we must avoid while making our way in the line. No one tells us that man's outburst should be a lesson to us all. We're expected to learn by example.

Twenty seconds pass between each step forward, indicating I'll be standing here another two hours before I'm questioned. Like most of the other men, I'm sent to the next room where more lines await. Before I hear the command, I assume what's to come as the others strip down bare before dumping their clothes into a rubbish bin.

"Remove your personal belongings," a voice shouts.

I unclasp Felix's belt from around my waist and reach into my pockets for the few belongings I always carry on me. The trousers drop to the ground, and I tug at my shirt, pulling the buttons from the seamed narrow holes.

What else can they take from us? If not for the sake of humiliation, what good are our clothes when every Nazi is donned in rich uniforms emblazoned with metals and satin trim. No one looks at one another, not out of a form of respect, but because we're all looking toward what comes next.

A man in a prisoner uniform holds a metal syringe the size of my torso, spraying a white fog across each person's body. They must be trying to kill possible bugs. But first, an electric blade is pressed to my scalp, removing every hair on my head before shoving me over to the man fogging the others in front of me. The white fog strikes my skin like jagged ice shards, stealing the remaining warmth from my body.

"Your belongings," a man demands, shoving a basket against my chest. He's in a prisoner uniform too, which confuses me.

"Can I—"

"All of it," he says, shoving the basket with more force.

I drop my wallet, identification, and passport, clinging to my pocket watch and small folded up note from Papa. A stick slashes at me, seemingly coming from out of nowhere, thrashing against my hand, forcing me to drop the pocket watch and note. My two prized possessions fall to the ground between the worn and torn black boots of the prisoner collecting items. I gaze at the watch, as if I were leaving another person behind in my past. I've had on a brave face until now but the weakness inside of me threatens to break me.

I'm torn from my distressing thought as a pile of clothes and a thin wool blanket are topped with a metal bowl, spoon, and cup. I'm shoved along in the moving line, trying to keep myself from staring back at the pocket watch I'll likely never see again.

"This is all you will need." The guard's words splinter through my spine, on a loop for every prisoner passing through the lines.

I believe every word.

TWELVE

DANNER

MAY 1942

Dachau, Germany

As if the questions I've been asked again and again throughout this registration process, or so they call it, haven't been enough, there's another SS guard standing in front of me with a clipboard in hand now. With an eagle eye, he stares at the number inked across my uniform and shakes his head.

"You have committed crimes," he says, clucking his tongue. "Hiding in an innocent family's house, endangering their well-being for the sake of your own. What a coward." His words seethe out between gritted teeth, but I can't react. It won't help. "We have a proposition for you. We don't have space for people like you, so you will be executed."

My bladder becomes heavy and urine spills down my leg. My head is hollow, empty, nothing but air inside as I try to keep myself upright.

"Such a coward," he says again, staring down at the damp stream, lining the leg of my uniform.

The moment reminds me of when I was a kid and Gerty read my fortune, telling me I would pee my pants at school. It was meant as a joke and never happened. Maybe she did know...just not when it would happen. If this tyrant is going to kill me, I wish he would just do to me what was done to the other man who tried to find his son. He was shot. It was quick.

"If you would rather avoid execution, there's a different opportunity you can take. A nice healthy man like you, despite being Jewish, can be of significant use to us—to our country, even."

"I do-don't understand," I say with a stutter.

"We need lab rats for medical data. If you agree to be a lab rat, we will spare you execution."

I want to ask him what happens after they use me...whatever that means, but I would receive an answer I don't want to hear.

"Okay, I'll do it," I agree without giving it much thought.

"You'll do what? You must say what you will be doing so I understand properly."

He's just a devil in a uniform.

"I'll be a lab rat to help my country." A cool breeze blows between my limbs, reminding me of the wet pants I'll have to sit in until they dry.

"Very good. Follow me."

After walking past several blocks, the guard opens the door to one on the right and shoves the heel of his boot into my lower back, catapulting me into a barrack with what appears to be over a hundred other men. I take in the surroundings, focusing on the two rows of three-tiered wooden bunks. Perspiration, sewage, and bile as pungent as skunked onions and eggs is all I can smell upon entering the musty dank space. The air doesn't move, only I do. I'm just another body to take up room, garnering me expressions that I try not to take personally.

I walk down the row, skin-covered bones dangling from every which way as I seek a small spot to claim for however long I'll be in this location.

"There's a spot over here," someone says. A man around my age holds his hand out so I can see where the voice is coming from. I imagine I must look eerily similar to the way he does with my shaved head, dirt-covered face, and this dingy uniform, left with nothing but eyes, nose, and a mouth to suit as my only form of identity.

"Thank you. I appreciate your kindness."

"You don't want to sleep on the floor if you can avoid it. The mice are relentless here," the man says.

"I can imagine." I toss my small pile of belongings up onto the third tier of the bunks and use the rickety ladder to climb up to the top. The available space is just large enough for my narrow body to lie flat, but it's all I need.

"They took a bunch of men out of here this morning, so an open spot is a sign of luck I suppose," the man says as I sit back against one of the wooden beams framing the row of bunks. "Hans Bauer." He holds his hand out.

"Danner Alesky," I reply, taking his hand.

"It's nice to see someone around the same age here. I'm not sure why they tossed us into the elderly men's barracks."

"I take offense to that," the man in the next bunk over says, swatting his hand at us. His voice wavers and crackles as if he hasn't spoken in a while, except he surprises me with a bout of laughter to follow. "I'm just messing with you. I'm Eli." He reaches his hand out to shake mine and I return the kind gesture.

"See?" Hans says, gesturing his hand out to the man before they both share a quick chuckle. "He thinks shaking hands is necessary here."

"I'm Fred," the man right below me shouts up through the fine crack between the platforms. "I'm not as old as Eli, but your new young friend thinks I am. Us old men know a thing or two. You'll find us useful. You'll see," he says with a snicker.

"Nice to meet you," I reply, wishing I could wave or shake

his hand, but I'd have to hang over the edge of the bunk to do that.

Once the three of them stop laughing at their old-jokes, Hans continues with his question, seemingly intrigued to know everything about me as quickly as possible. "So, where are you from?" he asks. "You must be about twenty-one or something, right?"

"I'm from Munich, and you're close. I'm twenty-two." *Not old enough to be considering this place to be where my body is found someday.* "How about you?"

Hans doesn't answer right away. He seems lost in thought, as if the question requires him to jog through his memory. He must have arrived here a long time ago. "Salzburg. I'm nineteen."

"Still the baby here," Fred speaks out.

"I'm from Prague," Eli adds. "I'm sixty-two—not quite as elderly as your friend described, and I arrived by a dark train crammed with a thousand other people. It wasn't the most comfortable trip I've taken." I see Eli is sarcastic and poking fun at this awful situation.

"I might have only come a short distance, but it felt longer in the back of a dark truck, alone with a skeleton." The memory of falling onto a body sends a chill down my spine.

"A skeleton?" Eli asks. "They don't get much more creative than that, I tell ya." *Creative?*

"They do like to disorient us," Hans says. "I take it you didn't arrive with anyone from home then?"

I shake my head. "No, I've been taking slow steps toward my ultimate destination for a year and a half now. I thought I was being heroic, leaving my mother and brother behind in search of my father, but that didn't end well as you can see."

With a sullen grimace, Hans palms my shoulder. "Even if you had done everything differently, you'd still be here, as would I, I'm afraid. Don't blame yourself for any decision you've made. The last thing we need is to live with guilt. I left my mother and sister behind because I had a chance to hide somewhere. My mother forced me to leave, despite it being an unthinkable decision I couldn't bear to make on my own. She wanted me to go if there was even the slightest chance I could be spared from what might come, especially for all the men where we were. I ended up hiding in a crawlspace of an attic, protected by the love of my life. Her father found out and called the authorities. Having known him most of my life, it's still a hard bullet to bite, knowing he handed me over the way he did."

"That's unimaginable," I tell him. Though nothing seems quite unimaginable these days.

"Poor lovesick kid," Eli adds. "She slept in the attic with him sometimes." Eli chuckles as his eyebrows dance around his forehead.

"At least he knows what love is. Life would be meaningless otherwise," Fred says, his words more serious than the last comments he made.

"I miss Matilda, every day, my heart just bleeds for her, praying she's still okay wherever she is. It kills me being away from her. We grew up together, never spent much time apart at all. We were best friends, and there wasn't enough time. There's never enough time," Hans says, staring through me. "Anyway." He shakes his head as if to push away his thoughts. "Did you leave a special woman behind?"

I think about the question, knowing there's only one woman I've ever considered special, but there would never be an opportunity in this lifetime to have what I wish we could have had together. Me as a Jewish man, and she as a German with Aryan roots...there was no hope for anything more than friendship.

"There was, but it was never meant to be."

"See, he's a smart man who wasn't looking to have his heart broken," Eli says, pointing at Hans.

I'm not sure about that, but I suppose I'd be in much worse shape now if I had been with her.

Hans hums with thought. "What's her name?"

The corners of my lips pucker into a small smile at the thought of her.

"Emilie."

Her name feels distant on my tongue, but I can imagine her beautiful face as if it were just yesterday when I said goodbye. I knew that was the end for us—I could feel it in my chest, but I didn't have the heart to tell her I didn't think I would ever see her again.

THIRTEEN
EMILIE
JULY 1942

Dachau, Germany

Over the last five months, I've become the silent housewife, the one waiting at home with a warm meal for whenever Otto decides to walk in through the door. Though he leaves his belongings scattered about in every room, he eyeballs every item if I don't tidy up fast enough. He must think his work clothes iron themselves because he always just walks up to the closet and pulls out what he wants to wear. The thank yous have stopped, not that I need one for keeping a clean house or cooking the meals, but I thank him for earning a paycheck to keep us afloat. It's the same difference in my mind.

The job he's doing has changed him over the course of the five months we've been here. It's been a slow progression, but a noticeable one. The frown lines along his cheeks have deepened and his brow sits low all the time, not just with certain expressions. His smiles are rare, and when I ask what I can do to cheer him up, he only shrugs.

As much as I don't have a desire for the role of a housewife, I should be able to look forward to my husband coming home at the end of a long day, happy to see me, happy to have a clean house, and a meal on the table. That was my only reward for putting my endeavors aside in favor of his.

Today, I didn't prepare dinner, or pick up his laundry, the newspapers scattered along the coffee table, his dirty bourbon glass on the side table, the envelopes from the mail he tore through last night, ashes from his cigarettes that didn't make it into the ashtray. There are dishes in the sink from breakfast this morning. Even the washroom is as he left it—toothpaste stuck to the drain cover, the cap left off the top of the tube, clippings from his shaven face peppered along the sink basin, spattered spit marks on the mirror, and a wash towel crumpled up on the ground.

My stocking covered feet are up on the coffee table. I have a magazine spread open on my lap and the gramophone is playing much louder than usual. If only it could drown out my anger. Anyone would call my behavior unusual, unconventional, and absurd, but something needs to change. We need to find our way back to where we were a few months ago when everything was still fresh and new.

While there's no definitive routine in which I can depend on him to walk through the front door every night, the time has narrowed down to between seven and eight. I've been reading and rereading a letter I received from Gerty, my one link to home aside from Mama and Papa. Or she *was* my link to home, before receiving this letter. She sent me a photograph too.

My Dearest Friend, Emi,

I should have written to you sooner but I've hardly had a minute to catch a wink of sleep. I've received all your letters and I hope you're aware of how much they've meant to me since I've written last.

I've included a photo of the most beautiful little boy in the entire world. Theodore Calvin Distler was born with a full head of curly honey-brown hair, and eyes the color of the South Pacific Ocean. He's healthy and perfect and I'm dying for you to meet him, but as your mom told you, Calvin and I decided to move south, away from the city. The moment Theo was born, I couldn't bear the thought of keeping him there with all the protests, riots, and fights breaking out. I'm sure once the war is over, we'll move back home. I suppose this is where I tell you, you're smart for waiting on bringing a baby into the world. Babies in general are scary enough, never mind the state of Germany.

I tell Theo stories about you every day so even though we aren't physically together right now, he will always know who his Auntie Emi is.

He's taking a nap right now, which is a rare occurrence even though I was told babies are supposed to sleep most of the day. That's the reason I haven't been able to write sooner.

I hope you're doing well and happy, loving married life, and I hope Otto is the same. I miss you so much and I can't wait until we can see each other again. Calvin sends you his best too.

With all my love,

Gerty

My eyes well as I stare at the beautiful little boy—not girl, as she predicted—in the photograph. He looks like a little doll, a perfect combination of Gerty and Calvin.

My heart aches and I'm not sure if it's because I feel terrible that I'm not with Gerty and wasn't with her when Theo was born, or if it's for selfish reasons. I could be sitting here with a baby in my belly, but nothing seems right, and that's enough of a reason to be sitting here holding a grudge instead.

The squeal of the Volkswagen's brakes alerts my attention, confirming Otto is home. My throat tightens and fists clench, preparing for his reaction. After the last few weeks, I don't expect him to be in a good mood, but learning I've done nothing all day will only dampen his mood more.

The front door in the foyer opens but I don't hear the click of his shoes move past the welcome mat. The scuff from the coarse texture of his trench coat is the only thing I can hear until the coat rack tilts off its three feet onto two, just by a hair, then falls back into place after recoiling from Otto's tossed coat and hat, which then slip off the rack and fall to the ground as he walks away.

Maybe he noticed the wet umbrella upside down, still dripping with water from where he left it this morning after stepping outside to put an envelope in the mailbox. He took a different, dry umbrella to work with him when he left a half hour later.

"Emilie?" He sounds unsure by the way he says my name, almost as if he's questioning if I'm even home.

The clicks and clacks from his heels commence, growing louder as he crosses the few steps toward the opening to the living room. Before another word comes out of his mouth, he scans the room, taking note of everything out of place. He swallows a lump in his throat and I might have heard it if my thumping pulse wasn't so loud.

"How—how was your day?" he asks. I was sure he'd ask me if I'm feeling okay or if something happened while he was gone.

"Wonderful. I've been sitting right here, reading for most of the day. How was your day?" I close the magazine and place it next to me on the sofa.

"Terrible," we say at the same time. I knew that's what he would say.

"Every day is terrible now." I grimace. "Otto, I'm not sure what to say about your job, but I want to finish taking my classes to become a certified nurse. I can't just sit around all day like this."

Otto takes in a deep breath and releases the air slowly through pursed lips. "Okay, I understand."

I don't think he does.

"There's a bus station down near the grocery store. I can switch buses at Rangierbahnhof and take the city center bus from there to Munich. It will take me over an hour to get to and from the university, so I won't be home until late, but it's what I want to do."

Otto's chest expands and he holds the air in his lungs for as long as it takes him to think of his next thought. "What will we eat for dinner? Who will do the shopping? Take care of the house?" I'd like to tell him to hire someone, but we can't afford to do that. "In fact, I was going to tell you tonight that we're having guests over tomorrow night, and I need everything to—"

"You need everything to what? Look perfect?" I finish the statement.

"My parents and uncle will be joining us, as well as the Schmitts, Deckers, and Fishers."

"A party of eleven with no warning?" I add. "What for? What are you celebrating, Otto? Your misery?"

"I just found out about the gathering today."

I drop my feet off the coffee table and jump up, trying to take a breath before steam comes out of my ears.

"No, no, you didn't," I snap, turning to find Otto just a footstep behind me. "Ingrid told me a week ago, and if you repeat that to Karl—"

"Emilie, threats aren't necessary, please."

"Can you not see that you're treating me like an unpaid maid. Otto, I'm your wife, and you seem to have forgotten that minor detail."

Otto cups his hands around my shoulders and cranes his neck to lower his gaze to mine. "I would never think of you as—

you're my wife, and I love you dearly. I didn't realize you were fed up with our lifestyle, and I'm sorry for not noticing it sooner."

I shove the tip of my thumbnail between my teeth, an old habit I had left behind long ago. I'm not sure how else to convince myself this is all much worse than I'm making it out to be. However, the questions keep percolating in my head and I can't stop them from spilling out. "Whose idea was this? I would think you would have at least spoken to me first if it had been yours, no?"

"My father insisted we boost morale within the research team since we don't work side-by-side most days. The work has been tedious and he said casual socializing would be great for all of us."

His father. Of course. I should have known. His father has been controlling our lives since the day we got engaged and I was too oblivious to notice it before. Otto's cheeks burn red, and he drops his hands from my shoulders, pressing them against his hips. He peers up at the ceiling in thought—*a thought I would like to hear out loud.* After a long moment, he takes my hand and leads us around the coffee table to the sofa and gestures for me to sit down. I do, and he sits beside me, retaking my hand in his.

"At what point will decisions be made between the two of us rather than you and your father?" I ask, keeping my voice quiet and somewhat calm.

"You're right. I was wrong to agree to a dinner without speaking to you first. I won't let that happen again. I can assure you."

"Thank you," I mumble.

"Emi," he says with a sigh. "I thought we were settling down and finding our way in the new life we're living together. I've kept telling myself that you will eventually find happiness here, but I can see how much you despise being stuck at home all day.

It was never my intention to make you unhappy, I hope you know that."

He's said this all before. "Understanding what is making me unhappy won't fix the problem."

"I know, darling. I have considered finding a way to get you back down to the city to take those classes, but I'm terrified of sending you there alone, knowing an air raid could strike at any time, a street fight could break out, a riot, an act of resistance. The risks are great and to not know if you're okay all day would leave me feeling sick, constantly. This might sound selfish, but I'm comfortable knowing you're safe in this house while I'm at work. I just didn't think that was the foundation of being a terrible husband to you."

"I would rather be home with my parents. It's the truth, and I'm sorry if you don't want to hear it, but you must understand what kind of life you're creating for me. I'm alone from early in the morning until late at night, worrying about you too, despite your desperate attempts to ease my concerns about you working in a camp."

Otto lets his head fall back against the top edge of the sofa as he lets out a long sigh. "Will you give me a day to think of options?"

It's the first time he's offered to consider finding a resolution to the way I feel. "Do you mean it?" I ask, a flicker of hope warming my insides.

"Yes, yes, of course. I wouldn't say so if I didn't. In the meantime, I'll clean up tonight. I realize I've been a bit of a slob lately."

"I didn't make dinner either," I add.

"That's okay. I'll find something to make for dinner tonight. You can stay right here with your feet up. I want you to. Then, tomorrow, I'll come home early, go to the grocery store, then prepare for our company." I'm not sure he understands how much work that will all entail. It wouldn't be fair of me to watch him do all the work, but to have help is a start—it's something.

"I'll do whatever I can to make tomorrow night successful. If you're truly going to try to find a resolution to what's making us both unhappy, I'll do my part until we can make changes."

"You mean it?" he asks, twisting his body to face me.

I stare at him from the corner of my eye. "Yes, but you need to clean up after yourself and stop expecting me to take care of everything aside from your job."

"Emi," he says, endearingly, taking my chin between his thumb and forefinger so I'm looking at him. "I love you dearly. I've only been trying to do what I promised your parents I would—take care of you. I didn't mean for you to become upset. I'll do whatever I can to fix this."

I bob my head, just enough for him to feel the movement against his hand. "Why didn't you tell me about the dinner party a week ago?"

"Because..." he hesitates, "because there was something I needed to work out with my father—a disagreement of sorts. But I think we've come to an understanding now."

"An understanding about what? What was the issue?" I ask.

Otto lowers his head. "I can't get into it right now. I hope you understand."

But how could I?

FOURTEEN
EMILIE
JULY 1942

Dachau, Germany

Otto has put Charlie & His Orchestra on the gramophone for background dinner music. We've never played this record. In fact, I'm not sure when we acquired it because it's not something I would have bought. He's made good on his promise to help prepare the house and food for our guests arriving shortly so I certainly don't want to stir up any tension, but this music is known for its controversial, pro-war innuendos.

"Otto," I call out, finding him in the kitchen wiping down the countertop.

"Yes, my darling?"

"When did you bring this record home?"

The circular motion he's pushing the rag around slows to a stop. "My uncle gave it to me yesterday and said it would be good dinner music."

Otto has mentioned seeing his uncle at work. He's said he hardly sees any one of the men including his father and our neighbors who are joining us tonight. They all work in different departments, assigned to a variety of roles integrating into the cancer-cure research.

"Have you listened to the words of the music?"

"Yes, of course. It's a neutral form of entertainment for all. It's just jazz music."

"I don't like it. The words are demoralizing to the Allied forces." Otto continues wiping the already clean counter, dragging the rag in a repetitive circular motion. "Our guests might find it to be offensive, as I do. I'll need to put on another record. Your uncle should know better than to suggest such precarious ideals."

Of course, ever since spotting the *Das Reich* newspaper folded over Ingrid's magazine rack the first day I stepped into her house, I've been questioning their level of loyalty to the Reich. Though, as for anyone in Germany now, it's impossible to truthfully know how everyone feels. The fear of speaking up against our country's imposed policies masks any division between the two sides. For most, at least externally, there's only one side—the Reich side.

From the time I was a child, I've been taught to avoid political topics of conversation similar to how we wouldn't share how rich or poor we were. I've remained faithful to keeping my beliefs private, but that's the problem this country has. Like Otto and me, all who despise Hitler's plans and beliefs are silenced with fear.

"Sure, okay, I see what you mean. We can play something else," he says. He doesn't seem aghast at his self-proclaimed diplomatic uncle for giving him this record to play tonight.

"Thank you," I say, spinning on my heels to switch out the record.

Upon returning to the kitchen, I arrange the hors d'oeuvre assortment and the meat and cheese platter, placing each selection neatly across each dish. As the clock ticks, my stomach tightens in anticipation of our guests' imminent arrival. After hanging my apron, I head to the washroom for a quick mirror check.

My cheeks are rosier than the blush I applied earlier, but my perspiration has washed away the powder. I retrieve my compact and lipstick from my dress pocket and freshen up my face, giving the appearance that I'm ready to host this dinner party. I'm not.

As I step out of the washroom, headlights flash through the narrow side windows framing the door, which triggers a flash of stress that heats me from my core. The only guests driving here tonight are Otto's parents, coming in from Munich. The others only have to make their way next door or across the street. I feel like I might need to physically force a smile onto my face before Otto opens the door. His parents make him feel uneasy. It wasn't always like that. Their household was as warm as mine, or maybe not *as* warm, but the difference wasn't noticeable unless one really looked. I've gone through life thinking people are who they were born as, but too many people have proven this to be false.

Otto reaches for the door, and I take in as much air as my lungs can hold before releasing it through my nose. I should have had a glass of bourbon with Otto, but Frau Berger would smell the liquor on my breath and ask me why I'm not pregnant yet.

"Mama, Vater," Otto greets his parents with open arms.

"So, you're finally settled in after a few months. We were wondering when you were going to have us over," Herr Berger says, eyeballing me at the tail-end of his statement.

"But we wanted to give you time to make your new house into a home, so we didn't want to bother you," Frau Berger adds, nudging her husband with her sharp elbow. "Emilie, dear, you look wonderful. How are you?"

Frau Berger reaches for an embrace; one I can't say no to. Along with her hug comes a startling aroma of potent rose-scented perfume. My eyes threaten to tear from the burn. "I'm doing wonderful," I answer through my tight throat.

"Something smells scrumptious, doesn't it, Marion?" Herr Berger says to his wife.

"Yes, yes, of course," she says, releasing me from her grip to see her way into the kitchen. She'll have her fingers in the hors d'oeuvres and the tinfoil off the roast so it can breathe within seconds.

"Son," Herr Berger says, slapping Otto on the shoulder. "I heard you took time off today for this dinner party." The scoff doesn't go unheard. "Emilie, how are you, dear? Otto says you've been a bit tired lately. I hope you're taking care of yourself," he says, pressing his hands to his hips, smirking down at me.

"Vater, she does more than I could ever ask of her, as I said earlier," Otto says in my defense.

"Yes, yes, of course. I want her to get well if she's been under the weather. That's all," he says, faux surprised by Otto's assumption.

"Where is Uncle Dietrich?" Otto asks.

"Ah, I forgot to mention...He sends his regards as he can't make it tonight. Something came up at the last moment."

One less person is fine by me, especially his uncle Dietrich who's known to make dinner conversations awkward.

As I go to close the front door, I spot three couples walking up the stone path with dishes in their hands. Their heels clap against the stone as they walk in, all chattering at the same time. I can hardly make out a word anyone is saying but arms are tugging at me and folding me to various wool and silk textures. It's as if we've all been lifelong friends, except I've only spent time with Ingrid on occasion. I've only met her husband, Karl, once, for a short encounter on the weekend when I was bringing groceries into the house.

Ursula lives across the street with her husband, Hermann,

who works with Otto. Ursula and I have exchanged words a few times, but we only cross each other's path once in a while. She seems kind enough, although a bit tough to warm up to. Each of the three wives who live around us looks distinctly different. Ingrid with her stark red hair, Ursula and her gaunt figure reminds me of a colored pencil with a white eraser. Whatever clothes she has on, the entire outfit, whether a dress or blouse and pants combination, is the same color and hue from her hat to her shoes, always in startling contrast to her flour-white chin length hair.

Then there's Helga. We've met three times to be exact, once as we were both about to slide into our husbands' cars, the second time, when we both arrived at the same restaurant, and the third time, when we arrived home and slid out of the cars that same night—none of which was planned. She's quiet as far as I can tell. Her husband does all the talking, but I've only seen them when they're together. She seems to have an artificial smile pinned to her face, one that doesn't fade. Her dark blonde hair is flawlessly pinned back into tight curls, not a strand out of place, and her makeup looks as if it's been professionally applied—so much so that I think her makeup does a good job of making her appear cheerful and energetic. Yet, I get the feeling she has a different story locked up inside of her.

Each of the women follows the same path as Frau Berger, into the kitchen with the dishes they graciously brought with them. Otto offers a quick introduction to Hermann, Ursula's husband, since he's the only one I've yet to meet in passing. After our quick hellos, Otto ushers the men off into his study, leaving me standing in everyone's dust between the room full of women and the one full of men.

My kitchen looks like it belongs to an upscale restaurant with the flurry of activity, hands on every dish, preparing plates and pouring drinks. The roast is the only untouched item, so I squeeze between the others and add the garnish I was waiting until just before serving time to sprinkle over the top. I glance over my shoulder as I replace the foil, spotting a cloud of smoke billowing out from beneath the closed door of Otto's study. It doesn't take long for the musty scent of cigars to fill the kitchen.

"You ladies must have done this a time or two," I say, unsure if my voice is loud enough to hear over the commotion of plates and dishes shuffling around.

"We sure have, and now you'll be joining us too. Another set of hands is never something to complain about when it comes to keeping our husbands happy. Am I right, ladies?" Ingrid says, her red curls bouncing behind her as she mixes up a bowl of greens.

"You're right," the two other neighbors echo each other.

"It's been a while since I've hosted a dinner party, but I must say, I do miss the camaraderie of being around other housewives," Frau Berger says. "See, Emilie, it's essential to make good solid friendships at the start of your marriage. That way by the time you have children, you'll have a village around to support you."

I knew she wouldn't make it ten minutes without mentioning children.

"She isn't wrong," Ursula says. "Our two kids are older now and we're lucky if they spend a night at home with us, but those early days were quite tiring, and I didn't have anyone to call if I needed a hand. Thankfully, you will have us, as your mother-in-law says."

Smile, I tell myself. "Yes, absolutely." I must sound like I'm biting down on a piece of leather with the way I'm clenching my teeth.

"Or you could end up like us and be content as a couple without children," Helga adds, her words meek and hushed.

"Nonsense," Frau Berger responds. "She'll have children. They'll have children," she says. Maybe Helga thinks the way I do in that the thought of having a child during a war sounds frightening and stressful, and likely the worst time to enjoy what should be the happiest time of one's life.

"Do you and Wilhelm ever plan to have children?" Ingrid asks, peering over at Helga with a hint of judgment.

Helga shrugs against her blonde shoulder-length curls. "I'm not sure. Only time will tell."

"I see," Ingrid says. "I might have some tips for you. We can talk more later."

Tips? Shouldn't pregnancy come naturally? I want to have children someday, but not now.

Frau Berger rinses her hands in the sink and dries them on one of my decorative hanging towels that Mama gave me when I moved out. They're my grandmother's and she told me if I have these in my kitchen, I'd always make wonderful meals. Frau Berger was there when Mama handed the towels to me and commented that it was such a sweet sentiment. I'll assume she forgot what the grape-purple laced towels looked like.

She claps her thick heels across the kitchen and down the hall to Otto's study. She gives a terse knock, pauses a moment then knocks once more. "Gentlemen, dinner is about to be served. You can have a seat in the dining room, assuming the table is already set." She mutters the last part under her breath, acting as though I can't hear her. She'll later follow her mutterings with the fact that her hearing has gone bad in recent years because aging has been difficult for her.

"Mother-in-laws are all the same," Ingrid says. "Don't pay any attention to her. She probably still sees Otto as a little boy and can't handle the fact that some woman—one better than she, as she probably sees you, stole him away."

She gave him away at our wedding with his father. They pushed us to move up our wedding since our engagement was lasting too long in a time of war. As soon as the ring slid onto my finger, it was like she suddenly despised everything about me. I'm not sure what made her feel differently after inviting me into her house from when I was a young girl, offering cookies and milk, or even help with homework if Mama was busy, but I often question if I've done something to offend her.

"I didn't steal him," I reply. "Otto asked me to marry him."

"She's being funny, dear," Ursula says. "She'll act like she loves you again after you give her grandchildren. I promise."

There's a fire burning inside of my chest as I take in the unnecessary amount of unsolicited advice and warnings.

"Well, you know what I said to that," Karl shouts as he steps out of the study. "The hell with them. What have they done for this country? Nothing. They can burn in hell for all I care."

"Karl," Ingrid snaps. "Watch your mouth. We are guests here."

"Who can burn in hell?" I ask, repeating his remark.

Laughter grows among the men but then Otto loops a lazy arm around my waist. "Sorry about him. He slugged two glasses of bourbon without rocks within the first two minutes of arriving. He just likes to hear himself talk."

"Well, what's he talking about?" I ask again.

"He's—uh, he's been going off about the overpopulation of rats because we were talking about testing in the lab and Hermann doesn't like to hurt animals. Ignore them, trust me. It'll be easier that way."

Animals? I wasn't aware the research had reached the testing phase...

FIFTEEN
EMILIE
JULY 1942

Dachau, Germany

Otto and I are seated next to each other, but somehow, I feel like there's a table between us. Most everyone seems like-minded, except me and maybe Helga. She's sitting to my right, and I would venture a guess that she's feeling the same way, considering how quiet she is.

I place my hand on Helga's forearm to grasp her attention so I don't have to shout over everyone else. "So, Helga, do you have any hobbies?"

Her pale face brightens as she glances in my direction. "Hobbies?" she repeats. "I do, in fact." She smiles and her eyes illuminate with elation. "I enjoy building furniture."

I'm stunned by her response, a brave response I'm not sure I've heard from any woman I know. "You build furniture? What kind? Where do you do something like this? That sounds enthralling."

She lifts her index finger to her lips and shakes her head with a subtle movement. "Wilhelm has asked that I don't overshare."

My face strains in response to confusion over her statement. "I don't see how talking about a hobby could be considered over-sharing. In fact, I'm jealous that you know how to build something—anything at all. I would love to learn how."

Her lips press together into a smile that appears to be holding in a response. "What about you, Emilie? Any interests you enjoy?"

"Wait, but what do you do with all the furniture you make?" Our houses are a decent size, but surely not big enough to store extra furniture.

"Wilhelm sells most of the pieces, but with his name attached, of course. No one would buy furniture built by a woman."

"Well, that's just nonsense. I would buy it from you. In fact, I want to see your next piece before you send it off to be sold. Would you agree to that?" I have a bedroom upstairs that is still in desperate need of furniture.

Helga gives her husband a casual glance, maybe wondering if he's listening in on our conversation, but he's caught up in whatever the men are all shouting about.

"Yes, of course. I'm almost done with my latest piece, a writing desk. Perhaps next week sometime, you can come over during the day and I'll show you." Helga's cheeks flush.

"I would love that."

"Wonderful," she says.

Otto reaches for my hand beneath the table and closes his fingers around mine.

"I have to be frank with you men, Dietrich made it clear to me today that if we don't find a solution in this research soon, we're going to have correspondence trickling down from Luft-waffe's commander in chief." Herr Berger's rigid interruption blankets the table with a coat of silence.

"We're doing everything we can, Herr," Karl says. "Many of our assistants have been needed elsewhere to keep up with the incoming patients. There aren't enough of us to cover all bases. Although, we do hope to have a breakthrough soon."

I pull my hand out of Otto's to rest my forearms on either side of my plate, wishing I understood more of what they were talking about. "I'm sorry, but what does the cancer treatment research have to do with the Luftwaffe?" Otto had asked that I not insert myself into business matters with his father present because the topics were always so sensitive, but I can't help my curiosity.

Otto squeezes his hand around my knee making his gentle reminder clear. Of all people, he should know that keeping quiet is not a strength of mine.

My question disrupts the flow of conversation much like it did for Herr Berger. I scan the table, taking a fleeting second to look at each person's reaction to my question. The women are all unitedly staring down at their laps, except Frau Berger. She's glaring at me, making me aware my audacity is not appreciated.

The men, however, don't seem bothered by my question. In fact, they appear intrigued. But for what reason, when they should already know the answer?

Herr Berger is looking at me with an assessing look. With his elbow pinned to the table and his palm holding up his chin, he lowers his index finger and points directly at me. "Emilie, let me ask you something. How confident are you that you can treat mild cases of...say a common cold, or a stomach flu, a rash, or a wound, perhaps?"

"Quite," I say, perking my right eyebrow up into a point.

"Vater," Otto speaks up as if he could close the door on the question.

"In a crowded setting, what is more important to you, speed or bedside manner?"

"I'm not sure I understand your question?"

"I think you do," he says.

"Both. A person can be both kind and diligent at the same time. Per my training, thus far, they are one and the same."

"Good answer," he says with a snicker. I'm not sure I'm reading his reactions properly.

"Vater, please. Let's discuss this later, perhaps?"

Herr Berger's scrutinizing stare pierces through me, making it known I can't slink away from the conversation that's become the center of attention at the table. Of course, he doesn't scare me like he does Otto. "*A boy should always have a certain level of fear in his father, or he will never know the meaning of respect.*" Otto's repeated mantras about his father still make no sense to me, even after all the time I've known them both. I'm quite sure the Bible states that one shall, "Honor thy father and thy mother." Period. there's no mention of fearing the people who put us on this earth.

"It's all right to allow your wife to speak, son," Herr Berger says.

I peer at Otto from the corner of my eye, watching his cheek move against his grinding jaw—a common reaction he has to his father's behavior.

"Emilie, let me ask you this...if a patient came to you with a case of hypothermia, how would you assess and treat them quickly and effectively?"

"Well," I begin. "Hypothermia occurs when the body temperature falls several degrees below our core body temperature. When this occurs, the heart, nervous system, and organs are unable to function properly. If hypothermia isn't treated immediately, heart failure or respiratory distress are possible—both could lead to death. However, there are methods of treatment."

"How would you determine the signs of hypothermia?" Herr Berger continues.

"Symptoms can include a weak pulse, shallow breaths, fatigue, and unconsciousness. Most often, hypothermia sets in so quickly that the person in trouble isn't aware of their symptoms and won't always speak up about them so it's purely based off an initial observation, measuring vitals, and interaction."

"Where did you learn all of this?" Otto asks, quietly in my ear.

"My nursing books. I've read them all several times from cover to cover. Just because I've had to stop my classes doesn't mean I've lost interest in what I plan to do someday."

Chirping sounds erupt from around the table—feminine choking sounds. I'll take them as quiet sounds of encouragement.

"Emilie, we are struggling to keep up with the intake at the hospital and are in desperate need of help. What would you say to joining Otto and the others, assisting and gaining experience as well?"

"What kind of help?" I ask, wondering why I'm even asking after fearing the fact that Otto has been working within the confines of a camp all day.

"I don't think that's a wise idea," Otto says, his eyes bulging through a grave stare at his father.

"Well, why not? What would I be doing there?" I'm curious why Otto is closed off to the idea before I've had a chance to respond properly.

"Each day is different, really. There's nursing assistance needed in many areas, obtaining data on patient vitals, and notating intake and release forms. You would be in a safe environment, of course."

"Vater, I'd like to speak to you in private," Otto says, raising his voice.

"That's not considerate. Emilie has a right to her own decisions, has she not?"

"Of course, but this isn't a common—"

"Son, your uncle is the one reporting back to the Luftwaffe's commander in chief and he's expecting answers from us as to why we have not submitted certain reports or patient data. We are behind and we need extra assistance."

"I wouldn't mind finding out more about how I can assist, dear," I tell Otto, finishing my sentence with a polite smile. I'm still not sure what their work on hypothermia has to do with curing cancer, and me assisting with ill political prisoners, but I'd at least like to know more before declining the offer.

"I think it's a fine idea," Karl says.

"Agreed," Hermann follows.

"We're all in this together," Wilhelm says.

Helga takes in a harsh breath and slings her head to the side to look at her husband. "We're all in this together? Since when?"

"Helga," he replies, shock lacing every syllable of her name.

Helga turns quickly to me, "I apologize, Emilie, but I'm afraid I'm not feeling well tonight. I'll see myself out."

I push my chair back just as she does, planning to walk her to the door. "Please don't leave," I say.

"Thank you for being such a kind host this evening. I'm sure I'll see you all soon. I can see myself to the door, Emilie. Please, stay here," she says. Her cheeks tremble as if she's trying to keep in a cry, and my heart breaks for whatever pain she's going through.

When the door closes, it's already been long enough to notice that Wilhelm hasn't stood up to follow his upset wife home. Though delayed, he soon realizes he should have gotten up too. "I'm sorry to cut the evening short. I'll see you gentlemen tomorrow." He stumbles around to push his chair and the napkin from his lap falls to the ground in the perfect place for him to step right on top of it and nearly go flying across the freshly cleaned floors.

Karl catches him by the elbow. "Take it easy, fella. She's just your wife. She won't kill you."

I don't know if I would be so sure about that after hearing

her confession about building furniture. I believe sharp, dangerous tools are required for such a hobby.

Once Wilhelm has left in Helga's footsteps, a vocal sigh of relief wavers around the table. "She's just jealous," Ingrid says. "Don't worry about her. She'll get over it."

I don't think her outburst had much to do with jealousy, more like resentment for the way her husband treats her. "We all have our moments, I suppose," is all I can think to say.

"Well, maybe their moment tonight will finally land them with a baby. None of us are getting any younger."

Helga and I are at least a decade younger than Ingrid and Ursula, so I'm not sure her reference to biological clocks is applicable, but I keep my mouth closed.

"I don't love this idea," Frau Berger says. "However, if this gets your brother to stop nagging you for assistance, take whatever help you can get."

Ingrid and Ursula appear bored by this conversation, inspecting the polish on their nails, acting as if they were wall fixtures.

"Emilie, if you think you could assist us in any way, it would be much appreciated," Karl says.

"Yes...so long as I'm not in any danger among the prisoners," I agree, hesitantly, but I'm not sure I want to decline with the hopeful look Otto's parents are giving me. If I had let the idea simmer for another minute, however, I might have debated the thought of being inside the prison that I've been worried about Otto working in every day.

"The prisoners aren't criminal convicts," Karl says. "They've just verbally gone against the Reich's beliefs in a public setting and the act is punishable by imprisonment, and that is why they are there—as unfortunate as it might be." Otto had said the same. I suppose helping them would be a good deed considering the prisoners feel the same way as many of us who choose to keep silent.

"That's good to know. Well, in that case, I suppose I can be of help," I offer.

"Perfect. You can start tomorrow, yes?"

"Uh—ye-yes, of course," I haphazardly agree, wishing I had taken an extra moment to think through the proposition.

Herr Berger says with a wink, "I told you she was a keeper."

If Herr Berger ever told Otto that I was a keeper, I'm sure the word "house" came before keeper.

I let out a quiet sigh while pushing my chair out once again. "Well, I'm going to prepare dessert."

I collect the nearest plates to where I'm sitting and Ursula and Ingrid follow, doing the same. Frau Berger trails the three of us into the kitchen, once again, empty-handed.

"You do realize you're going to have to report back to us what it is those men do all day long, right?" Ingrid says, the moment we're in the farthest spot in the kitchen, away from the dining room.

"Yes, you'll have to dish everything," Ursula says.

Frau Berger fiddles with a pin in her hair. "Ladies, some things should just be assumed and not told. Let's not get Emilie in trouble before she has a chance to set foot into that rat-infested landmine," she says.

Rat-infested landmine. How lovely. I should be up with nightmares most of the night.

"One of us should bring Helga and Wilhelm plates of dessert," Ingrid says.

"Are you sure that's a good idea? They might be having an argument. No one would want to bear witness to that at their front door," Ursula says, speaking as if she has experience.

"Good point. We can wrap something up for them and hold on to it until tomorrow," I say.

The word "tomorrow" sends a chill down my spine as I imagine myself walking through rows of criminals. I've heard the stories about men in captivity and the thought is enough to make me want to fake a headache tomorrow. But knowing how much we all want to know what goes on within those stone walls each day, I feel it's my responsibility to carry through with the plan, on behalf of us all who wait at home each day to receive nothing more than half the story our husbands choose to share with us.

SIXTEEN

EMILIE

Munich, Germany

With a finishing touch to my rose red lipstick, I stare into the mirror, my reflection backlit by a flickering candle on my dresser. I want to look nice tonight since it isn't often that we get to go out and have fun these days, but it's Danner's eighteenth birthday, and there was no way we were going to allow this occasion to go by without a proper celebration. He just doesn't know about it quite yet.

Munich hasn't seen its finest days recently, but I'm hoping a celebratory distraction might be a good break, especially for Danner who rarely gets out anymore. It feels like there's more than a street dividing our lives, and I miss my friend. It's been two years of fighting how we feel about each other, and when we cross paths, he's quiet, distant, and not the person I've always known. Regardless of all the rules we can't break, I haven't given up on keeping him a part of my life—our lives. I couldn't. Until a month ago, I always told him he was on my mind and that I was thinking about him, even that I love him.

Then, one night when we were all together, he pulled me aside and told me not to say things like that anymore. He told me I was breaking his heart in more ways than I could imagine. He pushed me away as hard as he could. It hurt, even more than the last time he reminded me of what could never be.

It's been four weeks since we've spoken but I wasn't going to let his birthday pass by so I rounded everyone up and planned what I could to celebrate him tonight.

Felix is responsible for bringing him to the pub while Otto, Gerty, and I handle the cake, gifts, and confetti. Felix's father knows the owner of the pub who was kind enough to let us section off a small area in the back to keep the setting more intimate, the way Danner likes.

"I should have gotten balloons," Gerty says, pressing her palm to her forehead.

"Danner hates balloons," I say, laughing.

"I didn't realize," she replies. "Interesting."

"Plenty of people don't like balloons," I argue.

"I meant, interesting that you remember such a small detail like that about Danner."

We've all known each other most of our lives. I know trivial details about Gerty, Otto, and Felix too.

A loud scraping noise startles me into spinning around, finding Otto pulling a collapsible folding wall panel across the floor. "Sorry I'm late. My uncle—the one who's been staying with us the last couple of months—just informed my parents he would like to live with us permanently." Otto lifts his brows and sucks in a lungful of air. "Anyway, my parents will be here shortly."

"Your uncle is moving in with you?" Gerty asks. Otto never mentioned an uncle existing before he arrived out of nowhere, and we've all met him. He's an interesting man, but a bit quirky, and he has a habit of mouthing the words we say back to us, as if he needs to speak to them to himself to comprehend. We've all made mention of it, but we shouldn't be so quick to judge. I know better.

"He's my father's youngest brother. He can't exactly say no to him," Otto replies to Gerty.

"Family is family," I add.

She gives me a wide-eyed look before straightening the streamer she's hanging up.

"I'm going to grab the other wall partition. They said we could borrow two tonight to section off the space."

"That's perfect," I cheer.

Otto finishes setting the first one down in place and scoots toward me for a quick embrace. "You look stunning tonight," he says, looping his arms around my back.

"You look quite dapper yourself," I reply, my cheeks burning, knowing Gerty is eyeballing us with a giddy smile.

"You two are—" she scoffs. "It's too much. It's too perfect. It took way too long but thank goodness you both stopped being so stupid."

Otto grins with a soft chuckle and leans down to kiss me—something we've been doing a lot of recently.

"You smell like vanilla," Otto mutters against my lips, ignoring Gerty.

"It's called perfume," I tease as he flutters his lips along the side of my neck.

All the while, Gerty's words trickle into my head, one by one, making me think about all the times Otto asked me to go somewhere with him or spend time with him because he had feelings for me. I turned him down with a dozen different excuses, but really it was because I was fixated on Danner until he closed himself up inside his house after pushing me away.

With all of us turning eighteen this year, we've become acquainted with beer and other spirits, giving us courage to do and say things we hadn't before—also the reason Otto and me, me and Otto, us, became a "we" two weeks ago. It's been a nice distraction.

A strand of hair comes loose from his slicked do and swishes between our foreheads, tickling my nose. I nearly headbutt him when I laugh from the sensation, but he holds me tighter, spins me around, and kisses my cheek. I fit perfectly in his arms with the back of my head against his chest. It's comfortable—something I've always known.

"You're making me wonder where Calvin is," Gerty says, peeking down at her watch. Calvin and Gerty have been an item for almost a year and despite what he might know, she already has their entire future planned out for them.

I wriggle out of Otto's hold to finish setting up the space before anyone else arrives. I asked everyone to get here fifteen minutes before Danner arrives so we can give him a big surprise.

Otto's parents, my parents, and Felix's all arrive within seconds of each other. The moms jump right in to help Gerty and me and the fathers center themselves in the middle of us all, not wasting a moment to begin their work-day chatter.

"My parents should be here any second now," she says, staring down at her watch. "They're always late."

"Don't worry," I tell her. "We have time."

I tack one side of a streamer up to the arched entrance, balancing on a wobbling chair.

"So your brother will be living with you?" I hear from the booming conversation behind me.

"Yeah, he's uh—he's always been the one without a clear direction in life. My other two brothers knew exactly what they wanted before they finished school, like myself, but Dietrich, he'd be in outer space studying the stars if he could."

"Long-term family guests always change the dynamic in the

household," Felix's father, Herr Weber says. "My wife's brother stayed with us for a couple of months and—I'll just say, I'm glad he found a job in Austria."

The men all share an understanding laugh.

"So what will your brother be doing for work?" Papa asks Herr Berger.

"Well, funny enough, following no direction for so long, he did actually settle down a few years back and went back to school to obtain his medical degree. He's been hired to research for a private governmental agency, promising him the world and more. I couldn't turn him down when he asked to stay with us. This opportunity could benefit our entire family."

"Oh, you don't say," Papa presses for more information. Papa likes to ask questions and by doing so, seems to manage to stave off questions he doesn't feel like answering about himself and his job that he doesn't care for.

"Yes, the agency he's working with has asked him to build a team. Various roles are needed and I've spent time in every department of the chemical plant, they've told my brother I'd be an asset to their team. So, I think I'm going to take the leap," he says, his voice veering off into a high-pitched question.

"Any opportunity nowadays is a good thing. I'd take it and run," Papa says.

"Absolutely," Felix's father says. "Good for you."

"I'm hoping I can convince my Otto to lean in this direction too. The kid has had his heart set on becoming a pilot, but I think we all know where the world is heading now and I need him to settle down with a stable job and career."

"I thought Emilie mentioned something about him starting medical school in the fall," Papa says. "Is that right, sweetheart?" It's become obvious to them that I've spent far too long tacking up this one streamer, but I didn't want to miss out on this conversation either.

"That's what he said," I reply, hopping down from the chair.

"She's right. He was accepted and will be starting in the fall just like Emilie. I think it's a good path for him to follow, especially with the promising opportunities my brother continues to talk about."

I move to the other side of the arch to finish tacking up the streamer. Otto doesn't seem too excited about the new direction he's taking, but anytime I ask him why he changed his mind about becoming a pilot, he says he'd like something more stable for his future. It's clear his father has been filling his head. I can understand where he's coming from, but a dream is a dream, and why should we give up on doing what we want to do just because our country says so?

Just as I hop down from the chair on the other side, I spot Danner's parents, Frau and Herr Alesky, arriving—or just Frau Alesky and David. Herr Alesky doesn't appear to be with them. Maybe he isn't feeling well.

Frau Alesky spots me and directs her attention to meeting me at the wall partition. "Thank you so much for arranging this celebration for Danner," she says, a tear forming in her eye.

"It's our pleasure. Of anyone, Danner deserves to be celebrated," I say, keeping my voice down.

Frau Alesky takes in a staggered breath and stares up toward the ceiling, her eyes filling with tears. "I wouldn't miss celebrating my son's birthday," she cries softly. "But—" she exhales and cups her hand over her mouth, "Abraham—he left early this morning to pick up a loaf of bread, and upon returning home, he was met by two Gestapo. They...they arrested him." Tears fall from her eyes as she shakes her head. "They took him away from us. He just went to get bread."

My heart leaps into my mouth. I can't stop myself from picturing the scene—how horrifying it must have been. I try to respond but the words feel stuck in my throat. "Why—no—no they couldn't—why..." My words squeaking as I press my hand to my mouth. "Herr Alesky has never done anything wrong. Not ever," I argue as if she has any say. She obviously doesn't.

"It's not fair," David says, his expression pinching into tight lines. He sniffles and swallows against the pain evident within his red cheeks. "The Gestapo aren't just taking people —Jewish people—to prison. They're sending them off to labor camps."

This can't be happening. Danner must be so worried and distraught, and we're here ready to surprise him with a birthday party.

Frau Alesky pulls in a heavy breath and releases the air slowly so she can try to compose herself. "The Gestapo said he had a traffic violation on his record, and it was means for an arrest."

Herr Alesky rode his bicycle to the farm most days. The car was only used if someone had to go out of town or across the city, and there couldn't have been a more careful driver than Herr Alesky. I can't imagine him breaking a traffic law. "That's absurd. He couldn't have—"

"He seemed to know what they were talking about, but it's hardly means for an arrest. He said he would take care of it, and he'd be home in a couple of days, not to worry—his famous words."

"I believe him," I say, unsure if I truly do. David is right. It's known that the Gestapo have been sending Jewish people to labor camps for crimes less than an unpaid traffic violation.

Frau Alesky tries to force a quivering smile and gives me a quick hug. "Only time will tell," she says, her words pinching at the end. "Danner said he would find out where he is and contact a lawyer, if one can be found. There aren't many Jewish ones left, and no one else will help us."

"I could help look for a lawyer too. Anything I can do, please—I-I will," I offer, speaking so quickly I'm not sure she understood what I said.

She nods and stares past me in a sad daze before walking away as if we weren't in the middle of a conversation.

"Frau Alesky, I—I can cancel the party. I'll—I'll send everyone home right away. I can't imagine sitting here—this is horrible timing. I'll take care of this all. Why don't you just—"

She turns back for me, her expression crumpling with grief as her toes meet mine. "Please, please," she says, placing her hand on my cheek. "It's his birthday. I'd rather he be with his friends tonight. What you did—this is special. Don't send anyone home."

She steps past me into the private space where more people are beginning to gather.

I grab a hold of David's arm and pull him in toward me. "Are you okay?"

He shrugs. "What if he isn't back in a few days?"

I reach up and grab his chin. "Look at me. Your father will do whatever he can to get home to you. You must believe that."

"Thank you, Emi," he says, leaning down to give me a lopsided hug. Fifteen and still awkward, but I love him as if he were my little brother. He was just two when I first met him.

"Is Danner okay?"

"You know him. He's fine until he's not. He's sure Papa will be home before tomorrow night."

"Good. Listen to Danner. He knows best."

David rolls his eyes at me and steps to the side to move into the room. A few brief minutes pass between the last person arriving and the sight of Felix's red fedora. I turn toward the gathered group and hold my finger up to my lips while pointing toward the entrance.

I count down with my fingers, creating a perfect moment for Danner to enter while we all shout "Surprise!"

Shocked, Danner's cheeks burn red, and he turns around to face away, taking a minute to collect his thoughts before spinning back toward us.

"For me?" he asks.

"Who else?" I reply.

He walks toward me, and I open my arms to give him a hug, but he takes my hand and squeezes it gently. "Thank you, Emi. This means so much."

"It was all of us. We all planned this party to celebrate you." It was my idea, and I coordinated most everything, but we're a pack—our group of friends.

He makes his way around the room, giving everyone else warm hugs and words of gratitude, making me wonder if I've done something wrong, or if he's putting on an act for everyone so they won't think something is upsetting him. No one else knows about his father.

What an awful birthday.

Otto returns to my side, wrapping his arm around me, and hands me a beer glass. I spot Gerty off in the corner, kissing Calvin as if she hasn't seen him in two years. Felix, David, and Danner are having a private chat off to the other side of the room, and Frau Alesky is sitting at one of the small round tables alone, staring at her reflection in a fork.

"Where is Herr Alesky?" Otto asks.

I stare past them, avoiding the topic their family might not want repeated. "He must not be feeling well."

"Well, I hope Danner has a wonderful time. It's a lovely party," he says, kissing my cheek.

The moment Otto's lips touch my skin, my eyes lock with Danner's and for the briefest moment, his eyebrows furrow and he fights a grimace before turning away.

"You know, now that I've decided to study medicine like you, next fall when we start classes at the university, we'll be able to have lunch together and walk to and from school together just like we always did. It'll just be the two of us, but it will be nice, won't it?"

My acceptance to the university has been something I've

had a challenging time wrapping my head around. Most women aren't accepted, and the nursing program is small. It doesn't seem real yet and I keep thinking someone will tell me my acceptance was a clerical error, but I pray that's not the case. I want to be a nurse more than I want anything else. Conversely, Otto just made the decision within the last few weeks to start medical school. He applied and was accepted almost at once, even though he's never picked up a medical book in his life—at least not that I'm aware of. In fact, he'd never mentioned anything other than the idea of becoming a pilot.

I notice my parents have made their way over to Frau Alesky and are sitting with her. I hope she tells them what's happened. They'll comfort her.

Papa stands up from their table only a moment after taking a seat and makes his way over to Danner, pulling him away from Felix and David. The two have a talk in the corner and I wish I knew what they might be talking about.

"Is everything okay?" Otto asks. "Do you like the beer?"

I shake my head, trying to release myself from this trance I'm in, and turn to face Otto. "Yes, of course. I'm just making sure everything is going the way it should."

"You seem upset."

"I'm not," I say, maybe too quickly to be believed.

"Okay then. I'm going to go check on the food order. I'm sure everyone is hungry."

"That's a good idea. Thank you."

Another kiss on my cheek from Otto is like a silent alarm for Danner to glance over at me while still speaking to Papa.

I can't do this. I can't act like this is okay. Just because Danner said there could be nothing more than friendship between the two of us, doesn't mean he should have to watch Otto taking his place. I know the truth and so does Danner. I decide it's going to be now or never that I speak to Danner because I'm not sure I can go through the night like this, acting like everything is the way it should be.

I try to pace my steps, rather than run to him like I would any other day. He and Papa notice I'm approaching, and Papa places his hand on his shoulder. "We'll talk later, son," he says before making his way back to the small table of parents.

"This is a great party," Danner says.

"Happy Birthday," I offer, as if it shouldn't be assumed.

"I wish," he says.

"I wanted—we all wanted you to have a wonderful birthday."

Danner stares at me as if I should be able to read the thoughts brewing behind his eyes. "Being here, with you...and the others, there's not much more I could ask for."

"We both know that isn't quite true. I'm sorry if I've added more stress to what you're going through today. I had no idea..."

"Don't do that. You have never added stress to my life, Emi. You have no control over the world right now, no more than I do, and you couldn't have known what was going to happen today."

"But you're in pain. I can see the pain in your eyes."

I recognize the feeling, but for a different reason. It pains me, knowing I can't do something to help him.

I used to lose myself in a daze, staring at his beautiful smile, eager to be near him. Now, I'm not allowed to feel that way, and knowing so silently breaks my heart every time I see him.

"I can see the pain in yours too, Emi."

My heart feels swollen, like it's pressing on my lungs, making it hard for me to breathe. "You'll always have me in your life. You know that, right?" I say, realizing my words won't make anything better.

"I'm not sure we'll always have anything. Nothing is set in stone anymore. Our city lost its synagogue last week. I lost my father to the Nazis this morning. I couldn't even say goodbye.

All I have left from him now is a note telling me he went to get bread. There's no more. So, I'm not sure what is certain now."

"Me, Danner. I'm not going anywhere. Don't you believe me?" I'm not sure offering myself up as something he can hold on to will do anything to fix the grief and worry about his father being taken away, but I want him to know we should always hold onto hope. I can offer hope, even if it's the least I can do.

"I can't have you, Emilie. Legally, I can't be with you. So, I'm glad you and Otto have found a connection because if you can't be with me, I'd be happy knowing you're with someone we both care about. Nothing will change, and it won't be long before it's illegal even to be friends with us Jews, trust me. I do appreciate you finding the one place that will still allow me inside though. I know it isn't a simple task."

"I've hurt you because—"

"Because I told you, I wouldn't put you in danger by getting any closer to you than I am right now. You fought me on the decision, and I fought back. I won, and I'm glad I did. It's the only way I can protect you."

I close my eyes, pain slicing through my heart. "I shouldn't have said yes to Otto when he asked me out a couple of weeks ago. He told me you encouraged him to go for it, and it hurt me, so I said yes. Things just kind of evolved from there."

"I did encourage him because I don't want you to be alone. You and Otto should be together. I want—you to be together. You deserve a happy and protected life."

My heart is shattering again just like it did two years ago and again a month ago when he reminded me that I'm not supposed to love him. Pieces of me keep disintegrating when I hear his words. They should make sense, but they don't. He doesn't mean them. I know he doesn't. But neither of us can change the world.

"Is that why you didn't give me a hug?" I bite my cheek, trying my hardest not to let my emotions get the best of me.

"Yes," he says, reaching around me to pull me in for the hug I didn't receive. If I could melt into him, into this moment, into a different world and life, I would without hesitation. "And I'm sorry."

"Danner, I can't stop the way I feel... Despite what we can or can't be, I'll always love you for the person, the friend, and the more you have been to me."

SEVENTEEN
EMILIE
JULY 1942

Dachau, Germany

I've been a firm believer in following what my gut tells me, even if it's a split-second decision. Otto has been quiet since everyone left last night, making his opposition to me being here with him this morning clear.

I knew I would be going in through the Dachau gates when Otto's father offered me this opportunity. I agreed without hesitation, and yet now, my stomach is in knots as Otto rolls down his window to request admission.

"Heil Hitler," Otto says, saluting the man.

"Heil Hitler," the man replies. "What is the purpose of your arrival to Dachau?"

"You must be a new guard. We haven't met. I'm Dr. Berger, working in Block 5. Dr. Dietrich has requested that my wife, Emilie Berger, aid him with his work as I've been doing."

Groups of male inmates wearing blue and white striped uniforms watch us as we walk along the muddy, rubble pathway. I can't avoid the dread and grief in their eyes. They recoil upon eye contact, turning away as if it's a sin to look in our direction.

A daunting wooden door with an iron handle stands between me and this solid confinement, a place I never imagined I would see.

Otto releases my hand to close the umbrella and steps inside after me.

A distressing moan echoes between the corridor walls and I can't tell how near or far from the source we are.

Otto stops in front of a wooden door and my heart thumps in my chest as he pushes against the slab to reveal what's waiting on the other side. Before he steps forward, he pauses and peers down at me but doesn't make direct eye contact. "There are patients in here, but we'll be continuing on to the lab where I work. Don't look at any of them. It will give them a reason to talk to you. We shouldn't converse. I know that goes against your good nature, but these men are still criminals, even if they aren't the dangerous kind."

"I understand," I say. But I'm not sure I do.

Men line the walls: some are standing, others are sitting on the floor, heads hanging between bent knees.

"Help," someone groans. "Please, miss. Help us."

"Ignore them. They do this to everyone who walks through that door," Otto mumbles beneath his breath.

I wish I could close my eyes or pinch my nose to avoid the stench of what must be a mixture of body odor and sickness, but I'm not that type of person. That would be rude and disrespectful, even to a criminal.

I do my best to block out the cries for help as we near the next door, but a distinct sound yanks me to a firm stop.

"A rare honeybee," I hear.

Groggily and softly spoken, those familiar words strike me like a punch to the gut. *A rare honeybee...the world couldn't survive without them.* I'd never forget that fact. I search for where the words came from. There are so many men, and they all look alike. My free hand flares to my chest and my breath catches in my throat as I search, knowing those precise words were meant for me to hear. I was sure there wasn't a single person here that I could possibly know. Not under these circumstances, but I must be wrong.

"Dr. Berger," another voice calls. Otto is addressed formally with a commanding inflection. "Might I have a word with you?"

"Yes, of course," Otto replies. "Go on and wait over by the office door ahead. I'll just be a moment."

From the corner of my eye, I see an inmate lift his limp arm, holding his palm toward me. I want to screw my eyes shut, to close off my ears.

Then I hear, "Is it really you?"

Unable to resist, I twist my neck slightly to the left, toward the man holding out his arm, and step in closer, his words pulling me over. My blood runs cold as I come to a stop in front of him, my brown leather day shoes scuffing against the dirty floor. He has no body hair, is malnourished, and pale. His eyes are heavy as if he hasn't slept in weeks, and...

Bile rises from my stomach, burning through my insides as I notice a small but prominent dent on the bridge of his nose. A dent along the bridge of his nose...that I know happened when he tripped on a knot-riddled log, landing face first in a pile of splintered wood, requiring eight sutures.

I shake my head furiously as my stomach drops. I'm mistaken. He wouldn't be here. He *couldn't* be here. With my eyes shut tightly, I pray that when I open them again, I'll see that my mind has been playing tricks on me.

But I know it's not.

Those eyes...I would recognize them anywhere—even here, in a place like this. My breaths become frantic, and my lungs struggle to inhale. A whimper rattles deep in my throat as tears burn at the back of my eyes. He looks close to death.

"No, no—" I whisper. The sensation of his name flickers across my tongue, a relic of nostalgia that sears in my brain.

"You're here," he utters, his voice dry and scratchy.

My brain catches up with what I'm seeing, and I hold a finger to my lips, signaling him to stay silent. A heavy wave of dizziness hits me, but I glance over my shoulder to find Otto still having a private conversation out of view.

I swallow against the thickness in my throat, keeping myself still so no one will notice our encounter.

"Why—why are you here?" I gasp. "Did you break the law? You wouldn't do that...you-you wouldn't," I whisper, my words fumbling as I try to ask everything all at once.

He tilts head to the side and the faint line of his eyebrows arch with despair. "Of course I haven't—"

"Tell me what's happened. Let me—" I swallow hard and peer back once more to see if Otto is returning, but he's not there. "Let me help. Why would anyone bring you here if you're not a criminal?"

His sharp, bony shoulders slouch forward, and he stares up at me for a long, painful second. A second I'll never forget.

"Emi, you must know why I'm here..."

I scan the other men around us again, taking a closer look— spotting the yellow star adhered to their uniforms with the exception of a few men who have red triangle patches. I'm not sure what the triangles mean, but the yellow star patches with the word Jude inked in the center that has branded all Jewish people of Germany for almost two years now, answers my question.

This camp—it's not just a concentration camp for political criminals, it's a camp for Jewish people. Until now, I'd only heard of Jewish people being deported to ghettos or labor camps outside of Germany. No one has ever hinted at them being sent to a barbed-wire, gated prison within Germany itself. I've only ever known Dachau to hold members of the resistance and political opponents following arrest. There are more yellow stars adhered to uniforms than not in this room. How many Jewish people have been brought here?

A cold numbness zings through my veins as bile swirls around like a tornado in my stomach. Why is Otto working in a place like this? Does he know about it? Does Otto know Danner is here? Is that why he didn't want me to join him? The startling perception sends a sharp shiver down my spine.

"Oh my God," I cry quietly, taking in the sight of my old friend, terrified to imagine what he's already been through.

I've never seen Danner without a full head of hair, never mind bald with mere sprigs of hair regrowing. His eyes are darker, lifeless but lined with terror, and his eyelids appear too heavy to hold open. His skin is pale and gray, and his cheeks are hollow. He's skeletal and his shoulders are drooping forward, causing his prison uniform to sit on him as if it's resting on a hanger. And his hands...they're hardly recognizable, just thin sticks covered in pale scratched up flesh. Dirt is caked beneath his nails, something Danner never allowed to happen before, despite all the time he spent working outside with his bees.

My chest caves in, pinning my heart to my spine. It's hard to breathe, and I must force myself to acknowledge that he—that Danner...Danner depicts the definition of being on the brink of death.

"Are you sick?" I ask, clutching the collar of my dress.

Danner shakes his head. "No, I was given a choice between execution or reporting to the sick bay. I have a feeling I made the wrong choice."

"Ex—" My breath catches in my throat, and I want to press my fingernails into the flesh of my chest and squeeze my heart until it stops throbbing. "Ex-execution?" I repeat. There have been rumors, carried through illegal broadcasts from other countries, but we'd been assured this wasn't the case. I take in a shallow, shuddered breath that fills my lungs with what feels like tar. "No. No. That can't happen. No. Jewish people aren't being executed. That can't be right. It can't be true." I'm not sure if I'm trying to convince him or myself, but along with the rumors, it's hard to forget Hitler's infamous words spoken three years ago, promising "annihilation of the Jewish race" if Germany were to end up in another world war. We've been led to believe this statement refers to the deportation of Jewish people. No one speaks of such a thing. I don't understand.

"Emilie," Otto calls for me.

My head slingshots to my other side, finding him waving me over as he continues his conversation.

"Emi, go. I'll be fine," Danner utters.

I shake my head as tears fill my eyes. I reach my hand out to his cheek, but he pushes it away while shifting slightly to shield me from anyone watching us. "You need to go. Listen to me."

"I can't—"

"Go now," he grunts. "Please. They'll likely kill me if you don't." As if lightning strikes the center of my head and writhes down to my toes, I drop my hands and try to swallow my pain. "Dry your eyes."

I shove my fists beneath each eye, doing as Danner says, and struggle to take in another shallow breath. There's no air to breathe. "I—"

Danner shakes his head dismissively then stares toward the corner where I'm expected to go.

I take a step away from him, trying to understand why we're face to face like this...why? Why is this the world we live in? Who allowed this to happen?

The world becomes dark around me as I stumble somewhat blindly over to Otto, my eyes still wide with shock. He'll ask me what's wrong, and if he looked across the room, he would see for himself, if he hasn't already. Otto didn't mention seeing Danner here. Surely that's something Otto would tell me if he knew. We're Danner's friends. He needs us.

With a cold numbing sensation bleeding through me, I reach Otto's side and he swings his arm around my back. "It turns out we need your help in the laboratory today, alongside me. Isn't that wonderful?" he asks, urging us forward to follow the other doctor—the man Otto was speaking to.

I glance over my shoulder once more, confirming that I've not hallucinated the conversation I just had with Danner. He's sliding down the length of the wall, burying his head in his hands. "Otto..."

"Yes," he says. "What is it, darling?"

"Danner—he's...did you...he's out there in the...the room. He's a prisoner. Did you know?"

"Doctor, I'll be just a moment," Otto says to the man we're following.

"Of course," the man says, continuing down the hallway.

Otto stops walking and turns around to face the direction we came from, a startled look in his eye. "What in the world are you talking about? No, Danner isn't here. Where?" He looks around. "Are you sure, sweetheart? Maybe someone looks like him?"

"Go see for yourself," I say, staring at Otto's chest, wondering what his heart feels like right now. Does it feel something? Anything?

He places his hands on my shoulders. "Wait here," he says, hustling down the corridor. He only makes it to the corner where he peeks around into the open area where the prisoners are waiting. His head recoils but so slightly, I might be imagining his reaction. Otto's facial muscles slacken and his shoulders drop. He covers his mouth with his hand, but then quickly scratches his fingertips down his chin and turns to face me, moving back down the corridor to where I'm waiting.

"I—uh—no, I—" Otto wrenches his arm around my shoulders and squeezes tightly. "We need to talk about this when we leave. I have not seen him until now. I had no idea," he whispers.

EIGHTEEN
EMILIE
JULY 1942

Dachau, Germany

The walls feel like they're closing in around me as Otto's hand trembles against my shoulder, telling me he's speaking the truth when he says he didn't know Danner was being held captive here. I'm just not sure I can wait until we leave the sick bay later to discuss this further. We can't just act as if he's not standing out there.

Otto urges me to move forward, further down the corridor alongside him. We both walk as if in a trance until we reach the laboratory, two doors down and to the left. He stops before entering, closes his eyes and stretches his neck to both sides.

His shoulders press back and he clears his throat. "Follow my lead."

Again, I try to swallow against what feels like sand in my throat as we enter a large room with sterile equipment, tables, lab desks, and tools. There are no windows, just a large room of stuff that could be used for an infinite amount of things. Where are all the other staff?

Once we're closed into the room, Otto gestures to another

man waiting in the room. "Emilie, you remember my uncle, Dietrich, don't you?"

My stomach twists and turns, cramping as I try to focus on the middle-aged man in front of me rather than Danner sitting on the other side of the corridor. "Of course." I met him several times when we were younger, and he was at our wedding. "How do you do?" I say with a hand wave, turning toward the nearest wall, wishing I could see through it to the other side.

"I'm well, thank you," he says just before letting out an explosive sneeze that recaptures my attention.

Dietrich is middle-aged, and although he's Herr Berger's younger brother, he could pass as ten years his senior. His horse-shoe of white hair is combed into patterns for more coverage and his thick, black-framed glasses magnify his eyes beneath his sharp, shaped brows. Then there's his smile that contradicts the rest of his face—it's kind and warm, but forced and unnatural.

"Dr. Dietrich," Otto says, clearing his throat again while emphasizing the doctor part of his title, "is heading up the new research study for aiding hypothermia. We'll be working with him to formulate studies that will encompass the trials of testing and follow-up reports."

"Here?" I ask, my word broken like a crow's squawk.

"This camp is not just for political prisoners?" Otto turns to Dietrich, forming his statement into what can be taken as an unknowing inquisition. "There are Jewish people here, too. I thought—"

"*This camp is not just...*" Dietrich silently echoes the words Otto is speaking, his way of digesting confrontational statements. "It's a concentration camp, Otto. You've been here since February. Surely, this isn't breaking news," Dietrich says, holding his arms out like this shouldn't be a confusing topic. "Jewish people, black people, homosexuals, handicapped, and political prisoners—yes. There isn't enough space in the camps to keep everyone segregated by their ethnic differences. Of course you know this. Everyone knows this, yes?"

"No," Otto says. "There are innocent people here, not just political criminals like I thought."

"No one is truly innocent. Not you, nor I, are we, now?"

"I—I—yes, people can be innocent—even if you're not." My words are broken and my voice hoarse. The struggle to think of words when all I can do is picture the tortured look in Danner's eyes is keeping me from saying anything firm.

Dietrich lowers his hand and glances over to Otto. "I'm not sure I understand the issue here, Frau Berger."

"You'll have to excuse us," Otto says. "I—uh—I didn't quite brief Emilie on much before arriving today as we hold a strong focus on classification for our studies."

"Ah, well, I suppose we should start from the beginning," Dietrich says with the return of a wide grin.

"Actually," I say, holding up my index finger. "I would like to speak to my husband in private before continuing this conversation."

Dietrich repeats my words to himself then shifts his stare down to his wristwatch. "I'm afraid I'm on a tight timetable today. If we could just chat for a few minutes first, you can discuss whatever you'd like with your husband afterward."

Otto remains quiet, allowing me to argue or agree to Dietrich's schedule.

I'll do nothing to help any staff, police, or whoever is here. Had I known this was a concentration camp to punish innocent people... Herr Berger asked me to assist with the overload of patients, but it doesn't really seem like that's why I'm truly here.

I should have questioned the logic behind arresting so many political prisoners, just to put them in impoverished living conditions. Only for them to end up in a bind when they become overwhelmed with medical issues. It makes no sense.

It's foolish. And worse, Danner isn't even in the sick bay because he's actually sick.

I'd like to know how many of the men waiting in that room are sick versus here for reasons like Danner's. With that answer, maybe I would understand what it is I'm supposed to be doing here, or worse...what Otto has been doing here all this time and how he didn't know the entirety of what was happening here. He may not have seen Danner before today, but how could he not have known this isn't just a prison for political criminals? I know he wouldn't want to tell me something so awful, but a secret like that...I can't fathom Otto keeping such a thing from me. Unless, he had an idea that there was more than just political prisoners here, and that's the real reason he argued with his father about me helping out with the sick patients. Another bout of nausea waves through me. I'm not sure I'll even make it to the trash receptacle from here, but I run and heave up the small breakfast I'd forced down my throat this morning.

Otto yanks at a metal paper-towel dispenser, grabbing a handful for me. I take them and press the dry napkins to my mouth. Otto's hand circles around my back, trying to calm me, but it doesn't seem to be working.

"Come, have a seat. You're as pale as a bed sheet," Otto says. "Do you need to use the lavatory?"

I shake my head, not wanting to wander around these halls anywhere. "No, I'll be fine."

"I understand this sick bay is a lot to take in at first, but I assure you we're here for valuable reasons," Dietrich adds, pulling a stool away from the lab table, and tapping his palm on it, gesturing for me to take the first seat. The only reason I sit is because I might fall over otherwise.

He pulls a second one out for Otto and a third for himself. Before Dietrich sits down, he makes his way across the room and opens a metal cabinet door, retrieving thick folders and pencils. He places one of each down in front of Otto and me, then finally takes his seat.

"Okay," Dietrich says as we settle in around the table. He intertwines his fingers together on top of his folder. "The nature of our research is in response to the request from the German Air Force, seeking additional aid tactics and solutions to combat cold-climate elements—particularly immersion hypothermia after suffering a loss of crew members who were recently shot down over the North Sea."

The hypothermia question Otto's father asked me last night makes more sense now. "I see," I reply.

"Otto was just telling me how brilliant you are with all the studying you've done beyond your time in nursing classes."

Is that what Otto truly thinks of me? Maybe it is. Now that I know the reason he hadn't wanted me to join him today, maybe it wasn't his level of faith in my knowledge I should have been questioning.

"I'm not so sure. I can tend to sick patients, but anything more than that—" I croak.

"Don't be modest, darling," Otto says, squeezing my knee beneath the table.

"Moving forward then. As you can imagine, we are already in a time of war and don't have an extended period to follow the research steps we might normally follow. We will be complementing our research efforts with experiments here in our lab, using prisoners who have volunteered to be case studies in exchange for a shorter sentence."

Even though I knew the truth was coming, it still hits me like I've just been immersed in ice-cold water. "Human experimentations," I repeat, knowing the spoken words may make me vomit again. I clutch my hand around my throat and wrap my other arm around the center of my stomach as if trying to physically prevent myself from purging again.

"Correct." I want to glare at Otto. I want to slap him and

scream at him, but all I can do is sit here as if I'm being held hostage. I can't get up and run. The entire camp is surrounded by guards. I need to be escorted out, and I want nothing more than to get as far away from here as I can right now.

Except, Danner just told me he volunteered to be here so he wouldn't be executed. We hear so much chatter over the radios but no one has mentioned the act of execution. Executed for being Jewish?

My eyes blur as I stare at a blackboard full of chalked chicken scratch. The blasts I've been hearing from our house—they might have been executions, not methods of redirection. It could be a scare tactic to force the Jewish people to comply with their demands, but I've heard the sounds. There's no choice but to believe the threats. Danner's ultimatum says it all—die quickly or suffer until you do. Danner's face—the pale, thin, sickly version—floats across my mind's eye and then another blast rattles through my core, a bullet shoots straight through Danner's forehead and his eyes bulge and remain in shock, frozen, lifeless before he falls. Another blast hits his chest, forcing his dead body to bounce. "No!" I scream, gasping for air.

"Emilie," Otto hisses, grabbing my hand. "Are you okay?"

"No—no, I—I need to leave. I can't be here. You can't—"

"I knew she wasn't feeling well last night when we went to bed. I was hoping it would pass," Otto tells Dietrich.

"Oh, dear. Can I get you anything? Some cold water, perhaps?" Dietrich asks.

"Please," Otto replies.

Dietrich pushes his stool away from the table and takes his folder with him. "Oh, I don't want to be carrying this around. Why don't you take this, Otto. The folder contains IDs for our experimental subjects, and you'll also find accumulated data given to us by the air force. All notes you add to this folder must be datemarked, and cited."

"Okay," Otto says, keeping his eyes glued to my unseeing expression.

Dietrich walks out of the laboratory to find me a glass of water.

"I know what you're thinking," Otto says, wasting no time in expelling his thoughts.

I drum my nails against the tabletop, collecting my thoughts before I say something I shouldn't within the confines of these walls. Anger is raging through me and I'm having trouble looking at Otto.

"Tell me you didn't know you were working in a death camp torturing innocent people..." I say.

"No, Dachau is a concentration camp—a prison for persecuted criminals," he replies, avoiding the answer he knows I'm waiting for.

"Did you or did you not know that Dachau was interning innocent Jewish people too, and not just political criminals?"

"I've just been assisting with note-taking and data entry on the research pertaining to the potential cancer cure until now, Emi. This new order just came in and everything shifted within days. I—I don't know what to say...This—it's complicated here and I'm sure you understand now why it's the last place I want you to be." Otto is obviously uncomfortable, shifting around his seat, a sheen of sweat glistening across his forehead. *He knew there were innocent Jews here.*

"Yet here I am."

"Because of my father, yes."

"It's always because of your father, Otto. Tell me why you decided to leave your dream of becoming a pilot behind. Why did you suddenly change your plans to attend medical school? I was so foolish convincing myself that it was because you wanted to share a common interest with me, but that wasn't it, was it? I knew your father had something to do with you choosing a different career path, but I didn't know he had hatred running through his veins until today."

Otto rests his elbows on the tabletop and drops his head between his clenched fists. "I don't know what you want me to say. Yes, my father told me I wouldn't be able to support you or a family on a pilot's income. He told me the only chance I would have at giving you a proper life was if I went into the medical field—that and that it would keep me off the battlefield. I fought him on this, Emi. God, I fought him for weeks about this, but the man is relentless. You know this. I never intended to end up here. I didn't know before it was too late. I swear to you."

"You knew yesterday, and the day before that. You've known since February and didn't say a word."

"Because—I'm already in too deep. If I walk away...I'll be a loose end. Hitler's army does not have any loose threads. Do you understand?"

"So, you let me walk in here to also be trapped by what I'd find, rather than telling me the truth and giving me the choice to stay away."

Otto stares into my eyes and I can read his thoughts of blame. *You're stubborn. You would have forced me to leave, getting us killed. You wouldn't listen if I told you this was a bad idea last night. I tried.* If those are his thoughts, he's right.

"So it's my fault." His sarcasm is clear and unnecessary. "Look, if either of us walk out now—it will end as badly as you can imagine. There are two sides of this war. There's the side that lives and the side that dies. Which side are we going to be on?"

"Not this one. I'd rather die than be the cause of someone else losing their life. This isn't a world I chose to live in, nor will I take part in crimes against the innocent."

Otto stands up, shoving his stool back, the metal legs

scraping against the wooden floor. "You don't understand what you're saying. This order—it's from the Reichsführer."

"Your father did this to us," I utter, breathless as tears run down my cheeks. "I have an excruciating headache and need to get home. Now."

Otto holds his hands up in defense as if I'm threatening to physically assault him. "Emilie, we need to talk about this more. You can't just run away, and I can't leave for the day."

"I understand your situation perfectly. However, I need to take care of my headache so I can think straight. So, please, take me home at once."

Otto slaps his hands against his hips, closes his eyes, and paces two steps forward, pivots, then two steps back, again and again, until he stops. His eyes open as he squeezes his hand around his temples. "Okay, okay, but this is all confidential, and—"

"I'm aware of what the consequence entails," I tell him.

NINETEEN
DANNER
JULY 1942

Dachau, Germany

Days ago I worked alongside men, drowning in our own sweat, digging holes with tools too flimsy to dig sand, never mind the wet dirt we were working with. I cycled through various jobs until the SS called for me this morning to report to the medical block per my agreement to avoid execution.

I thought anything would be better than the forced labor I was being subjected to.

I was wrong.

Twelve hours into this never-ending day, I've done nothing more than stand in a room full of men waiting to be called. Anyone would choose this option over digging a hole.

Not me. Not after my heart disintegrated in my chest upon spotting Emilie following in Otto's footsteps around the sick bay, working alongside the evil tyrants of this hellhole. They were on that list of all the people I had never expected to see again. They were also on the list of people I could never imagine in Dachau, especially Emilie.

Upon spotting me, she looked like she'd seen a corpse, her

expression was unfamiliar. In all our years, she'd never looked at me that way. She also seemed surprised by my presence and the fact we'd seen each other here. Otto, on the other hand, walked through the doors and right past me as if I was a ghost. Despite our shared feelings for Emilie, he supported me, unlike the majority in this country who had turned their backs. But now, he was amidst Nazis who found pleasure in torturing innocent people.

I told Emilie she would have a good life with him. I was sure of it.

How could I have been so wrong?

My eyes are still set on the corner she disappeared around when Otto called for her. I've been waiting for her to return, but she hasn't. I need to know why she's here. It just doesn't make any sense.

"You won't be seen today," a guard shouts. "Return to your barrack." After standing and staring at the corner of the room, wavering like a flag that could blow away with one slight gust of wind, I learn it was all for nothing. For today, that is.

Some men here are truly ill, and I'm just trying to avoid execution. Every man in the holding room exits in a single file, heading out of the block and into the sticky, humid night air that adheres to my skin like oil. We stumble along, stiff, tired, hungry, and weak, toward our barracks. Lifting each foot feels like someone's tied a brick to my soles, the thuds on the wooden floors reinforcing that notion.

Most of the men in my barrack are curled up under their thin blanket despite how hot it is within these walls. I know the feeling. We just need something that symbolizes the idea of comfort, even a prickly wool blanket.

"Please, God, I beg of you, spare me of these days. Take me from this pain. Take me in my sleep so I can go in peace," Fred, the man in the bunk below mine whimpers. I stop on my way up to my bunk and tap his ankle.

"Don't say that. We can do this together," I remind him. "We have each other. Remember that, okay?"

"He's right. I can smell the chicken casserole now. The potatoes, boiled just right, and the bread warm with honey dripping down the edges," Eli adds.

"Don't forget about the apple tart for dessert, the sweet and sour freshly plucked apples from the orchard, sliced and sugared just before being baked. A heavy plop of cream melts over the side of the slice and it tastes like heaven. Doesn't it, Fred?" Hans asks.

Fred's heavy breaths come and go, slowing slightly as seconds pass. "Yeah," he says, panting. "Yeah, I can taste it now. I can."

Other moans and groans clash around me like an untuned orchestra and I wish I could block it all out. Most have been here longer than me, which makes me believe I'm staring into a future where I'll be crying myself to sleep, praying for death to find me painlessly. However, if I can give comfort and hold others up, even just with hollow words, I will. It's what we do for each other.

My muscles struggle against the rungs leading to the top bunk, my wooden plank between Hans, who's writing out a note with a pencil the size of a match, and Eli, who's staring at the growing spider web glistening along the ceiling.

"Danner," he says, "I was worrying where you might be this late into the night."

"They sent me to the sick bay."

"Are you all right? Are you sick?" Hans says, pushing up on his elbows to take a closer look at me.

"No, no, I was assigned to go there."

"For what reason?" Eli snaps. "Those damn Nazi monsters thinking they can use us like pin cushions."

"I'm not sure yet. I stood there all day, wondering the same." I'm leaving out the part where I was offered exemption from execution in exchange for whatever medical research they want to use me for. I don't think Hans was given the same offer.

He shakes his head in disbelief. "They just want to mess with your mind. That's the only game they know how to play."

"I think you're right about that," I agree, folding my blanket halfway down the wooden plank.

"I was just writing a letter to Matilda. Another one that may or may not ever reach her," Hans says, with a sigh that ends as a dry cough.

"If you ever need paper. I have a friend," Eli says, tapping me on the back.

"Thanks," I offer.

"Hans, you never know. Maybe Matilda does receive the letters," I argue.

"It's getting harder by the day to hold on to hope, brother," he says, lowering down to his forearms to continue writing on a scrap of paper.

I pull my knees into my chest and stare across the barrack. The lights are off but there's an orange glow from the exterior field lights, allowing me to see the surrounding bunks. Then every thirty seconds, the rotating strobe light from the closest watchtower flashes the barrack with a blink of light that blinds anyone who's still awake, leaving flashing spots floating in its trail.

"I saw her today, here," I say quietly.

"I have visions like that, too. My late wife, Belle. I see her all the time," Eli says. "Those are nice moments."

"They are, I'm sure," I reply, knowing we're talking about two different visions. Still, I don't want to disregard that he sees his wife in his dreams. We all need something to keep us going.

Hans pops his head up again. "You saw her—your Emilie? She's here?" The whites of his eyes glow in the faint light coming through the windows.

"I did. I'm not sure why she was here," I lie, knowing she

was helping the doctors of evil. I'll keep that part to myself for now. I'm still trying to convince myself I truly saw and spoke to her.

"You mean, you saw her here as a prisoner?" Hans continues.

There aren't many female prisoners here as it is so I'm not sure if it's more likely to see her as one of those or someone escorting the master race of followers.

"She isn't a prisoner. She was in the sick bay, dressed as if we weren't in a prison, and there's no war." And she was with Otto.

"I thought she was anti—"

"She wouldn't ever choose to support war efforts. Emilie would never follow the regime's beliefs, but that doesn't explain why she's here."

"Did you talk to her?"

"For a moment but the words didn't matter. Nothing truly matters now."

"Danner, tell me...did you ever tell her you loved her?" he asks. I'm sure he's confused about why I would care so deeply for someone and not fight to keep them. I ask myself the same question too, but I remind myself it was because I loved her that I let her go. So she could be safe and not subjected to a life with a Jew. I didn't know she would later be subjected to the influence of a Nazi sympathizer. I must believe Otto is to blame for them being here in their capacity.

"No, I didn't. It was easier for me to believe that love is something two people silently share, and though it's often expressed out loud, I never questioned if she loved me the way I love her. I knew she did, and it was enough for me, I guess."

"Do you think if you had, it would have changed anything?" Hans asks. I can tell he isn't pressing me for answers for my sake, but his own processing of thoughts.

"No, I don't. I think it would have made life harder for her."

"My Matilda was relentless. I tried to tell her I would end up getting her into trouble, but she wouldn't give up and I couldn't stay away. I tell myself I'll find her someday. That's the thought that gets me through each night. I might be lying to myself, but hope is all we're allowed to have here and though it might be a reverie, it gives me strength to keep going."

"That's fair," I tell him.

Hans clears his throat and readjusts his back against the beam he's leaning against, arching with a squint in his eye. I imagine it won't be long before I'm feeling the effects of sleeping on solid wood while taking part in forced labor.

"Will you be going back to the sick bay tomorrow?"

"I believe so." I wasn't told otherwise. "I was told this would be my fate after arriving here." I swallow air into my hollow stomach, wishing the hunger pangs would become less noticeable. "My options were execution or volunteering for an experimental medical trial." I'm not sure I feel better confessing this difference between the two of us, but he might as well know why I don't return at some point, assuming that to be the plan.

The outer corners of Hans's eyes sink with sorry, pity, or maybe both. "And you don't know what the trial is for?" he asks, his voice hoarse.

"I'm not sure. Perhaps I'll find out tomorrow. I'm to return to the sick bay each day until I'm needed—if I'm needed, and I'm not sure what that might mean either."

He's looking at me as if someone should already be digging a hole to bury my body. "None of us know what the next day will bring. All we can do is pray to make it through another, right?"

"Yes, I'll agree with that," I say.

Hans pulls something out of his pocket and unclasps his hand. "I saved some from this morning. Want half?" It's a sliver of bread. Though I would offer a limb to taste anything now, I won't take this man's food from him. I wasn't allowed to eat today in case I was needed for testing at the sick bay. He doesn't know that but we each have our own hurdles to jump over at the moment.

"I can't take that from you. It's yours, but thank you," I say.

Hans gives a dismissive shake of his head and tears the slice in half. "No, take it. I insist."

He holds out his trembling hand, waiting for me to take the bite. My stomach gnarls at the thought of saying no once more so I take the bread. "I owe you," I tell him.

"No, you don't," Hans says, holding up his piece.

I hold mine the same. "Cheers to brotherhood and finding a friend in hell."

"Cheers to that," I reply, taking the stale texture into my mouth. If I tell myself it's toast, I'll believe it's toast.

Hans pulls his ratty wool blanket covered in threads of hay over his body. "Dream about something far away from here," Hans whispers.

There's no right side, but I'll do as he says to avoid one less stench. "Thank you for the tip."

The moment I lie down and pull my thin blanket up, thoughts of earlier rush through my mind, of staring at every person surrounding me in the sick bay. Some of them were truly sick, not there like I was, waiting to find out what I'm needed for. Many were coughing for hours; expelling fluids without anything to clean up with. A few fell asleep on the ground and couldn't be woken.

My throat burns at the thought of how quickly illnesses must spread here, making me wonder how critical the medical trial must be if they didn't keep someone like me separate from the ill. I'm no scientist or medical professional, but it seems counterintuitive to whatever they are trying to accomplish.

I imagine I'll have vials of blood sucked out of my body, leaving me even weaker than I already am after going all day without food, except the scrap of bread Hans was kind enough to share.

Then there's Emilie and her innocent promises from grade school. She constantly tried to give me hope even when there was no hint of any. Her promises used to give me a unique perspective—ones I could believe in more than my own. However, there came a time when even the most optimistic person couldn't rely on another person's promise. Her words became words I wanted to hear—words she felt better to speak, but we both knew we had no control over what was inevitably becoming a future we both feared.

I want to believe she has no control over her being here, but that's a harder truth to accept.

TWENTY

EMILIE

Munich, Germany

I've been studying for an exam on the nervous system for the past four hours, and my eyes are beginning to cross while rereading the pages of my textbook again and again. Seeing as the nervous system is the most complex system within our bodies, I would think this subject would come a bit later in the year, but we're moving along at a fast pace in the classes I'm in. I can only imagine what Otto must be learning in the doctor's program.

"Emilie," Mama calls for me, shouting louder than the static riddled radio.

"Yes?" I reply, matching her volume.

"You have company. Danner is here."

His name is enough of a reason to slap my book shut and take a much-needed break. He hasn't come to visit in a while. We typically just see each other outside when either of us are coming or going from somewhere. Ever since his surprise birthday party, he's been spending more time locked up in his house. I assume it has something to do with the fact that his father hasn't been released yet. I know they're all worried sick about him.

"It's so lovely to see you. You look well. How are things at home?" Mama is plying Danner with questions, which is the last thing he needs. If he's found enough reasons to stop visiting, Mama's curiosity isn't going to entice him to visit more.

I find Danner at the front door, his dark hair swept to the side, sunlight highlighting his hazel eyes, and a hint of a smile I haven't seen in a long time. He's dressed in long dark slacks and a gray-blue button-down shirt. He looks different somehow, but I'm not sure what it is about him that's changed. It's only been a few days since we've crossed paths outside, but we didn't have the time to talk for long.

"You're looking quite handsome," I tell him.

"Emi," he says with a chuckle. "I'm sure your mother has told you to allow a gentleman to compliment you before you start throwing flattery out to him, hasn't she?"

"She doesn't listen to a word I say, Danner. You know that..." Mama says, flicking my braid to the side.

I grab Danner by the shoulders and push him back out the door while glaring at my mother over my shoulder. "We'll be back. We're taking a walk," I say, closing the door.

I look him up and down, still trying to figure out what's different. "You know, you haven't stopped by in so long, I was beginning to think we weren't neighbors anymore," I say with a sigh.

He doesn't respond right away, but we silently agree to take a familiar shortcut between the houses that leads to a grove of trees that encircle half of our street. It's as far from the city as we can be while still living in the city. It's always an enjoyable escape.

"I haven't been by your house because you're a taken woman. It would be inappropriate to stop by as much as I used to," he finally says.

"Taken? I'm not taken by anyone, and that's a silly reason."

Danner clasps his hand around my shoulder to stop me from walking. I already know what he's going to say, though. "You and Otto are dating. You're together, and that calls for a bit of distance between you and other men," he states.

"We were together. I guess you and I haven't had a proper conversation in a while."

"You aren't together now? What happened? I thought everything was perfect."

I appreciate that he's able to make such a statement without cynicism, because I might not have been so mature if I were in his shoes, and he was with Gerty. But that's neither here nor there because we are by law, incompatible.

"Well, when my nursing classes began a couple months ago, I became overwhelmed with the workload, and all the while, he wanted to spend all his free time with me. I guess he doesn't need to study as hard as I do." Maybe he's studying more now, at least. "Anyway, I told him I need to focus on classes right now. We still see each other every day but the 'together' part is on hold until I can get a handle on the amount of homework and studying I have."

Or that's what I've told myself. It was all too much to balance at once. I thought I might suffocate. I glance over at Danner, wondering why he's so quiet and unresponsive to what I'm saying, but there's another hint of a smile. I think he's desperately trying to hide this one.

"You're the smartest woman I've ever met, Emi, and I know you will always make the right choices in life." I don't think he was thinking that when Otto and I were together for those few months, but he said otherwise.

"I don't know about that, but I think it's important to focus on this opportunity with nursing school. I don't want to risk getting kicked out before I've made it through the first year."

Danner scuffs his shoes against the freshly fallen leaves and hums with thought. "Well, whoever ends up in your caring hands will be better off after. The world needs a nurse like you."

"I hope so," I tell him. We continue to walk further into the settlement of trees and the silence grows for a short minute. "Danner, did you just stop by to let me talk your ear off?"

He lets out a heavy sigh, one that sounds full of relief. "No, but you know I'd listen to you for hours before you realized you've been doing all the talking." Finally, a real smile to admire, one with pearly whites, and all. He was the friend with all the jokes, the infectious laughter, and the person who I couldn't help but smile at. Then, his voracious personality began to fade, alongside the acceptance of Jewish people in this country. I know the real Danner is still there, buried beneath layers of fear.

"You listen better than anyone I know, but you know I can stay quiet long enough to listen too, right?"

Danner screws his lips to the side and shakes his head. "I don't know about that..."

His comment garners a nudge from my elbow to his waist. "So then...what did you want to talk about?"

Sun beams break through the branches in front of us, pinning us in a blinding spotlight. I hold my arm above my forehead to shield my eyes, wondering why he's been quiet again for more than a long breath.

Danner's hand seems to fly out of nowhere, wrapping around my elbow to pull me out of the direct light and behind one of the larger trees so we can see each other in the shadow. "Emi, my mother received a letter."

"From your father?" I ask, hoping that's what he's going to say.

He drops his shoulders following a sharp grimace. "I'm afraid not."

"Then, who from?"

Danner tilts his head to the side, his eyes lingering on mine as he takes his time putting his words together. The pause makes my stomach twist and turn in pain. "The Third Reich has decided to force all Germans with Polish blood to return to Poland."

"Polish blood?"

"My grandparents on my father's side and my grandmother on my mother's side are all Polish, and I guess it wasn't a secret from the government."

I place my hand over my eyes, bewildered. "Wait, so...you're saying—you're moving out of Munich?"

Danner shrugs and puffs out his chest. "It's not by choice. We aren't even sure where we'll go when we get there, but they made it clear that we shouldn't plan on returning."

All the blood in my body rushes to my chest and my limbs tingle into a cold numbness. "I—but you can't—" without another passing thought, tears spill from my eyes.

I can't be here without him. We've always been here together.

"I don't want to go, Emi."

"Then don't," I cry out, my statement reckless, knowing none of us has a say in anything anymore.

He presses his hand to his chest. "I'm—I'm leaving in three days."

I shake my head as my lungs constrict, preventing air from coming or going. "No, you can't—"

Danner wraps his arms around me and pulls me into his chest—a place I always long to be, even when I shouldn't be. He's my home. I can't compare the feeling to anything else. He lowers his forehead to rest on my shoulder. "I'm sorry. I'm so sorry," he says, his words trailing into a raspy sob.

"This isn't fair," I whimper, clutching the back of his shirt into my fists.

"Nothing is fair when it comes to war," he says.

I try to breathe through this new sense of grief, but I can't find enough air to fill my lungs. "My heart is broken. I'm broken. This hurts too much not to fight. We must fight this. You can't leave, Danner. We're supposed to be side-by-side, the best of friends for ever and ever. We made that promise." I know my words are just words. All our words have only been words. Words spoken by children and teenagers, and now... whatever we are on the brink of adulthood.

"I'll do whatever I can to get back to you, but if I can't, please don't ever think it's because I didn't want to."

His hands slide away, the touch of his fingertips fade as he steps away.

"No," I whimper. "You can't leave me without you."

"Emi, listen to me," he says, submitting to his distance. He doesn't understand that I don't think like many of the Germans. I'm not afraid. I'll love who I want...if that person allows me. "I want you to work things out with Otto when you're ready. He'll take care of you, and give me peace of mind. Will you do that for me?"

"I want to go with you," I say.

"I want you to come with me too, but you can't. You must listen. Please, Emi. If you love me, you will settle down with Otto and live the life you deserve. I need to know you'll do this for me." He's suggesting a forever plan. He isn't planning to return.

The tear-filled-eyes blur his expression, but I know he's waiting for me to agree. "I love you. I love you more than I could ever love another person." He'll return the words, but I don't need to hear them because I feel it every time he looks at me.

Love is a feeling, not a word.

"So, you'll do that for me?" he presses.

I've been afraid of saying goodbye to him so many times throughout the years, but this time...it's real. It's happening, and there's nothing I can do or say to stop it. The heaviness in my chest is weighing me down, forcing me to fight gravity.

"I must go. Do you want to walk home with me?" he asks. "I don't want to leave you here like this."

A cry hitches in my throat as I try to respond. "I'll be okay here on my own. I can't go home yet. This all hurts too much."

Danner takes a step away, then another, and I can feel the distance growing between us like two magnets pulling us from opposing sides. We're losing each other, even though we never quite had each other.

I gasp for air through another sob, clutching at my chest, wishing the pressure from my hands would release some of the pain. I clench my eyes shut and fall back against the tree, letting the tears flow.

But as I'm about to sink to the floor, the sunlight disappears and a force pins me against the trunk of the tree, strong arms tangling around my waist. The world spins around me in a fog as his lips crash into mine, for the first time in the thirteen years we've known each other.

I've lost the ability to breathe, think, or be anything but inside this moment. He's squeezing me so tightly, holding on to me like I'm a crumbling ledge. I feel like we've become one person. The pieces of my shattered heart burst inside of me, like a snow globe being shaken with all of someone's might.

"You will always be mine," he mutters against my lips. "No matter what. You're mine. Forever."

I lock my arms around his neck, desperate for another touch of his lips. I've spent too many years imagining this moment, but now I know it's always been an unrealistic reverie. His hands cup my cheeks, making the tears dry and disappear.

But like every living, breathing thing, we need air. We need to part and go back to our separate paths. There cannot be an us, only me and him.

"This can't be over...we never got the chance for it to begin," I utter.

He presses the tip of his nose to mine. "We have this memory to keep."

"I need more. I need more time, more memories...more of you. Please," I cry, knowing it isn't he who has the final say.

"I'd spend forever with you if I could, Emi. But, since we can't have that, I just want your promise that you'll be happy, content, and cared for. By Otto."

I tighten my arms and press up on my toes to rest my cheek on his shoulder. "Danner..."

"Promise me, please. I beg of you..." he says, breathlessly.

The words swell in my throat. "I..."

"Say it," he demands in a hoarse whisper.

"I promise..."

Danner kisses me once more—so briefly I might have imagined it—then turns to leave, disappearing between the trees as if the wind has carried him away.

My knees give out and I slide down against the tree, resting in a pile of leaves. "I promise to always do what my heart tells me to do, Danner."

TWENTY-ONE

EMILIE

Dachau, Germany

Ingrid's children are playing outside on the street, laughing, and cheering without a care in the world, and yet we live within blocks of an electrified prison fence. The innocence of Ingrid's children is still pure because they don't know what I know. Though innocence can be obliterated in the blink of an eye, apparently.

If I could convince myself I imagined the inhumane scene I was witness to, I would. Danner in the prison sick bay, labeled a criminal because he's Jewish. There could be an alternate reasonable explanation, but the harder rationalization is to believe that he's truly guilty of anything more than being Jewish. Rather than leave the sick bay with a "headache," I should have tried to find out more of what was going on there. Not all the prisoners gathered in that hall were volunteers. Many of them were obviously sick. Danner appeared healthy; therefore, a volunteer makes sense. Why have a sick bay and a lab inside a prison if we aren't going to help the so-called prisoners live? To think I was fearful of being around all those poor men today. They are the ones who are living in fear.

As if my life is well-balanced like the contrast of night and day, I'm back here, at "home," in our kitchen, an apron secured around my neck and waist, and a noodle casserole simmering in the oven. The savory aroma fills the room, but it can't cover up the unease gnawing at me. My options are this or aiding in human research trials. It wouldn't be apt to use an animal for testing, never mind a person.

When Otto dropped me off here earlier, per my request—or demand—we didn't say much to each other before going our separate ways. He was in a hurry to return to work. I've been in a trance for hours now, staring out the kitchen window toward the curb that meets the corner of our street. I've washed the paring knife pinched between my fingers half a dozen times, soothed by the running water cascading over my hands.

Through the window, I see Ingrid shuffling along the curb with an oven mitt dangling from her right hand. She's in her favorite navy blue, polka-dot dress, stockings, and pink house slippers.

"Gunter and Ada, what did I tell you?" she calls out. "Your bedroom is a mess. You aren't going outside playing until you've completed your chores. Your papa will be home soon, and you know what he will do if he sees the mess you've left."

Every day, Ingrid chases her two youngest children around, trying to get them to comply with rules. Those two children just want to play ball and ride their bicycles all day during their summer school break, and I can't say I blame them. However, they're growing up in a world where broken rules are punishable without the chance of forgiveness.

I twist the faucet dial to stop the running stream just as I hear Otto's Volkswagen come to a stop in front of the house. With a quick glance at the clock on the wall behind me, I notice I've lost track of time today, but he's home at the time he promised. I reach for the crumpled dishrag set down on the counter beside me and dry the knife until my reflection sharpens along the blade and I place it back into the drawer I took it from.

My heart drums against my chest as I count the seconds down until Otto makes his way in through the front door. Strands of hair tickle the sides of my face as I whirl around to untie the apron and straighten my dress. I pat my hair back into place and hurry into the foyer to greet my husband like every good housewife ought to do. Although, I suppose in his mind, I'm no longer considered a housewife—just a fellow unlicensed nurse.

As I approach the front door, the weight of the unknown hovers over me while I continue to ponder what other secrets lie behind those prison walls, and within my husband's mind. I want to believe he's trapped in this situation like me, a person who has never agreed with the atrocious laws and regulations our country is being forced to follow, and a person who refuses to support this corrupt government, their antisemitism, and hatred for so many. The Otto I've always known would never agree to take part in anything supporting the regime. But he told me he wouldn't be working alongside the prisoners, and yet, they were there. Innocent Jews being labeled as prisoners in the same hall. How could he be okay with this?

The door opens and as usual, I'm greeted with a smile—today, the smile is more fearful than loving, but nonetheless, he's trying to act as if nothing out of the ordinary happened today. "Hello, darling," he says, removing his fedora before leaning down toward me with a kiss. He doesn't look worse for wear after finding out one of our closest friends is a volunteer waiting to sacrifice God knows what in the name of Hitler. "How is your head feeling? Better, I hope?"

"Yes, I'm fine, thank you."

"Oh good. I'm glad to hear it," he says. Otto smells like cigarettes and rubbing alcohol—not my preferred combination, yet our new normal. "It turned out to be a lovely day, didn't it? I was sure that rain wasn't going to let up." It's clear his tactic is to be abundantly cheerful in the hope that I'll mirror his mood, which tells me he hasn't come up with a better idea in the six hours we've been apart. And as for the weather, I haven't paid much attention to it. My thoughts are too cloudy.

"I suppose so," I reply, taking his briefcase to drop it off in his study. His eyes burn into me as I hurry away, but the moment I return, a more complacent expression conceals whatever he's truly thinking.

"I'm so sorry for—for this morning," he says, loosening his tie as if it were a noose restricting his air all day.

"I understand your father has put you in a tricky situation."

Otto tilts his head to the side, raising an eyebrow as he twists his lips into a scowl. "You look pale, Emilie. Are you sure you aren't coming down with something?" he asks, reaching for my hand to draw me in closer to him. He touches his palm to my forehead, checking for a fever I don't have. His steel-blue eyes pierce into mine, trying to read the thoughts between my responses. I can't see a single thought when looking back at him.

"I'm quite well. My headache went away. I just couldn't bear the thought of being in there for another minute."

"I know the prison was an unsettling sight for you this morning. It can be jarring the first time you walk in through those doors, but after a while you learn to focus on the tasks at hand," he says.

I'm not sure the sight of ill people ever becomes easier to witness, never mind the healthy who are volunteering to *become* ill. Nurses are supposed to learn how to put on a brave face to keep patients calm, but how could I be brave in a situation like this?

"It wasn't what I was expecting? Is that all? What about the fact one of our very best friends is being held there as a prisoner? We haven't seen him in years, wondering what might have happened to him, and now—well, now we know, and it's the most horrific answer to our questions possible." I don't understand why he's curtailing the blatant issue. "It's a concentration camp, imprisoning innocent lives. *Danner, my God.* I refuse to take part in anything that jeopardizes a life, and if you choose to continue to do so...I'm not sure—I don't even know what to say to you."

Otto walks past me, following his nose into the kitchen. "I understand how jarring it is to know Danner is within those gates, and us, essentially on the other side. But we aren't Nazis, Emilie. We're assisting with scientific research, and offering medical care to sick patients, prisoners or not—we aren't hurting anyone. We aren't the people who decided to create internment camps, but we can take care of the people who are prisoners in them."

"You aren't hurting anyone? You must be fooling yourself if that's what you believe. Human experimentation is not research, research does not involve testing theories on living people."

"You're making this sound much worse than it is," he says, his words so unconvincing there's no way he believes what he's saying. He must be in denial or trying to convince himself that this isn't as deplorable as it is.

I follow at his heels but remain in the open archway. "With so many...prisoners, we'll call them, I imagine many must die under Dietrich's treatment, all while you're doing research, yes?"

Otto pulls open the oven door to peek inside. "Emi, I'm not a monster."

"I think this would define the act of a monster, Otto. How can you not see it that way?"

He moves down the counter to where he keeps the glass

ribbed bottle of brandy and takes one of the clean glasses that I've left out for him to pour a pre-dinner splash.

"Working within those gates makes you—would make me an accomplice."

"Emi—we can help them. You know I support your endeavors and studies just as you support mine, and it must seem unfair that I'm working in the field we both planned to be a part of while you've been here at home, but now...we have a chance to make a difference."

I make my way to his side and take the second glass in front of the bottle of brandy, pouring myself a small serving.

"Life isn't always fair. Isn't that what they say?" I reply.

A common housewife wasn't written into my life plans, but neither was another world war. One thing shouldn't have anything to do with the other, but here, it does, and for reasons I can't understand. People need medical care—all people, and if help is needed, I shouldn't have been pulled away from the opportunity.

"I know you're upset that we had to uproot our plans and place a pause on our classes, but while this current opportunity isn't something I would have chosen, it's experience we can use when moving forward later. Maybe it's best if we look at this as a situation we were meant to be in to do the right thing and help those who need us."

"We aren't helping people. We'll be hurting them, Otto."

"No, we won't. We won't hurt anyone." He sounds much less defensive now as if he thinks he's proven his point, but there's no way to make this sound any different to what it is.

With his final words, he will continue thinking I'm not disgusted by the idea of what's happening within those walls. I keep so many of my thoughts bottled up inside lately that I'm not sure he knows what I'm truly thinking now. I take a sip of the brandy, allowing the burning liquor to trickle down my throat. I'd rather go back to being naive about his job that I thought was so dangerous.

Otto has a kind heart. He will never just agree with someone else's opinion if his doesn't match. But that's with the exception of his father and uncle, who he just can't seem to fault or argue with. The Otto I've known most of my life would never volunteer to spend his time in a concentration camp where innocent people are being held captive, nor would he consider what he's doing an experience he could use in the future. I would know if I was married to a man capable of forgetting his morals. What wife wouldn't know this about her husband?

"Has your father brainwashed you? Because I can't even begin to think of what to say to you right now. Who are you, Otto? I feel like I'm married to a complete stranger."

Once upon a time, I wouldn't have thought his father would set foot inside a concentration camp either, but it's becoming clearer by the day that he has betrayed his morals on behalf of his brother's promises to be world renowned for curing cancer if that's even still a work-in-progress now. I don't understand how Otto has walked through those gates day after day without noticing the truth of the people being held within them. It seems impossible to avoid, and to withhold it from me for five months is unfathomable. I have tried not to fault him for being so loyal to his family, until today.

"Yes, Emi. Yes, he did, and now I'm stuck, so I'm going to do what I can to do right by those who deserve help. That is my answer to you. I'll help Danner, and whoever else I can to keep the odds of their current inevitable outcome as far away as possible. However, I need you to return with me, or we're going to face issues—terrifying ones."

He wants to help.

He wants me to help.

I would walk through a rain shower of bullets if there was a chance of protecting Danner. I've never been one to shy away from bravery but we're all so small in the face of what's taken over our world. Nothing is black and white, or maybe it is, and that's what scares me the most. I clench my hands and release them continually, feeling the sweat pool as I consider what's to come. I fan my hand in front of my face and lean against the arched wall.

"Despite the desire to help whoever we can, I can't move past the idea of us facing 'issues' if I don't return with you. Your father and uncle are responsible for setting up this supposed research trial and yet, you're afraid for our lives. Am I understanding you correctly?"

I thought I was at a loss for words, but in truth, I'm doing everything I can to bury my rage. No matter what he responds with, nothing will change because his father is a man of his word and when he commits to something, it's done. He expects Otto to act the same. I never considered that I might have to question who Otto would be more loyal to—his father or me. Regardless, if there's a chance to help Danner, I have to hope Otto will indeed be a man of his word.

"You understand perfectly well and I'm unable to make an excuse for him. I believe many people have been blindly led into situations without knowing what's around the corner and everyone is afraid for their own lives. My father and uncle are likely feeling the same way. I'm not sure what to think, Emi. That's the truth."

My heart is pounding so fiercely, it's hard to portray any sort of calmness, but I can't let myself explode. It will only make things worse.

"I'll return with you, but let it be known that I'm only returning to do whatever I can to help Danner and the other innocent people there—however possible. And I'm terrified that this will all end badly. The thought of what can happen... I can't wrap my head around the fact that we're in this situation. I can't."

"Understood, and thank you," Otto says, dropping his head, a sign of the shame he must be feeling. "I can't fathom the thought of Danner being among those men. Of all the people in the world... You know I wouldn't want anything to happen to him. He doesn't deserve this or anything he's had to deal with over the last four years." He lifts his glass from the table and takes a long sip of the bourbon. "Danner was in Poland for a while, wasn't he?"

I shrug because I don't know much of how Danner ended up Dachau, but he's there.

"What is this prison camp doing to Jewish people, Otto?" He must know they are executing them.

He shakes his head and closes his eyes. "Everything is so covert. I only see the people who are in the hospital block, but until last week I wasn't crossing paths with anyone except other medical professionals working on the research I had been assigned. I told you we were being shuffled around."

Otto seems to have a challenging time finding his voice and clasps a hand around his throat. He can't possibly be in a state of denial. These camps that hold Jewish people don't have a reputation of giving them simple jobs, a place to sleep, and enough food to survive. It's the opposite, and worse. Much worse.

"What does this research truly entail, Otto?"

"I'm not sure. I mean—I think we may be...I just—" Otto averts his gaze to the popcorn plaster on the ceiling. "There are papers we have to sign tomorrow before any further information will be given."

"What will I be signing? What will I be agreeing to?" I ask. I'm not sure whether he knows and would rather not say or is in the dark like me, but he's been there. He should know how they operate.

"I don't know."

It doesn't matter. Knowing Danner is there, I can't sit here and do nothing. I'm not sure what I'll be able to do but anything will be better than remaining ignorant to the truth of what's happening behind those gates.

When Danner was forced to leave us four years ago to go to Poland, we had no way of helping him. I can't let him down again. I won't.

Dachau, Germany

The next morning, the heavens above bear witness to me sliding into the passenger seat of the car, knowing we're returning to a prison camp. There isn't a right decision to be made. All I can do is pray I find a way to help the innocent. I'll need to mask every emotion, each sawing pain in the pit of my stomach and the hiccups in my racing heart. No one can know I have ulterior motives. I have never considered being untruthful, unfaithful, or disloyal to someone I love, but now I'm forced to question whether Otto is capable of betrayal when it comes to his family.

"Are you feeling better this morning?" Otto asks, placing his hand on my knee.

I exhale sharply through my nose, still unable to fill my lungs. "I'm not sure I'll ever feel better."

He sighs and nods in agreement. "I didn't sleep well. Hopefully, I didn't keep you up," he says. "My mind was racing much of the night, worrying about you—us, and this job."

"You're right to do so," I tell him, hating to be so pointed. Otto has said there are two sides to this war, but there aren't, and we can't walk by as if innocent people aren't being terrorized through a dictator's orders. It's Hitler against the world. We are all on one side except for him.

"Emi, if—" he begins to speak but clears his throat as if something is stuck.

"Yes?"

His hands tighten around the steering wheel, the plastic scrapes against the inside of his palms. "If you see Danner again today, I need to know you won't interact with him. It will be a violation of the agreement."

"What agreement are you referring to?"

"One that you will be asked to sign today about the research."

I twist my head, staring at his pale profile, his veins bulging in his neck, and the tremble moving through him. "Did you acknowledge Danner yesterday after I left?" I ask rather than respond to his statement.

"I couldn't, because I signed the agreement back in February."

"You signed an agreement stating you wouldn't be caught communicating with a man you've been friends with most of your life?"

"I agreed not to fraternize with the inmates, Emilie."

"With the prisoners, you mean?" I lash back.

"Yes, you're right."

"Otto, you're a brilliant man. So please, do tell me the definition of a prisoner before you continue to act so confused as to why Danner is here."

Otto clears his throat and straightens his shoulders. "Good God, Emilie, I didn't mean..."

"What is the definition of a prisoner, Otto?" I repeat, staring at the side of his face as he continues to drive. My pulse is racing, my blood boiling, and my face is on fire. I promised myself I wouldn't do this because it wouldn't help anything, but it's impossible to act like this is all okay.

"I don't know, Emi, a person who is entrapped as a form of punishment?"

"What did Danner do to deserve this form of punishment?" I ask, holding my stare over him. He needs to admit it out loud—to hear himself speak the unthinkable words.

I watch Otto's Adam's apple bob up and down against the taut skin of his neck. "Because," he says, his word hitching in his throat. His eyes water as he covers his hand over his mouth.

"Because he was born Jewish, remember?" I say.

No response. Only more bobbing of his Adam's apple.

We're about to pull into the exterior entrance to the Dachau prison and Otto presses on the brakes. "Are you going to sign the agreement, or not? I would rather you not go inside again if you don't plan to adhere to their requirements."

I'm not sure if Otto will feel more concerned if I agree or disagree at this moment. "You said if I don't return, there will be consequences. Did you not?"

"Yes, and not ones my father or uncle will be able to control, I'm afraid."

"So do I have a choice?"

Despite my desire to help Danner, walking back in there, knowing what I know, will forever change me. I'm already a different person to the one I was before yesterday. It will only become worse. Maybe I should run. What if that's the only way to keep everyone safe?

"No, Emilie. No. We can't turn back. You've already seen what's behind the gates. By not returning, you and I will be in more danger than we've ever been in. I assure you."

"I won't say I agree. If I don't have a choice, then do what you must and I'll do what I'm told. But I don't agree."

My chin quivers and I stare out my window, desperately avoiding the reflection of my tear-filled eyes. This is how everyone takes part in a revolt. This is why our country is turning on itself. I've fallen victim to the trap just like many others.

"Okay then," he says, parking the car and opening the door.

I slide across the seat to follow him and brace myself for another haunting walk through the barren block leading to the sick bay.

"What is that?" Otto asks, pointing to a notepad I'm clutching tightly to my chest.

"My notes on hypothermia." I continue to walk alongside him even though he seems to be stumbling over his feet.

"We have books here."

"I have books written before 1933 at home. They're more reliable."

"Shh, Emilie, you can't speak like that here. Someone could hear you."

I squeeze my notebook tighter against my chest and scan the surrounding walls, expecting to find peepholes, proving we're being watched and listened to. Otto's breath shudders as he holds his hand against my back and ushers me forward toward the same hallway we walked through yesterday.

Upon entering the main area filled with prisoners, the sight is now familiar, except for a few new faces in addition to those who were here yesterday. Danner is back in the same spot too. How long has he been here? I'm not sure if they made him sleep here last night. Where else would he sleep? I bite the inside of my cheek as my temples throb. I can't cry. Someone could see. I swallow hard and try to take in a mouthful of air to hold on to.

As we walk past Danner, Otto keeps his head up and eyes set forward, ignoring Danner's existence as if he's an uninteresting portrait collecting dust on the wall. The behavior enrages me, but I bite my tongue as I peer at Danner through the corner of my eye, giving him a subtle glance just so he knows I'm acknowledging his presence. Of course, he may assume I've been brainwashed overnight to think along the same wavelength as Otto, but I would like to think Danner knows me well enough to know I wouldn't collapse under pressure so easily.

We pass Dietrich in the final hallway that leads to the lab we were in yesterday.

"Good morning. Welcome back, Frau Berger. A pleasure to have you here. I've left the paperwork on the table for you to review and sign. Once you're through, you can leave it on my desk in the office across the hall," he says, speaking to me as if we only met for the first time yesterday. He stops short in his steps and points to what must be his office. "Ah, one more thing." He pivots his stance to walk in the direction we're heading, leading us to the lab. I glance over at Otto, curious about his expression. I find him unusually pale and jittery as we enter the lab, finding three unfamiliar uniformed men. "The commander in chief has enlisted three servicemen to assist. These men have helped with previous assignments and will be of great help to you."

They aren't doctors either.

"Heil Hitler," Dietrich greets them with a salute.

"Heil Hitler," Otto follows, peering at me to hint that I do the same.

"Heil Hitler," the servicemen say.

I utter the same words while biting my cheek.

Hearing Hitler's name grows older with each passing day.

I spot the papers on the table and plan to sign them without reading through the gibberish because I don't quite care what is written. I'll imagine the worst. I continue to clutch my notebook against my chest and allow my handbag to slide off my shoulder so I can take that in my hand too. With the pen resting on top of the papers, I lean forward, feeling all pairs of eyes in the room staring at me as if there's an alternative to what I'm about to do. I scan each paper, sliding the tip of the pen under each line, reading every other word on how my agreement is legally binding and prosecutable if falsified or objectified. With my initials scripted along the bottom line I place the papers back in an even stack and set the pen on top.

"I'll bring that to Dr. Dietrich's desk," one of the uniformed men offers.

"Thank you. I'm looking forward to the outcome of your work, Frau Berger," Dietrich says, disappearing from the doorway of the lab.

"Emilie, we discussed the idea of beginning our research with our test subjects to determine our baseline data including body temperatures prior to immersion in varying degrees of water," Otto says. "All of our test subjects are in fair health without medical complications or history of medication conditions."

We should have discussed this at home so he wouldn't have been embarrassed by my response to his plan.

"Do they all have records of heart rate, weight, age, and rectal temperatures?"

Another one of the airmen slides a folder over to Otto as if to help him with the vital stats he should know.

Otto takes the folder and thumbs through the pages, searching for the data that must be hidden in the pile.

"We don't have time for this," the third airman says. "We're filling the submersion tubs, as discussed."

"Submersion tubs?" I repeat. "There's much to be done before testing contrasting temperatures."

"They're right. We don't have time," Otto says.

"Yes, we do. It only takes a second." I take the folder from his hand and thumb through the pages, finding no records of heart rate, age, weight, or body temperature for any of the subjects. We're talking about living, breathing people who chose this option over execution. "Without baseline knowledge, we won't have—"

"Okay then," Otto interrupts. "Fill the submersion tubs to

34°C/93°F. We should be gauging the rate of change for body temperature when immersed into water about five percent colder than average body temperature."

The last of the airmen to leave the room nods at me with an agreeable gesture and continues into the adjoining lab where I assume the tubs are located. By starting at 34°C/93°F, a temperature warmer than a pool or summer ocean water, I'll be able to measure the gradual change of heart rate and body temperature without causing hypothermia. If we move at incremental rates, I'll know when to stop before endangering anyone's health. If they are looking to me to educate them on this process, they shouldn't expect a quicker way of getting these results.

"They aren't going to give you the leisure of time," Otto says, taking the folder back from my hands. "They're going to think you aren't moving quick enough if it takes too long, and they'll take matters into their own hands."

He's speaking so quietly, it's hard to hear every word of what he's saying, but it's the first time in the last three days I've felt like we're on a semi-common side on this. I won't hurt those men out there, and I won't let Dietrich or the selected servicemen do it either.

"What water temperature will cause hypothermia within minutes?" he asks.

I lower the notebook I've been squeezing in my hand and glance at my notes, reading that 5°C/44°F will cause hypothermia within a few minutes. We can't brush up against that number.

"16°C /60°F."

Otto glances at my notebook but I pull it back to my chest. "Okay," he says.

"Prisoner number: 13415 and 13286, come forward," someone shouts. "Go down the hall to room twelve, strip out of your clothes then report to room ten."

The sound of scuffling feet moving down the hall grows

louder as they pass by the lab, then quieter again as they continue down the hall. I take a guess that they're preparing our first two test subjects before we've had a chance to even fill up the tubs and regulate the temperatures against a thermometer.

"The second submersion tub needs to be set just slightly over the patient's original body temperature, so we don't scald anyone when switching them over."

"Okay, okay, don't worry. We'll check the temperatures before going any further," Otto says.

"Do you understand what happens to a freezing body when it is overheated within minutes?" I don't know if he grasps the importance of what I'm saying and I'm scared he's going to think I'm being overly cautious and do something reckless to appease these people.

"Of course, I do. I took similar classes as you, didn't I?"

Neither of us spent enough time in our medical classes to learn about this subject matter. My knowledge is from personal research using the books I have at home, which is why I know more than Otto. Why I've been asked to help. "So, you know it causes arrhythmia, stroke, cardiac arrest, and/or death?"

"Yes, I know all of that," he says, clearing his throat with a clear expression of unease.

"You, over here," a guard shouts in the hallway. "Do you have any current medical concerns we should be aware of?" They are close enough for me to hear every word so must be in the corridor.

"No, Herr. I don't have any current medical concerns that I'm aware of. I've always been quite healthy. I have volunteered to be here," he says.

His voice—it's Danner. Of all the prisoners, volunteers, or whoever is waiting here to take part in this horrific test, why does he have to be the first on the list?

"That's Danner. Did you hear his voice? Do you remember his voice, Otto? Our friend? The boy you used to play ball with as a child, and then ran track with as you got older. You helped each other with school subjects that you struggled with. He was always there for you, and you were there for him. What about now? How do we go about helping him now?"

"Emilie, enough!" Otto snaps. "Maybe it's best if you go home again so I can take things from here. Just tell me you have a headache and I'll send you back to the house. Go on."

"No. I won't leave Danner alone with you here."

TWENTY-THREE

EMILIE

Dachau, Germany

Otto is immersed in the paperwork, taking his job more seriously than I can stomach. "We need several subjects for this first round," he says, his voice monotone, emotionless.

"So you're responsible for choosing the subjects?" I ask.

"Yes. I have a list in front of me to choose from. What makes for the best specimen for this test? Is it someone with more body fat? Is there an age range we should begin with? What about a certain pulse rate range?"

My heart drops when I realize we haven't chosen people for this test yet, which means Danner's number must have been called for a different reason. In truth, the selection should be varied to get valid data to cover a broader range, but if Danner wasn't being called for this particular study, he could be put into one much worse—one I can't control. I should request vitals that likely would match up to Danner's just in case he's still in the running as a candidate. That way I can make sure he remains safe.

"I would start with an age range of eighteen to twenty-five.

All body weights should be considered, but they all seem fairly consistent in their state of frailty." Danner is twenty-three and though he's thin as a rail, he's not as emaciated as some of the others I saw out in the corridor. It's clear none of the prisoners here are eating well, and not for a while. God only knows what Danner has been through over the last few years.

Otto peers up at me over the folder, narrowing an eye as if questioning my decision to be purposeful rather than logical.

"The general age of air force crew is eighteen to twenty-five. Someone with a greater body mass will have a wider time range of how long it takes to warm and cool. A lean person will reach a level of hypothermia faster than someone obese so I'd like to start with the leaner people and shorter time periods before testing too closely to a degree of risk. I'm trying to preserve our subjects as there will be further requests for additional data."

Otto clears his throat. "You're right. I'll inform the administration of what we need. I'll be requesting twelve subjects to start, which is in accordance with the first test we need to complete."

"I didn't see any paperwork requesting particular data sets..."

"I was informed of what we need," he continues, avoiding eye contact.

"By whom?"

"Dietrich. I'll be back in a moment," he says, holding up the folder and heading for the door.

Left with nothing to review, I decide to join the servicemen in the room next door.

My heart rate increases as I reach for the doorknob, again unsure of what I'll be facing even though I know there are no subjects in the room yet. I spent a considerable number of days observing operation theaters and taking notes, but that was different. I wish I could tell myself it wasn't, but we were watching experienced surgeons do what they do best.

I push the door open, my heartbeat pulses in my head as I step into the open space to find two large submersion tubs on opposite sides of the room beneath hanging spotlights. The assistant servicemen handle the hoses as gurgling water fills each tub, the pressure becoming muffled the closer the water level rises to a thick black strip of tape adhered to the inside.

I'm out of my element, standing here clueless. Everyone seems to have direction except me and I'm still wondering what I'm doing here if I'm not being given any information. I've only been asked simple questions that surely Otto could have answered himself.

"Welcome," one of the servicemen says. I nod, not wanting to converse. "You'll get used to all of this."

"Really?" I ask, sharply. "Have you been here long?" I seem to have interrupted their task of watching the tubs fill with water. God only knows how many innocent inmates have come in and out of these rooms.

The three of them share a look, followed by a pause. One of them bursts into laughter. "We were all prisoners here once, then sent to the front to train as soldiers. Our petty crimes could be paid for with our service. Since we were familiar with the camp, we were sent back here to work."

"Shut up," one of them snaps. "You run your mouth like a little girl. You'll get us killed."

"I won't say a word," I promise, desperately trying to protect myself from becoming one of the loose ends Otto was talking about.

"He's lonely. Forgive him," the other soldier says.

I fidget with my wedding band, hoping the lonely one will notice so I don't have to share anything about myself.

"Just to confirm...what temperatures will you be setting the water to?" I ask.

"34°C/93°F, as mentioned earlier, Fräulein," the lonely soldier says.

"Frau," I reply. "Frau Berger."

"My apologies."

Otto bursts into the room, his expression intense, his arms wrapped tightly around a mess of supplies. My throat tightens and the muscles in my limbs lock as the reality of what's about to happen crawls in closer. With a trembling hand I can't conceal, I reach over to take something from his full arms, finding the supplies to be life vests and uniforms. "What—wh—what are these for?"

"We will be testing the difference between summer air force uniforms and the winter ones, with and without life vests," he says, a grimness lining his voice.

Twelve subjects won't be enough to gather sufficient data, but I'm not going to be the one to suggest we bring in more people. "I see."

"Emilie, could you prepare the notes for data collection?" Otto asks, with a flashing plea in his eyes.

He needs a transcriber. That's why I'm here.

"Yes," I say, trying to keep myself composed though my insides are shattering like fragile glass. I clutch the notebook and a mess of life vests against my stomach, pressing against the never-ending nausea that started when this situation began, and has yet to dissipate.

"We need to know the water temperatures, Herr Berger," the lonely soldier says.

"Yes. The freezing water should be set to 16°C /60°F and the hot water should be 40°C/104°F." I'm thankful Otto didn't question my numbers, but this experiment could result in significant damage if not properly monitored.

"Are we planning to warm them in blankets in between immersions?" I ask, worried about the sudden shock a person would experience with exposure to extreme temperature changes.

"No, we're to move them straight from one tub to the other," Otto says, firmly.

"And for how long?" I continue, shivering as I stare at the water.

"Until their body temperature reaches 26.5°C/79.7°F."

"How will we monitor their body temperatures?" I press, noticing there's nothing around us that could give us that reading from inside the tub.

"We'll get thermometers," he says.

There's no proper equipment and there's no in-between life and death. I can only stand here, watching helplessly as we attempt to freeze a bunch of men only to then try and warm them back up without an ounce of science behind this theoretic remedy. We aren't trained to be doing this. We could cause serious damage, or worse, and that's not why I'm here. I came to help, but I'm not. I might as well be restrained to a wall with what little control and power I have.

"Go on, bring the first twelve in," Otto tells the lonely soldier.

In the moment I have before I need to find a way to lock all my emotions inside, I scan the room, taking note of how sterile the environment is. The door opens and twelve men shuffle in, still clothed in their prison attire, all disheveled, bald, weak, thin, hollow eyes, with frail frames. Each one of them has a Jude patch sewn to their shirts. These men aren't prisoners. Danner is not in this group and at the moment I'm not sure if that's good or bad. I'm sure each of these men has someone who loves them dearly, who would do anything to help them get as far away from here as possible.

Otto won't look at them. He keeps his head down, buried in the folder. The man I know...the man I've always known is hiding inside the cloudy soul that has taken over. His ability to shut out emotional ties to humanity must be genetic. I didn't think he would become like this. This is my fault for assuming wrong.

"Look at them, Otto. You have no choice but to look at your subjects. You should be studying them so you know every single detail for each one of them before you go any further," I whisper to my husband.

"Emilie, please," he replies, "I'm trying to read something."

"The water is set to the requested temperature," one of the soldiers says. "Would you like us to immerse the first prisoner?"

"Yes, with the winter air force uniform and the life vest," Otto says.

Dr. Dietrich enters the room, scuffs the heels of his shoes one by one as he meanders in, weaving in and out of the men in line. "Are the temperatures set?" he asks.

"Heil Hitler," everyone but the Jewish prisoners shouts in unison.

"Yes, both," Otto answers.

"Yes, both," Dietrich says, repeating Otto's words in a whisper. "Good."

The first man in line is stripping out of his uniform to switch into the air force uniform, complete with the life vest.

"Are we immersing the first subject entirely?" Dietrich asks.

"Yes," Otto says.

"Yes. Good. As a reminder to your prior instructions," Dietrich says, facing the men in line, "You are not to move from the position you are placed into. Do not fight against the water or anyone measuring your vitals. If you try to stand up, you will be removed from this trial as you will no longer be needed here. Or anywhere, for that matter..."

He's going to threaten their lives if they attempt to fight for survival? This is abhorrent and inhumane. I clench my fists by my sides, trying to find my voice. "Are you planning to fully immerse this man?" I snap. "He'll drown, and you know so." I can't control the growl beneath my breath.

"Is there a problem, Frau Berger?" Dietrich asks.

"Doctors are aware of the brain stem and how fragile the head and neck can be. Surely, a crew member's winter gear would include a head cover and scarf, yes?"

Dietrich makes his way over to me, leaving little space between us, making me uncomfortable. There's nowhere for me to go if I were to run away. "Doctors are aware of..." he repeats. "Frau Berger, seeing as you seem to have the most medical knowledge aside from myself..." He pauses his statement to raise a brow at Otto, obviously displeased. "...please come with me—let's discuss more of this knowledge you're hiding in that beautiful head of yours." He wraps his arm around my shoulders, urging me toward the lab next door, where we started.

I doubt Dietrich's medical degree would have left him with so little knowledge. It's maddening to watch lives rest in the hands of people who don't know what they're doing. It's as if life is worth nothing to these people, reminding me I'm no different.

He closes the door, isolating us in this awful room. "What you said about the brain stem, tell me more..." he says, pulling out a small notepad and pen from his pocket.

"Aren't there more qualified people to help with this research? There must be doctors with degrees who are willing to contribute to the importance of this data." A true doctor wouldn't willingly put someone's life in jeopardy. Except for Dietrich.

"More. Qualified. People," he repeats, airing out the words. "Many doctors who were experts in this field of study are or were Jewish, dear, and they are of no use to us here or anywhere in Germany. Germany is suffering from a shortage of medical professionals so we're making do with what we have, and what we have here is my intelligence and yours, yes?"

We are likely going to freeze and boil Jewish doctors among the subjects. There are so many people trapped within this godforsaken camp who would be an asset to our scientific and medical knowledge, but anyone who holds a handful of power in this country is apparently blind to common sense. "I'm not confident—"

"*Not confident*—Nonsense. You are, and we're relying on you, and me, of course."

I can hardly conjure a clear thought. I can't argue with him, and if I make myself out to be any less knowledgeable than what he has been told, he'll consider us to be liars, pushing us back to those loose ends we can't end up as. My chest aches as I plead with my mind to process the thoughts I need to express but the pressure will break me.

I close my eyes, recalling the information about temperatures affecting the head and neck region. A nervous gurgle in my throat reinforces my lack of ease and comfort around this man, but I need to spit out what I know so he leaves me alone.

"Studies have shown that autopsies of diseased people who died from immersion hypothermia had extra blood flowing through the cavity of the cranium, thus causing intracranial pressure which can quickly damage the brain tissue, resulting in a stroke or brain damage. Any man or woman traveling as crew aboard a mission over the Black Sea should take caution in keeping their head and neck covered in case they are shot down."

As if he's taking oral notes, repeating my every word to himself, he stares up at the ceiling seemingly baffled.

"That's quite fascinating, young lady. I earned my medical degree not too long ago, but I don't recall this. You learned all this from a book?"

"Yes," I say, trying not to let a cry shoot out of my throat.

An ear-piercing scream gushes through the cracks of the adjoining door before the sound becomes muffled—suffocated. I stare past Dr. Dietrich, lost in thought, trying to shut off my imagination that is gathering an image to fit the awful, tormented sound. The scream returns, but after a loud gasp of inhalation. I lunge for the door, my hands are ice cold as I grip the knob tightly.

"This is part of the trial. They'll be all right," Dietrich says, following me to the door.

I shake my head as the sensation of pins and needles rushes through the flesh of my face. "No. This isn't the way. They are drowning him and freezing his brain, Dr. Dietrich," I grunt, attempting to tear open the door Dietrich has his foot pressed up against. "Stop, stop! This isn't the way! Can you hear me in there?"

Dietrich places his hand on my shoulder, a gentle touch that feels more like a knife piercing my skin. "*Stop, stop!* No, no. We need the data, Frau Berger. I can't draft a complete report unless I have complete data. You understand this, don't you?"

If I say no, he will send me away. I won't have to stand by and listen to more torture, but I'll have no chance of saving anyone, including myself.

"Don't you see—this is inhumane, it's torture," I cry out. "They're people like us. They don't deserve this."

"*Don't you see*—Frau Berger." He waves my pleas aside, "I'm pleased with your astounding amount of knowledge. You will be quite an asset to us here. I know it." He finally moves his foot and I tear the door open, making my way back into the experimental room, spotting a man submerged in the tub. Not one of the assistants is within reach to help the drowning man. I run to the metal tub and pull the man up by his arm. He is heavy, even with his body floating in the water. I press my hand under his chin to keep his neck above the water line but he isn't breathing.

"Emilie," Otto calls out, his voice deflated.

"Get him out of the water," I shout, tossing my hard gaze toward the three assistants standing around me.

I try to pull him out myself, but I can only get him to the lip of the tub when he begins to slip back out of my arms.

"Cardiac arrest," Otto says. "He's gone."

"You can't declare him dead until you've warmed his body temperature back up to normal. Get him out and warm him up now!" I shout. My body is shivering just from submerging my wrists into the water—water that must be colder than freezing. Otto is the first to step up to my side and help me pull the man from the tub. The other three men follow Otto's lead, lifting the man up and out, then immersing him in the heated tub.

I pace the room, catching the terror-filled eyes of the eleven other victims waiting to meet their assumable demise. At first glance, they all appear to be the same person—bald, tired eyes, and skin and bones, but just a second later, I see freckles, scars, and sprigs of facial hair in various colors. They're people just like us but the assisting servicemen are acting as if the inmates are already dead. The worry lines are prominent between many of the men's brows, chins are trembling, bodies are shivering even though they haven't yet touched the water. I want to help them. I have to put a stop to this.

"How warm is the water now?" I ask, pivoting around to face the pale man with blue lips draped over the side of the tub like a doll stuffed with hay.

"38°C/100°F with the body temperature being 27°C/80°F," Otto says, his words barely forming completely. I check my watch, noting it's been seven minutes since the man was removed from the cold. "There's still no pulse."

I drop to my knees next to the tub and place my hands behind the man's lifeless neck, rubbing tersely to create more heat. I'm holding his head up like an infant's but there's no hint of movement. I continue my efforts for several more minutes. "What's his body temperature?" I utter.

Otto shakes his head. "It hasn't changed much."

I rest my arm, the man's head still in the crook of my arm.

His eyes are open wide, his shock apparent as he stares into another world that I'm not a part of. My stomach coils and my lungs struggle to take in a breath, grieving for a man I didn't know but who probably had a significant life story to share. "I'm so sorry," I whisper.

"*I'm so sorry*," Dietrich mocks me. "Take him out." He shouts the command to an assistant.

My eyes burn, staring at this helpless person, knowing I've been convincing myself I can stop this, but I'm nowhere close.

My blood freezes in my veins. Is it my fault we ended up here, like this? I battled the societal changes affecting my life internally, but now I'm not sure I ever fought hard enough to make a difference.

TWENTY-FOUR

EMILIE

Munich, Germany

The city is heavy with silence, frozen beneath a fresh layer of snow. There's no stomp of marching boots, rallying parades of camaraderie, or laughter. There hasn't been any semblance of laughter in more than two years, or so it seems. No one speaks to one another, every person on the street is a stranger, and even if they aren't, no one lifts their head up long enough to figure out whether they know who they're passing. To speak out loud means we must have an opinion: an opinion on this city, on the country, the war, the fairness, and unfairness alike. It's easier to keep our heads down.

Typically, I walk home from class with Otto, but he had a surgical observation at the hospital today. He's likely already home by now. The times when I walk home alone, my mind fills with memories of the days when this amount of quiet seemed impossible, given how loud us kids were together. Even though there were five of us, we always somehow paired off—Danner and me in a conversation or debate about a subject in class, Otto and Gerty arguing over scientific theories that neither of them knew anything about, and Felix with his head in the clouds, thinking of his next story to interrupt everyone with.

I miss my conversations with Danner. Sometimes it almost feels like he's passed away because his departure left such a gaping hole in my life. But if he had passed away, I could still talk to his soul, and he might hear me. Instead, I know he's somewhere a country away living a different life to the one he wanted and I have no way of reaching him. It's been over a year since he and his family were forced to leave, and I haven't heard from him since. I check the mail daily, but there's never anything addressed to me.

Back in a relationship with Otto, I often feel guilty for thinking about Danner as much as I do. Otto doesn't speak of Danner, and he doesn't know that Danner made me promise to rekindle my relationship with Otto. Gerty and Felix talk about him whenever I see them. They talk about him like they just saw him yesterday. Time just keeps passing and nothing seems to get any brighter.

I turn onto my street and my eyes float to Danner's house first as they always do. I'm quickly reminded that someone else has moved into his house with the pea green interior, curtains, and red and yellow bird ornaments dangling down each window. The Alesky family were never eccentric, they just blended in like the rest of us with their neutral color curtains and lack of flare for window treatment.

Everything in this little corner of the city is the same except for Danner and his house. A twinge of pain strikes through my chest as I force myself to look away and face my front door. The aroma of fresh bread distracts me for a moment but I remember that Mama rarely bakes bread in the middle of the week. I step inside to a frenzy of Mama running around the kitchen in circles, pots and pans bubbling, sizzling, and a timer buzzing with a squeal. Flour coats the counters and Mama's forest green apron.

"Mama, what are you doing? You look like a mad woman."

"Oh good, you're home. I wasn't sure what time you'd be home today but I'm glad it's on the earlier side because Herr and Frau Berger are joining us for dinner. It was a last-minute plan,

but—"

"Wait, Mama, since when do you make plans with Otto's parents?"

They're friendly, of course. We live next door to each other, but it's rare we share a meal with them. In fact, I don't recall the last time we did. It would have been a gathering with Felix, Gerty, and Danner's parents too. It was never just two families. It was all or nothing.

"Well, Frau Berger knocked on the door this morning and asked if we were free for dinner tonight. She's invited us over. I told her I would make a loaf of bread, a pie, and dumplings."

"Is this dinner party just for you, Papa, and Otto's parents?" I'm still confused by the last-minute plan.

Mama stops and pulls a dishrag off her shoulder, flour snowing everywhere as she wipes her flour covered hands off on the fabric. "No, of course not. You and Otto will be there too, obviously."

Otto didn't mention this to me last night when we had dinner together then went for a walk through the square in Altstadt. For that reason, I must assume this was Frau Berger's idea.

"Are we celebrating something?" I ask, the nerves in my stomach growing angrier with the questions floundering in my head.

"Not that I'm aware of. Do you know of anything we might be celebrating?" There's a smirk on her face and it sends a chill down my spine.

"I don't see what's so funny about this. I don't like surprises,

Mama. If you know something and aren't telling me, please don't keep it from me."

Mama steps in closer to me and places her flour covered hands on my shoulders and kisses each of my cheeks. "You need to be calm, darling. Everything is fine. There's nothing you should be worried about."

"I didn't say I was worried, but I don't like the unexpected."

"Even if it's something wonderful?" she asks, her smile still present.

"You know something," I state.

I realize I'm clenching my fists tightly by my sides and my neck is starting to sweat. Otto must be behind this. We've been dating on and off for a while and he talks about the future as if it's already here, but I always thought it was just talk, not something that would really start now. Even when we got back together, it was with an understanding that we both needed to focus on our studies and put us second.

Maybe I'm getting ahead of myself. It could be that Otto heard some good news between late last night and this morning. My stomach just says otherwise.

"I don't know any more than you do, but Frau Berger did seem more chipper than usual so I figure the invitation has to be for a good reason, right?"

"You mean, as in, perhaps Danner came home?" The thought brightens my mood, lifting my hope when I know it shouldn't, but without hope...there's nothing.

Mama reaches behind my neck for my braid and pulls it over my shoulder, sliding her fingers down the silky weave. "Emilie, you speak as if you're a heartbroken widow. I know you miss your friend and I miss mine too, trust me, I do, but I think we both know that until this war ends, they won't be coming home. It isn't safe here for them and even if they could come back, from what I've heard, the borders are locked down. To care about Danner means to want him to be somewhere safe, and Germany is not a safe place for him."

Everything she's saying is true, but my heart *is* broken regardless of whether I'm a widow. It hurts just as much today as it did a year ago. I don't want to imagine a pain much worse.

"Yes, I know, Mama."

"Okay," she says, sweeping a fallen strand of hair behind my ear. "Go freshen up. Dinner is soon."

Papa closes our front door behind us as we set off to make the quick walk next door to Otto's house. I hold two fingers against my opposite wrist, counting the beats of my pulse. My heart is racing. I would never expect anyone to assume how little I enjoy surprises so I'm forthcoming about what causes me discomfort, which is why I can't understand why anyone would knowingly cause me stress. Maybe this is a bad omen for becoming a nurse. I suppose nurses need to be able to handle the unexpected, but in those cases, I work better under tension. My mind just likes to contradict itself, I guess.

Mama knocks on the Bergers' front door, and we hear the scampering of feet as someone comes closer to the other side. I wrap my arms around my stomach, squeezing at my nerve pain.

Frau Berger opens the door, a red lipstick lined smile stretches from cheek-to-cheek. "Welcome. I'm so glad you were able to come over for dinner at such short notice."

Why was it short notice? There must be a reason.

"We're so flattered you thought of us," Mama replies.

I glance over at Mama, realizing my hands are empty, aside from holding my own body upright. She has two stacked serving dishes and Papa has the pie and loaf of bread in his hands. This is unlike me. I'm usually the first to offer to hold or carry something, especially for my parents. My head is just floating in a thick set of storm clouds right now.

"Come on inside. Stefan is pouring drinks and Otto is setting the table." Why didn't Otto greet us at the door?

The moment we step inside, the warmth of burning firewood embraces us. Frau Berger takes the serving dishes from Mama and rushes them into the kitchen before returning for the pie and loaf of bread. The three of us remove our coats and hang them on the tall rack next to the large brass mirror.

Herr Berger turns the corner and dips his hands into his pockets. "Welcome. Come, have a seat in the dining room," he says, waving us toward him.

I've been inside their house more times than I can count, and though everything looks as it usually does, nothing feels familiar. Otto greets me as I step beneath the arched entryway to the dining room, taking my hand in his.

"You're here," he says, as if it's a surprise to him too.

I press up on my toes to lean in closer to his ear. "What is this all about?" I utter beneath my breath.

"It's a bit of a story, but there's nothing to worry about," he says, placing a soft kiss on my cheek. The grip of his hand eases my nerves a touch but not enough to mask the panic pinching at my stomach.

"May I help you in the kitchen?" Mama asks Frau Berger.

"Yes, I could help as well," I follow.

"No, no, sit down. You're our guests tonight," Frau Berger says, disappearing into the kitchen.

We all take our seats around their large oval shaped table, covered in a gold satin tablecloth, and set with fine China.

Frau Berger returns with a platter of deviled eggs and salmon-cucumber bites and places them down on the table.

"Would anyone care for a short glass of Schnapps? We also have Fanta, mulled cider, and beer," Herr Berger asks, peering around the table with a pleased expression. Any time I see him, it's after a long day of work and he appears worn, tired, and less than enthusiastic to be doing much more than sitting in his smoking chair near the radio.

"The mulled cider sounds wonderful," Mama says.

"Yes, it does. I'll have the same, please," I follow.

"I'll have Schnapps with you," Papa says, nodding toward the glass in front of Herr Berger's seat.

"Me as well, Father," Otto says.

The process of pouring drinks and Frau Berger settling down at the table feels like it took days rather than minutes. The urge to bounce my knees has my ankles crossed so tightly, I might be bruising myself.

"There must be a lovely occasion for a spread like this," Mama insists.

"In fact, there is," Herr Berger replies. I peer at Otto from the corner of my eye, watching him take a drink from his glass of Schnapps. "As you know, my brother, Dietrich, moved in with us two years ago. He's at a meeting tonight so we thought it would be a good time to have some intimate family time, just the six of us."

"That man must be at a lot of meetings. I hear him leaving before the sun rises and return late into the night," Papa replies.

"He's certainly a busy man, as hard as it is to admit, my youngest brother has become quite a success in his medical career. As of late, he's been involved with an extraordinary study, working on cancer diagnostics. I've been working with him in a different capacity over the last year or so, and he's already been asked to expand the team. We've been accomplishing wonderful future-changing progress and Dietrich's agency is eager to invite Otto to join the team."

Confusion is an understatement to what I'm feeling, but with an explanation such as what I just heard, I think I might have been wrong about this occasion having anything to do with me. I should feel relieved at that thought, but I'm still not sure what this has to do with my family.

"How wonderful," Mama says. "What a marvelous study to be involved in—just the thought of being a part of something so vital to humanity is quite refreshing to hear at a time like this."

"Agreed," Papa says, taking a pull from his glass of Schnapps. "Good for you—all of you. Wonderful news." Papa's short statements hint at his confusion too. He isn't sure what to make out of this announcement, especially with Dietrich out for the evening. I thought Mama might have known something earlier, but she must have been making assumptions too.

Otto still has another two years of school to complete. "How will you work while you're taking classes full time?" I ask Otto, trying to understand the gravity of this exciting news.

Herr Berger holds his finger up with a gleeful smirk. "Ah, this is the best part. There's time. The evolving program is in a constant realm of development and the agency, Dietrich, are able to wait until Otto receives his degree. You see, with the support my brother is receiving, anyone who works with him will be given many benefits including high level wages and housing for he and his spouse. The opportunity is one in a million."

He slipped the word spouse into his sentence and didn't think I would hear him, maybe. I don't see how a spouse fits into this opportunity.

"A spouse, you said?" Mama repeats. I wish she hadn't, and so does the napkin on my lap because I've unraveled a thread so far and the hem is coming loose.

"Yes, Frau Marx," Otto says, pushing his chair away from the table.

My body turns to ice as I stare between Herr and Frau Berger, focusing on the chevron pattern of the blue and green wallpaper. I can't figure out how to move.

"Emilie," Otto says, his words soft, shy, and intimate even though we're surrounded by our families.

My hands begin to shake but I tear my gaze away from the wall and turn toward Otto, finding him down on one knee. *I don't like surprises. He knows this about me.* I should be ecstatic, over the moon, and eager for the impending question. Yet, I feel like I'm under a surgical lamp being observed by a class of medical students. Everyone can't feel this way when someone is about to ask them to marry them. I have no one to ask and I wish Gerty were here. She should be here. I would have said I wanted her here if I had known what was happening tonight.

"I know we have time and we're young, still working toward our career endeavors, but when my father was telling me this wonderful news, I began to imagine you and me living together in a beautiful home, sharing meals at our dining room table while babbling about medical research. Down the road, we'd have a family of our own, and my imagination got the best of me because I could picture it all too clearly. When I snapped out of my daze, I thought about how fickle life is now, how fast everything changes, and what if you didn't know I wanted to spend the rest of my life with you, and we drifted apart somehow. I don't want that. I want to be with you, and if I know that for certain, I couldn't think of another reason to delay asking you to marry me, even if we have a two-year long engagement first so we can both finish our classes. I know you want to focus on your studies, and I do too. I just want us to be able to support each other as we work toward our future together." He reaches for my hand, likely noticing my trembling fingers. "Emilie Marx, will you do me the honor of becoming my wife?"

Time. Time is everything and I love that he has considered my desire to focus on my classes before moving on to the next big event in my life. I'm not facing my parents, but I can sense their desire to shove me into Otto's arms, knowing I'll be stepping into a well-cared for life just as they wanted for me. Just as

Danner wanted for me. He made me promise I would land here with Otto if possible. He told me it was all he wanted for me.

I consider my options, the yes, or the no, and with the no, it's clear my life won't be anything like what I imagined. It would be a series of surprise events because I'll have chosen a different path. This path is comfort, known, with plans set in stone. It's with Otto, and I do love him dearly.

I do.

I shake my head before the word "yes" forms on my tongue, but I know he noticed the trail of thoughts running through my mind as I came to a decision.

"I'd be honored to be your wife." The words tremble against my tongue with a foreign sensation.

Our parents are shrieking with cheers and clinking glasses as Otto slips a beautiful gold band onto my ring finger then stands up, blushing with a smile that warms my heart.

"I love you," he whispers into my ear. We haven't shared these words before. The only man I've ever confessed my love to was Danner, but he didn't reply the same.

"This was all so unexpected, but I couldn't be happier," I say.

I wrap my arms around his neck, and he arches down to kiss me.

"I promise you that will be the last surprise from me."

TWENTY-FIVE

DANNER

Dachau, Germany

Back and forth each day, pacing like a rat in a glass cage until I'm needed. Maybe the waiting, watching, and listening is part of their intended torture. It's becoming harder to tell who is sick and who is waiting for their assignment per their so-called act of volunteering. No one looks well, including myself. We are surviving off little bread, coffee, and potato stew, and only if we're released from this barrack at the end of the day. The rations are hardly enough to keep a body functioning. Still, it's enough to sit here in this medical barrack, listening to men screaming out in pain, crying as if someone is tearing off their limbs, and moaning after they are left alone. A permanent chill writhes through my spine with the thought of the horror that exists on the other side of these walls. Yet, I remain here, returning like I'm supposed to each day as if it's the only job left in this life. I don't see people walking out of the rooms they are taken into, making it clear I've chosen to take part in a slow, violent death in exchange for a quick execution.

It's been a couple of weeks since I began waiting in this room for someone to call my number. It was called once the second day I was here, but that was for another round of prisoner registrations where a Nazi jotted my name, birthdate, prisoner number, former profession, and health vitals onto an index card before shoving the paper into a box with thousands of others. It didn't go unnoticed that they wrote in pencil, making their notes easily erasable. Like me, I'm also easily erasable.

Otto has walked past me twenty-three times this week, his eyes locked ahead as if he is wearing horse blinders. If he doesn't see me sitting here, I must not be here. He'll be entering the room again any minute now after having slept comfortably all night in a bed next to the woman he doesn't deserve. Emilie will follow behind him with swollen eyes, red cheeks, and her hair a little less tidy than it was the day before. Each day she walks through this room, she's losing a piece of herself.

Each day, she stops before me and smiles through her pain. She whispers words such as: "I can't give you much, but I'm here..." It's her warm smile that she's truly giving me though. She's also slipped me slices of cheese and bread, even a couple of notes with reminders of good memories we shared in the past. Anything she could do, she has done, and though I fear for the brief interaction each day, I live for the moment. Her last note struck a nerve, and despite her intention, it tossed me into a darker place than I've been since I arrived here.

Danner,

This note is dangerous and could get us both into trouble. It's important you destroy it after reading.

I didn't walk into Dachau knowing what was happening here. Herr Berger mentioned needing assistance with medical research taking place in a lab separate from the space being utilized by the political prisoners held here. I didn't know there were innocent people, like you, here. Otto didn't confess this truth after finding out the same way I had, and therefore, I walked in blindly like him. His uncle is tied up with high-ranking commanders, putting us both in jeopardy if we were to rebel.

Please know that what you see or hear here is something I'm desperately trying to stop. Whatever I can do to help you, save you, and protect you, please know, I won't give up.

I'll find a way. I must.

With love,

Emi

She was fooled into joining Otto and now she can't find a way out. I want to take the blame. I told her she belonged with him. I see now I was wrong, utterly wrong. I never imagined her father-in-law being blindly led into this world, and then bringing his son along too. I'll try to forgive myself for being ignorant once, thinking a friend was just that—a friend, nothing more and nothing less. It turns out, a friend is someone who knows you so well, they know exactly how to fool you into believing whatever they want you to believe—including that of being a friend at all.

It's eight in the morning and the door opens, as I predicted. Otto walks in, his feet heavy from carrying so much evil on his shoulders. His blinders are in place, and he continues down toward the corridor fifteen steps ahead of his terrified wife. He must not notice she isn't following directly behind him. Emilie has the same look in her eyes as she's had every morning this week, but beyond her fear, I see my sweet, beautiful, innocent Emilie, the girl who scooped me up from too many silly falls when we were children, taking care of me with the most gentle hands until I was bandaged up, then later becoming the woman I wanted but could never have. My best friend, my forever friend, and yet, in this moment, we look nothing more than strangers.

Emilie's footsteps are slow and light as she walks on her toes, her gaze darting in every direction, looking for whoever might be watching her. Otto has already turned the corner by the time she stops beside me to adjust the handbag dangling from her wrist. "Hi," she mutters beneath her breath. "Are you still okay?"

"Yes," I respond quietly. "Are you?" Our lives aren't comparable, but I know she's living in her own form of hell too.

"I'm fine." She drops her handbag, and several items spill out onto the floor. She grumbles out loud, "Oh, good God." Then kneels to pick up what has fallen, and I debate what to do because if I'm caught helping a civilized woman, I'll be beaten. If I'm caught watching a civilized woman struggling to pick up belongings from a prison floor, I'll be beaten. At the moment, there are only prisoners standing around me, so I bend down quickly and scoop up the remaining items, handing them to her. A cloth wrapped object falls into my palm and she stands back up, replacing her handbag over her wrist.

"Emi—" I whisper.

"Hush. Take this to the far-left corner and face the wall." It takes me a moment to piece together her words with the air masking every other syllable, but the cloth wrapped object is cold and malleable. I believe it's food and she doesn't want me to be seen with it, hence the facing the wall in a corner. "There will be more to share."

She leaves, her heels heavy, clacking against the wooden floor with each step as a warning to Otto that she's still behind him, or at least I assume that is what she intends.

I rush to the empty corner, feeling eyes slant in my direction. I don't think anyone saw the exchange, but they may be wondering why I've just moved so fast across the room just to face the corner. My hunger has taken control over my usual thought-out decisions.

The other corner has the metal bucket used to urinate in, so I move there to make myself less conspicuous. I unwrap the cloth, finding a large hunk of Swiss cheese. I break a piece off and shove it down my throat, barely tasting it as I consume it. I take another piece, and one more before staring down at the remnants. If my number is called today, I'll hand it to whoever is beside me, but I need to take care of Hans first.

The cold cheese chills the inside of my stomach, making it known there isn't much else in there, but there's at least that.

There was one time in my life when we had too much cheese in the house. We didn't know what to do with it all. I was only ten, but I remember that week as if it was yesterday. It was the beginning of the Great Depression when Papa bartered cases of honey for other produce. There was a misunderstanding with his request, and we ended up with three times as much cheese as any other item. It was too late by time he noticed so Mama made us eat cheese for days so it wouldn't go to waste. I remember thinking I could never take another bite in my life. We went door to door offering all the neighbors a helping. I even brought some to the square and handed it out to the first people who approached me. We didn't want it to go to waste in a time of so much need, despite our need for income.

Mama always told me the more good deeds we did, the better our lives would be. I'm not sure she predicted the world turning upside down years later though.

I haven't seen another female in this barrack since the day I arrived, but all I can hear now are a woman's heels clunking up and down a hallway. I know it's Emilie. I can tell by the way she walks, the first heavy step, followed by three lighter ones. Then she'll pivot and repeat. I wish I could walk around the corner and find out why she's pacing and what has her so upset.

A door opens and closes, rather tersely, before I hear their voices.

"Did you report what happened to Dietrich?" Otto asks. "We have to report our findings."

"No, Otto, I didn't, and I won't. You can go in there and tell him yourself."

"Neither of us is watching this study. What's he going to say if he walks out of his office right now? We need a replacement, Emilie. The data—"

There's silence and I can imagine a million reasons why but none of them will be true.

"The data is correct, Otto. Don't question me."

"They saw—" he continues. "You can't change or undo that. Do you realize what will happen if you try?"

"Well, they saw incorrectly. It happens," she replies, stomping her foot before walking off to wherever she's going next.

Emilie is being Emilie, and it terrifies me. She'll never give up, never back down, and never stop doing what's right, which is the one thing we're all expected to stop doing.

I'm taken aback when Otto turns the corner into the waiting area, facing my direction and the exiting door to this corridor. If I moved two steps to the right, I would be in his direct path. He would be forced to stop and look at me. We, the prisoners, know not to stand in the way of anyone with authority but I take one step to the right. He'll have to brush shoulders with me if he continues forward.

Within steps of each other, he lowers his eyes, setting his glare toward the ground. "I know you see me," I whisper.

"I can't—Danner. I—I'm so—" he says in nothing more than a mutter disguised as a cough.

I've heard enough, so I move back to the left, allowing him

out of the corridor he appears to be suffocating in. If he were
starving and had nowhere to sleep, I might think he would
understand how I felt, but even if we were living identical lives,
Otto still wouldn't see me as an equal, not like he did all those
years ago.

TWENTY-SIX

EMILIE

Dachau, Germany

As my pen glides along the paper, jotting down the tangled threads of thoughts spinning through my head, I notice Otto has been watching me from the hallway for the last five minutes. I'm not sure he knows I've been sitting here like this at the kitchen table for hours, staring at the imperfections in the wood grain, unblinking. I've been afraid to lose my train of thought, but at the moment, I'm not sure I want to discuss the notes I've made, if he were to ask.

Otto's wingtip shoes clap against the linoleum tiles as he starts to pace in small circles. "Are you going to be much longer?" He finally breaks his silence.

"One moment," I say, continuing with my notes. I try to contain the hint of annoyance that pokes at me. He can see I'm busy.

"We haven't had a warm meal in days," he continues. "Is there something I can put together?" He opens the cabinet doors above the counter, the squeal of the metal hinges zinging down the back of my neck.

I brush off the sensation and try to refocus my attention on my notes. "I'm not sure what we have, but if you can find something, by all means."

"You haven't gone to the grocery—I mean, neither of us has gone to the grocery store recently." I'm not sure how he's just realizing this fact, but he's correct.

"There's no time. We're on a deadline, are we not?"

"We still must eat..." He opens the oven door to glance inside as if something might just appear out of thin air.

"Of course, I understand, but I need to finish my notes right now."

"What notes, Emilie?" he asks, closing the oven door.

"The counter action of resistance to balance the viscosity of blood flow when a body's temperature drops to 30°C/86°F," I spout.

"I'm not sure I'm following you," he says. "I didn't realize you had broken down the data so far within your analysis."

I take in a deep breath to tame my frustration with his purposeful disruption. "What do you think I've been doing?" I ask, flipping through the pages of my notepad, the pages fanning the fallen strands of hair framing my face.

"I thought you were furious about what we were doing, not invested to the point of analyzing the numbers. In fact, I was wondering why you've hardly said a word to me about the number of deaths we've seen recently." Anger doesn't describe all the emotions I've experienced. The constant tightening of my chest and lack of appetite says it all, but I'm not sure he's aware of what I'm feeling inside. His words are eating away at my soul because whatever he thinks of me is inaccurate. The deaths only mean I'm not working fast enough to solve the issues at hand, or slow down the process of the trials.

I huff out the breath I've been holding in my lungs. "Otto, I'm focusing on what needs to be done."

He moves behind my chair and places his hands on my

shoulders, rubbing at the tight muscles I can't seem to relax. "I think it's wonderful that we're doing something so ground-breaking to solve such a large crisis. We'll be known for the work we're carrying out. It's inconceivable."

I wish I had the capability to dream of a truth such as what he's talking about. To be recognized for any form of medical research at such an early age would be unheard of, an accomplishment so far out of reach for someone like me. However, the only reason this research could be seen as an accomplishment would be because it hadn't been trialed on humans before, and for obvious reasons. I'm not in this for the recognition. I'm in this to save as many people as I can, despite the freight train soaring toward us, aiming to take down anything in its path.

"I'm not sure I'd refer to this as groundbreaking—it's death defying—that's about it, Otto," I reply.

Otto steps to the side and drops his hands into his pockets. "So, if this means nothing, why are you putting all your time and effort into it? Surely there's a reason you're so invested in all of this."

I drop my pen and swivel around to face my husband. "Otto, what was it about me that made you say: *I want to marry her?*"

Otto might have thought I wouldn't make it through nursing school if I were given the chance to fall happily into the role of a housewife. I must not have been clear on the importance of having a career of my own.

His face contorts with anguish, reacting as if I've accused him of something. "Well, that's a fairly simple answer. I couldn't picture myself spending my life with anyone else, Emilie," he says, the clear pain idling in his eyes. "Is there a different response you're looking for?"

"No, I'm not."

He pulls his hands from his pockets and folds his arms over his chest. "And you, why did you agree to be my wife? Wasn't there something better out there for you? Did you just settle for me?"

His question hits me like a blast of frigid air, forcing me to consider the answer to his question. If I tell him it's because it felt like the right thing to do, it would sound demoralizing to my character. If I say it seemed like the comfortable choice, I might hate myself for admitting so out loud. It wasn't a question of settling for Otto. I hadn't looked elsewhere for someone, and our paths came together in such a way that I could only assume it was meant to be.

"You're taking an awfully long time to answer my question," he mutters.

I clasp my fingers together, squeezing the discomfort into my tight grip. "I don't know how to answer you."

Otto lifts his head, his cheeks flaming red, and squats down to be eye-level with me. "I can tell you why, Emi. It's because we know the answer," he says. "There was someone better out there for you, but you couldn't have him. Isn't that right?"

I try to swallow against my parched throat. My stomach hardens like stone and my heart pounds heavily against my ribs. He might as well be accusing me of being unfaithful to him with the way he's speaking. "Who are you referring to?"

Otto snickers and nods dismissively. "You think I don't see the way you look at Danner every day you pass by him? I've always known how much you loved him when we were kids, and even until a few years ago when we were all split apart. I knew he wasn't an option for you then. You knew that and so did he. I didn't steal you from him, but I did see my chance to finally have the girl I always had eyes for. That's my truth, Emilie."

There isn't much else to say seeing that he clearly knows me so well.

"I need to be alone right now." I lift my books and notepad from the table, watching my reflection as I pass by the red polka-dot teapot on the way out. I scurry out of the room and stop when I make it to the second step, listening to the floorboard moan from my wavering feet. I turn back and retrace my steps into the kitchen where Otto is now standing, staring toward the hallway as if he can't believe I left.

"I was wrong not to respond to your question," I say. "While I don't understand what you gain from accusing me of looking at Danner in some way, I'll say this: When I see him, my heart shatters into a million pieces—the same way it did when he was forced to leave Munich four years ago. My feelings for Danner weren't a secret. You knew I locked myself inside my house for weeks after he left for Poland. I'd never felt as much pain as I did then. Not until now...upon seeing him wither away, knowing I can't do anything about it."

My throat tightens around my words as tears burn the backs of my eyes. I try to be strong, to keep myself together, but I'm only human.

"I have loved you and still do love you, Otto. But the life I had hoped for with you, it didn't look the way it does now. I also loved Danner, and I still love him. I love you both differently and I can't say that will change, and I can't pretend to be unaffected by my grief."

"You still love him?"

"Love doesn't just die."

"It fades, Emilie."

"True love—it doesn't fade. I'm sorry for you. I'm sorry for me, and I'm sorry for him."

"I guess I didn't realize I was marrying a woman with a taken heart," he says, pressing his fingertips against his chest. I know I'm hurting him, but I won't lie. I never have. If he had asked me these questions two years ago, I would have said the same.

"There's nothing you didn't know about me. We have chosen—" he has chosen, "to see what we want to see and that's okay too." I step closer to him, feeling guilt for never being able to offer him my entire heart.

"I see," he says, sniffling.

"I've been a good wife and loyal to you. I gave you my word and I wouldn't go back on that. I'll continue to live up to the promises I made to you even though now, it seems, they aren't enough. And for that, I'm sorry. But he has been *our* friend, not just mine. When you look at him, what do you see? Because if you for one second imagine what his face might look like if a Nazi fires a bullet through the center of his head, how—how would you feel then?"

Otto's chin juts out, dimpling as he gasps for air. Tears flood from his eyes and he falls to his knees, clutching his chest before pressing his forehead into the ground. "Oh God, I can't—" he cries out. "I never wanted life to be this way. I wanted to be a goddamn pilot. That's it. I wanted to fly and see the world from above the clouds, feel the wind take me where I'm supposed to go. That's what I wanted. I don't want to watch the torture of innocent people, especially not someone who grew up like a brother to me. I was jealous of him before, of course I was, but I want him to live and have an equal chance at life like we do."

I cross my arms over my chest, embracing myself with the hug I desperately need. Nothing will make this relentless pain stop and we can't avoid the truth set out before us.

Otto struggles back up to his feet, clenching and unclenching his hands repetitively. "I can admit this was my father's doing, or honestly, my uncle's, for that matter. You know the influence he has over my vater," he confesses, a known issue that goes unspoken about.

"And the influence your father has over you," I add gently.

Otto's red-rimmed eyes meet mine, his brows sewn together above the bridge of his nose.

"Everything made sense when your reason for coming here was simply to avoid being called into battle. But what we're facing now isn't a battlefield. War is a fight between opposing sides. This is abuse of power and control, cornering the helpless and taking Germany's losses out on them."

"I know, I feel it too," he whispers with a shallow gasp for air. "But what can I do to free us from this hostage-like situation?"

"Your father and uncle should be protecting you—us, not shadowing our lives with threats if we disagree," I say, boisterously. "Your father should have found a way for us to break away from this. He made a mistake by pulling you in with this agency, he should be correcting it. That's what a father does for his son."

Otto shakes his head and grits his teeth. "My vater, he's a coward," he says bitterly. "He's afraid with Dietrich answering to Himmler. Himmler is Hitler's right-hand man. We are in the direct line of fire."

"I don't believe that," I argue, slapping my hands down onto the tabletop. "I assure you we're on no one's radar." No sooner than the words escape my mouth do I doubt my response. No one knows who is in Hitler's crosshairs, and no one should assume. I just can't wrap my head around the fact that we ended up here. I press my fists against my chest, wishing the inflicted pain would subside. "You promised to protect me."

Otto's eyes flutter closed, his wet lashes brushing against his cheekbones. "I tried to stop that conversation at dinner. I didn't want you involved but you made it clear you have your own voice."

"If you had been honest with me before that night, I never would have opened my mouth," I say, my words sharp against my tongue.

With a pale complexion and a tremble in his chin, he says, "You're right. I thought I was protecting you by not telling you what I was led into, but it's clear to me now, I was wrong."

I drop my gaze because it's all too late now. "Whatever the

case, I want this to be over and final. It's torture and it's murder too. Do you understand that? When you look in the mirror you must see yourself as an accessory to murder, Otto. How can you not?"

"I haven't murder—I'm not responsible for anyone who—"

"Yes, you are, and so am I."

"How was I to know a certain body temperature or a particular part of the body being submerged in cold temperatures could cause immediate death?"

His question infuriates me, stiffening every muscle in my body as I try not to lose my temper. I've been digging my fingernails into the flesh above my knees, and I fear I might have punctured my skin by now. "Because I told you so. I told you, and the three assistants, but the experimentation continued despite my plea to rethink their decisions based on the research and notes I had in front of me. You, yourself, told me to stop arguing. Do you recall?"

"If I argue with those three men, they will report back to Dietrich, who will send his findings and notes to Himmler, and if it's mentioned anywhere that either of us were a roadblock in the experiment, what do you think will happen?"

"Could it be worse than what those innocent subjects are being put through?"

Otto exhales heavily, his shoulders dropping in defeat. "I'll speak to Dietrich and explain that we're close to a solution and that we shouldn't be wasting any more subjects until you find what you're looking for."

Relief floods through me, just a mere promise of attempting to put a stop to this allows me to breathe a hair deeper. The look on his face, however, tells me he has more to say.

"Thank you. Now I'm going to continue with my research so I can find the answers I need."

"One more thing," Otto says. "Then I'll leave you to your work and find something for us to have for dinner."

"What's that?"

"You need to stop communicating and making eye contact with Danner. You're putting us all in danger, Emilie, including him. So please, I ask that you stop testing boundaries."

My heart shoots into my throat and my body weakens at the thought. Speaking to Danner is not an act of pushing my luck. We're all running out of luck.

TWENTY-SEVEN
EMILIE
SEPTEMBER 1942

Dachau, Germany

Dietrich gave me one week, two days, twelve hours, and sixteen minutes to complete my research prior to testing additional subjects. They placed a temporary pause while they waited on the pending data necessary for the research. I'd been terrified they'd take Danner for other purposes, but I passed him in the waiting area this morning. He's still alive thank God.

There are more subjects lined up today than usual. Otto has decided to walk into the sick bay side-by-side with me, likely to ensure I don't glance in Danner's direction, or hand him the scrap of food I had set aside for him, which I don't think he's aware I've done daily. If he is, I assume he would have said so the other night.

"Are you sure you're ready with your data?" Otto asks me.

"Yes," I reply, turning the corner toward the lab.

I'm not surprised to find Dietrich and the three soldier assistants waiting on us as we arrive.

"Good morning to you both," Dietrich says, clearing his throat.

"Heil Hitler," Otto shouts, saluting his uncle.

"Heil Hitler," I add, muttering the words.

"Heil Hitler," he responds.

"I'm sure you're eager to hear the data we'll need to work with this week to conclude our findings in your report," I say.

"Indeed," Dietrich says.

I place my notepad down on the table, ready to begin talking about my findings, but the three soldiers are having a private conversation, chuckling among themselves as if I'm not standing here waiting for their attention.

"Well, I'll begin," I say, ignoring them. "Despite original theories stating that rapid re-warming tactics are the best way to treat hypothermia, there are other factors to take into consideration. While rapid rewarming does aid in the rejuvenation of blood flow, it depends on how low the body temperature had reached. With an increase of hemoglobin and leukocytes, there are regular and common cases of heart arrhythmia at 30°C/86°F, which can lead to stroke, heart failure, or a heart attack, regardless of the attempt to rewarm a patient quickly."

"Wait, wait," Dietrich says, interrupting my report findings. "You forgot a key solution."

"I haven't finished," I say.

"Which solution are you referring to?" Otto counters, allowing Dietrich to speak before I'm through.

"*Which solutions...* Well, you haven't mentioned the idea of animal warmth. Have we tested what would happen if the action of rapid rewarming was produced through the heat from animal bodies? Or perhaps...women's bodies?"

His question garners laughter from the male audience in the room except Otto. His words unravel down the length of my spine, sparking me with fury. The things I would like to say to him would put me in a dangerous situation. "I'll touch on that subject, yes," I say. More inappropriate laughter echoes. "Skin to skin contact is a valuable tool in circumstances where a person's internal body temperature has dipped too low, but not to the degree we're speaking about. The speed of rewarming a body with another person's body heat would take far too long, and the patient in a state of hypothermia wouldn't be remedied." The continued laughter makes it clear I'm not being taken seriously, and this is a joke to them.

"*I'll touch on that subject...* I see," Dietrich says. "But have we tested this theory?"

"No, Doctor. It won't be necessary."

"*No.* Hmm," he grunts.

"It's become clear that patient recovery depends on whether a person is clothed or bare skinned. Therefore, improvements in aviator uniforms, which could include headgear and neck protectors with a foam insulation could prove to have a dramatic lifesaving result."

"*Clothed or bare skinned.* Compelling," Dietrich says. "I would like you to prove your theory on the choice of subjects we will have lined up for you shortly. If you're correct, they should all be alive when you're through, yes?"

"Yes, Dr. Dietrich," I reply, feeling the tightening knot grow in my stomach.

To be a nurse is to save patients from pain and sickness, not to deliberately inflict pain.

Dachau, Germany

I've been focusing on my notes, ensuring that whatever I do today won't result in even a chance of injury to anyone. The others have been preparing the subjects and are waiting for me in the next room over where the tubs are set up. I lift my belongings to my chest and hold them tightly as I make my way across the empty lab into the adjoining room, finding a line of twelve prisoner volunteers, the three soldier assistants, Dietrich, and Otto.

Among the prisoners is Danner. My stomach burns and acid rises into my throat. I've treated every volunteer with the same level of respect as the next, doing everything in my power to ensure we spare them from torture. However, I'm aware of the continuation of testing after I've left for the day, which has resulted in deaths. I can't let that happen to him.

Each of the men are already dressed in air force uniforms, but not the proper headgear and neck covering, which are critical to this part of the trial. "Do we have the additional protective layering?" I ask.

"Additional protective layering," Dietrich utters. "Yes." It's clear he's shooing off the question. His focus frozen on Danner as if he's trying to place the recognition. He's met Danner before, in a lifetime where Danner could still walk around with some freedom. I would think it would make him feel something. Anything. But Dietrich's mind belongs to the SS now.

"What temperature are the tubs set to now?" They've added three more testing tubs to this room to save time.

"Station one is set to -12°C/10°F, station two is set to -7°C/20°F, and the third is set to 2.5°C/36.5°F."

"No, no, that's an unnecessary range. The average North Sea temperatures range from 2.5°C/36.5°F to 12°C/53.6°F depending on the depth and seasonal climate. We should be testing between that range. There's no need for minus figures." If someone sinks to a level below these temperatures, revival won't be possible. Therefore, there's no need to prove that theory here, now.

"*Unnecessary range. The North Sea,*" Dietrich mumbles. "Except, just two years ago, we hit record low temperatures that reached far into the negative temperatures, so it isn't out of the realm of possibility that we could see those temperatures return."

"Those temperatures were a direct result of the number of battleships and torpedo blasts stirring up the unreached depths of the sea with surface temperature water. Ice formed, making the sea unnavigable, much like what's still occurring now. No matter the clothing a person wears, no one will survive in temperatures below 2.5°C/36.5°F for more than a few moments, which has already been determined," I argue.

I notice Danner staring at me with wide, unblinking eyes. I'm not sure if he's surprised to hear these numbers, or fearful I'm going to lose this argument. Maybe both.

"If there's no chance of survival below 0°C/32°F there's no purpose of testing below that range," Otto says, supporting my theory. To hear him agree comes as a shock and I peer over my shoulder at him, noting his downward gaze to avoid eye contact with anyone in this room.

Dietrich throws his arms up in the air. *"If there's no chance...there's no purpose,"* Dietrich whispers, chewing on the words. "Nonsense. Whatever you do, however you get the data, just get me the numbers by the end of the day."

"We will," Otto replies. "Change the water temperatures of the two tubs with temperatures below zero up to $4°C/40°F$ and $12°C/53.6°F$." The assistants jump to his command, altering the temperatures. Otto steps up beside me and peers at my notepad. "We'll need three volunteers to step forward."

I drop my gaze to my notepad, praying Danner doesn't step forward. One set of clogs steps out of line and a cold sweat covers the back of my neck as I glance up, finding him standing directly across from me. It takes everything in me not to shake my head at him.

Otto clears his throat and takes a step forward. "We need two more. Come on now."

One of the soldier assistants ignores Otto's request for volunteers and pulls two men out of the line, tossing them toward Danner. "Done," the soldier says.

"I'll go into the lowest temperature tub," Danner says.

The same soldier who grabbed the two volunteers shoves each of them in front of a tub.

All I can do is the one thing Otto told me not to do—stare at Danner. I want to scream at him, ask him why he would volunteer for the more dangerous of the three tests. Is it to make a point to me or Otto? What if my calculations were off? I've been under so much pressure and I'm not a scientist. All of my studying has been out of my area of knowledge and it's all new.

I grind my teeth, clamping my tongue between them so I don't do something I'll regret.

"What are the durations for each?" one of the assistants asks.

My hand shakes as I run the tip of my finger down the text on my notepad. I swallow against the thickness in my throat and try to take a breath before speaking. "The tub measuring 4°C/40°F will be for..." My notes say: Twenty minutes for data collection. No more than twenty-five minutes as thirty to ninety minutes of immersion will result in death. "The fifteen minute mark will give us time to collect data and remove them from the water," I speak out.

My body rushes with heat, sweat beading beneath my collar, knowing Otto is staring at my notes still. He's probably seen the time is set between thirty and ninety minutes, knowing I've lied. Otto's breaths are loud, sharp through his nose.

"The second tub 12°C/53.6°F will allow for a thirty-minute time marker, and the third tub at 16°C/60.8°F should have a seventy-minute time marker. All three volunteers must be wearing neck and head foam protection." All of my altered time markers have enough padding to spare the lives of the frailest.

"And the heated tubs, Frau Berger?" the lonely soldier asks.

"Set those tubs to 40°C/104°F." The soldier tends to the tubs parallel to the cold ones and I know I'm running out of seconds to make any last-minute decisions. I scan my written notes repeatedly, flipping the page back and forth. "Body temperatures need to be monitored as well as their heart rates," I say as a reminder of what was ignored last time.

"Dr. Dietrich said that information wasn't necessary for his report," Otto says.

"What is the purpose of any of this if we aren't collecting the proper data to back up our findings? I would like three thermometers." I can check a heart rate without an instrument.

"Emilie," Otto says.

"Do you know why the internal body temperature is so imperative to this data?" I question Otto.

"Well, yes, but—"

"I don't care if the report doesn't require it. There's no purpose in monitoring time without temperature," I whisper to him. "They can't survive past a certain point. We need to protect them."

"Find three thermometers," Otto directs the soldiers then turns to reply to me quietly. "Rectal temperature is the only accurate way to measure, and we can't do that when they're underwater."

I clench my hands, feeling the pressure of all these lives on our shoulders. "On average, there's a two percent difference between oral and rectal temperatures. We can manage the math while they are in the water," I say.

"Based on averages, the data won't be—"

I whip my head toward Otto, staring at him with what I can only hope he sees as a demand to be quiet.

"Then go find the appropriate rectal thermometer for when they are removed from the water," I argue.

Otto strides along the rim of the room until he reaches a drawer of supplies, returning quickly with the rectal thermometers, setting them on the table between the cold and hot tubs.

"Let's begin." Otto checks his watch and holds his focus on the time, avoiding the scene of the soldiers tossing head gear and neck protection at the three men. They're prepared within seconds and are shoved toward each tub with haste.

I watch Danner step into his and my heart falls flat. I make my way closer to the tubs, clenching my notebook in one hand by my side.

Despite the varying temperatures, the three of them grunt and groan the moment they are immersed up to the base of their skulls, mimicking a person floating in the ocean, awaiting aid.

These sounds of abuse and torture haunt me at night. I've heard the sounds so many times now with each round of experiments I've been forced to watch.

Time seems to be moving at half the speed it should as I watch the paleness grow across their faces, each shivering, creating small ripples across the water.

I start with Danner and approach him with the thermometer from a tray on a table near him. He opens his mouth, keeping his watering eyes locked on mine as I place the thermometer beneath his tongue. "Why did you volunteer for this?" I whisper so quietly, I'm not sure he heard me.

I might never know if he did because he doesn't respond in any way.

While the thermometer is beneath his tongue, I slip my fingers against the carotid artery beneath his neck protection to measure his pulse. He's ice-cold to the touch.

Why is this happening? Why are we here?

He's still staring at me, and I want to say so many things, but I can't say a word, and nor can he.

"Pulse, 120. Oral temperature, 36.11°C/97°F," I speak out, pulling my fingers from beneath Danner's neck protection. I glance around to make sure someone is jotting down the data, finding Otto with his head still down, writing the numbers.

Tears burn the backs of my eyes as I stand up and replace the thermometer on the tray, needing to move on to the next subject.

"Please follow me with the simple questions to gauge their brain function," I tell the soldiers who are lined up, waiting for instruction.

After a few minutes, we've gotten into a rhythmic pattern consisting of me checking vitals and the soldiers asking the three volunteers a series of questions while Otto transcribes the information.

At the ten-minute mark, I return to Danner to conduct the third round of vital checks. His temperature has dropped to 32°C/90°F and he's beginning to convulse rather than shiver. It's quicker than the estimated rate and temperature fluctuation from 36.11°C/97°F. With five minutes left, my heart races and my breaths quicken as I try to think up a plan quickly. Everything in my body aches as I watch what's happening to Danner. *Why are we here, like this?* I'm not sure he'll make it the full fifteen minutes before his temperature falls too close to 28°C/82.4°F, the life-threatening temperature for hypothermia.

"Can you tell me if you can hear me?" I ask, placing my hand on the top of his headgear. His eyes roll up behind his eyelids and his body stops convulsing. "Danner, look at me!"

"Emilie," Otto shouts over me. "Stats for Prisoner 13415." I spoke out his name. I'm not supposed to know him as anything but a number.

"We need to get him rewarmed at once. His vitals are falling," I shout.

"The test is scheduled to run fifteen minutes. There are four minutes left," one of the soldiers reminds me.

"He's going to die if we don't remove him from the water now."

"He won't be the first," a soldier replies. "We must finish the test for accuracy on Dr. Dietrich's report."

I move behind the tub and drop my arms into the water to lift Danner up, but his body is lifeless. "Help me!"

"Drop him," a soldier shouts. "You're tampering with the data."

"Emilie," Otto says.

"Help me," I snap at him.

"We're not supposed to have any deaths today. The data will be smudged," Otto says. I'm not sure what he's talking about or what he means but he's moving toward me, and it better be to help me lift Danner out of this tub of ice water.

I stare at his familiar lips, becoming bluer with every passing second...

TWENTY-NINE
DANNER
SEPTEMBER 1942

Dachau, Germany

Waking up to thrashes from what feels like hundreds of serrated knives, each slicing across every hair on my flesh, is enough to make me question whether I'm truly alive. If I'm dead, I've been thrust into the depths of hell, despite not believing such a place exists. But my mind has been catapulted into a sleep-like state. I'm not dead but I'm not sure I'm alive either. I can't speak or move, imprisoned within my body.

I distinctly recall stepping into a tub of ice-cold water, a decision formed by spite, heartache, and despair. Regardless of the degree of torture, I had no say in the matter, aside from choosing an execution instead. I preferred the darkness I'd slipped into before reawakening in this state. Now, the torment is unbearable as I burn on the outside while my bones remain frozen inside. My breaths are running away from me at a pace I can't catch up to, and my heart is pounding like fists against a locked door that won't open in time to save my life. My vision is nothing more than a blur, leaving me to the crux of my imagination—where I am, if I'll get out alive. Every hint of sound seems distant yet obtrusive. Nothing is clear aside from the high-pitched squeal piercing through each nerve-ending.

I saw her, though. At least I saw her before I ended up like this. This must be my punishment for receiving the gift of her presence when I should have been experiencing nothing but torture.

Hands attack me, shoving me every which way, my body slamming against metal, back and forth.

"His temperature is still dropping. We're getting too close to our bottom line." The first clear words I make out are not the ones I would want to hear, but they are hers. I know this much. "Turn up the temperature."

"You may not be second-guessing my theory of body heat now, are you?"

I'm not sure who else is here speaking to Emilie or whoever, but the sinister tone doesn't give me a sense of optimism.

"No. That's ridiculous," another person says. "Body heat won't work fast enough."

Body heat. Papa taught me about skin-to-skin contact when I was younger. He was teaching me survival skills for when we would go camping in the mountains. I never had to use that technique because we were never lost or stranded.

"What if it will help?" Emilie shouts.

"It won't!" The response is clear, and I know it's Otto now. The two of them have been working here together, she for one reason, he for another—or so it seems.

If only I could scream for the release of this agony that's ravaging my body, but instead I remain still like an inanimate object, left to spectate the result of extreme opposing temperatures.

Strong hands lift me out of the tub before swinging me onto a solid surface. Each touch might as well be blades stabbing through my core. The clothes I was forced to wear are torn from my body, leaving a freezing dampness behind. The wet, heavy materials fall to the floor, sounding like a body is still inside of them. The exposure to air stings like salt in an open wound, and the time between losing the clothes and feeling a dry sheet of fabric settle over my body feels like an eternity. The aggressive hands return, shoving me around, attacking me from every side.

"You're going to make it," she says. "You need to slow down your breaths. One breath every five seconds..." Her last words form in a hush of a whisper. I've heard them from her before, but I can't control the air coming and going from my lungs this time. It's hard to imagine the hands all over me belong to Emilie. I've never known her to have anything but a gentle touch. Yet, the force against me is great enough to push me off this surface. "Help me, Otto!"

"I am," he replies. "Any more pressure and I'll end up breaking his bones."

Weight bears down on top of me and hair flutters over my face, a tickle rather than a piercing sting.

"What are you doing?" Otto shouts.

"He needs more heat," she grunts in response.

"Maybe you should take your clothes off," another voice suggests.

The hands that were knocking me around disappear, a breeze left in their place, garnering pinpricks, a thousand at a time on the left side of my body.

Another hand presses against my face. "Danner, can you hear me?" she whispers.

A thud on the floor shakes the table and the sound of wallops against flesh tell me what's happening to the man who spoke out of turn.

"What are you doing?" Emilie hisses.

"That soldier has served his purpose here," Otto replies.

"Can you focus on what we're trying to do right now?" she replies.

"He's just another volunteer. Why are you so concerned about this one?" another unrecognizable voice says.

"The—uh—post-trial data is imperative for completion of the report on this subject," Otto says.

It's hard to tell if he's trying to protect me or protect himself.

The searing pain begins to subside at a gradual pace, giving me hope that I won't feel like I'm being mauled by knives soon. I don't know how long I've been pulsating in pain, but my vision is beginning to clarify. Though it feels as though my eyes won't remain still within my head, I'll accept the double vision when I spot Emilie.

"Your temperature is rising," she says, her eyes trying to fixate on me, but with the lines of her forehead dipping between her brows, I can read the concern that says I'm not considered remedied yet. I want to tell her I know why it's rising. I want to tell her a lot of things. I've gotten good at keeping my thoughts to myself though. "How's the pain level?"

The sharp burn has subsided, just a hair, but enough to convince me the pain will continue to lessen. I'm able to stretch the muscles in my legs, giving me hope that I might regain proper sensation as well. "Nnn-not a-a-s ba-ba-bad," I stutter, between chattering teeth and a numb tongue.

She places her hand on my cheek and gives me a small smile. "Good," she whispers. "You're going to be okay. I'll make sure of it."

I knew someone would find themselves the lucky patient left in her caring hands someday. For this one moment that may be short lived, like myself, I can rest knowing my journey was worth something. I'd left everything else behind with a promise to bring my family back together. I failed.

THIRTY

DANNER

Gorzeszowskie Skałki, Poland

Here in the crevice of two mountains, I could convince myself there's no such thing as war, which might be easier if we hadn't left people we love behind in Germany. We can't send letters or make any phone calls. We eat off the land and rely on candles, gas lamps, and firewood—much different to living in a city. However, Mama, David and I are safe here, for now. There's no saying when or if the SS will find their way through this unpopulated area, but Great-Uncle Igor and Great-Aunt Eunika believe we will remain safe throughout the duration of the war.

After the Gestapo sent us to the German/Polish border, we had no choice but to find refuge or rot with only what we could carry in a suitcase. Mama had her address book, something I wouldn't have thought of bringing among the few items we could fit. Though we hadn't spoken to Papa's aunt and uncle in over a decade, we could only hope they would welcome us into their home.

The three of us walked for days, living on nothing but berries and lake water, and when we arrived in the empty town, we were sure it had been taken over as there were less than a handful of people to be seen as we continued through the valley. Only one of the people knew who our family was and pointed us in the right direction. Our arrival came as a great shock to our long-distance relatives, but thankfully, they took us in without hesitation. We've been here just over two years now, and aside from helping with their small land of crops, the few farm animals, and tending to the bee hives, I've done little else but try to devise a way to find Papa.

The front door of the cottage opens and slaps shut, wood against wood, echoing between the walls. "I have good news," Great-Uncle Igor says.

"You found Papa?" David asks, jumping up from the straw woven chair he's been sitting on.

"No, no, I'm—I'm so sorry. I shouldn't have excited you. I'm sorry, son."

Great-Uncle Igor is known to speak before he thinks through his thoughts, so I've gotten better at withholding my reactions to whatever he's about to say until he says it. He has more hope than any of us combined, and I wish I could borrow some.

"Where have you been, Igor, oy, you're going to give us all a heart attack one of these days. Calm yourself down," Great-Aunt Eunika says, throwing her hands up in the air. That's her typical reaction to much of anything Great-Uncle Igor does. I suppose fifty years of marriage will do that to a couple.

Mama places a teacup down on the handmade, worn wooden table and returns to the wood stove for the kettle of water. "Have some tea, Uncle Igor," she says.

"I was visiting my friend who lives about an hour south of here in a small village, one still untouched by the Germans."

"The man you listen to all of the radio broadcasts with?" Great-Aunt Eunika asks. "You haven't spoken to him in ages. What made you decide to go searching for him?"

"Yes, I know," he says, shaking his head.

Great-Aunt Eunika folds her arms over her chest, a scowl outlining her lips. "Why didn't you tell me you were going so far from here?"

"There was no reason to worry all of you. We need to know what's happening outside this village, dear. Being in the dark won't help us."

Great-Aunt Eunika steps up to her husband, standing a head length shorter than him and slaps the side of his head. "You're a putz, Igor. For God's sake. Imagine how worried we would be if you didn't come home? My heart just can't take this for much longer," she groans, clutching her chest. "Well, get on with it...what did the man say?"

"He had exciting updates."

"Igor, what updates? What is it?" Great-Aunt Eunika shouts, losing her temper with him as she often does.

"There was a group of Jewish prisoners in Munich released because of overcrowding issues due to the resistance fighters. The release may only be temporary until another solution comes about, but there may be a chance Abraham was sent home."

My heart drops to the bottom of my stomach like a heavy rock. "You think Papa might be back at our house in Munich?" I ask.

Igor shrugs. "I can only tell you what I've heard. The details are scarce, but what else would they do with these people?"

"What about the concentration camps? Is that where they're bringing all the Jews now?" David asks, his voice hoarse. We all know about the concentration camps intended for political prisoners, but there have been rumors of Jewish people being sent there too, and assuming that's where Papa has been weighs heavily on all our minds.

"My good friend's knowledge does rely on Polish radio waves, but only Polish radio waves, which don't receive the most detailed updates from Germany." Igor holds his hands out as his eyes fill with a sense of hope. "However, from what he said...the concentration camps are also overpopulated and running out of space. So what else is left for them to do?"

The mere thought of Papa being released and going home to find we're no longer there, tears through my chest. He would think we'd abandoned him or forgotten about him. After everything he's been through, most of which I'm not sure I can imagine, I can't allow that to happen. "I must go home. Somehow, I need to find a way back there to find Papa. Then I'll bring him here," I say without a second thought. There's nothing to consider. If there's a way to find him, I must.

Mama says, "Danner, that's absurd. There's no way you'll make it across the Polish border. This is impossible. I want to find your father more than anything in this world, but we're just one family fighting against an entire country. They don't want us, and they won't bend rules for you, I assure you of that."

"There's a way," Igor says, pacing the length of the kitchen.

Mama stares at him, her eyes bulging and cheeks burning red. I can see she wants to tell him to stop whatever thought is brewing in his head before he says it out loud, but he knows better than to make eye contact with her when there's something he wants to say. Mama would protect David and me from everything if she could, but I'm a grown man now and it's time for me to be making the decisions for what's best for us.

"What is it?" I ask him.

"Igor," Mama hisses.

"I don't like whatever thought is burning through your head," Great-Aunt Eunika says. "Don't suggest something you will regret."

"The man I receive my radio updates from has a brother. He's a notary with impeccable penmanship. His notary skills haven't been needed much in recent years due to the war, so he has taken up other—eh—jobs, so to say."

We are all staring at Igor as if he's telling us the most thrilling story and about to reveal the major twist. "What kind of jobs?" Mama grunts.

"He has been working underground, altering identification cards and passports for many Polish people who need to leave the country. Not one of them have been caught due to their identification."

Mama places the teakettle down heavily onto a hot plate, clattering the metals against each other. "No," she says. "No. We have no need for false identifications."

"Yes, we do, Mama," I say. "If there's a chance to bring Papa here, it's what I must do."

"I'll go with him," David says, a sickening eagerness in his eyes. My stomach burns with the thought, likely the same as Mama is feeling at the mention of just me going through with this.

"No, you must stay here to take care of Mama," I correct him.

"But she has Uncle Igor and—"

"No, David. You need to stay here in case they need you."

"I won't agree to this," Mama cries out. "There's no way. How will you get your father back to Poland? We don't know if they are allowing more German Jews into the country."

"It's Papa," I say, staring at her with the dread I feel inside. "I'll do what it takes to get him back here."

The argument ensued for the rest of the afternoon and evening until Mama couldn't argue anymore. I would never dream of pushing her to the point of throwing her arms up in defeat, but this is one fight I couldn't afford to lose.

Despite knowing how the disagreement ended, Igor was gone when we woke up this morning, as were my forms of identification. I decided to keep that part to myself until he returned. Mama was not in the mood to speak or converse about the topic any further. David was still bitter about the idea of me leaving him behind. I would never intentionally hurt anyone in my family, but I know this is something I must do for the sake of our family.

Great-Aunt Eunika, Mama, David, and I have been sitting at the kitchen table in silence, all looking toward the two front windows every time we hear the sound of a twig crunching. It's just a family of squirrels running circles around the nearby trees.

Great-Uncle Igor's footsteps are much louder and too quick for anyone to spot him out the window before the front door flies open. He closes us inside and draws the curtains. He's out of breath and a bit pale as he approaches me. "I've got everything you need," he says, reaching into the inside pocket of his coat. He retrieves my forms of identification and hands them to me with a trembling grip.

I scan through the papers and booklet, finding my name changed to Albert Amsler. My occupation is listed as: Cook, rather than the blank space that was there before.

I've taken more than enough time to inspect the papers, dreading the thought of peering up and finding the look on Mama's face.

"When—" I begin to ask.

"I've purchased you a train ticket for later today, but first, you'll want to use this..." Great-Uncle Igor reaches into the front pocket of his coat and pulls out a small container with a brown label I can't make out.

"Is that hair dye?" Mama snaps.

"Blonde hair will be best to avoid unnecessary questions. Many women have been doing so and it works just fine."

"Listen to you. What do you know about what women are doing?" Eunika lashes out at him.

"He's right. It's been happening for years," I agree. "I'll use the dye."

My deep-set brown eyes and long nose are enough to look at

and question.

I'm unrecognizable even to myself after coloring my hair, giving me hope it will do enough to help me through this train ride without being questioned.

While combing my hair into place, Great-Uncle Igor steps up to the door of the washroom. "Listen to me carefully, Danner," he says. "You're a personal chef for an SS-Obergruppenführer, sent to Poland on a special request to collect bottles of Dwójniak Mead for a dinner party you're responsible for preparing. You're returning to Germany from your quest. You will have four bottles of Dwójniak in a crate to carry with you as your proof."

Dwójniak is a mead only made in Poland because of their access to honeydew and heather honey. The rest of Europe is used to paying a hefty price for such a valuable brand of mead. Great-Uncle Igor had a different experience in his years of raising bees than Papa did. Being in Poland was a great advantage to contributing to a product constantly in demand. Before the war, we would receive bottles of honey from the uncle from Poland, who we had never met. I always asked Papa why his uncle would be sending us honey if we made our own, but I quickly came to learn the difference between Polish honey and German honey.

"Okay, I'll use that story if approached," I agree.

"You mustn't look nervous or unsure. You will stare them in the eyes and tell them this is your job and believe it as well as they should."

"I understand." I've never been a good liar, but my life will depend on it now.

"We need to be going. The train leaves in a couple of hours."

I swallow against my dry throat and leave the washroom to collect my suitcase and coat. On the cot I've been sleeping on, is a small wooden crate.

With my hands full, I make my way to the front door, finding Mama in tears and David with a stiff jaw. "I'll find him and bring him here," I tell them.

"What if you don't find him?" David asks.

"I won't give up."

"I can't lose you too," he mumbles.

I place the crate down between my ankles and slap my hands down on my brother's shoulders. "You won't lose me. You're safe here, and we will be together again soon. I promise."

"You always said to me that a brother never breaks a promise," he says before pressing his lips together tightly.

"And I'll stand by that promise forever," I tell him, wrapping my arms around his neck and squeezing him with all my might.

Mama is next and the sobs quaking through her chest pound against me as I hold her in my arms. "I'm proud of the man you've become, Danner. I've always been so proud of you. You're just like your father." She pulls away from me, tears streaming down her chapped cheeks. "I have something for you." Mama reaches into the pocket of her white apron and pulls something out, concealing it within her clenched hand. She places it in my palm and closes my fingers over the beveled round piece. "Your father's pocket watch. He told me it brought our family good luck and kept us safe. He didn't have it with him the day he was arrested, and I don't know why, but I know he would want you to hold on to it for him."

I circle the pad of my thumb across the dated golden embellishments I have traced hundreds of times before, enamored by this pocket watch Papa always kept with him.

"This is all I need along with your understanding and faith in what I'm going to do for us."

"You have my blessing, even if it is covered in tears, my sweet boy," she says, kissing my cheek. "I love you, my son."

THIRTY-ONE
EMILIE
SEPTEMBER 1942

Dachau, Germany

I walk across the wooden floors of the hospital block on my toes, trying to silence the heaviness of my heels as I make my way to the room at the end of the hallway. I glance behind me, making sure I'm still alone and slip into the dim-lit room, closing myself inside. Dietrich knows I'm collecting vital data, but I'd rather no one knows how long I spend in this room.

"Emi." A man's voice croaks, still weak. A smile presses into his frail cheeks and his eyes flutter open wide.

"How are you feeling?" I whisper.

"I'm okay," he says, air punctuating his words.

I pull a wax paper wrapped sandwich out of my pocket. "Eat this," I tell him.

He struggles to push himself up onto his elbows, so I help him, noticing how easy it is to maneuver his declining weight.

Danner unwraps the sandwich as if it's a mirage that may disappear if he doesn't move fast enough. I take the wax paper from him and fold it up to place back in my pocket, and he shoves the sandwich into his mouth. Watching him eat following his long bout of starvation, my chest caves in as if boulders are toppling down on top of me. He's hardly taking a breath between bites. This is the fourth day I've been able to give him larger portions of food. I was scared he might get sick the first couple of days, so I've been slowly increasing the portion size. I'm just not sure how much longer I'll be able to keep him here. It's not under my control.

"This is the most delicious sandwich I've ever had," he says, his mouth full.

"You said that yesterday," I whisper along with a soft laugh.

"They just keep getting better."

"So are you," I tell him.

He takes the last mouthful and chews for a long minute before swallowing the last of the bread. I wish I had something more to give him, but it would be too much for his stomach. He rests back into the thin mattress covered table and sighs. "Thank you. Thank you, a million times."

"Please, don't..." I knew he would be thankful regardless, but I don't deserve gratitude.

"I'm alive because of you," he says.

He's recovering because of my assistance, which means he won't be kept here once he's well enough to leave. "I'm going to find a way to help the others too. I'm going to do everything I can. I swear to you."

"You're an angel, Emi," he says.

"Let me jot down your vitals," I say, pulling a small kit out of a nearby drawer. I've been keeping track of his temperature, blood pressure, and heart rate. It's the data Dietrich needs to compile his final report.

The numbers I add to my notes aren't exact. They're lower than they truly are as I try to drag out the upward trajectory of his recovery period.

"Everything looks good," I tell him. "They don't need to know that just yet though, okay?"

Danner nods in understanding as I drop my notepad into my pocket. He reaches for my hand, still struggling to lift his arms. I wish I could get him up onto his feet and help him walk around, but rehabilitation isn't a part of the procedures done in this asylum of a hospital. I give him my hand and he pulls it down against his chest, his bones protruding sharply against my palm, his heart beating tersely against his flesh and my mine. "A rare honeybee," he says. "How lucky am I to know you?"

"I'm the lucky one, Danner. It's me."

THIRTY-TWO

EMILIE

Dachau, Germany

My back aches as I stretch my shoulders, the result of sitting hunched on the edge of my bed for so long trying to read medical texts, questioning every decision I've made up until this point.

Danner's vitals match the picture of health, meaning there's no reason to keep him in observation any longer. Until now, I've been able to see him each day following his near-death submersion because I've made it clear that post-testing data was as important as the other information garnered along the way.

Now that the research trial is officially over, I'm not sure where Danner will end up once he leaves the sick bay, and I'll lose control over keeping him safe, fed, warm, and healthy.

The sunlight has dipped below the window, leaving me with only a pinpoint of light to continue obsessing over my data. Otto's heavy footsteps pacing up and down the hallway downstairs isn't helping my concentration either.

Otto's hand claps down against the banister in the stairwell, his wedding band causing a vibrating echo between the walls. I close my book and slip it into the drawer of my nightstand as he hollers, "Emilie, we need to leave. We're going to be late."

I push our bedroom door open wide and make my way to the top of the stairs, clasping the railing as I imagine tumbling forward in this haze I feel trapped in. Otto is staring at his watch, a dozen steps below me. "Go on without me. I'm not feeling well." I've made no attempt to prepare myself to leave the house tonight and still have an apron tied around my neck.

Otto makes his way up the steps, two at a time, taking my hand as if ready to plead. "Emi, I know you hate me. I know I have destroyed our marriage, and I know there's nothing I can do to fix all of the things I have done, but my father and uncle will be there tonight and—"

"I send my regards," I say, gritting out the words.

"If you don't show up with me, you will seem like a loose end to those in command. I will too," he adds. The genuine fear in Otto's eyes prickles at my flesh because I know he's speaking the truth. I've been numb, scraping up all the anger I can muster to shield my pain from everything we've witnessed.

"We are and always will be loose ends. Do you not see this?"

"Loose ends are removed quietly and inconspicuously. Is that what you want?" he asks, replying as if I didn't just tell him it's too late. If that's our fate, there isn't anything we can do to stop it now.

Staring at Otto, I recall the look on his face when he was arguing with me as we were fighting to save Danner. Weeks have passed and I haven't wanted to be in the same room as him, never mind put on an act and a phony smile to please a bunch of Nazis tonight.

"I'm going to tell them what I know," I threaten. "It'll only take a glass of wine or two, and I won't be able to stop myself."

Otto's knuckles turn white as he squeezes the banister. "Please, Emi. I know what Dietrich is capable of—what he'd do to his own blood if I so much as blinked the wrong way in front of them. If we don't show up tonight, and I won't go there without you, he'll be at our door within the hour in a rage."

He lifts his hand from the banister, leaving a dark ring from where sweat remains. How much do I have to give in before this will end? I have refused to accept that there's no way out at this point, but I'm growing closer to the realization. I have no say in anything. I'm doing as I'm told.

"I won't smile. I won't take part in small talk. I won't act like all's right with the world, but I'll go and sit at the table quietly to be seen with you, for you, as an obligation to our marriage. I'll be dressed and ready in a few minutes."

I pivot on the bottom step and make my way back upstairs. Knowing this is how the conversation would end, I already had my dress hanging up and my shoes polished.

* * *

How else to celebrate a momentous occasion than to have upbeat static-ridden jazz filtering through speakers, and the heavy aroma of smoked and seared hors d'oeuvres while prancing around an SS banquet hall. The room could be mistaken for somewhere pleasant, as it only takes linen, polished silverware, and dim lighting to hide the truth of what this building represents.

"You're here," Ingrid calls out, holding her gloved hand toward me as she makes her way across the room. Helga and Ursula follow her. "Come let's get you a drink."

"I'm not drinking tonight but thank you. Flat water will be fine."

"I know what that means," Ingrid snickers. "Is there something you want to tell us?" She reaches to my stomach, caressing the silk ribbon belt draped around my waist.

"I'm not with child," I say dryly.

Ingrid pulls her hand back, and places it over her chest, covering it with her other hand. "I apologize for my grubby hands then."

"No apology necessary," I say, glancing around the room to see what other familiar faces I recognize.

"It seems as if it's been two months since I've seen you last," Ingrid says, a red silk curl bouncing against her forehead.

"Yes, it has been a while. They must have kept you busy at the sick bay," Helga says.

"Are you going to tell us what it is our husbands truly do all day at work?" Ursula adds, her cat-like eyes peering over her shoulder, seeking out eavesdroppers.

I had full intention of reporting back to them on the life they weren't a part of while their husbands are at work all day, but if I tell them the truth, I'll void the reason for agreeing to be here tonight, and I'll ruin their marriages too.

"To be fair, over the last two months, I never spotted any of your husbands, not even once. The medical building is large and divided up into several sectioned off areas. There was little intermingling."

"I guess they were telling us the truth," Helga says to the other two.

"Emilie, could I borrow you for a moment," Otto says, approaching the group of wives. He waves me over and though I would rather refrain from running to him like a lovesick mistress, I have to follow his lead.

"If you'll excuse me, ladies. I'll return her to you shortly." The way he speaks makes me feel like a shared object. I'd rather just return home.

"My vater and Uncle Dietrich would like to have a word with us—a congratulations of sorts."

I might need to bite off my tongue.

The room isn't large enough to steal more than a few seconds before we're in the presence of his father, mother, uncle Dietrich and wife, Ginny. Dietrich and Ginny have only been married a couple of years and have been eager to grow a family in a brief time, especially considering their older ages. She looks quite uncomfortable to be standing here in heels. In fact, the longer I gaze at her, I consider the thought that I've never seen a mother-to-be carrying their baby so high before. I can't imagine she's comfortable whether sitting or standing. Hopefully, she was given more of an option to be here tonight than I was. She never says much, but Otto heard a rumor from his parents that she used to be close with high-ranking members of the Reich. I can't help but wonder if she's quiet because she's shy or quiet because she knows more than she's able to let on.

"Well, if it isn't the golden child and his wife," Dietrich says.

His wife has a name.

"Heil Hitler," Otto regards him with a salute.

"Heil Hitler," I say, begrudgingly.

"Heil Hitler," he responds.

I wish I could refuse to salute him, but it would be a "sin" to do so.

"I've been told you two have accomplished quite a bit," Herr Berger says, holding up a glass of champagne. Frau Berger clinks her glass to his.

"That's wonderful," she agrees, clearing her throat as she eyeballs me from the corner of her eye.

"*That's wonderful,*" Dietrich repeats quietly. "Emilie, I do hope you will continue to work with us in the lab. We have another study coming up that you would be quite useful for."

The fire inside me burns up through my throat and I know if I open my mouth to speak, flames will shoot out.

"Oh, that's kind," Frau Berger says. "But—"

"Brother, I think we've taken enough of Emilie's time. In fact, I think I might like to see the two of them finish their medical classes before moving any further into a long-term career path," Herr Berger says.

Otto's parents take my breath away, shocking me like never before. I'm not sure what has changed their mind, but their rebuttal is welcome.

"That does sound like a wonderful option for us," Otto says, swallowing hard as he peers at his father's unreadable face. It's clear he's as taken aback as I am about this sharp change of agenda.

No one appears more stunned than Dietrich. "*A wonderful option*," Dietrich grumbles. "Well, why bother with that if they can have hands-on experience with us? The work we're doing is life-altering. What more could someone with our knowledge ask for?"

"A good conscience," Herr Berger says, speaking quietly beneath his breath. "Dietrich, you hid many of the details from me, masking my awareness from an office building outside of Dachau. Had I known what Otto and then Emilie were stepping into, I would have—"

"*A good conscience?* Enough," Dietrich says. "I've been nothing but honest with you. I didn't realize I needed to define the conditions of our country and confirm what it is we're working toward. You won't find yourself in many places where there isn't a war in the background. It's something we must all live with. To put our lives on hold—well, it's a waste of time."

"Human experimentation was never mentioned to me," Herr Berger utters, stabbing his finger toward Dietrich's nose.

I have so many questions I want to ask Otto's parents. Most importantly, how long they've known about what we were subjected to—what we've been forced to subject others to.

"Blame it on me," Herr Berger says. "Tell Himmler you need to corral a new team, and if he asks why, tell him it was my doing."

"Stefan," Frau Berger hisses, her inflection makes it clear he should stop speaking.

He's protecting us, yet putting himself and likely Frau Berger in grave danger while doing so.

"Vater," Otto says. "I should have spoken up sooner. This is my fault. I'll take the blame."

"No," Frau Berger shouts.

I grab Otto's arm, pinching my fingernails into his flesh, wishing he would stop talking.

Dietrich shakes his head and takes a swig of the clear liquid drink he's been washing green olives down with. "*No!*" Dietrich mocks Frau Berger. "You're going to get me killed. That's what you're doing. I'm your brother. Do you have no understanding of the fact that we've all been blinded at some point," he says, his voice carrying through the hall. Dietrich lifts his glass to the Reichstag flag hanging above our heads. "We all live under the same mind, and there's no way out. We can live or die."

The growing argument between Otto's family settles into the back of my mind as I imagine what will become of Danner if Dietrich complies with us stepping away. I'll have no way of helping him, or anyone else. There's no hopeful ending here. Someone will suffer the consequences we're all tossing around, hoping it isn't—

"We can't lose Frau Berger of all people," a man says, passing behind us. "She's the only one who truly knows how to work with her hands."

Me. I'm the one with the grenade.

I whip around in search of who would say such an awful thing, spotting only the back of a soldier's head as he walks away.

I slip my hand out of Otto's and rush toward the man, grabbing a hold of his wrist to stop him from going any further. "I beg your pardon?"

The lonely soldier. I should have known. Seeing that he was

dismissed from duty, I'm not sure why he received an invitation to this event. "I watched you bring someone back to life," he says. "That's all I meant, of course."

"Is that true, Emilie?" Herr Berger asks, showing interest, not disappointment.

My mouth is open, but words don't form. What am I supposed to say?

"Yes, it was for the conclusion of our data," Otto says. "If we lost the volunteer, we would have had to start from the beginning of that trial and we wanted to make sure we had all our information in on time."

The soldier makes his way into our circle with a sly crooked smile. His hands are in his pockets, and he looks like he knows he's about to win the jackpot. "Oh, come on now, I wouldn't say that was the exact reason your wife went through the trouble she did," the soldier replies. "We just have a Florence Nightingale on our hands, don't we? Or was it something more—something a married woman shouldn't be so concerned about?"

"*A Florence Nightingale...*" Dietrich grumbles. "What is the meaning of this?"

"There's no meaning. Emilie was doing what she needed to complete the task. In fact, Private Krieg here was relieved of his duty for his inappropriate behavior in the lab. I think it might be best that you see yourself out the door, Private. Your invitation must have been a clerical error."

Dietrich is staring at me like an owl watching a helpless mouse who has backed herself into a corner.

"As you wish, Herr—pardon—I meant to say Doctor Berger. I must say, I find it fascinating that you would defend your wife after her covert behavior."

Otto's father whistles to a man standing guard by the door. "Please see him out," he shouts. "Do not return. I know where you came from, and I'll have no quandaries about sending you back to where prisoners belong."

Mortification wraps me in a cold sweat, wondering what Otto, his parents, aunt, and uncle are thinking. If I make a peep to defend myself, I'll appear guilty. I know it's best to remain quiet. "Emilie is the only woman working in our lab. This kind of behavior was bound to happen with the straggling soldiers coming and going. Private Krieg fondly approached Emilie the first day she arrived, but she kindly told him she was a married woman. Apparently, that wasn't enough of a reason to satiate his jealousy," Otto explains, squeezing my hand with a clammy grip.

"Young soldiers will be young soldiers. We just need to ignore their pettiness, isn't that right?" Frau Dietrich asks Frau Berger.

"We've both seen our days of this," she agrees.

I wasn't aware Otto knew about the lonely soldier—Private Krieg—approaching me that first day. Someone must have told him.

Otto wraps his arm around me and pulls me in tightly to his side. "I suppose it isn't easy being so beautiful, or being married to someone so beautiful, is it?" he jests.

"So beautiful..." Dietrich mutters. "Well then." He abruptly steals the conversation back. "I'd like to speak with you both in the morning to discuss our plan for moving forward, Stefan, Otto." The formality is gone, and I've been weeded from the equation. "My office at seven." Dietrich twists on his heels and casually makes his way over to another gathered crowd, lifting his glass to start a new toast.

"What now?" Otto asks his father.

"We'll have to see in the morning. I don't know where this leaves us. I apologize for trusting him and putting the two of you in this situation. I understand why you didn't approach me until now. I'm a coward of a man when it comes to my brother, but I assure you I'll be putting a stop to that at once." Herr Berger drops his gaze to his feet and shakes his head. "Marion, let's see ourselves out."

"Herr Berger," I say, stopping them from leaving. "The man I was saving was Danner Alesky, a Jewish prisoner of Dachau."

"Danner?" Frau Berger repeats, shock widening her eyes.

"Yes. They were going to execute him if—"

"No more," Otto says. "Not here."

Frau Berger clamps her mouth shut, her cheeks trembling and her forehead puckering over every age line. "Please excuse me," she says.

Herr Berger clears the phlegm from his throat. "I—I, uh— I'll see you in the morning, son," Herr Berger says, following his wife out of the function room.

"Someone could have heard you," Otto whispers. "Why did you do that?"

I don't have answers to any question anymore. I don't know why I'm here at all.

THIRTY-THREE

EMILIE

Dachau, Germany

A thin layer of dust covers the half-filled bookcase in Otto's office. It's obvious I haven't gotten around to tidying up in here in a long time, but there's been no time. Until now.

Otto and I have been working for Dietrich as if gagged. Yet, the cards are all out on the table after last night's discussion between Herr Berger and his brother, Dietrich. I'm left wondering if Dietrich would throw his own brother to the wolves, bury him alive, or do whatever is necessary to be seen as a hero in the eyes of Hitler's men. It's impossible to know how much danger we might all be in now, and yet, all I can think about is the fact that I may have lost access to Danner and all the other innocent prisoners who I want nothing more than to help somehow.

I've been sitting at Otto's desk, drawing circular patterns on a piece of notepaper while my mind follows the maze of pen strokes, wondering what is being discussed in the Berger family meeting early this morning. It's nine and I would have expected to have heard something by now, but I'm not sure if silence is a good or bad sign.

An unfamiliar squeal of brakes abruptly stops outside of the draped window behind me. It's not Otto's car. I twist his desk chair around and peek out, unable to see the car because of the shrubbery blocking my view.

A knock on the front door shouldn't startle me into jumping out of the seat, but it does because I don't know who would be visiting at this early hour of the day. I tiptoe over to the front door, staying out of sight from the side windows so I can steal a glimpse of who is at the door before having to confess anyone is home. I spot the pinched look on Dietrich's face and pull away, concealing myself directly behind the door while I debate whether to open it.

He's the last person I want to see or speak to, but he's supposed to be with Otto and Herr Berger. Something must have happened to them.

Something could happen to me if I open the door.

I might lose my last chance of helping Danner if I ignore Dietrich.

Nothing good will arise from either option. A man of power gets what he wants.

I open the door enough to see his face, enough to exchange words. "What are you doing here?"

"*What are you doing here?*" he mouths the echoed words. "Emilie, good morning," he says. "I'm wondering if I might have a word with you."

"For what reason?" I ask, expressionless. The less he knows about what I'm thinking, the better off I'll be.

"*What reason...*" he whispers. "A proposition of sorts." I thought that's what he was alluding to last night, bluntly asking me to continue aiding him with whatever experiment might come next. Rather than reply with a hard no like Herr Berger did last night, I remain silent, waiting for him to continue. "I have received a request to prepare a written memorandum for the air-force troops, outlining our findings and direction on how to utilize such measures to protect themselves during extreme cold conditions."

I've already given him every bit of research and data I documented during the trials so he could compile a report. "You have all the information needed to create a memorandum," I reply.

"*Information needed*," he mumbles. "Yes, I do, but I'm not sure I'm able to convey the information in a proper outline structure as eloquently as you did with your notes." He must have copied my notes to use in his letter if he's suggesting he doesn't have the ability to write in a way that speaks of his so-called expertise.

A chill from the wind blows against us in the doorway and though I would typically invite someone in for a cup of tea, I won't allow him to come one step further.

"As my father-in-law mentioned last night—"

"As my father-in-law..." he repeats, hissing the words. "Emilie, I'm going to cut to the chase here. I heard all topics of conversation last night and am aware of the extra efforts made to save one particular volunteer. It has become clear that you have a personal connection with this man, and therefore might be more willing to sacrifice your time to help me if it were to mean keeping him alive."

"How so?" I ask, trying not to cry at the thought of this threat—another threat.

"*How so?* The other volunteers won't be returning to their barracks. In fact, they're already dead. They knew too much, saw too much. They are of no use to us now. The only one spared is Prisoner 13415. His survival will depend on you and your decision to help me."

My stomach burns as acidic bile rises into my chest. I should have been more cautious but that would mean giving up on him when he's on the verge of death. I grit my teeth to avoid showing a reaction but I'm sure he sees the tension in my jaw.

"I—" I know what my answer has to be.

"Your husband knows this volunteer prisoner too, doesn't he?" I swallow against the growing lump in my throat. "Of course he does. You all lived on the same street as children."

"Why are you asking if you already know?" I should be more careful with my words but with my life teetering on top of a mountain peak, I'm not sure anything I say will end in my favor.

"*Why?* Because your husband and my brother have refused to continue aiding me in my efforts—efforts my life depends on as I still answer to the Reichsführer. I'm afraid if I have no one to assist me with this data, we might all be at risk for an end none of us wants to see."

"Otto won't be assisting you anymore?" I ask, baffled by this revelation.

"*Won't be assisting...*" he echoes. "Correct. Apparently, my brother has already secured a position for Otto at a nearby field hospital outside of the camp."

"So, you're here because you think you can convince me when you couldn't convince Otto or Herr Berger?" I question him.

He pauses, mouthing my words back to me. "Yes, in fact, I'm quite sure I can convince you."

"No, not a chance."

Dietrich tilts his head to the side and furrows his brows. "Even if it meant saving that lone standing volunteer from death? Of course, I don't have say in much but there are certain areas I have control." Dietrich straightens his wool scarf and shrugs his coat into a flat line against his shoulders. "As a married man, I know there are secrets we keep from those we love, to protect them. Just as Otto has done for you. In return you'll do the same. No one will have to know my team has split apart, you'll stay in your beautiful house, and your friend will be spared."

"I'm not sure," I say, the words coming out on their own. "Otto will ask you why we haven't been kicked out of the house."

"*Otto will ask...* My agreement with Otto and my brother is that their names remain on my team roster, but they won't be assisting. Otto won't question the house." Dietrich drops his head back and stares up at the sky, choking out a laugh. "Emilie, I'm no stranger to the truths we aren't supposed to know, but still, somehow, find out. Even my darling wife has a past she cannot speak of, but that's for her to dwell on, not me."

I'm not sure what he's alluding to, but I certainly wasn't aware there was any tension between him and his wife, especially since she's carrying a third child with him. They had a set of twins less than a year after being wed and then fell pregnant again just months after giving birth. I thought their marriage was on the up-and-up given they're so eager to grow a family.

However, he isn't wrong about the secrets Otto kept from me, and I'm not sure if they were because he wanted to keep me safe. Despite everything—lies, truths, deceit, and faithfulness—I would never choose for Danner to die because of my resentment toward what Dietrich has been doing and will continue to do.

"I understand," I say.

"*I understand*," he mimics. "Wonderful. We are in agreement, then. You will assist me with writing this memorandum and I'll ensure that volunteer remains alive." He reaches his hand out to solidify the deal, and as if I'm possessed, I take the agreement. "Aside from the two of us, no one else will be privy to this information."

With each blink, the image of Danner with blue lips and skin as white as frost sinks deeper into my mind's eye. I would do anything to keep him safe. He would do the same for me. "Yes, I agree with the terms."

"*I agree*," he confirms to himself. "As I said before, Emilie, you're a brilliant young woman. I realize this memorandum will take some time to write up, so I ask that you leave written portions on my desk daily so that I have time to review and re-type promptly. You're still listed as an approved counterpart working with me in Block 5 and won't have any problems entering the prison grounds or the building."

I pull my hand from his, feeling as though I've just made a deadly pact without knowing who will die in the end. How many innocent German citizens have stepped over the line between good and evil? It seems common to be blackmailed into doing what most would never consider.

My throat tightens as I stare into his dark beady eyes, wondering if there's even a soul left within his being.

"Enjoy your day, Emilie," he says, stepping back from my front door and jovially hopping down the front steps.

I close the door, secure the lock and drop my forehead against the wooden trim.

My marriage doesn't need added burden, and every day seems a step closer to a place we won't come back from.

In the kitchen, I scribble out a grocery list. If Otto has taken on a new job so soon, surely he'll be on board with me re-enrolling in classes.

If only I could truly do so.

He just has to think I am so he doesn't find out I'm helping Dietrich of all people. He wouldn't understand why I'm doing what I'm doing after everything we've been through. I'm not sure I could make him understand that I'm willing to risk my life if it means possibly saving Danner's.

Since I haven't had the time to make a satisfying meal lately, I'll put together a nice dinner. It will be the perfect setting to inform each other of the changes we'll both be taking on. One thing is certain, I'll need to start taking frequent trips to the library to brush up on any forgotten material before stepping foot into a classroom. Otto will understand that part.

I complete my list for the store and grab my coat, purse, and scarf, to make the short walk to the bus stop. The winds are brutal today, making me think about the prisoners who must be working outside in their thin layers of clothing.

I pull my gloves out of my pockets and slip them on over my hands before tightening my scarf once more as I approach the full bench of people also waiting for the bus.

"Emilie Berger," a familiar voice speaks out from behind me. "Where are you heading?"

I turn around, finding Helga, dressed similarly to me, blowing cold puffs of air out of her mouth. "Hi, Helga. Oh, I just have to make a quick trip to the grocery store."

"Me too," she says. "I went to start making dinner and found out I had a bad batch of potatoes and I'm out of cream. I didn't have any intention of weathering this cold today."

I smile at her rather than think up something to respond with. I wish we were closer or had spent more time together since it seems she and her husband, Wilhelm, have a similar marital setup as Otto and me. He keeps her in the dark and assumes she'll be okay with it, but she's not. Just like me.

"I prefer warmer weather too," I finally blurt out.

THIRTY-FOUR
DANNER
OCTOBER 1942

Dachau, Germany

To be separated from the other few surviving volunteers has left me wondering where they have gone. The Nazi guard had only ever guaranteed I would avoid execution by volunteering. But they expected me to die freezing in the tub. With the help of Emilie, I've defied the odds and I'm not sure what will become of me now. That, and I've been left wondering what will become of Emilie.

A guard releases my arm in front of the barrack I had been living in prior to being observed in the sick bay. "If you speak a word about anything you heard, saw, experienced, or know, you will be executed immediately, without warning."

I assumed I would be placed under a gag order if I returned to the barrack. I'm surprised they've let me come back here. It doesn't seem to be the way they operate. They use us and then likely dispose of us, which is why I know now that execution would have been a better option in the first place.

I trudge into the barrack, toward the back, seeking through the darkness for the wool covered wooden plank I'd used as my bed. The others are already asleep and aside from the faint glow from the moon, there's no light. Not until I pass by the narrow vacant spot do I know I've arrived at my bunk. It's much harder to make my way to the top with the fatigue and weakness I'm now battling, but I manage to make it up and roll onto my side, praying sleep will come easily.

"You're back?" Hans peers through squinted eyes, the reflection from tired tears captures a bit of light. "I thought you were done for. It's been weeks."

"Yeah, I'm back," I reply.

"What did they do to you?"

The memory of ice-cold stabbing knives slowly tearing my skin to shreds flashes through my mind. The screams within me are still present. "They didn't need me," I lie. Even if my life weren't threatened, if I were to speak of what occurred, I'm not sure I'd be doing Hans much good by sharing my nightmares.

"Thank God, brother. Thank God you're back in one piece. I can't tell you how happy I am to see you. What about Emilie, did you see her again?"

I have the urge to hug this man, a man with a heart and soul, still living like me—just one person who knows I'm still alive is somehow more important than being alive. "I appreciate your concern. It means a lot," I say. "And briefly, but it was too dangerous to talk."

"A vision is worth a lot of words. I'm sure you were exchanging thoughts. It's something, right?"

It's something. Life is cruel.

"You're right. I'm lucky to have at least caught a glimpse," I say, knowing he would do anything to see Matilda too.

Hans shuffles his arms beneath his cheek, resting in the way he often tries to sleep until we realize how hard the wood truly is against our protruding rib cages. "While you were gone, I couldn't help but think at least I could tell people someday that I knew you and you were one of the good ones. I could keep your name alive if given the chance. Then, of course, my thoughts led me to wondering if anyone would remember *my* name if I didn't survive. The thought of never letting a loved one know what has become of us is more heartbreaking than the thought of losing this battle."

It seems we're all on our way to losing hope.

"I don't know what the future holds, but if I somehow manage to walk out of here, I hope you do too, and if not, I promise you I'll make sure your name is not forgotten and your loved ones know what became of you."

It feels like I'm making an empty promise when I don't see how any of us will walk away from this prison, but to die thinking no one will ever know our stories leaves us without any purpose.

Hans pulls his arm out from beneath his cheek and pats my back. "You're an honorable man," Hans says.

"As are you," I reply.

"You two are something else," Eli says, groaning as he turns to face us. "It isn't often you find a friend in the depths of hell, and it speaks well of you to know there are still good men left in this world. Depend on each other until you can't. Life can disappear in a second. Go ahead and ask him, Hans. Don't wait any longer."

"Ask me what?" I ask, looking back and forth between Abe and Hans.

Hans drops his gaze to his lap and sighs. "Could I ask a favor in case something is to happen to me?"

"Of course, but don't tell me you're giving up now..." I say, scolding him as many of us often do to each other.

"No, I'm not giving up, but if I lose that choice, would you try to find Matilda Ellman? According to a letter I received from her, she's somewhere in this town. She said she would be waiting for me. My worst fear is to leave her waiting...if I'm gone." Hans reaches beneath his blanket and pulls out a thin tube of papers. "Also, do you think you could give her some-thing I need her to have?"

"Of course, but there's no saying one of us will outlive the other. I don't want to lose anything precious if it's me who goes first."

"I have more notes. I'm a writer. It's all I can do when I'm not asleep or working. Please, if it isn't too much to ask…"

"Of course. I promise I'll do that for you if given the chance to walk out of here," I say, tucking the rolled-up papers beneath my blanket.

"What about you? Is there something you want to make sure Emilie knows?" he offers. "I'm familiar with a guard who takes and delivers mail on occasion. I can see if he'll send some-thing for you too."

I didn't know anyone received mail from outside of these gates.

"As much as I would like to take you up on the offer, I'm afraid that won't be necessary as I don't have an address for her." As for the rest of his question…the answer isn't difficult, and though something I've refused to tell Emilie many times for selfless reasons, she should know the truth. "But if I don't make it, and you find the time to seek her out, I would like her— Emilie Marx is her full name—to know that I spent my life falling in love with her, being in love without her, then dying in love with my memories of her."

Hans repeats my words under his breath as if he needs to hear them once more to remember them. "If I make it out of here without you, I'll make sure she knows. I promise, and a promise between brothers is something to rely on."

"You boys need to hold on to your loves if given the chance. What keeps you alive in here will be something you can never live without if you make it back out there," Abe says. "Trust me, as an old man…I know a thing or two."

I've suffered the pain of distance, living a world apart,

knowing my love for Emilie was something we could never share—something I'll always live without despite my survival here. To think I once mourned over her loss while merely moving a country away from her, makes me realize there's no hope of surviving anything worse.

THIRTY-FIVE

DANNER

Munich, Germany

I've spent many days on trains in my lifetime, but none have felt quite like the ones I've been on since yesterday when I left Poland. This final train to Munich is no different to the others. There are more members of the SS and Gestapo police than there are civilian passengers, making my appearance, blonde hair, and all, stand out among the crowd. Great-Uncle Igor made it clear I had to avoid showing any signs of stress or nervousness because the Nazis pinpoint those particular people and run them through the question mill. If I can avoid the questions, I'll have my best chance of making it off this train into the city, which won't be much better.

My hands are raw from gripping this bulky crate of mead. Every seat on the train is taken so I must keep everything with me, on my lap. All the while, I continue to repeat the story I should use if questioned by authorities.

I'm a cook for an SS-Obergruppenfuhrer, sent to Poland to collect bottled Dwójniak mead for an elite dinner party.

I've done what I can to remain awake, but particularly

during the daytime hours as the sun casts a spotlight over everyone seated on the left side of the train.

* * *

This next stop is Oberschleißheim. Oberschleißheim will be our last stop before arriving at the final destination, Munich.

The shrill screech of metal grinding against metal sends a phantom pain down my spine. I've become tired of hearing the sound so often over the last day. The doors open, only a few step off, and twice as many board, all of which are in uniform. I've never considered what it takes to appear unfazed and calm, but avoiding eye contact seems like the worst way to behave. I force myself to peer at each man passing by, giving each a quick nod of respect while praying the heat burning through my limbs isn't apparent in my face.

My pulse slows as the train doors shut and the brakes are emphatically released. I rest my head back in the seat, trying to breathe through my tidal wave of panic. *Unclench your fists*, I tell myself. *Drop your shoulders. One breath every five seconds is a sign of a contentment, as Emilie used to tell me. Anything more would be a sign of stress.* I'm not sure I had ever wondered how many breaths I take in a minute's time, but it's been a helpful practical fact to hold on to over the years.

I count my breaths like seconds ticking on a clock, giving me something to focus on while we travel the last kilometers to the train station in Munich.

The screaming halt from the brakes doesn't bother me this time. The awful sound is more like music to my ears now. I stand from my seat, my satchel secured across my torso, and the crate locked within my grips.

"Papers!" I hear just before stepping onto the platform. It's not that I didn't know I would have to present my fake identification again, I was just putting the thought off until now.

I hoist the crate over my left leg and pull my papers out of my coat pocket.

I'm Albert Amsler. People call me Al for short, I remind myself.

I hand the papers to the police officer reaching for them. He scans them, takes a look at me, returns his gaze to the papers, then again, back at me. *A third will mean he's spotted something*...or so I tell myself.

"Albert Amsler," he says, "what are you traveling with in that crate?"

The words tango on my tongue as I try to place in them in the right order as quickly as I can. "I'm a personal chef to an SS—"

"Okay, move along," he says before shifting his gaze to the next person in line.

I feel as though I've gotten away with murder, giving me the extra bit of energy and confidence I need to make it back to my old neighborhood in the hope that Papa has made it home. The walk feels much longer than it ever did before. Everywhere I look, red flags wave, loudly claiming this city as a home to the Nazis. I haven't felt welcome here since I was thirteen. I shouldn't feel any differently now.

One block left to walk before reaching my old, enclosed neighborhood. What once smelled like firewood from piping chimneys and a faint scent of pine from the outer encirclement of trees, now only reeks of horse manure left behind from whatever parade must have come through here last.

The street I lived on looks the same until I reach my house, first up on the left. Mama's curtains in the front window have been replaced with green linen. I'm not sure Papa would do something like that. I grab the doorknob and twist to push my way inside, but the knob doesn't budge. I knock while keeping my gaze on the window. The curtains billow against the glass a brief second before the front door opens.

"Yes, can I help you?" A tall, thin woman with rigid stone-like features stands before me with her eyebrows angled to a point.

"Uh, yes, are you—do you live here now, or—"

She glances over her shoulder as if she needs to check her response with someone but when she returns her cold hard stare, she says, "It appears to be so, doesn't it now? What can I do for you?"

"I apologize for bothering you. I was only looking for my father."

"The only man who lives here is my husband, and he's most certainly not your father."

She closes the door without giving me a chance to apologize again.

This doesn't mean he isn't around here somewhere. The house could have been occupied as soon as we were forced to leave. I knew it would be unlikely to find him here in our home after all this time, but it had to be the first place I'd start.

I spin around, debating which door to knock on next, wondering if Emilie's parents still live here, and Felix's, Otto's and Gerty's parents too.

I choose Emilie's door first and my heart thunders as I lift my hand to knock. Seeing her again after all this time would more than make up for the disappointment of not finding Papa right away.

There isn't a sound from the other side of the door, but I wait another moment before knocking again. The stillness within the house seems clear so I move on to Felix's front door. *Please, be home.*

Seconds after I knock, footsteps scuttle along the wooden floors until the door opens, leaving me face-to-face with Frau Weber, Felix's mother. The sight of a familiar face stiffens my chest as I want to jump into her arms and steal a moment of what feels like home from her.

"Danner?" she whispers.

I glance around, nervous about who might be listening, hearing my name is something other than Albert Amsler. I shake my head. "May I come inside?"

She scoops her arm behind my back and pulls me in at once, then draws the curtains inside just as quickly. "What in the world are you doing back here? You should be in Poland with your Mama and David, yes?"

I place the wooden crate down between my ankles, happy to free my hands for a moment. "I was there, but there was news that some of the Jewish prisoners were released due to overcrowding. I thought Papa might have..."

By the mere look on her face, I can already tell she hasn't seen Papa and hasn't heard a word about this news.

"You thought he was back home," she says, placing her warm hand on my cheek. "Sweetheart, we haven't seen him at all. I'm so sorry you've traveled all this way."

"Thank you, I just need to find him somehow. He's somewhere and, well, if anyone will find him, it will be me."

"Of course," she says. "I hadn't heard about the police releasing any of the previously arrested Jews but that doesn't mean it's not true."

I contemplate what to do next. I put all my hope into walking back into my home as if we had never left. "Thank you for letting me know," I offer, reaching down to lift my crate back up with my sore hands.

"Where will you go? Who are you staying with?"

Emilie's parents might take me in. "Do the Marxes still live down the street?" I ask, curling my fingers around the wooden frame.

"Of course," she says. "Although they've been quite busy lately with planning a wedding and all. They hardly ever seem to be home much these days."

I release the crate again and stand back upright. My hands

become ice cold, so do my legs, back, and torso. They're planning a wedding.

"You weren't aware, I see," she says. "Oh, Danner, sweetheart. I know you loved her…"

"She's to be wed to Otto, I assume?" The words taste like vinegar on my tongue, knowing I'm the one who made the suggestion to her years ago.

"Of course," she says. "Who else?"

Me. In another life.

"Do you not have a place to stay?"

"I'll find somewhere," I say.

"Nonsense. You'll stay here with us."

"I can't insist on that. No one wants to house a forbidden Jew." Emilie's parents were the only other couple on this street who never treated me any differently to the other kids. They didn't see religion when they looked at my face and now, I see how rare that sentiment is.

"Well, we'll have to work out some details, but you're welcome to stay with us." She combs her fingers through my hair. "You're already blonde." She chuckles then pinches my cheek.

"I have updated identification papers too," I say, reaching into my pocket to show her. "They worked at the train station."

"Felix will be so happy to see you when he gets home from work," she says, seeming to be choking on her words. "And Herr Weber will be just as thrilled. Does Gerty know?"

"No, you're the only one who knows I'm here. I think it might be best that Emilie, Gerty, and Otto's family don't know."

I plan to remain inconspicuous, for the sake of making sure I don't overstay my welcome or make anyone uncomfortable. The thought of not telling Emilie I'm here is torturous, but I would only disrupt her life and it may only be for a brief time that I'm able to remain here.

"I understand, and I'm happy to keep the secret in our

home. You don't need to stress about making us feel uncomfortable, though, okay?"

I know the look on her face. It's the same look anyone has when they're trying to act as if they aren't afraid to be seen with a Jewish person. I can't blame her. Fear is fear, no matter what the cause.

"Okay, but if anything changes, I can find somewhere else to go," I offer. "I truly don't want to be a bother."

"You have nothing to worry about, dear." There's a questionable inflection in her voice.

It's understandable. No one truly means the words: "You have nothing to worry about." Not anymore.

THIRTY-SIX

EMILIE

Dachau, Germany

Four months of wondering when Otto might decide to make a stink about me spending time at the library so many nights a week—in what he believes to be preparation for my return to nursing classes. He even taught me to drive so I could take the car after work, rather than having to ride my bicycle in the cold.

To prevent his discontent after a long day at work, I've made sure to prepare casseroles and nights' worth of leftovers. The nights I leave the house, we're much like a revolving door. He returns home from the field hospital and hands me the keys to the car, and I leave for the next few hours.

Before leaving tonight, he asked me if everything was all right because I looked flushed. My guilt must be becoming more obvious.

To my credit, I do actually spend a fair amount of time in the library, writing up my notes for Dietrich's memorandums. Except, when I leave the library, I don't go directly home. The guards at the tall black iron gates know who I am, briefed by Dietrich with instructions to escort me to Block 5 with the paperwork pinched between a daily edition of the *Der Stürmer* newspaper. Once the guard on duty unlocks Dietrich's office door, I step inside, pull open his top left metal desk drawer and conceal the papers within a folder he's left for me.

I walk the same path back every time I'm here, along the far side of the rows of blocks, then pivoting a sharp right at the final block, before the land opens into the roll-call pit in front of the service building. I spot the last metal rubbish bin I'll pass before exiting the prison, roll up the newspaper tightly and toss it away as I do every night. The guard doesn't care about my disposing of the paper within the prison gates, because the paper is the perfect propaganda for them, something the prisoners here will find no use in reading...except one.

The newspaper was originally a way to conceal the papers I was delivering to Dietrich, per his instructions. However, two weeks after I begun shuttling papers to Dietrich's office, I found additional use for it. It was the night my true purpose became quite clear.

One hollow clang after another, metal bouncing off knees as men lug large metal trash receptacles through the wet gravel beneath a heavy downpour. The sky always seems to be crying here—crying in a way that steals all the wind from the sky. There aren't many lights lining the rows of blocks but there are enough to spot groups of men still working late into the night. They all look the same for the most part: thin as tree branches, lanky like puppets dangling from string, and quiet. They're quiet as if they aren't humans who struggle to move heavy objects or exert the energy they don't have, or hold in their emotions when they want to cry their hearts out like the sky.

Some have hair, others don't. I spot a lighter color of brown, curling into one barrel wave before flipping up at his temple. That's Danner. It's him. I clench the newspaper tighter within my grip and hug it against my chest. He spots me for the first time since he survived the deadly experiment. I didn't know where they'd sent him next, but Dietrich promised me he would remain here and be kept out of additional experiments. I wasn't convinced the man was capable of keeping a promise.

Is he here at this time every night? If so, I could do something. I could help him somehow. With a glance down at the newspaper rolled up in my hand, I'm struck with an idea—a dangerous one, but one that could help him and the others. I could hide something or somethings in here. I wish I had something to leave tonight, but I have to warn him that I'll be back and hope he'll somehow figure out there will be something in the newspaper next time.

With Danner's momentary attention, I curl the corner of my lip ever so slightly, careful not to be seen by the guard but noticeable enough for Danner to grasp the hint. I push the cuff of my coat up to check my wristwatch. I nod once and glance at him again then tap the newspaper against my opposite hand. The gesture might make no sense to anyone, but the newspaper...it's all I have to conceal things, anything he or the others might need.

Danner glances away, takes in a breath and nods, repeating my gesture.

"Is it okay if I just toss this in the rubbish?" I ask the guard as we pass a half-filled bucket.

"Yes, that's fine," he says.

I drop it into the bin from high enough that the papers fan down the sides, making a swooshing noise.

"My timings have been a bit staggered these last two weeks, but this hour seems to work best for my schedule, so will you be available to escort me at this time going forward?" I ask the guard.

"Yes, Frau Berger. Not a problem."

From the corner of my eye, I see another man in a prisoner

uniform elbow Danner in the side, both silently laughing. Once more, Danner glances in my direction as I shift direction toward the gates. It takes everything I have not to break into a full smile, but this passing moment is all I need to get me through to tomorrow.

It was hard to predict if Danner would go fishing for the newspaper the nights following the first sighting between us, but I see him each night now, lugging metal bins at the same time in the same place. Sometimes, when his eyes graze mine, he places a hand on his stomach and pulls the corner of his lips up into his cheek.

Tonight, he takes a second longer to scan past me. I do what I can to keep my focus set ahead while making sure not to miss a second of whatever he may try to tell me. He presses his hand to his heart and sucks in a breath. Pain burns through my chest, wanting nothing more to stop the charades and run over to him and hug him with all my might, but the consequence will be deadly. We are deadly to each other.

All I can do is leave him food concealed in a rubber-band wrapped newspaper. Whatever I can roll in between the pages, whether it be cheese, bologna, or thinly sliced bread, I put in as much as I can. It isn't enough to sustain his life, but it's more than what he's trying to survive off. I would give him more if I could, but as always and like everything else, it's a risk and I wasn't sure if he was receiving the scraps until last week. One fateful rainy night when I was walking out from between the iron gates, I twisted to close my umbrella away from the guard so I wouldn't splash him. That's when I spotted Danner taking the trash receptacle that I'd just dropped the newspaper in. He knew. He was bringing it up to the line of other men dragging bins. The relief I felt that night, it was euphoric. I knew he was getting what I was leaving for him, and for that I'll keep this up for as long as I can.

In response to his simple gesture, I place my hand against my chest and force out a small cough, masking the true meaning behind my touch. Now that I'm confident he's receiving what I leave behind, I slipped a note in with the food the other night, just so he knows what I'm thinking.

My feet feel like they're walking over air as I reach the perched open gate. Until tomorrow...

"Have a pleasant night, Frau Berger," the guard says, the only exchange following his simple greeting when I arrived.

"You as well," I reply, keeping my tone even, lacking any hint of emotion. I despise the thought that any of the guards here think I might share a similar hatred for human life, but the act is all I can give to offer Danner the slightest hope of surviving.

My palms slip on the steering wheel as I take the familiar streets back home, wondering how Otto will greet me this evening. With the look he gave me before I left, I'm afraid of what has been stirring in his head all night. The brakes squeal as I come to a stop in front of our house, noting the faint glow from a light toward the back—either his office or the kitchen. I tuck my hair tightly behind my ears, feeling the curls bounce against my shoulders as I make my way up the path and to the front door. My heart races like a clock running out of time and something in my stomach tells me I might be better off sleeping in the car tonight.

I twist the doorknob but lose my grip as the door flies open. "You're so punctual," Otto says, "arriving home at the same time every night."

I don't think it's been the same time every night, but within the hour, yes. "I'm a creature of habit, I suppose," I say, walking in and unbuttoning my coat.

"You are, indeed," he utters. "You don't have your books."

I think about the front bench of the car, knowing my purse was the only thing resting there when I got out.

"Oh, I must have left them in the car. I can grab them before you leave in the morning," I say, spinning around to hang up my coat on the rack.

"Actually, Ingrid stopped by about a half hour ago with them. She said her daughter found them at a table in the library and saw your name written inside the front cover. They're on the kitchen table."

He knows I left the library more than a half hour ago, and the drive hardly takes five minutes.

"That explains why I forgot them. I went to the restroom and then went to look for an additional book I needed. I must have searched the medical research shelves a dozen times because this book was supposedly available to borrow, but I couldn't find it. I got so frustrated that I went back to my table, grabbed my coat and purse then left. I can't believe leaving my books behind didn't cross my mind for even a second. I never do that."

Otto's shoulders lower and he tilts his head to the side, a hint of relief on his face. "Darling, I think you're studying too hard. If you cram all this knowledge into your head at once, you won't retain it all later."

"I know. You're right. I'm just eager to get back to my classes."

Otto leans forward for a kiss and circles his thumb along my cheekbone. "I'm proud of you. You never give up, and that's what I love most about you."

He wouldn't be proud of me if he knew the truth, he would feel deceived. It's only a matter of time until he can no longer convince himself to believe the words I tell him, and I fear the outcome. I don't know how long it will be before the storm clouds hanging over us burst into a flood that might just drown us.

THIRTY-SEVEN

DANNER

Dachau, Germany

I climb up to the top tier of the bunks in my block, holding the rolled-up newspaper tightly beneath my arm. "Hans, I've got more," I whisper.

"Am I truly hearing these words?" Hans utters, shimmying around to face me. I hold the paper out to him so he can smell the mouth-watering aroma of sliced beef.

"I've died and this is heaven," Hans says.

"Eli, wake up," I say, shaking the old man's shoulder. He doesn't stir right away, so I give him a moment.

I unravel the newspaper beneath my wool blanket, knowing I don't have enough to share with anyone other than Hans, Eli, and Fred.

"Have you seen that guard who looks like he's seen masses of goblins every day? You know, the one who's always sweating and shaking when giving orders?"

"Yeah, I think I know who you mean. He's by the second watch tower most afternoons, right?"

"That's him," Hans says. "He's been the one delivering

letters to me over the last year, but I hadn't seen him for months until these last few days. He had a letter for me today, but said it might be the last for a while. He told me I could find Matilda at The Shop of Wonders in town. He said he couldn't tell me anything more and he was sorry for that."

"What do you think that means?" I ask, eager to find a reason to hope of getting out of this place.

"I wish I knew," Hans said. "The look in his eyes didn't paint a good picture, but to know that he's seen Matilda, she's still okay, and had a good enough reason to give me her location...it has to mean something." It could mean many things, things that I might try to avoid thinking, but all we have is the idea of possibility and I won't take that from him.

I split the food beneath the blanket and pass Hans his share, turning back to Eli to give him his. I give him another nudge, but he doesn't flinch.

"Has he just gone to sleep?" I ask Hans.

"I think so, but he was already there when I got back from labor duty."

I shake Eli a bit harder and he flops from his side onto his back. His eyes are closed, his mouth open, and his face pale— not necessarily unusual for when he's asleep. "Eli," I call out again.

Hans dives over my bunk and shoves Eli harder than I did. "Wake up, old man," he says, his voice croaking. "Come on, wake up. I have more old-man jokes. Don't you want to hear them?"

I stare at his neck, wishing there was more light filling the area here, but there isn't enough to make out fine details like the sight of a pulse. I reach my hand over, clenching my fist before stretching out two fingers, and place them over his carotid artery beneath the shadows of his chin. My entire body shivers as I move my fingers around, hoping I wasn't lucky enough to find his pulse at the first try, but his skin is cold—too cold.

My head shakes from side to side before I can find the words.

"No...he can't be gone. He's fine. He's fine."

I rock back and forth, keeping my hand against his neck. I told myself we'd all get out of here together or none of us at all. Now I know how this will end.

"Papa!" Hans shouts. "No, you can't leave me again."

I grab Hans' shoulder as he tugs at his ears. "Papa?"

Hans curls his hands into fists and presses them against his ears. "He's been like a father to me since I arrived. I lost my father. I lost him. I can't lose Eli, too," he cries.

"Me too," I say, pulling him into my arms. "Me too." I clench my eyes, expecting tears to fall down my cheeks, but nothing comes—just the ache in my chest. We see people fall to their death every day, but we hold on to each other as if we're the keepers of one another's last breaths.

Eli has done nothing but gives us fatherly advice, words of wisdom we may need if we somehow survive the odds here. A familiar, comforting face. I didn't think—I don't know why I didn't think—anything could happen to him.

"I'm so sorry," I tell Hans, choking on my words.

"We needed him. He needed us. He had nothing outside these gates. He already lost his wife. This isn't fair. It's not fair!"

I choke back the sobs threatening to burst from my chest as the tears finally slide silently down my cheeks. We all try to avoid the truth of how slight the chances are of walking out of here, and how much less of a chance we have at finding anything we left behind. We are free-falling between heaven and hell and I'm not sure there's a stop anywhere in between.

THIRTY-EIGHT

DANNER

ONE YEAR AGO, FEBRUARY 1942

Munich, Germany

Everyone will be there, celebrating a wedding that has been moved forward an entire year for reasons no one seems to know.

In this house alone, I've heard thoughts of:

"Maybe she's with child..."

"Could be the war..."

"Maybe he's joining the service..."

I'd rather not think too deeply into there being a reason other than convenience. Regardless of it all, there's a celebration of love amid a war. It seems paradoxical, unlike anything Emilie would agree to. However, I no longer know the Emilie I grew up with, loved, and left behind.

"Are you sure you don't want to join us?" Felix asks, still not understanding my desire to remain in the shadows here at home. I've spent too much time trying to avoid everyone to show up at a wedding unannounced.

"I'm sure but thank you. I hope you all have a good time. Don't forget not to mention me, all right?"

"I know," he says, straightening his tie. "We'll be back soon."

Herr and Frau Weber are already waiting in the car for Felix. They asked me the same question, making sure I hadn't changed my mind about revealing my presence in this anti-Jewish city. I'm bitter. It's unlike me to be so miserable.

I'd be worse off sitting in a church watching Emilie confess her love to Otto for all eternity. Of course, I was the one who made her promise to do what she's doing today.

I should be there.

I should have told her I was home.

She should know I've been searching for Papa over the last two months that I've been back in Munich, and without an inkling of hope. She would care. She would listen. She might have had advice that could minimize my misery a hair. If that had happened—if I'd made different decisions, I would have been there for her today, to support her, because that's what love is.

I stroll across the drape-darkened house, into the kitchen to find the wedding invitation. My stomach tenses at the sight of Otto's name where I wish mine would be, but I force my eyes to scan down the formal words until I spot the name of the church. It isn't far from here.

I glance down at my borrowed clothes, knowing my options are limited but at least I'm in all dark colors so I won't stand out. With a coat, scarf, hat, and gloves, I step out into the raw temperatures, the wind hitting me like a bat to the face. A February wedding is another part of this that has me scratching my head. Emilie loves the summer, flowers in full bloom, greenery, warmth, the sun high in the sky. Not this.

The walk feels much longer than I remember it being. I would always pass this church on the way to the local butcher shop, but it was condemned due to being owned by a Jewish family shortly before we were sent to Poland.

I tuck my head down as usual, keeping to myself like a lurking shadow of the boy who used to live here. The church bells ring, announcing the noon hour, and the start time for the ceremony. Everyone must already be inside, which is what I prefer. I've only been inside this church once, when Emilie's grandfather passed away about ten years ago. I remember there being two sets of doors, so I won't be walking into the service straight from outside. I believe there were interior side entrances too, which would be best.

I open the large wooden door, feeling the warmth from inside pull me in. I see flower petals scattered along the floor and hear a minister define the value of a marital bond, his voice echoing along the high domed ceiling on the other side of the doors I'm staring at. There's another door down to the right, so I carefully pull it open, just enough to see where the door leads. No one is sitting in the last row. I duck in and move along the chairs until I'm seated behind a tall man just in front. I peek down the side of the man's head, spotting Emilie donned in white ruffles and lace, with a veil as long as her dress. I can't see her face. If I did, I might lose all desire to be here.

Otto is sharply dressed in a black suit, his hair shorter than I remember, and a rose pinned to his lapel. His cheeks are nearly the same color as the flower, but I suppose mine would be too if I was standing where he is.

I haven't heard much the minister has said but I clearly hear: "Should anyone here today know of a reason why this couple should not be joined in holy matrimony, speak now, or forever hold your peace."

I'm not sure why I'm staring directly at Otto, but in what feels like a long second, he catches my gaze. His head falls slightly to the side as a look of recognition dashes over his features. I hold my index finger up to my lips and shake my head. I'm not sure he understands that I'm silently pleading that he doesn't tell her I'm here, but I'm sure he won't want to tell her anyway.

The minister continues and I block the rest of his words out because I came here for her, to silently do the right thing. I can live with that. The minister's voice grows louder, showing a formal celebration of the newlyweds, so I take the moment to slip back out the doors and hurry back to the Webers' house before anyone sees me. Not once did I see Emilie's face or have the chance to decipher whether she was truly happy. I must tell myself she is, because that's all I want for her. Even if I feel as though my heart just shattered into a thousand tiny pieces.

THIRTY-NINE

EMILIE

Dachau, Germany

I should have known what usually follows a threat or bribe. Once a person knows they can claim another as a puppet, boundaries cease to exist. Dietrich has approached me monthly for the last year and a half since showing up at my doorstep the morning Otto was sent to his new place of employment—when we made our dangerous deal to write up his report on the hypothermia testing. Then he came to me with new studies he was conducting, ones I hadn't witnessed. He wanted me to write up the reports in the same format I wrote the original. It was the only way to keep our deal of ensuring Danner remains safe. I ask for proof that Danner is still alive, so he doesn't become suspicious of the other ways I'm helping him and others, and he shows me a list of numbers still living in his assigned barrack.

I didn't know how many research studies there could be, but they seem to be never-ending. My only benefit to him was my ability to transcribe data better than the few who remain on his team. While it isn't something I've strived for, it's a form of control whereby I can muddle data and paint a perfect portrait for the results being sought. The strategy of tweaking data is nerve-wracking, dangerous, and the only thing keeping many of the subjects in Dachau alive. That part, Dietrich isn't aware of. If I can save some of those innocent people, I'll continue acting loyal with the hope I'm gaining more from this than he is.

My objective in life has moved on from completing my nursing classes to making every attempt possible to protect the innocent and check on Danner whenever possible. Otto's questions have tapered off. We've settled into our routine of coming and going, ships passing in the night. Every time we pass one another, I wonder if he questions what I'm truly doing. Though I've become proficient at sneaking around, I don't feel any less deceitful when I come home each night. Of course, I'm not being unfaithful, and I still conduct all my wifely duties, but that façade isn't for me, it's for him—and for Danner.

Another night, the same time, same location, one of four guards I've come to know greets me at the window of my car. "Good evening, Frau Berger." My door opens and I step out, a newspaper pinned beneath my arm and my purse dangling from my right hand.

"It was a good evening, wasn't it?"

My eyes widen as I turn toward the second voice, and I can't manage to take in a breath when I find Otto standing behind our car, his bicycle by his side.

Eight months have passed since his last obvious suspicion that I was doing something other than studying at the library. I didn't expect so much time to pass before it would happen again. Even knowing this great possibility, I continued doing what I was asked to in return for the promised favor from Dietrich. The thought of what I would say to Otto in this moment has kept me awake many nights, leaving me restless in the morning without a clear thought as to what I would say, here, now. I was living one day at a time because that's what we're all doing in this war—surviving, minute by minute.

I can see him clearly, beneath the bright watchtower light. Each new age line earned over the last couple of years rests in the shadows of the sharp edges above his cheekbones and forehead. He doesn't blink, just stares.

"You're here to see him, aren't you?" Otto asks.

"To see who?" I ask, doing my best to play the part of an ignorant woman, even if only for the sake of the guard who doesn't need to know any of our personal business.

"What the hell are you doing here, Emilie?" Otto grunts.

"Perhaps I should be asking you the same question," I reply, arching my brows despite crumbling into a million pieces beneath my skin.

"Frau Berger," the guard interrupts, "we can reconvene at another time."

"What is that supposed to mean?" Otto snaps at the man. "What do you know that I don't? Huh?"

"I know nothing, Herr Berger. I'm not privy to information that goes beyond these gates."

"But you are," Otto says, staring me straight in the eyes.

"Let's go home and finish our discussion there," I suggest, hopefully buying myself a few minutes to formulate a reason for being here at this hour.

"I would much rather follow you into Dachau to see what it is you do every night when you claim to be at the library." This guard has already heard far too much.

"Yes, thank you. I'll follow up at another time," I tell the man, and reach for the car door.

My heart shudders between each breath, leaving me weak in the driver's seat as I wait to see what Otto does next. I close my eyes and grip my gloved hands around the wheel as the guard closes my door. The passenger side door opens, and I peek out through squinting eyes, to find Otto dropping into the seat and slamming the car door shut. The scent of whiskey fills the car, the liquor that makes him angry. He knows as well as I do what happens to him after only two glasses. He can't control anything that comes out of his mouth, and whatever he has been thinking for however long he's kept it inside, will be spoken, loud and clear.

The car ride home is unsurprisingly quiet as he refuels his anger. It isn't until the front door closes us inside our house that I see he's managed to take the *Der Stürmer* newspaper from my possession while I was driving.

"You've been going to see Danner, haven't you?" he asks, his voice oddly calm considering the raging glint in his eyes. He rolls up the newspaper and shoves the tube into his back pocket.

"I haven't seen Danner," I say, lying through my teeth. "I'm not even sure he's still alive." The thought burns through me, thankful I don't have to truthfully feel that way.

Otto tears his coat off and throws it to the ground, the buttons clapping all at once against the wooden floor.

"God dammit, Emilie. I'm not playing this game with you. Tell me why the hell you were at the gates of Dachau."

"I've been sworn to secrecy," I reply. There's no way of getting out of Otto's way tonight. My only hope is honesty and to make him see life from my eyes, which may be impossible after living and working on the same side as the world's enemy.

"Sworn?" he asks, his voice a hair softer.

"Does the word 'threatened' make you feel better?"

Otto grits his teeth and pinches his hands around his neck. "Who threatened you?"

I tug at the fingertips of my leather gloves, sliding each one off my hand before placing them down neatly on the small entryway table. "Someone you made a part of our lives," I say, moving to the buttons on my coat. I refuse to react the way he'd like me to because I wouldn't be in this situation right now if it weren't for the decisions he'd made, and the secrets he'd kept.

Otto releases his hands from his neck as I hang up my coat and slip off my shoes. He tilts his head to the side as an idea or realization seems to strike him. "Dietrich?"

"Of course. Who else would do such a thing to me?"

Otto picks at his bottom lip, squinting past my shoulder, but the question isn't something he should be too surprised about.

I take a few steps toward Otto, forcing him to look at me instead of past me. "When did your uncle join the SS? Was it before or after we got married?"

I know the answer to this question now, having access to Dietrich's biography inserted at the bottom of his memorandums. Otto must be aware of such a significant year in this timeline.

"I—I don't know...It was after...I only knew he was forming a team of medical professionals to assist him in his research to cure cancer. His connection with the Luftwaffe had nothing to do with the regime," Otto says. It's easy to say stuff like that when everything in this country is so carefully swept under the rug, but it's easy to see our military forces have been taken over. There's nothing left of us now. There's no hope.

I unclasp my earrings one by one and clutch them in my hand, allowing one of the posts to pierce into the flesh of my palm. "Did you ever question how easily Dietrich let you off the hook?"

"No because we agreed to remain members of his team but not take part in what he was conducting. That was to protect you. And all this time, you've been jeopardizing yourself and me. Our families. And for what?"

He pulls the rolled newspaper out of his back pocket and holds it up. "*Der Stürmer*? You're reading Nazi propaganda now? We've been married two years. Two years, this week, in fact, and stupidly, I thought we were going to make it through all this together. I'm wrong, though, aren't I?"

"No," I say. "That isn't what it seems, which you of all

people in this world should understand quite well." As hard as I'm trying to keep myself together so I don't shatter and fall to my knees for forgiveness after going against my morals and lying to my husband, all I can do is pray that he doesn't unravel that newspaper.

"What has Dietrich threatened you with?" he asks, slapping his free hand against the newspaper. "What?"

I stare at the newspaper, wondering if there will come a time when I'm the newspaper, rolled up, swung around, and slapped. Would Otto become that person? After all this time, I still don't know what makes a human become a monster like so many have become here. I still feel every bit of pain for the suffering, especially when I step through those gates, greeted with cries, moans, and bodies hitting the inside of walls. The putrid scents that fill the sick bay, so strong they can't be concealed with ammonia. I've walked past dead bodies strewn like pieces of rubbish against the exterior of a block, presumably left there until they are carted away in the daylight hours. I've risked everything in my life because I know what is at stake.

"Danner's life."

Otto huffs through exasperation and drops the newspaper to the ground. He was holding it so tightly, he didn't stretch the rubber band, and I'm thankful for that. "I should have known Dietrich would use him as a weapon."

I want to lunge for the paper and remove it from his sight, but I know better than to raise another question right now, except one. There's one question I must ask him...

"Well, what's Danner's life worth to you?"

He chuckles against a grimace of discomfort. "Jesus, Emi, how am I supposed to answer that?"

I look up at Otto as tears burn behind my eyes. "You just did."

FORTY

EMILIE

Dachau, Germany

The agreement between a man and his wife should be solid enough to trust, even after both parties have been neglectful. I'm not sure Otto and I will ever see eye-to-eye when it comes to our agendas for survival in this cold time, but the options for us are limited. He wouldn't jeopardize my safety for the sake of Danner, and I'm supposed to understand this notion.

My response was that Dietrich didn't want him to know of my involvement because he and his father came to an agreement, one that excluded my assistance, kept Dietrich safe with his team still appearing intact, even though neither Otto nor his father would have to be physically involved in his efforts anymore. If Otto were to tell his father I've been involved in writing reports being sent to Himmler, Herr Berger may see the opportunity to renege on their agreement, ultimately creating a spotlight over Dietrich's head from high command. The outcome could be Dietrich's head on a platter and the loss of my opportunity to help Danner and the others suffering within the camp walls. Therefore, nothing can change, and Otto has to accept our situation for what it is—blackmail.

Despite anger and resentment towards me for keeping this information from him, Otto has promised to keep quiet in the hope that it will keep us safe. It's been a month now and though the plan sounded simple at the time, I've come to realize it was much easier keeping the secret to myself than ensuring Otto and I had stories that lined up for whoever else we encounter. We've dodged dinner invitations from neighbors and our parents, becoming loners in our house, except for work. I keep asking myself whose fault this is, but when I draw the line back to the beginning, I can only believe Otto's word, that he didn't know what trap he was stepping into, which puts us on the same page, with the same problem, facing the same fears.

I sprinkle more flour over the ball of yeast I've been kneading and continue to stare out the window in a trance, watching leaf covered branches sway along with a gentle breeze. The moments I'm cooking or baking are the only tranquil slices of time I have during my day.

A sudden knock on the kitchen window startles me into tossing a storm of flour and clutching my chest. I only saw the blur of a clenched fist before gasping for air, but now I see Ingrid's face, her sharp pointed eyebrows, and pursed lips. "Open the door, Emilie," she demands.

I knew my avoidance would only last so long, but I've also run out of excuses and ignoring the relentless rings from the doorbell has landed me here, covered in flour.

I spin around, frazzled, looking for the dishrag pinned beneath the flour jar. While making my way to the front door, I dust myself off and tell myself to say that we've just been busy and I've been studying to prepare for my return to classes, which must seem like a joke at this point with how much time has passed since I began studying in the library at night.

Studying. It's my only motive for hiding indoors.

I open the door, still cleaning myself off. "You scared me half to death, you know," I say.

"Good. Now, you know how Helga, Ursula, and I have been feeling about how distant you and Otto have been. Something is clearly wrong, or one of us did something to upset you, and we need to know."

I'm not surprised Ingrid is the one to confront me. The other two seem to have more understanding for privacy.

She steps in, forcing me to take a step back.

"I apologize for causing any worry, but that wasn't my intention. Otto and I have just been so busy and quite frankly, exhausted."

Her gaze drifts down to my stomach, and I'd like to tell her she can just stop looking there every time we see each other because it isn't happening, not now.

"No, I'm not pregnant," I utter.

"Okay, then what is it?"

"I told you; I've been studying every night so I can return to my classes."

Ingrid presses her hands to her hips and tosses her head back. "Did we offend you? Just tell me, I can handle it...Things haven't been right since that dinner event and that soldier said all those awful things about you." Ingrid places her hand on my shoulder, her nails clawing at my skin. "Emilie, are you having an affair?"

I pull away from her grip. "No, Ingrid, I'm not. If you're worried that I've been offended by something you've said, why would you suggest something like that?"

She shrugs. "You leave the house every night. We've all noticed."

"To go study at the library," I continue.

"Ingrid's eldest daughter, Marie, has been going to the library these last couple of weeks and I asked her if she ran into you. She said the library was empty aside from herself and another couple of students."

With the front door still open, I see and hear our car pull up and come to a sudden stop. Otto jumps out and races to the door. He's never been home at this hour of the day.

"Goodness, I hope everything is okay," Ingrid says, pressing her fingers to her lips.

"Ingrid, hello," Otto says, breathlessly.

"Is everything okay, dear?" I ask him. His gaze darts between my face and Ingrid's. "Yes, yes. I forgot to take my lunch this morning and wanted to come by for it quickly."

"You don't hand him his lunch on the way out the door?" Ingrid asks.

Otto shuffles his weight from one foot to the other. "Ingrid, would you mind if I have a moment with my wife?"

"Oh," she says, touching her fingers to her chest. "I'm so sorry. I beg your pardon. I'll just see my way out. I was worried about the two of you, so I—"

"I appreciate your concern, but there's no reason to worry." Otto opens the door wider, re-enforcing his request. All the while I worry what has him so wound up. He wasn't missing his lunch. I *did* hand it to him as he walked out the door this morning.

Ingrid, wide-eyed, and probably offended, walks stiffly out the front door before Otto closes us inside.

"What is it?" I ask him, noticing he's pale, and the whites of his eyes are stained red.

"Something isn't right. I've been light-headed and cold to the bone. I took my temperature in the sick bay, and I have a high fever."

I take him by the arm and bring him into the living room to sit him down on the sofa. "It could be influenza," I tell him, placing the back of my hand on his head. He certainly does have a high fever. "Did it all come on at once?"

He leans back into the sofa and stares through the coffee table as if he's trying to recall when these symptoms began. "I suppose I felt a bit weak this morning, but I was fine after a while. A dizzy spell hit me just an hour ago and then the chill."

"I'm sure it's nothing. You work in a hospital. You're bound to pick up germs. I'll make you tea and get a cool compress for your head."

"I've never felt so awful before," he says as I walk out of the room.

I run the teakettle under the faucet, filling it halfway before placing it down on the stove top and igniting the burner.

"Emi, what if it's something contagious?"

He's right. "Don't worry, just close your eyes and try to relax. Everything will be okay." The words just emerge on their own, a side-effect of having a nurse's mindset.

I pull a handkerchief from my pocket to cover my mouth and nose and return with a rag I ran under the faucet. I'm quick and it's been less than two minutes, but he seems to have fallen asleep. I place the compress over his forehead and stack the decorative pillows by his side to keep him from getting a neck ache. He could have been exposed to anything at any given time while working at the field hospital.

I sit down beside him on the sofa and hold the handkerchief over my face and the compress on his forehead. The innocence of his panic isn't something I've seen in him for longer than I can remember.

* * *

I've been tending to Otto for days, working for Dietrich at home and making my trips to Dachau to drop off Dietrich's paperwork. While slipping the folder into his desk drawer the other night, I came across half a bottle of penicillin and swiped it to give to Otto in case he has an infection. My assumption is that he might have contracted streptococcus, but he hasn't complained of a sore throat. Still, even after several doses of penicillin working through his system, there hasn't been much of a change. I have him resting in bed, trying to give him as much liquid as I can, but he's been refusing to eat, saying he's not hungry. None of this makes sense. What kind of nurse am I if I can't help my own husband? With all the studying I'd done and should have been doing, I feel as though I should be better at diagnosing him, but the list of possibilities is beginning to grow, rather than shrink.

"I'm so sorry for keeping you up all night," he mumbles, reaching his hand out. I lean toward him from the chair I've settled next to his bed side and take his hand, first spotting his wedding band overlapping mine. While shifting my gaze to his eyes, I notice a pink welt forming along his wrist. I push up the sleeve of his pajamas, finding more pink welts and small bumps scattered between.

"What is it?" he asks, focusing on the expression I didn't hide well.

"You have a rash. Does it itch?"

"Now that you mention it, I have been itchy."

"Don't scratch any of it," I tell him, dropping his hand to run downstairs. "I'll get ointment."

"Emi, it's okay. It's just a rash," he says, calling after me.

I make my way into Otto's office then fall to my knees in front of the bookshelf full of medical textbooks. I pull out several and flip through the pages until I reach the diagnosis of rashes, finding several different variations to compare his to.

Just as I'm tracing my finger down the center of the text, there's a knock at the door. I'm beginning to hate that godawful sound. Ingrid has come back three times since Otto asked her to leave. She's wanted to extend an apology for her behavior, which I accepted and told her was unnecessary. She heard Otto moving around upstairs so I had to tell her he's ill, but likely with a case of influenza. She then returned with soup, then dumplings.

I open the door, feeling as though I just ran up and down the stairs a dozen times. "Ingrid, now isn't—"

Instead, I find Dietrich standing in front of me. I would much prefer Ingrid over him.

"I'm here to check on Otto. He must be quite sick if you made the decision to steal a bottle of penicillin from my desk drawer. At least, I assume he's the one who's sick, since you appear perfectly healthy."

"Yes, he is," I say, running my fingers through my knotted hair. "Otto is sick with symptoms of influenza and a fever, but I've just spotted a rash that I'm trying—" I can't believe I'm explaining anything to this man. I would like nothing more than to kick him all the way to the curb. "I have everything under control. He'll be back on his feet in no time," I say hastily, still gripping the doorknob in my hand. "I'll give you money for the penicillin I stole."

He repeats my words in a quiet mutter before replying. "A rash?" he questions.

"Yes," I reply.

"*Yes...* Good God. I was afraid it was serious," he says. "Where is he? Upstairs in bed?"

More than anything in this world, I hate that Dietrich is the only certified doctor that either of us know. I wouldn't trust him if my life depended on it, and I don't think he knows much more than I do with my year of nursing classes and self-studying.

"Yes."

He rushes past me and storms up the stairs. I close the door and follow him, worried about what he'll say or ask Otto, who isn't thinking too clearly at the moment. I find him inspecting the rash on Otto's arm.

"Did you touch his rash?"

"No, and I had my face covered until today in case he had been contagious, but he's been taking the penicillin for three days now." I lift his shirt sleeve.

"*No...* That's odd," he says.

"What's odd? What is it?" I shout, demanding a clearer answer.

"*What is it?* We only see rheumatic fever in children, but this jagged rash is most definitely a common symptom. It's good you started him on penicillin, but unfortunately with this rash, it means the strep has already spread to other parts of his body."

"I had rheumatic fever as a child too," Otto says, coughing against his words.

"*As a child...*" Dietrich repeats to himself. "Making you more susceptible as an adult."

"It can affect the heart and liver sometimes. I had a sore throat a few weeks back—it must have been strep throat," Otto says.

He knew he was susceptible and surely knows strep throat is the most common precursor to rheumatic fever, but ignored his health for the sake of work. I can't wrap my head around the logic.

"Why would you ignore symptoms like that?" I ask, perplexed.

"I—I don't know. I guess I was too busy to concern myself over a silly sore throat. The pain subsided and I didn't think anything of it again."

"Shouldn't the penicillin be working by now?" I question, knowing it should.

There must be something else wrong. Something serious.

FORTY-ONE

EMILIE

Dachau, Germany

For the last six weeks I've watched my husband lie in our bed, groaning from joint pain, chronic headaches, and weakness that won't allow him to get out of bed on his own. I took him to the hospital when we figured it might be rheumatic fever, but every hospital was overfilled, understaffed, and facing far worse issues. We were sent home with simple instructions to keep Otto hydrated and off his feet until the symptoms subsided. Like a cruel joke, I've been nothing more than his bedside nurse, doing as instructed and keeping him fed as well as I can. At this point, I'm fearful of the complications that have come about from whatever infection he must have let linger. He should be showing improvement by now. He should be better.

Our families are always here, trying to help, making my house a central station for non-stop visitors. It is late afternoon every day when the abdominal pains grow to an intensity that sends him into tears. I'm not sure I've read anywhere that stomach pains are a symptom of rheumatic fever, if that's even what he has. Aspirin hardly takes the edge off, and I've tried every other natural remedy I could think of. I'm left with simply waiting to see how he progresses because there's no way of knowing. I've only managed to slip out of the house once or twice a week at night since Otto got sick. I wouldn't be able to explain leaving the house while either of our parents is here. I've done what I can to ensure Dietrich's paperwork delivery as well as supplies for Danner within the rolled up newspaper continue smoothly. It doesn't feel like enough. Nothing I'm doing feels like it's enough to keep anyone alive and well.

"I brought you some tea," Mama says, walking in as Otto rolls into the fetal position, groaning for help. I take the cup from her hand and take a small sip. "Go get fresh air. I'll sit here with him."

I shake my head. "It's okay. He's embarrassed to be seen this way. I don't want to leave him like this." Frau Berger was also picking up new tea leaves she heard about. There's a kind of beneficial bacteria that helps heal inflammation. Everyone has been trying to find a way to help him, but nothing works.

"How is the patient today?" Dietrich shouts, stomping up the stairs. He must have heard the moans and groans from outside the front door. There's no reason to ask. "Good after-noon, family." He greets us with a conniving grin. I'd like to tear off his face. "I have new medication I'm going to give Otto. It might do the trick."

"What medication? He's already been on two rounds of penicillin?" Mama asks, pressing her hand to her chest.

"Oh, my apologies. In some cases of rheumatic fever, internal inflammation can cause blood vessel walls to narrow, thus blocking his blood flow to vital organs. This condition can cause many of the symptoms he's presenting at the moment. I'm going to give him a dose of chloroquine phosphate to see if that helps him out at all."

Mama looks over at me because I don't think she under-stood much of what Dietrich just said.

"Chloroquine can be harsh on the stomach. I'm afraid that will cause him more pain," I argue.

"*Chloroquine can be harsh on the stomach,*" he repeats. "Yes, yes. The benefits outweigh the side effects. If we can reduce the inflammation, all issues will be solved."

The front door slams from down below and another set of feet charges up the stairs, followed by two more. Papa, Herr and Frau Berger all jolt into the room together, panic-stricken and soaked in sweat.

"Air raids are inbound. We need to get him downstairs," Herr Berger states. He and Papa move to Otto's side, both cradling him as they work together to move him off the bed. Otto's body appears locked in a frozen state of pain, stiff and tangled.

"Ladies, downstairs right away," Papa shouts between ragged breaths.

Dietrich runs out before the three of us women, unsurprisingly. We're all making such a racket that I don't hear any hint of a storm coming toward us, but I won't question their knowledge.

This house has so many windows, I'm not sure where they think might be a safe sheltering spot, but when we reach the bottom floor and scan the area, we find them cramming into the utility room where I have lines of laundry hanging. There's a back door but no windows.

I pull bulky clothes from the line to cushion a spot for Otto to lie down. I'm not sure much of anything will help his pain now, but a cold hard floor will only make it worse.

"Who is it? Who is attacking us?" Dietrich shouts.

"The Americans," Herr Berger says.

"*The Americans,*" Dietrich echoes. "Are we trying to stop them?" His question comes with haste as if Herr Berger would have that level of information. Dietrich is the one who solidly belongs to the SS. If he wasn't made aware before the radio broadcasted the news, I'm not sure how much information is available.

"Yes, the Luftwaffe is pushing against them, of course," Herr Berger says.

"We should be far enough away but it's best to take precaution," Papa says.

Though my mind is running rampant with fear and concerns for everyone's well-being, Dachau seems to have been purposely hidden away from the city for a reason. Therefore, Papa is likely correct about his assumptions.

"Did you warn the others?" I ask. "Gerty's parents? And Felix's?"

"Yes, yes, of course. We warned everyone to get out of the city if they could," Papa says.

Once the commotion settles, our focus solely returns to Otto, who is in the process of being injected. "Wait!" I shout at Dietrich.

"*Wait!* You must listen. This will help him. He's my nephew. I don't want anything to happen to him, my dear," Dietrich says, calm as he always is when the world around him is in a panic.

"You said you've been doing everything you can these several weeks," Herr Berger says to his brother. "He hasn't shown any sign of improvement. Is there something you aren't telling us? Because if so, I suggest you say it now." Herr Berger's face is beet red, and his veins are pulsating at his temples. I've never seen or heard this level of anger from Herr Berger before.

"Hasn't shown any signs of improvement," Dietrich mutters. "There's no official cure for rheumatic fever. I've told you this. Each patient reacts differently. Some have milder cases than others. Then, there are some who end up with complications from the initial manifestations, which is what I'm trying to resolve with the chloroquine phosphate."

"Is he going to die?" Frau Berger asks, her voice high-pitched, caught in her throat.

"No," I reply before Dietrich does. "No, he's not going to die."

Dietrich's gaze fixates on mine and though I want to look away, I feel frozen, stuck, being forced to accept a truth I'm not ready to come to terms with.

The room becomes quiet after the last round of ramblings, and Otto has fallen asleep, likely as a result of the injection. I watch his chest move up and down at an even pace and try to focus on the moment instead of what may or may not happen.

Papa leaves the utility room and steps into Otto's office down the hall before returning with the radio he keeps on his desk. He turns the power dial, finding nothing but static. I know Otto keeps the radio on one frequency but depending on where the broadcast is coming from, we may have to find another source. It takes Papa a couple of minutes before finding a broadcast clear enough to make out.

...under fire. Airfields and manufacturing facilities from Friedrichshafen to Leipheim have been hit. The German Luftwaffe is in flight on the defense from the Swiss border to Stuttgart and Munich. With the head-on, heavy artillery battle, it is recommended to take cover, get to low ground, and move away from the center of cities, airfields, and manufacturing facilities immediately.

Once Papa turns down the radio, the distant alarm of sirens grows louder outside. Jets fly overhead, leaving us with nothing more than a zing following in the path of their engines. The floors vibrate, sometimes mildly, other times more aggressively, and the screams of speeding engines sound much closer than they are, but I can't convince myself we aren't within a target zone. What if someone is aiming at Dachau? Does Danner know to take cover? I don't know if there's somewhere to hide there. After all he's survived, he could be sitting beneath a falling bomb. I close my eyes and pray.

Please, keep us safe—keep the innocent at Dachau safe. Spare us after we have fought so hard to stay alive. Please, God. Please.

I've been sitting in a corner, holding my knees to my chest as if my legs will protect me like armor, but I'm scared. Any second could be the last and that will be it, and I don't know what comes next. There's no next. We don't get another chance, ever. Forever, is an infinite amount of time to question what becomes of us after we die.

The night has caved in on us, wrapping the house in a blanket of darkness with only the glow from a gas lantern in the center of the room. All four parents and Dietrich have fallen asleep, somehow, despite the continuous rumbles. To be asleep is better than to be awake, in case we're hit.

"Emi," a hoarse whisper sharply grasps my attention. Otto is awake and staring at me through the flickering glow.

I crawl over to his side and take his hand within mine. "How are you feeling?"

"Tired," he says.

"Your stomach?"

He shrugs, the movement so slight I'm surprised I noticed. "Not as awful as before."

"That's great. Maybe you're turning a corner." I haven't seen him this complacent in weeks. "Wouldn't that be nice? We can get our lives back on track and—"

"Emi, why are we down here? What's going on?"

I smooth his hair off his forehead. "It's okay, don't worry. It's just to be safe," I tell him, not wanting to add any unnecessary stress to his clouded mind.

"And our parents, Dietrich? Why are they all here?"

I squeeze his hand a bit tighter and keep my voice soft to avoid startling him. "Munich is under attack."

"Oh God, I think death might be chasing me," he says, his voice shuddering against his throat.

"Don't speak like that," I tell him, despite thinking the same.

"Emi, I don't deserve to live. This illness happened for a reason. It's punishment for what I've been a part of." I would like to know why Dietrich isn't being punished too if that's the case. "I never thought our lives would end up like this here. I was ignorant to follow—" he looks over at his sleeping father. "Them, but I thought it was an open door to a good future for us. It wasn't. I've ruined your life, stolen your hopes and dreams, and haven't found any way to undo what I've done."

"No one could have known what the future of this war would bring."

We'd had many hints and warnings, but we were thirteen when our world began to change, making life before that age disappear into faint memories. It was easy to get lost in the way of life we have referred to as common. I too should have known better. I didn't have to agree to an engagement proposal or give in to the force of dropping out of classes to move here, but I hadn't found my strength yet.

"It's not just that. I haven't done right by you. I wanted to secure our future because I imagined it to be perfect with you. We just always seemed to fit, but I knew you loved Danner, though you weren't a fit per society. I know love can't be masked. I knew you would never love me as much, but I thought maybe over time, our life together would be what we both loved most."

"Otto, you don't have to say this..."

"I have to. I need Danner to know how sorry I am that I didn't do more to help him. I should have done more."

"Otto, you don't need to focus on Danner right now."

"I need you to tell him I'm sorry. Okay? And I need you to know how sorry I am, too."

"Stop talking like this, just stop," I scold him.

"What I've put you through here is something I'll never forgive myself for, and I'm undeserving of you, this life we have been playing the roles of, and I won't take any more of your future away. Whether I make it through this or not, I—"

The ground erupts with a quake that sends us flying into the wall. The chandelier clatters in the dining room and the glassware in the kitchen rattles, picture frames fall, and it all happens at once. I dive on top of Otto and cover my head with my arms, not knowing if the roof will cave in over us, or worse. Another rumble shakes us around and fills the air with a sudden onset of white noise.

"Are you—" I can't hear myself speak, only a loud ringing. I push myself up and Otto grabs my hand.

He's mouthing something, but I can't hear him either. I pull my hand from his and step over the others who are trying to figure out what's happening as they pull themselves upright. I reach for the nearest wall for stability, throwing myself from one wall to another until I reach the front door, noticing the glass from the windows has all blown out and shattered. My head is heavy, or maybe my brain has been shaken around too fiercely. I try to wrap my hand around the doorknob but miss twice before securing it in my clutch. I pull the slab open and hobble down the front stone steps. Smoke and smog cloak the sky, an ominous telltale sign of what has happened. When I reach the street, I spot flames growing from the row of houses behind ours. The pungent odor of jet fuel burns my nose as I make my way to the corner of the street.

A hand on my shoulder startles me and I scream, but I don't hear that, either. Ingrid, Karl, and their children huddle together, pointing but not speaking. Helga and Wilhelm, and Ursula and Hermann make their way out of their houses and spot the rest of us on the corner. Helga is holding her ears like Ingrid's three children.

Ursula comes toward us with an unblinking stare, her eyes full of shock.

Karl, Hermann, and Wilhelm group together and hold their hands up for us to stay where we are while they venture down the street. Ursula, Ingrid, and her children are crying as they reach out for the men. Helga takes my hand in hers just as a wave of fighter jets flies overhead, lower than I've ever seen. The force from their engines pushes us to the ground and again...we take cover.

We've all become deafened by the war, but not everyone had noticed until now.

FORTY-TWO

EMILIE

Dachau, Germany

Three weeks ago, a U.S. airborne plane was shot down, and crashed a street away from where we live in Dachau. Fortunately, it missed us, and it missed the Dachau camp. No one was hurt or killed from the explosive crash and flying shrapnel except the poor U.S. pilots. However, the heart of Munich was not as fortunate. The shot down plane was part of a large U.S. attack serving the city over three million bombs. Half of Munich has been destroyed. It was the first time in my life I thought it might be my last night on earth. There was no telling how wide the targeted area would be.

We all hunkered down together in the utility room of our house—the neighbors, and our family. It was too hard to consider the possibility of another explosion hitting one and not all of us so for that one night, we all showed our true selves, the weaknesses we each carry, the hopes, dreams, and futures we all would like to have, and most importantly, the mistakes we've all made. We've all made wrong decisions.

We must have been let off the hook, but not Otto. He's

remained weak and fragile. The headaches have become more prolonged, and he can hardly keep his eyes open. No matter how many times I read through my medical books, I can't find a solution.

"Can I get you anything other than aspirin?" I ask, kneeling by his side, stroking the side of his face with my knuckles.

"There's nothing more you can do, Emi." His eyes are half-lidded, his lips downturned into a grimace. He alternates between staring at me, and shifting his gaze back to the wall. He rests his hand on his head and squeezes at his temples. "I can't take much more."

"Yes, you can. You're a fighter. You can handle much more than you give yourself credit for."

I grab the bottle of aspirin from the night table and pour two into my hand. "Here, it's time for another dose," I say, handing him the pills and a glass of water.

He takes both and tosses the pills into the back of his throat then washes them down, finishing his glass of water.

I take the glass from his hands and set it down next to the aspirin, and turn back, finding him squeezing his head between his hands so hard his fingers lose blood circulation. "Stop it. You're going to hurt yourself," I scold him. "I'll get you another cold compress."

"No, no, I don't need another compress," he groans. "I—I want to go fly a plane."

"What?" I ask, moving closer to his face, wondering if I'm misunderstanding him.

"I just wanted to be a pilot. I wanted to fly and see the world from the sky. I wanted to feel the rush of the wind taking me on its back and soaring me through the cloud drops. I never got to do that."

"There's still time. You will be able to fly. You don't have to be a doctor. You can be a pilot or whatever you want to be. We're young. You still have your whole life ahead of you. It's not too late to change our direction." I speak as if it would be so easy to pick up and choose a different life, knowing it's impossible. He might have options and yet Danner and all the others in that camp seem to have had their fate already determined. No one knows if this war will end. It's not even a matter of when… it's just, if…

"I'm not getting better, Emi. Something inside of me is dying. I can feel it."

"No, you're going to get better. You need to stay positive. You need to fight. That's the way through. We fight for what we want."

"At whose expense?" he asks, his mouth hardly moving along with his words.

"Emi," he cries out. "Help me, please. Make it stop."

I cup my hands around his cheeks, staring him in the eyes. "Take a deep breath, try to relax your muscles."

"Stop," he cries again. "I need to tell you that Danner was at our wedding. I don't know why, but he was there, and I'm sorry for never telling you that he came back from Poland to be there."

I choke on my breath, trying to inhale. "What do you mean?"

"He was in the back. He loved you that much. He just wanted to make sure you were happy. I know. I just know. If you can help him, you should… Promise me you will?"

Danner was there. I repeat the words in my head several times, my face burning with pain and anguish. Why was he back in Germany? What if it was because of me? God, I hope that wasn't why. He could be in the camp because of me…I'll have to live with that now. If I'd known Danner was in the church that day…I'm not sure our life would be what it is right now. Maybe I could have spared him from suffering in that horrid camp. But the other prisoners should have been spared too. They all deserve to be saved and helped. I can't understand why Danner wouldn't want me to know he was there. Did he know I was thinking about him in the moment I took my vows? How guilty I felt for what I was feeling and not feeling. And Otto kept this from me.

"I—why—I don't understand."

"Promise me," he demands again.

"Okay," I whimper. "I promise, but we can talk about this later..."

"We won't," he says, sniffling. "I *do* love you with all my heart, and I should have been a better husband. I should have supported your dreams. I have so many regrets, Emi, but you aren't one of them."

"Otto, you are—"

"Could I have more water please and ice for my head," he cries out.

In a frenzy, I glance at the pitcher of water, finding it empty. "I—we—I ran out of ice this morning—I'll go next door...just take a—take a breath," I say, grabbing the pitcher and running out the door. I should have refilled it earlier. I race down the steps and out the front door to bang on Ingrid's door. She's quick to answer.

"Emilie, is everything okay?"

"No, I—I uh—" I press my hand to my forehead. "Do you have any ice?"

"I don't, but I believe Helga does. I'll go see if she does. Is it for Otto?"

"Yes, please, hurry," I say. "Thank you." Before she can say another word I rush back home to fill the pitcher of water.

I return and fill his glass, my hand shaking as I do. "Here you go," I say, holding up the glass.

He doesn't take it from me. He just stares forward, passed me toward the wall.

"Otto?" I whisper, placing the glass down on the nightstand. I move to wrench his shoulders and shake him out of this motionless position, but his head falls back against the pillow, his eyes still open, still staring. The medical bag I left on the chair beside him is open on his lap. I lift it and two glass bottles roll off the bed and hit the ground. One shatters, brown glass sprinkling the tops of my shoes. I glance down, spotting pieces of an empty aspirin bottle that was full the last time I gave him a dose. The other bottle didn't break. I scoop up the empty bottle of phenol antiseptic, staring at the stark skull and crossbones warning. I shake my head as my throat tightens. I toss the medical bag to the ground and grab Otto's arm, finding a syringe dangling from his fingers.

"No! Otto! No!" I wrench open his mouth, finding a trace of white residue around his larynx and a drop of blood around his carotid artery. "Why? Why would you take your—" I cry, shrieking at him as I press my fists into his stomach and pump my hands up and down, to expel the bottle full of aspirin he's ingested.

I yank him to his side and drag him to the edge of the bed, so his head hangs down. I thrust the heels of my palms into his back, hitting him over and over, relentlessly without success.

"Why would you do this? Why?"

I slide off the bed, dropping to the side of the shattered glass bottle and his hanging head, grabbing his face between my hands.

"Otto."

A sob bursts from my chest and the thought of everything that has become my life—our lives—over the past however many years has been enough torture and pain to last a lifetime, and now this. This wasn't the answer. It didn't have to be the answer.

"I failed you. I'm sorry, Otto. I'm so sorry."

I lift his hand, pressing my first two fingers against his wrist to check his pulse.

There's no pulse.

I reach for his neck, my hand shaking so hard I'm not even sure I'm near his artery. Foam snakes out of the side of his mouth and I glance at my fingers, knowing they are where they should be to feel for a pulse.

"No, no. Otto. No. I lean my ear up to his mouth, listening for the air that won't pass through his lips.

He's still warm, but he's dead. He's gone, and I never loved him the way I should have. Maybe if I had, he would have taken a different path. I could have shown him a different way. "I'm so sorry. I am. I'm so sorry."

My chest aches, and the pain is relentless no matter how hard I press my fists against my sternum. I don't know what to do.

I need to get help.

I run downstairs and check our phone, not expecting it to be working since the line was damaged during the explosion. It doesn't connect. There's just silence...like the rest of my house at this moment.

Spinning around again, gasping for air, I race out the front door, spotting Karl's car out the front of their house. I'm barefoot, running over debris, trying to get to their front door as fast as I can, but it's as if the front door keeps moving away from my reach.

I trip up their front steps but catch myself on their door and bang as hard as I can. "Help!" I scream. "Help, please."

Marie, Ingrid's eldest daughter, opens the door, horrified to see me like this, and I should have thought better than to come here and scare the poor children after what they've already been through this month. "Mama!" she shouts, pointing behind me where Ingrid is running back from Helga's with ice wrapped in a rag.

"What happened?" she yelps, panic lacing her eyes as she reaches me. She pulls me in against her chest to offer me comfort but that's impossible right now.

"He's gone. He's gone. I don't know what to do."

"Who's gone? Who? Otto?" she cries back.

"Jesus," Karl says, sprinting out of their kitchen. "Is he upstairs in your house?"

"Yes, yes. He was in so much..."

Karl runs out the door and Ingrid continues to hold me in her arms, spinning me in a slow circle, hushing me and cradling her hand against the back of my head. The tears clear from my eyes for a moment, and I spot the picture frame across the room —the one she didn't want me to see the first time I came over. It was face down every time since.

And now I know why.

A photograph of Ingrid, Karl, and Adolf Hitler smiling in front of the Dachau iron gates. She's pregnant in the photo.

"I should go help Karl," I say, trying to catch my breath.

"Of course. Come back once—well, I'll come check on you in a bit. I'm so sorry, Emilie. I can't imagine—"

"I know. There's a lot I haven't been able to imagine too," I utter before stumbling back out her front door, knowing I'll never be able to set foot in her house again.

I stumble, like I'm blindfolded, into this nightmare of a life. I have been trying to save Danner at whatever cost.

I believe the cost might have been my husband.

And it's because I didn't give him enough to live for.

FORTY-THREE

EMILIE

Dachau, Germany

Millions are already dead in Europe. A funeral is no such thing today, not even a service. My parents and Otto's are downstairs, mourning, grieving, sitting silently and staring at a wall. I'm still staring at a wall with a bronze-emblazoned frame embracing the Monet painting I've always loved. If I loved it so much, why would I have hung it in a room we hardly used?

Otto thought it looked like it belonged in his grandmother's house. He called it outdated. I call it a visual escape. I wish I was sitting in a field of flowers, water lapping over lily pads, frogs chirping, birds singing, but instead I'm here, wondering what I should have done differently—not just now, but a decade ago. If I'd made different choices, how would life look now?

I'll forever be known as the widow of a man who took his life. People will speculate and judge me; assume I wasn't enough—think the worst of me. As they should. Gerty is beside me, combing her fingers through my hair, hair that has gone unwashed for days. She's been here two days, arriving the day after Otto passed. She hasn't left my side since. We've been sleeping in my guest room, so I don't have to be in the same spot I watched Otto die. She's been reading me mindless magazine articles and telling me stories about her son who's growing up so fast.

"Your stomach is growling so loudly, it's beginning to make me think there's a monster living inside of you," she says. "Please, will you eat something?"

There's a monster living inside of me. That's why Otto didn't want to share a life with me anymore.

"I'm not hungry," I tell her.

"Do you remember that time you had influenza and you were in bed for over a week, refusing to drink even a sip of water?" Gerty says, swinging her feet off the side of the bed.

"No," I say. I do remember, but I don't want to think about it.

"Well, I do. It took your mama and me an hour to trick you into having three spoonfuls of soup. You're as stubborn as they get. Still are, I guess," she says, forcing a small smile. "But I love you, so I won't give up. And I'll force-feed you if I must. I'll sit on you and—"

"I know. I know. That's why I had those three bites earlier. I didn't want you to sit on me," I reply.

"I'll be right back. I'm getting more. Don't run away."

I've only moved to use the bathroom so far. The thought of running or walking farther than across the hall is not something I'm considering. Gerty's bare feet clap against the steps as she makes her way downstairs and I turn my stare toward the window, the sunlight casting a faint glow against the corner, and a slice of the blue sky I can see above the tree line.

Why, Otto? Why did you do this?

How many last breaths have been taken in this town since I arrived here? Ones not by choice? And yet, Otto made the decision to take his last breath here, and from what only I know is guilt. My words, my recollections and retellings are just that—a story people can choose to believe or not believe.

"I've brought pastries," I hear from downstairs. Dietrich's voice echoes up the stairwell, making me snarl. Maybe if I start locking the door...I can keep him away. Our working arrangement is only tolerable because I never have to see him. "Where is Emilie?"

I can't bear the thought of looking at his face. He wasn't here when Otto passed away, but he assured me there was nothing to concern myself over. He might have been right about whatever virus or illness Otto was fighting, but he wasn't right that there was nothing to worry about.

His heavy footsteps march up the stairs and he takes the corner into the guest room, a brown bag of pastries in his hand. "You must be hungry, dear."

"I'm not hungry," I tell him.

Dietrich pulls up a chair, facing me from the other side of the empty bed, whispering my words to himself.

"Emilie," he says with a sigh. "If you had a secret—one that could destroy your life if shared, what would you do to protect it?" I'm not sure what he's alluding to, but I can only assume it has something to do with our secret about me authoring his papers in exchange for keeping Danner alive. "I don't need you to answer because I already know. You don't tell anyone your secret. You've been a trustworthy woman, and trustworthy women are hard to come by these days."

"What is your point?" I mutter.

"*Your point?*" he repeats. "Nothing. In fact, I'm quite grateful for the clandestine relationship we've kept regarding—you know what..."

"Then why are you here?"

He mouths my words before answering. "Well, I thought it would only be right to let you know that I plan to hold up my end of our agreement still. However, your parents have made it clear that they would like to take you back home with them."

They haven't said a word to me about this plan. They didn't ask. "No, I'm not leaving. I have to—I'm just...not ready to leave —my life with Otto behind. I can't...I'll just keep delivering your papers," I say.

I've already destroyed one life, and Danner is still depending on me, despite everything else that's happened.

He taps the toes of his polished shoes on the ground, staring at them for a long moment. "*Keep delivering papers...*," he says with a sigh. "No. To be honest, I'm not sure how much more work I'll have for you."

"Why?" I ask breathlessly, knowing my bargaining chip is growing weaker by the minute and I'm practically begging this awful man to allow me to keep doing his dirty work.

"*Why?* It's nothing you need brood over right now. For the moment, we'll continue on, business as usual."

FORTY-FOUR

EMILIE

Munich, Germany

A little girl sits on a sofa as her parents stand before her, staring at her with their arms crossed and a look of disappointment stamped across their faces. I don't even have Gerty to back me up. She had to go back home to Calvin and their son.

"There's nothing for you here," Papa says. "I need to know that you're not alone all the time, not now. It's too dangerous."

"I don't want to go home. I'm sorry," I say, uttering my words as I stare between them. They don't know about Danner. They don't know what I've been doing, keeping him alive all this time through my work and through the small things I can get to him—the hope I try to instill in him. I do know they would do the same, but they wouldn't want me walking into Dachau every night. Papa would tell me he would do it instead and wouldn't tolerate an argument.

I've never kept anything from them until Otto and I moved here.

"There's something you aren't telling us, Emilie," Mama

says. "You might be a grown woman living on your own now, but a mother's instinct only grows stronger with age."

She's staring at me with a sharp glare—a glare I could never peer past as a child. I knew I would be in less trouble by being honest up front than if I lied.

I close my eyes and swallow against the dryness strangling my throat. "Danner is a prisoner in Dachau."

The color drains from both their faces, and their jaws fall open. Their expression is something beyond the description of shock, and I've shared this information as if I were telling them it might rain later.

"I don't understand... How do you know this?" Papa says, stepping in closer to the coffee table between us.

"What did you think when I told you Otto bought us a house in Dachau? Where did you think we'd be?"

They weren't concerned when I told them I was leaving. They were happy I'd married a man who wanted to take care of me and keep me safe.

"That he would be conducting research with his father in a field hospital, as he said," Mama replies, a brow now raised as anger pinches at her forehead.

"Isn't that where you've been helping him all this time?" Papa follows. "That's what you've told us, is it not?"

I drop my gaze to my lap, my interwoven fingers, the golden band still encircling my finger. "Yes, but the field hospital was inside the Dachau concentration camp."

Their shock and anger transform into a state of horror, their eyes bulging, unblinking as if they've been shot in the back. Why is this expression familiar to me? It's one that haunts my nightmares, but I shouldn't be familiar with this dead expression.

"I've been covertly trying to save prisoners by altering data to avoid further human experimentation that continues to be ordered by the Luftwaffe. Danner was one of the initial subjects. I managed to save him, and I've been leaving him rations of food rolled into a newspaper nightly as I deliver reports to Dietrich's office. He'll die if I stop."

Papa drops down onto the side of the coffee table and Mama ambles to my side, sitting next to me on the sofa. "Why in the world did you keep this from us?" she asks.

"Everything is a secret, Mama. Shared secrets result in death."

"Otto knew he was pulling you into this situation and kept it from you?"

"Stefan and Marion knew about this," Papa grunts.

I shake my head. "No, it wasn't like that. Dietrich is the mastermind behind it all. Herr Berger pulled us away from Dachau once he found out what we were being forced to take part in, but Dietrich knew I had a connection with Danner and promised to keep him safe if I helped him." The more I say, the more nauseous they look. Mama is holding her stomach and Papa has his head cradled in his hand. "If I leave here, I won't be able to bring Danner any more food. He'll starve to death. He'll lose hope."

"There's so much I need to say, want to say—so much I can't comprehend," Papa says. "Stefan knew about Danner?"

"Yes, but not until Herr Berger confronted Dietrich."

"And he did nothing to help pull Danner out of that godforsaken prison camp?" Papa stands up, pinning his hands to his hips while pacing the living room. "He's as bad as his brother. You're the one who continued to help Danner. The only one?"

I lower my chin, dropping my gaze because saying anything more won't calm him down.

"I need to get him out of there. I'll deal with Dietrich," Papa shouts.

"Andreas, that man is—he's not right in the head," Mama snaps back at Papa.

"He's part of the SS with his role beneath Heinrich Himmler. I'm not sure anything you say will make a difference."

"I won't sit here and make assumptions while Danner rots to death," Papa says with a grunt, his veins pulsating along his temples.

His words squeeze at my chest, adding to the insurmountable amount of pain I'm trying to cope with. But if he has a chance at saving Danner—the risks, I don't know what's right or safe. "Maybe I should just continue delivering papers to Dachau for Dietrich and leaving the food for Danner as I've been doing. I don't want to make this worse. That's my fear," I say, mumbling my words.

"I'm just going to speak with him," Papa says, huffing from his nostrils like an angry bull. "The two of you stay here until I return. We'll pack some bags and come stay here with you if that's what's needed for Danner. We'll help take care of him."

"Andreas, you should take a moment to think this all through," Mama says.

"I already have. That boy has already lost his father, and I'm sure he isn't even aware of it yet. I saw his name on a list recently. He's dead. I don't know about his mother and David, but so help me God, I won't sit back and let something happen to him, too."

"Herr Alesky is dead?" I whisper. My body turns to ice, knowing it's something more Danner will have to move on with —if he moves on. "This isn't fair." Endless tears streak down my face, the saltiness burning my raw cheeks.

"Just stay here. I'll be back shortly," Papa says, his voice calmer, his breaths more even. He leans over the coffee table and presses a kiss against my head, then gives Mama a kiss, too. "I love you both. Stay here."

Munich, Germany

Hours have passed since Papa stormed out of the house and burnt the rubber of his tires against the gravel while leaving the street. Mama is quieter than she's ever been, and I believe she might be in shock. Nothing shocks me anymore. The world is falling apart. No one has been untouched. We're all affected. I've been telling myself that losses are inevitable. I didn't tell myself they might be preventable—that one day I should have tried to stop Otto's death. My grief has become anger, and I can't control much of what I'm feeling. All I know is, I'll keep helping and saving those I love. But I don't know who I am now. I'm a hollow person, filled with nothing but turmoil.

"Mama, stop dusting. There's no more dust," I tell her, watching as she makes her way around the living room for the fourth time in the last hour.

"I need to keep busy," she argues.

"Papa will be okay."

"It's not just your father, sweetheart," she says, turning toward me with the feather duster held out by her side. "You—

this is all too much. You're twenty-four, and a widow. You've seen nothing but brutal hatred for the last ten years of your life, and it's only grown worse by the day. I—I as your mother," she says, "I know what you've wanted throughout your life, and I've had no choice but to sit back and watch all of those things fall out of your reach."

"It's life, right?" I ask. "We live, learn, and die."

"No, my darling. There's so much more."

A car door slams and the doorknob jiggles before Papa storms inside. He turns the corner into the living room, pinches the top of his hat and tosses it to the ground.

"What is it?" I ask.

Papa's face is beet red, his neck, verging on purple. "I caught Stefan just as he was getting into his car, ready to leave for wherever the hell he and Marion are going. They're getting as far away from here as possible, so they won't be found associated with Dietrich."

I stand up from the sofa after sitting for far too long, but my lungs feel constricted, and I need to be able to breathe. "What do you mean...associated with him?"

Papa paces in small circles, his hands clutching his hips, his chest rising and falling too fast. "Dietrich and his wife have been arrested by the Gestapo."

The breath rushes from my lungs, leaving me clutching at my chest for air. "Arrested..." I won't ask why, because I can think of many reasons why, but not while he has been working with the German government.

"He and his wife had kidnapped a baby. She was faking a pregnancy for data on women of an older age who are able to conceive and give birth to a healthy child. During a thorough investigation and home search, it was discovered Dietrich also had an assistant years ago whose remains were discovered beneath a dirt pile in a wooded area behind his house. Her identification card was found in the corroding dress pocket."

My heart hammers against my rib cage as another unexpected revelation sinks in. I drop back down onto the sofa and clutch my arms around my stomach. My entire body becomes limp as I process how anyone could be so heinous and cruel, but I shouldn't be surprised. I know what he's capable of, what he did. He committed crime after crime, and yet he kept his word about Danner. Except, that word means nothing now. "He knew he was close to being caught. That's why he said he didn't know if he'd have much more work."

Papa holds his hands out, palms down. "Most likely," he says, making his way over. He pulls me back up to my feet and wraps me in his arms. "Stephan said Dietrich told him and Marion to get as far away as they could, and he said he had sworn never to mention your name as he has already predicted his fate."

"How can we believe him? The man is a liar. He doesn't have a heart. He's selfish and wants what's best for himself. It's obvious."

"We need to leave. We can't be around here," Papa says, not arguing with my statement.

"Papa, no! I can't leave Danner behind. We must help him."

"The guards at Dachau know who you are, and they now know about Dietrich. I fought with Stephan until he nearly drove over my feet to get away. I told him I need his help to get Danner out of that hellhole, and without a hint of remorse, they just left. You're our daughter. We need to protect you too. I'm so sorry, darling."

"No, I can't—"

"We need to leave now. Please, don't make this harder than it is. I'm sorry I have to do this to you. I'm so sorry," Papa says.

"I won't go. I need to get back in through those gates, at least once more. Just once more, please. Papa you can't—"

Papa pulls me away from the sofa and I do everything I can to resist, fighting to pull my hands out of his.

"Let go of me, Papa. You can leave me here. Just leave."

"Emilie, Emilie, sweetheart. You're in danger," Mama says. "Danner wouldn't want you to put yourself in danger for him. He would blame himself if something happened to you and you can't put that on his shoulders. You can't. It isn't fair to him."

"This isn't fair to him! This isn't fair to me! I've lost everything! Everything, can't you see?" I cry out, realizing I've become too weak to fight. Papa has managed to pull me across the living room. "I'll come back to get her belongings. Let's just get her in the car," Papa says.

"Please let me go. Why would you do this? Not now. I can't take any more, please!" My knees give out and I fall, but don't hit the ground as Papa sweeps me up into his arms, cradling me like a child. All I can do is cry, feeling as though I'm purging my soul as I do so. Through thick tears covering my eyes, I spot blurry figures, my neighbors, watching this scene unfold.

"She'll be okay," Mama says, following behind Papa, waving at the neighbors who are standing outside their front doors.

I don't think I'll ever be okay again.

FORTY-SIX
DANNER
APRIL 1945

Munich, Germany

When I wake once more in the darkness, I question if I'm alive or if this is the abyss. My internal clock winds up a couple minutes before the siren alerts us to all wake up. If I were dead, I don't think I'd still smell the rotting flesh, bile, and sewage that lingers like a fog between these walls. I also wouldn't hear purrs of snoring, wheezing, or delirious mumbles. My spine wouldn't feel like it's fused to a metal pole, and there wouldn't be stabbing hunger pains writhing through my stomach.

Three-hundred and eighty-four days have passed since I last saw Emilie. I read the last of her words every night before bed, hoping I'll dream of a better tomorrow as she taught me to do. Emilie was full of promises for a hopeful future, of the war coming to an end, of the happiness I'd find when this was all over. I waited at the location she passed each night, but she never came again. Night after night, I waited, but Emilie never returned.

The girl who would never give up has left me wondering what has become of her. I fight off nightmares of her being caught on the way out of the gates after sneaking me food. Even worse, there have been air raids and planes crashing in the not-so-far distance, telling me anything could have happened to anyone outside of these walls.

Here, people are dying, dropping face first into the dirt or onto a wooden floor by the hour, left pulseless by the time someone can move fast enough to check for the trace of a heartbeat. Every second of every day, I question how—why I—of all the people here—have managed to defy the odds and survive.

But there's nothing left of me now except the skin sagging from my bones.

The morning siren rings, screaming at us to move faster than we're capable of, to make it outside in time for roll call. A light bulb flickers to life by whomever was asleep beneath that spot of the ceiling. Hans doesn't sit up right away like he usually does. It's hard to avoid being startled by the ear-splitting alarm. I grab his thin arm, squeezing between his frail bones and tug him. He doesn't budge, so I shake him with more force.

"Get up, brother. We have to move."

He groans and struggles to open his eyes, his thin eyelashes wavering like a wing that can't take flight. "I can't move," he says.

"You have to. We have to." Without a morsel of fat or muscle left on my body, I'm as good as useless while trying to pull him toward the ladder, but I continue pulling anyway. "Come on, Hans."

"Go without me," he says, the sound of his voice hardly forming.

"No, I won't." I grit my jaw tightly and yank him over my shoulder, pulling him down to the ground with me. My knees threaten to buckle, but I keep my focus straight ahead, trying to remind myself mind over matter will win. I shove my shoulder under his arm and keep him upright as we shuffle our way out of the barrack.

The lineups are different this morning, for as far down the column of blocks as I can see against the sun's glow peeking over the horizon, people are being shoved in different directions and shouted at. Yet, we will sit here and watch until they do the same to us, likely without any further explanation.

"No, I can't—" the man in front of me moans before falling to the ground, face first.

I bend down to try to and help him back up, but he doesn't budge. I can't move him, and Hans is swaying beside me. I close my eyes and take a breath, holding it within my chest. "Please God, take care of this man laying here before me. Let his soul rest in peace," I mutter.

"No, he's—Fr—Frank, wake up," Hans stutters. "You promised you wouldn't die today. You told me last night."

"Brother, he can't—" Hans gently sways back and forth like a toy top about to make its last round. "Hans, look at me," I tell him, grabbing his shoulders. He peeks through one squinted eye and shakes his head. "You *can* make it another day. Focus on tomorrow."

I clap my hands around his face, trying to spark him into standing up straight. He gasps for air and winces. "How much longer?" he asks.

"Not much," I lie. I lie like we all do, telling each other we're going to make it, and that this is almost over even though there are no clues pointing to this possible end.

My vision blurs as I try to see more of what's happening down the line of people, but the sun scalds my eyes like metal rods.

"Thank you for dragging me out here," Hans mumbles. "Thank you."

"Don't thank me. We're in this together. We're making it through this. We are." I don't believe the words, but I believe they may help someone listening.

The group of guards makes their way to our section, grabbing shirts and arms and tossing people like rubbish off to one side of the dirt path.

Before I can consider what will happen if Hans and I are separated, it happens. My body is thrown up against our barrack and I fold in half, recoiling from the pain shuddering through my bones and skull.

When I regain my focus and try to push through the consuming pain, half of us are gone, out of sight, as if they'd never existed in the first place. "Hans?" I shout. "Where are you?"

"Get to work," a guard screams at me and a few others who are trying to pick themselves up. I scour the area, looking in every possible direction to see where the others must have gone. It's as if my mind is playing tricks on me, but there's a stick shoved into the center of my back, stabbing at me to move faster. My head is heavier than a cannon and it's nearly impossible to hold it upright. My feet trip over each other no matter how hard I try to walk in a straight line. I'm not sure I'm still living.

I pass Block 5, the sick bay block, staring at the wooden door as if I could burn a hole through it with my eyes. Would Emilie be inside? Is she still here? Is she still alive?

Or is this place hell? She wouldn't be there. People like her don't go to hell. People like me, Jewish people, don't believe in hell, yet, here I am, not sure what else to call this place.

"Emilie!" I shout, wishing she could hear me. "They took Hans. He's gone too."

"Shut up, rat. Keep moving," a guard shouts from behind me, throttling his stick into my back again.

FORTY-SEVEN

DANNER

Munich, Germany

With a weightless body drooping between my tired arms, I shake and wobble while bringing yet another deceased man to the wagon where the other bodies wait. The few remaining SS guards on site told us to move these people away from the crematorium that can't be used at the moment. No one said why and no one knows where the rest of the guards went. They've just told us to move the pile of bodies.

The repetitive motions are mindless, allowing me to multi-task—work and dwell while I tell myself that I'll soon be one of those bodies, strewn like a dirty rag. Then I switch thoughts to worry about Emilie—where she is and what she's doing, if she's forgotten about me, or worse... There are never answers, and there have been plenty of questions circling around the barracks because only half of us remain of the population that was here a few weeks ago. We don't know why.

Last week, when most of the SS left the camp, they took half of us and sent them marching away to God only knows where. They took my only friend—the only person I had left.

There was no reason why it was him instead of me, and I'll never know. I just know that I'm here and he's not, and there must be a reason for why there are only a few guards remaining here.

"Do you hear that sound too?" the guy standing next to me with a matching shovel asks through a hoarse whisper.

"Gunshots?" another grave digger replies.

"Those aren't blasts coming from German guns," another says.

"If not a German weapon...something is happening," the man beside me says, his voice cracking.

The seconds between the last statement and a growing roar of commotion feel like an eternity as I consider what we're hearing. One by one the six of us, who had been digging, drop our shovels. The dry dirt bursts up into fine grains from the ground, covering our shoes.

"Amer... ...diers," someone cries out.

We all exchange a look, trying to decipher what we're hearing. "Ameri-diers?"

"They've come," a stronger voice shouts from nearby. "They've come for us."

The six of us stumble, dragging our toes in the dirt with each step, holding our hands above our heads to shield our eyes against the blinding sunlight.

Others spill out of various blocks along the way. Some trip but continue forward, crawling. Others fall to their knees, holding their hands over their hearts and stare up to the sky as tears leave white streaks down their faces.

We pick up our pace, walking past another shout. "God has sent the Americans to save us!"

Remarks bellow through a megaphone, remarks most of us can't understand since they aren't speaking German. The English language is enough comfort beyond whatever they are trying to convey. We continue forward, each step like lifting an iron weight tied to each foot, but we're close to the rest of the crowd. When the exterior barbed wire gate comes into view, I watch a soldier take the megaphone from another and begin to speak. This time, the words are in Yiddish, which I can understand. "Medical aid and food are on its way; we need you to stay put until assistance arrives."

The cheers become silent as if someone has turned down the volume on a radio.

"Emilie," I cry out. "You were right. Emilie! Where are you? Can you hear me?" I buckle to my knees and roll to my side before folding over like a pancake. "Can you hear me?" Is she there with the Americans? Did she bring them here? Someone must have saved me, must have saved us. It had to be her. She promised, even though she never came back. I knew she wouldn't break her promise.

More American soldiers line the exterior gates, all staring at us as if they don't know what we are. They shouldn't be afraid of us. We aren't going to hurt them. "Have you seen Emilie?" I shout toward them. "Is she out there with you?"

No one answers me. They look like they can't hear me. They're staring through me like I'm a faint patch of fog. "Hello?" I shout. "Tell Emilie I'm here. I'm still here."

I can't hold myself up while I wait for them to respond so I curl up on the dirt-covered ground, pulling my sharp knees into my rib cage, but I keep my eyes open, staring at the soldiers so they don't disappear.

"Please help," I cry.

Munich, Germany

I turn up the radio, even though I'm not sure the volume can go much higher. I'm afraid I'll miss something.

"Emilie, please turn it down. It's so loud and they aren't saying anything different from what they've been saying for days," Mama says, pinching her fingers around her forehead.

Gerty is here, watching me pace the kitchen, but she's staring at Mama who's bouncing Theo on her hip. He's Gerty's spitting image, but with vocal cords twice as loud as hers.

"The noise is upsetting Theo too." Theo isn't crying or screaming. He's making a racket like he enjoys doing, as per most three-year olds.

"There's more noise in the streets than in this house and I don't want to miss an update," I argue.

Between learning about the death of Hitler and the war coming to an end here, there have been so many announcements, but new broadcasts seem infrequent compared to the repetitive announcements being played.

"I should go down there. I can help," I say again.

"Have you not heard what they're doing to the German guards who were caught at Dachau?" Papa shouts at me. "There's a reason we got you out of that town, and it's not safe there for you."

Do I deserve to be kept safe when so many have been killed and tortured to death?

"No one knows who I am, not at this point. Danner could have been liberated. He'll need help. I must go."

"They're caring for the liberated," Gerty says. "The Americans are taking care of them."

"I don't even know if he survived. I can't sit here and wait this out. I need to know," I say, running out of breath.

Gerty grabs my arm and pulls me over to the kitchen table, shoving me down into a seat. "Calm down," she says, pointing at me. "If he's alive, he's under care. If he's not—" Gerty closes her eyes and wraps her hand around her throat. "We can't change that, Emi."

As I go to argue, the radio crackles.

This just in:

Just ten days ago, members of the U.S. Army uncovered forty railway cars filled with human remains.

In the following days, U.S. soldiers interviewed many residents of Dachau, inquiring about their knowledge of what was taking place within steps of their homes. The general response was: "What could we do?"

At this time, the U.S. Army has requested all residents of Dachau to report to the Dachau prison camp to assist in reparations of the deceased.

I keel forward, clutching my stomach, feeling an acidic burn rise to my throat. "I lived there. I knew," I utter.

"You tried to help," Gerty says.

I shake my head. "It wasn't enough. I should have done more. I should have—"

"You would have been killed, had you done anything differently," Mama says.

"What if Danner is—"

"Emilie, you can't assume..." Gerty says, wrapping her arm around me. I can do more than assume. The only hope I had that he would remain alive was Dietrich's word, and he was executed.

"I need to go," I tell them.

"Emilie, you cannot go back there," Papa says, making his way into the kitchen, blocking me inside with Gerty, Mama, and Theo.

My blood boils, knowing I can't sit here any longer. "I'm going."

"Emilie, please, think about this..." Mama says.

"You know that's all I have been doing," I say, standing from my seat. "Let me by, Papa."

"You're not going there alone," he says. "Give me a minute. I'll take you."

"Andreas," Mama shouts. "What are you doing?"

"We aren't going to stop her. So, I'm going with her." Papa steps out of the doorway and leaves the house.

Without a second thought, I give Mama a hug, feeling her heart pound against mine, chest to chest. "Please," she cries once more.

"I love you, Mama. You've raised me to do what's right. This is what's right. Danner could be there." He could be a body among the thousands found. He could be one of the many who were sent marching away from the camp days before liberation, he could be in a hospital bed, or he could be a handful of ashes left behind.

I give Gerty a hug and wipe away a falling tear. "I wish you still had your crystal ball," I cry out.

"I wish it had worked, if I did," she says.

Papa collected Felix and Herr Weber to join us. I haven't had much to say to Felix over the years after learning he was hiding Danner in his home, keeping his existence a secret from us all. He confessed to his error in exposing his whereabouts to a friend, which led to his arrest. I know Felix punishes himself for the decisions he's made. We can all take blame.

"I know you hate me," Felix says, sitting beside me in the back seat of Papa's car.

I turn my head to stare out the window, unable to respond. I don't hate him, no more than I hate myself.

"He was my best friend too, and I would never wish for any of what happened."

I nod, assuming he notices the slight gesture. He places his hand on top of mine and then squeezes it tightly. I tighten my fingers around his hand, appreciating the gesture, trying to forgive him as much as I've tried to forgive myself.

"I'll help you find him, Emi."

* * *

Citizens are lined up along the road leading to Dachau's gates. Papa parks a distance away and we make our way up to the end of the line, like a funeral procession. Cries howl in the wind, gasps of shock and terror, moans and groans, and bouts of sickness are what we witness before we even approach the railway cars.

The pungent rotting stench is much worse than anything I smelled while making my way through the camp night after night.

I smelled the unimaginable then, but this is something different. A wave of nausea envelops my stomach. I try to swallow against the sick feeling, breathing in through my mouth and out from my nose but when we pass the first car, witness stacks of bodies strewn like piles of laundry, flies swarming like vultures, and pairs of eyes staring directly at me from every direction, I hurl forward and wrap my arms around myself, trying not to let out the sob wailing through my lungs. Felix puts his arm around me, pinching the tips of his fingers into my flesh. His body shivers against mine and our fathers continue forward, leaving us to watch their shoulders jerking up and down as they release their pain too.

"Danner?" I utter. I'm not sure why I call out his name when there's no living Dachau prisoner in sight, but I can't stop myself.

"I know," Felix says, rubbing his hand up and down my arm.

U.S. soldiers stand guard, watching us, inspecting our reactions to something no person should ever have to bear witness to. "Every one of these people will be properly buried," a soldier shouts. "Your assistance will be needed."

Felix and I share a look. His complexion is so pale, it's almost green to match the way I feel inside.

"We can help. We should," he says, speaking the words I was already thinking.

FORTY-NINE

EMILIE

Dachau, Germany

We've spent days making our way through the railway full of cattle cars, moving bodies that barely weigh a thing, frail bones with thin skin merely offering a hint of who the person once was. We've been placing bodies in wagons to transport them to a burial site—one body after another. I inspect every person, wondering if I would recognize Danner's face if I were to see it again in this way. I know Felix is doing the same. I can see by the extended glances he gives certain bodies before his shoulders slouch forward in defeat.

I'm not sure how many wagons of bodies we have filled, but with the amount of people brought here to help, we're coming to the end. I doubt there will ever be a time where I'll forget the look in every set of open eyes I have stared into these past few days, nor should I. No one should forget what they've seen here.

The car Felix and I have been working through is empty and we climb down, finding most of the citizens standing in front of the line of railway cars, staring into oblivion. We do the same until our fathers return from their daily search within the campgrounds, coming back without news of Danner. It's clear by the dull looks in their eyes as they walk toward us.

"So that's it. We give up trying to find him?" I ask as they step toward us.

Papa places his hands on my shoulders. "We'll never stop. There's just no record of him here."

The sun is setting and it's the time of day we leave. "I'm not leaving yet," I tell them.

"Emilie, there's nowhere for you to look here. You can't stay," Papa says, frustration quaking through his voice, along with how exhausted we all are from the labor of moving bodies.

Papa takes my hand and pulls me away from the empty tombs we've cleared out. But I need to be here. What if Danner's here somewhere?

Papa doesn't release his grip, ensuring I get into the car with the three of them. "I don't want to go home," I tell him.

"I know, but we have to."

No one is saying much because there isn't anything to say. We've done what we can do and there's no other option but to essentially give up.

I can't do that.

I endure the ride home, walking into the house as night settles in. I'm hollow inside, unable to process anything around me. The feeling has only gotten worse in the last year as I've sat here in my childhood bedroom, staring out the window that looks onto Danner's old house. All I feel is guilt, pain, grief, remorse, and emptiness. This can't be it—all that I'll feel for the rest of my life.

* * *

Later that night, with everyone asleep, I make my way out the front door, careful not to make a sound. I take the gas lamp from the front stoop and walk between the houses, toward the tree line. Years ago, there wasn't much that could convince me to walk into the woods alone at night, but now, the darkness is the least of my fears.

I place the lamp down on a flat tree stump in the middle of the bee farm and pull open the metal trunk where the supplies have always been kept. So much of this city is in pieces, destroyed, needing to be rebuilt, but Herr Alesky's supplies, the hives and tools, are all still intact.

I slip into my protective gear and light the smoker. The bees are less frightened at night and find a new hive to burrow in quicker than in the daylight, which has made the process of retrieving the honeycomb filled wooden frames much easier. After placing the frames into the metal bin, I get cranking. The habitual pattern of cycling the machine brings me comfort. Being left helpless and hopeless when it comes to not doing much of anything except sit around and stir with worry, Danner's words play in my head every night that I'm here: "It's true. Albert Einstein said that mankind would be extinct within four years if we lost all the bees." The explosions and air raids scared most of the bees away, but some had gathered in a swarm nearby. I remember Danner telling me about a special wooden box his dad had, which contained drops of lemongrass oil to attract the bees. If he found a tree hive, he'd shake the branch with the box below and capture the swarm. Then he'd bring them to the farming hives at night.

It's been up to me to make sure the bees have a home here. We're depending on them.

I'm depending on them.

If there are bees, we have a chance of surviving. It's all I can do now.

Once my arms give out for the night, I return the tools to the trunk and take off the protective gear, closing it all back up tightly. I take the lantern and hold it out toward the path home, but my heart aches and the grief weighing me down returns.

The only place I find any semblance of peace is here in the woods.

I turn back toward the opening between the trees, making my way over to the knotted stump responsible for Danner's scar. I promised myself I'd stop spending nights alone in the woods, but I can't get myself to go home yet.

I lower myself onto the moss-covered ground and lean against an old oak—my memory tree. I can still remember the first time Danner showed me how to extract the honey. It feels like it was yesterday, the day that was supposed to be perfect per my fortune. Except, Danner fell and ended up needing sutures. He always referred to that day as one of his all-time favorites, and it made me laugh, knowing it ended in the hospital. It was also the same day he told me he was sure I would become a nurse. It was a pivotal day, I suppose, but neither of us should have been trying to predict the future.

FIFTY

DANNER

Dachau, Germany

The world around me is a blur of people coming and going, some dressed like me, others in ordinary clothing, and soldiers in various uniforms, all here to help. It's been two weeks, or so I've been told. Bits and pieces of jagged memories flicker through my mind, but I only remember staring at an American soldier from the ground before waking up sometime later, being carried and then transported to another location. Today is the first day I'm awake in time to see the sun rise. The pinks, purples, and oranges all clashing together like a fire in the sky.

In recent days, I recall being fed, bathed, and given clean clothes. Nurses have said we need nourishment to refuel our bodies. I asked if there was a nurse named Emilie. There was.

She wasn't my Emilie. The Emilie who kept my mind alive.

"There is aid..." I keep hearing the announcement. "We will help you..."

I want to go home. *I don't have a home.*

"We can assist with relocation and help you find your families."

There are tents set up all over and the one offering to help find other living family members is the first place I'm walking to after being bedridden ever since the Americans arrived. I'm finally on my feet.

There are many people assisting, trying to avoid long lines. I only wait a few minutes before a woman with a book of papers approaches me. "Who can I help you find, sweetheart?" she asks. Before the name forms on my tongue, I wonder if she's someone's mother—if she knows where her children are, and if she knows how terrified I am to ask about my parents and brother.

"Alesky," I say. "I'm searching for Abraham, Sarah, and David Alesky from Munich."

A tight-lipped smile edges the woman's mouth as she flips through the pages. "Certainly," she says, drawing a line down the center of the alphabetized page. "And your name?"

"Danner, Danner Alesky, son of Sarah and Abraham. David is my younger brother."

The smile fades, her chest rises, and she looks directly into my eyes. My heart swells, or maybe it stops beating. My stomach, which has been feeling much better, twists and turns, moaning loudly in pain.

"Your father," she says, "Abraham Alesky...he perished in Auschwitz two years ago."

I couldn't convince myself the four of us had survived somehow, not after what the police told me upon my arrest. But now I know for sure, and the pain seeps out like blood from a wound that has only just closed.

"My mother and my brother?" I choke out.

"They also perished in Auschwitz, last spring. Other family members in connection to them are listed as Igor and Eunika Alesky." The woman closes the book slowly and she pulls it in against her silver-daisy brooch pinned over her heart but continues to hold her stare against mine. "I'm sorry for your losses. We have displacement services to aid you if need be."

Frozen in time, in this spot on the ground somewhere far away from my family, I turn away from the woman as if pushed by the wind.

"Danner. From my heart—from one person to another, I'm truly sorry."

I tap my chest and walk away. I walk toward the sun—the only thing I know how to follow now. I didn't get a light like the three of them did. Why didn't I get a light?

After circling the small area of Dachau, I step onto a bus, unsure of what I'll find at the next stop. Every step I take seems mindless and without a sense of direction. Nothing is familiar. Nothing is the same.

Life as anyone knew it is gone and I need something new to make me feel alive.

FIFTY-ONE

EMILIE

Munich, Germany

Warmth from the sun hits my cheeks, but I keep my eyes closed, wanting to avoid the day. A breeze sings through the tree limbs and bees buzz around me. I can almost hear Danner's voice... "A honeybee's entire purpose in life is to keep our world from falling apart. Kind of like you."

I hear Danner's voice often. My imagination is vivid and sometimes painful, filling me with hope I shouldn't depend on. Despite the words playing through my mind, they still bring tears to my eyes. He would say that, but I would argue that the world still fell apart. I'm nothing like a honeybee.

A stick cracks near my outstretched feet and my eyes flash open, blinded by the darting rays of sunlight filtering in around me. I jump from the ground, enduring an ache in my back from falling asleep against the tree. I rub my eyes, trying to see through the haze. It feels like minutes have passed by the time I spot someone stepping out into a patch of shade.

"Please don't hurt me, I—I fell asleep—"

"Hurt you?" he asks.

I blink again, my eyes still struggling to focus. I stare at the man, my heart still pounding at my vulnerability, until I notice the scar, his eyes, his lips. I clench my fists by my side as I step closer, trying to understand, trying to make sense...am I still dreaming?

He reaches out and touches his knuckles to my cheek. "You may not recognize me..." he says, whispering through a faltering cry.

I try to react, say something, anything, tell him I recognize him, but the words lodge in my throat. I step forward and place my hands on his cheeks, breathing so heavily my head becomes heavy. "Am I dreaming?" I croak.

"If you are, then so am I," he says.

"It doesn't matter," I cry out and throw my arms around him, pressing my cheek into his chest. He embraces me tightly and places a kiss on top of my head.

"If you're not real...if this isn't real, I can't pretend I'm still living. I can't live without you," I utter.

"I'm real. I'm here because of you. Because you never gave up on me. You're all I have left, Emi. You're it for me," he draws a shuddering breath.

"I'm all you have left?" I ask.

He closes his eyes and sniffles. "They—they're all gone. David...too." His words fall into the air, carried away with the wind.

"No, no, no," I whisper. Please God, don't let that be true.

Danner confirms with a nod. "I'm sure."

I can almost hear his heart splintering as he whimpers against me. I feel like breaking too but I squeeze him harder, trying so hard to be strong for him. I gasp for air, trying to say, "I'm—I'm so—so sorry."

"Just stay with me. Like this. I need this," he says, trembling within my hold.

"I never wanted to leave you. I wasn't given a choice," I say.

"I've been so scared—I visited Dachau days ago and helped with the bodies in the cattle cars. No one knew anything about you. I tried to find you."

"You did find me, and look, you've kept the bee farm alive."

"I—I had to capture a new swarm, using your papa's—"

Danner's brow furrows and he holds his head against his chest, peering around the edges of the clearing. "You did that?"

"Without bees, there was no hope for any of us, right?"

"Without you, there's no hope," he corrects me, his chin trembling as he peers through the high tree-branches as he composes himself.

"Without you, nothing has been right. Nothing has been right. The only thing that has ever made sense to me is you," I say, pressing onto my toes to kiss him. His arms loop around me and he spins me around until my back is against the tree, then presses his forehead to mine before reclaiming my lips. The side of his nose sweeps against mine as we inhale the same air and our hearts dance against each other's.

We might both be blue in the face when he pulls back enough to look at me again.

"I'm sorry. I shouldn't be kissing a married woman," he says, stealing another kiss, nonetheless.

I close my eyes and press my hands against his chest. "There's no sin. It's just you and me now. The rest—it's what brought us to this moment."

There's perplexity written across his face, but he shakes it away as he brushes a strand of hair behind my ear.

"Whatever has been or will be, you need to know that I love you. I've loved you forever, and I'll love you forever, no matter what comes next."

EPILOGUE

Munich, Germany

A daytime moon hovers over the horizon. People say it's rare to see the moon in daylight hours, but when I see it, I know it's the mirror to the other side where Mama, Papa, and David are—where they somehow keep the stars aligned just right.

Emilie and I are sitting outside on the front step across from her childhood house, watching our two little girls, Daisy and Lily, play hopscotch, giggling without a care in the world. What more could I ask for?

I have Emilie and this place that feels like home. It's all I wanted for so long. We may not live here forever, but while our wounds continue to mend, and the girls are young, I know this is where we need to be.

The nightmares continue, the memories haunt me even when my eyes are open. I still fear a certain look in people's eyes, and distance myself when my thoughts become over-whelming. I'm trying to recover, to grow stronger, to leave the past behind. But those are my scars, like the one on my nose—the reminder of where I've been and why I'm still here. Emilie has relentlessly nursed me back to life, all the while fighting off her own nightmares, regrets, guilt, and sorrows. We've been through a lot and saw too much. But together, we can move forward, letting the people and events in our past pave the way for a life we deserve—a life we will always fight for.

"Ten more minutes, my sweethearts. Dinner will be ready soon," I shout over to my daughters. I pretend not to hear their little grunts of frustration, and instead focus on Emilie's laughter.

"Thank you," Emilie says.

"I know you have an early shift at the hospital tomorrow. I'll get them settled early tonight so you can rest."

She kisses me on the cheek and brushes the pad of her thumb over the scar on my nose. "I love you," she says with a sigh. "My parents will watch the girls for us on Friday so I can go with you to the shop and help prepare for The Dachau Farmer's market this weekend." Emilie sighs. "You know, the one featuring the infamous Alesky Honey people can't stop talking about."

Hearing the truth of our reality out loud always brings a joyful expression to my face. Alesky Honey. I'm carrying on my family's legacy. "You'll be able to help?" I ask, feeling immediate relief. Both of us have so much going on all the time, but Emilie refuses to sit still.

She nudges her elbow into my side. "Of course, and besides, Matilda told me this weekend is expected to have the largest turnout yet for you and the Shop of Wonders. You've worked so hard for this, and your Papa was right...he knew you'd make it big."

From the increase in business lately, I have a good feeling. I think this might be a big weekend. I might sell out of all my inventory. "He would be proud—over the moon and beaming to know his dream was being kept alive when neither of us had so much as a promise of tomorrow," I say, wrapping my arm around her. *My Emilie. Always mine.*

The door across the street opens and Gerty steps outside with a dripping mixing spoon in her hand. Theo rushes past her like a tornado.

"Can I play too?" he shouts across the way to Daisy and Lily.

"Okay, but only for ten minutes," Daisy says with a huff.

"No, I won't be ready in ten minutes," Lily says. "Maybe twenty."

"I think she gets her stubbornness from you," I tell Emi.

"Girls...ten minutes," Emilie says, firmly.

Gerty holds her hand against her forehead, shaking her head. "Yup, that's all you, Emi," she says, laughing.

"Oh, hush," Emi says.

"Danner, Calvin has a buckwheat honey order. His market needs to double their stock inventory."

"I'm on it," I tell her.

"I'll let him know," she says, waving her spoon. "I'll see you at the Farmer's Market Saturday."

Just as she goes back inside, we hear a crash and a bunch of clanging bangs come from next door, followed by the front door flying open and twin boys chasing each other down the front steps with paper swords. "Keep it down," Felix shouts after them.

"They're boys. Let them have fun," Herr Weber argues with her son as the door closes.

Just another typical early evening on our road.

"I'm going to count the seconds before your parents' door opens a crack and the girls disappear inside," I tell Emi.

"Every night," she says. "Mama can't stop herself."

Like clockwork, we hear, "Psst," from across the street. "Girls..."

"Mama, no. Wait until after dinner. They won't eat!" Emi shouts across the street.

"Are you sitting there waiting for me to open the door?" Frau Marx says, opening her front door all the way. "I'm their grandma. I get to do what I want, and if I want to give them treats...I will!"

"Don't argue," I tell Emi. "She'll still win."

"See, you've got a smart husband there. Listen to him. You'll learn a thing or two," Frau Marx says.

"You know, she's been saying that since you were a few years older than the girls are now, but I'm not sure I've taught you much, have I?" I ask with a raised brow, staring directly into the beautiful eyes of my outspoken wife.

"Well...to be fair, you've taught me about patience," she says. "Forgiveness too, and perseverance. I always knew the words to speak. It's easy to tell someone never to give up, to be strong, and that everything will be okay in the end, but I didn't understand what it took to prove the meaning of those words until you showed me."

It didn't come easy. I didn't know how or if we could find a way here, but even on my darkest day, I knew she was my guiding light, the nurse with caring hands who brought me back to life. I'm the lucky one. I had a light all along...

A LETTER FROM SHARI

Dear reader,

I'm incredibly excited that you've chosen to read *The Nurse Behind the Gates*. If you enjoyed Emilie and Danner's story and are curious about what happened with Hans and his love, Matilda, make sure to check out *The Bookseller of Dachau* to read their story.

There's nothing I love more than sharing my books with readers from all over the world. If you would like to keep up to date with all my latest releases, just sign up at the following link. Your email address will never be shared, and you can unsubscribe at any time.

www.bookouture.com/shari-j-ryan

This past summer, I was fortunate to be able to visit Dachau and Theresienstadt, both concentration camps where I lost family members during the Holocaust. To touch my uncle's name on a placard, walk over stones he and my other family members walked, touch walls that caught many from falling, was an experience that will stay with me forever.

I'm grateful for the life I'm living and take pride in bringing light to these stories, hoping to keep the memories of those who have passed stay alive.

Among the many books to choose from, I'm very honored you have chosen to spend your free time with my characters.

There is no greater joy for me than the opportunity to connect with readers and share the passion I have for bringing history to our present day.

I hope you enjoyed reading *The Nurse Behind the Gates*, and if so, I would be grateful if you could write a review. Since the feedback from readers benefits me as a writer, I would love to know what you think, and it makes such a difference helping new readers to discover one of my books for the first time.

There's no greater gratification than hearing from my readers – you can get in touch with me on social media or through my website.

Thank you for reading!

Shari

www.sharijryan.com

 facebook.com/authorsharijryan

 x.com/sharijryan

 instagram.com/authorsharijryan

ACKNOWLEDGMENTS

The months of writing *The Nurse Behind the Gates* was an emotional journey, immersing myself into each page to create a true-to-life story based on the horrors of World War Two.

I'm incredibly grateful to Bookouture for the opportunity to continue my writing journey with such a wonderful team of experts. Your unwavering kindness and commitment have been invaluable throughout my publishing journey.

Lucy, my editor, I'm so appreciative for your skill, eye for detail, and talent. It has been a complete pleasure to work with you, and I look forward to working on more books together!

Linda, your steadfast positivity and unwavering belief in me have been a constant source of comfort and support over the years. Our friendship means the world to me, and I cannot thank you enough.

Tracey, Gabby, Elaine, and Heather, my longstanding confidants, I appreciate your time, support, and wonderful friendship. Your presence in my life has been more important than I could truly explain, and I am eternally grateful.

To all the ARC readers, bloggers, influencers, and readers who comprise this incredible community, I extend my heartfelt gratitude for your endless excitement, passion, and influence.

Lori, the best little sister in the universe, I'm grateful for your never-ending support and for always being my number one reader. I love you!

To my family—Mom, Dad, Mark, and Ev—thank you for

always believing in me and supporting my wildest dreams. You all mean the world to me. I love you!

Bryce and Brayden, my wonderful boys, thank you for believing in me and always supporting me even as a tornado-mom who promises I can do it all. You will always be my #1 pride and joy. I love you more than words can say.

Josh, I love you and feel very lucky for the endless support and patience you have always given me.

PUBLISHING TEAM

Turning a manuscript into a book requires the efforts of many people. The publishing team at Bookouture would like to acknowledge everyone who contributed to this publication.

Audio
Alba Proko
Sinead O'Connor
Melissa Tran

Commercial
Lauren Morrissette
Hannah Richmond
Imogen Allport

Cover design
Debbie Clement

Data and analysis
Mark Alder
Mohamed Bussuri

Editorial
Lucy Frederick
Imogen Allport

Printed in Great Britain
by Amazon